GREYHOUND DREAMS

Greyhounds Thru Time series
Book One

HOPE CHASE

GREYHOUND DREAMS

Greyhounds Thru Time series
Book One

HOPE CHASE

GREYHOUND DREAMS

Greyhounds Thru Time series, Book One

For information, please contact Hope Chase at https://hopechase.com. To receive book news, free stuff, and interesting tidbits, please connect with her through her email newsletter.

Follow Hope on Pinterest at *Hope Chase Author*.

Book ISBN: 978-1-7347713-1-2

ACKNOWLEDGMENTS

This book is dedicated to my husband, Larry, whose love and support helped make this book possible. He always said, "You could write that..."

Thank you to our daughters, Tara and Lisa, for your unending support, and to my sister, Sandy, who told me to keep writing.

My thanks to Ursula for being brave enough to start the writing journey with me.

I extend my gratitude to Anna Questerly for her initial reads and encouragement and to Kris Tualla and Jordyn Kross for their kind mentorship.

Thank you to my many wonderful beta readers and friends for your time and encouragement, Bonnie, Candace, Cathey, Dunja, Kathy, Jeni, Linda, Lisa, Milica, and Suzanne.

Thank you, Jared, for your legal information which helped to make this manuscript more accurate.

Thanks so much to my many friends at VOS and LERA from whom I learned so much.

And thanks to my editor, Judy Kurtz, whose superb knowledge helped make this book much easier to read.

CHAPTER 1

"You're firing me?" A rush of adrenaline shot through Liz Nottingham and sent torturous needles throughout her upper body.

She climbed down from the stepladder she'd been using while dusting the gallery's paintings, brushed something from her left eye lashes, and coughed. Scottsdale, Arizona, certainly seemed to have more dust than money right now.

"No, you do not understand me, *ma chère*." The gallery's owner, Jean-Luc Lafitte, waved a bent and wrinkled hand at the white gallery walls. "If these artists do not sell, I cannot pay you. You know this, *oui*? I need you to find me a salable talent just now to keep the gallery open. This year has been *merde* so far, *non*?"

Liz stared at the Frenchman who'd been a mentor to her. For the last five years she had sold art and managed his gallery successfully, but the last six months had shown minimal profit. Maybe she'd lost her edge. Or the poor economy was to blame. Or maybe a little of both. It's not like Jean-Luc's plea surprised her. She did the bookkeeping after all.

"You know I've been looking, but there must be some other avenue I can research. I'll work on it this weekend." If Liz couldn't keep Jean-Luc's gallery alive, how could she ever hope to own one of her own someday?

Jean-Luc rested his hand on her shoulder like he always did when he wanted to make a point. "Take the rest of the day off to think about it, *s'il vous plaît*. Also, the weekend days are good if you are not too busy." Jean-Luc gave her his one-sided smile. "We shall speak next week, *oui?*" He turned and shuffled his way across the artfully stained concrete floor back to his office. "*A Lundi.*"

You'll see me Monday, right. That doesn't give me enough time to find someone.

Dizziness engulfed Liz and she knew one of her frequent memory episodes would soon follow. She sat on the ladder and waited for the vision to start...

A slick-haired man in a Zoot suit yelled at Liz about something, but she couldn't follow all that he said, given his strange vocabulary. The old-time gallery space behind him drew her attention. There was something she needed to remember about a painting on the far wall, by someone she knew quite well. She stared at the painting and tried to figure it out.

All too soon, the scene faded, and Jean-Luc's gallery came back into focus. All seemed normal except that the existing art hung like colorful black holes, draining money and energy from the business.

Liz waited for the usual heat and tingling that followed the episodes she'd had most of her life to dissipate. Moments later, she stood, tugged on her pencil skirt, folded the step-ladder, and made her way to the storeroom. Maybe the memory would return later and she'd have her answer. Or had that just happened and she'd obviously missed the point?

Some old-fashioned magic would be welcome right about now. She needed to go home where she could concentrate. She'd find a solution, and do it as soon as possible.

As Liz drove down Scottsdale Road, a silver Corvette in the next lane swerved into her lane. Liz jerked her wheel to the right to avoid the impending collision. Her SUV bumped over the curb and into the parking lot of an upscale strip-mall. She slammed on her brakes and stopped inches from a parked car—a Lamborghini, no less.

Her heart beat faster than the thump-thump of the windshield wipers that had come on when she whipped the steering wheel. For a short moment, she couldn't breathe.

"Dumbass," she yelled over her shoulder.

When she got out of her red Kia Sorrento to check her vehicle, a white Dodge Charger pulled in behind her and parked. A brown-haired man got out and headed in her direction. The fleur-de-lis printed on his t-shirt stretched over his well-formed pecs, strong, but not too body-builder big. Then her eyes locked onto a familiar pair of *café au lait* eyes staring back at her. Those eyes set in that same angular face with its perpetual five o'clock shadow. He said something, but she became woozy and her weakened knees began to buckle.

He reached out and grabbed her elbows to help steady her.

She clasped his firm biceps in response.

"Are you hurt? Did you hit your head? Should I call someone, 911?"

"I'm okay." Her head cleared and she forced herself to let go of him.

"I saw that car run you off the road, but I didn't catch his plates." The man shrugged his shoulders. "I watched you instead."

"Are...are you Michael?" A slight breeze ruffled his hair, and the ends danced along the back of his shirt collar.

He tilted his head and furrowed his brow. "Yes, I'm Michael Donovan. Have we met? You look familiar, but I can't place you."

A shiver teased her senses. She knew those eyes, the ones from her memories, so many places, so many times. It had to be her Michael. But how could it be? She must be crazy. Or had she hit her head?

Liz shook the thought from her head. "Um, I don't think so, but you seem quite familiar as well. Perhaps I mistook you

3

for someone else. I'm Liz Nottingham." She stuck out her hand to shake his, not taking her eyes off his face. "Thanks for stopping."

"You're welcome. Can I check your car?"

"Sure, thanks." She followed his every move as he rounded her vehicle and then peered underneath. She sucked in a breath when his jeans stretched tight across his slim butt as he bent down. She remembered how firm it felt in her hands. As her face grew hot, she smiled, and closed her eyes. Could that be another memory? She wasn't sure, but the February day just got warmer.

"I think everything looks okay on the surface, but you should probably have it towed or at least take it in to a repair shop for a closer look. You might have problems with your front-end alignment or tires after hitting the curb." He brushed the dirt from his hands as he stood, and then wiped them on his jeans. "Do you have far to go?"

"No. I'm heading straight home and I have a phone if I need it. Thanks again for your help."

"I'm glad I was behind you. Be careful on your way home." He waved, climbed into his car, and drove through the parking lot toward the elegant shops in the plaza.

Liz waved, sorry to see him go so quickly before she could solve the deep feeling of déjà vu.

Ten minutes later, Michael paced the well-appointed office in Richard Radu's jewelry store and ran his hands through his brown mane. "She took Priscilla again. How could Bethany do this? I'm not keeping the dog from her. I need the name of the locksmith you suggested. You were right. I should have changed the house locks long ago, when she first left." He walked past a painting he had done for Richard's new location, half-imagining that it should have a safe behind it, although he knew it didn't. The bejeweled 16th century king in the painting stared back at Michael as if to scold him for his stupidity. "Yeah, I know," he whispered to the colorful king.

From the comfort of his executive chair, Richard watched his friend pace. "Apparently, shared custody is not good enough. You said she wanted the dog all along."

"She has her damn boyfriend, and I agreed to the divorce on her terms, so why does she have to have our dog, too?"

"Good thing the house isn't in your name."

"Yeah, she's pissed that it's my uncle's house. She can't get her hands on it." The two had moved into one of his uncle's upscale properties so Michael could supervise the remodel in exchange for free rent. His uncle would sell the house upon completion and split the profits with Michael, although his soon-to-be ex-wife didn't know that. He had planned to surprise her. Luckily, their confidential verbal-only agreement should keep the house out of the courts and the money out of Bethany's hands. He could live there until it sold if he wanted to.

"I should have seen this coming given her high-maintenance ways. She sure changed the minute we got married. You called that one right; I don't know why I couldn't see it then."

On Michael's way home, Adonia called. "Hello, Angel Boy." She alternated between calling him that or Michelangelo, depending on her mood or the art Michael created for her greyhound rescue group. "Are you having an interesting day?"

"Of course, you would already know or suspect that wouldn't you?" Adonia had shared some of her 'special gifts' with him, including the fact that some of her dogs were gifted. He didn't know if he truly wanted to find out how

5

many more abilities she possessed. He knew she read his mind on a regular basis.

"Yes, well, that's true. I'm calling about the new flyers. I need you to bring them with you to the Renaissance Festival tomorrow. I'm running short of the old ones."

"No problem and I think you'll like the new graphics."

"I'm sure I will, and thanks. Please bring them to me first thing. See you tomorrow."

Perfect. Just perfect. After Michael drove away, Liz looked up to see the *Secure Trust Bank* building, the gallery's bank, looming right in front of her. The imposing bank didn't make her feel secure at the moment. She needed to quit stressing.

She pulled the phone from her purse to dial Morgan Russo, one of her two best friends. "Hey, Lady, do you have a minute to chat?"

"I'm just completing my day. I recognize that shaky voice. Are you experiencing a dilemma?"

"Yes." Liz gave Morgan a detailed account of her Friday up to the crazy driver and her worry about finances. She excluded the encounter with Michael for the time being.

"I'd say that seeing that particular financial institution, at this particular moment, represents a lucky charm. Your dilemma is not insurmountable, Liz, and you know you can handle it. Relax…Breathe. Now enlighten me. How may I be of assistance?"

Liz had grown to appreciate the overly educated cadence of her friend's vocabulary over their many years of friendship. It always made her smile.

"I'll deal with it, but tell me if one of my 'past lives' has any clue to fix this." Liz had recently opened up to the possibility that her frequent visions and dreams might represent snippets of past lives as Morgan believed they did.

"Oh, and do you wanna buy a painting?"

"Perhaps I can carve out time next week between clients and peruse your current stock. Jean-Luc is probably in need of some cheer at this point. He adores me, too, you know."

"Thanks, Morgan, but I wasn't serious about the painting." Liz knew Morgan would do anything for her, as she would in turn.

"Just the same. I'll pick up Chinese food *en route* to your house tonight. I assume your vino stock is still adequate?"

"Can I take a rain check? I need to start an internet search tonight and I should probably skip the Renaissance Festival tomorrow as well."

"Unacceptable. You need nourishment, and I need to validate your sanity. In addition, tomorrow is your first Saturday off in eons. Your situation will resolve itself the moment you stop dwelling on it. Let fate take its course. *Que sera, sera.*"

"From your lips…." Liz looked skyward with her eyes closed as she envisioned Morgan's angelic features reassuring her. She always knew exactly what to say to put Liz at ease.

"I won't tarry and you can continue your search efforts after you're sated. I'll be there momentarily."

"Okay. Bring me two cookies. I could use the extra fortune in more ways than one and I need the crunch factor."

Liz took the 101 freeway from Scottsdale to her North Phoenix home. The descending sun glared in her eyes, but it also began a magnificent fuchsia, orange, and cerulean sunset.

A horrific noise suddenly exploded throughout Liz's vehicle. The front-end bucked and shimmied. Surrounding cars slammed on their brakes and dodged her. Fighting to keep her SUV under control, she took her foot off the gas and struggled to pull over onto the shoulder of the freeway— all in a span of a few seconds.

"Crap!" She mumbled clenching the steering wheel. Once again, adrenaline shot through her arms—her usual reaction to stress. "What was that?"

Liz panted for a few moments before she climbed out of her vehicle on shaky legs. She wrinkled her nose at the stench of the blown tire on the front driver's side. The rim still sat on the tire, barely, and the inside of the tire had all but disappeared. Another second and she would have been driving on the rim.

Liz paused to calm her turbulent heartbeat before she extracted some tools and a blanket, and then attempted to remove the full-sized spare mounted underneath her SUV. The pencil skirt she wore made the task almost impossible, and the gravel hindered her efforts as well. Kneeling on the blanket with her butt in the air, she tried to keep from getting too dirty from the dust and freeway grime.

"Can I do that for you?" a familiar male voice asked.

Turning around with the sun in her eyes, Liz squinted up, but couldn't see the man's face clearly. Her eyes dropped and she noticed the strong thighs straining his jeans. She averted her eyes and grinned. She hadn't even heard Michael drive up with all the traffic noise.

"Okay, I give up. Yes, please." Liz stood up and brushed her hands together letting out a deep sigh. Michael stood there in the flesh. Again. "You're back."

"Yep, it seems to be my day to watch over you. The 101 is my way home." Michael motioned at the freeway, near the upcoming intersection of Cave Creek Road.

A semi-truck thundered their way kicking up bits of road debris and dust. Michael pulled Liz closer to him and quickly spun his back to the traffic, shielding her from the gravel onslaught, however minor.

"Um, thanks," Liz managed to say as the heat from his body warmed her breasts and clouded her mind.

"Are you okay? And do you smell tea?" Michael sniffed the air.

"Tea?"

"Yes tea. Earl Grey, specifically. I drink it every morning and I know I didn't spill any on myself, but that scent is everywhere."

"That's probably my perfume. It's made with Bergamot and lemon."

"Bergamot?"

"Yeah, that's what gives Earl Grey tea its special smell."

"Oh. I thought I liked it because it tastes good, so maybe it's the smell I'm after." Michael smiled and slowly let go of her after he brushed a slight smudge off her arm. "Can I borrow those obviously too-large gloves?"

His touch had awakened her senses. An instinct. A knowing. He had to be the guy from her dreams and visions, from a past life. Her heart knew it, her eyes knew it, but her logic fought to deny it. That would require magic, a miracle, or a fairy tale. Her mind couldn't, wouldn't accept that *her* Michael could possibly exist, even though her heart knew better.

Too stunned to speak, she removed the gloves and passed them to him, unable to tear her eyes away from his face, until he turned toward her vehicle. She stood and simply watched his every movement, each more familiar than the next.

With the task finally complete, Michael stowed the shredded tire, rim, and tools in the back of the SUV.

"That was fast." Liz had recovered her manners. "Thanks for being a knight in a shiny Charger," Liz motioned to his white car, pleased with her altered cliché.

"T'was my honor, Milady," he said with sweeping bow and stunning grin.

"Straight out of time or the Renaissance Festival, aren't you?"

"I'll be there tomorrow."

"Us, too. Maybe we'll see you there."

"Us?" Michael's brow furrowed.

"Yes, my friends and I."

"Oh. Maybe. Drive safe and get your car checked." His gaze remained on her for a time before he slowly turned to leave. Michael waved as he climbed into his car.

"So, chivalry is not dead," Liz whispered to herself. Her heart soared as her head puzzled. In spite of her aversion to romance lately, she should have found a way to make him stay to solve his identity. Yet, she didn't want to start something she'd be too afraid to continue. What if he wasn't a knight, but a con man like her ex-fiancé?

Before she could make up her mind, her decision became a pair of tail lights heading down the freeway.

Back in his car, Michael pulled out, and glanced in his rear-view mirror after he passed Liz. His mood unsettled, he pondered her odd behavior and her wonderful smell.

He spoke to himself out loud. "She acted as if she really knew me, and she did seem familiar, but I just don't remember her. Maybe it's her natural beauty. Those wispy bangs above her compelling hazel eyes. She isn't what you'd call drop-dead gorgeous. More like pretty. More like cuddly. Long hair, soft clear skin, and the perfect size to fit in my arms. She felt like she belonged there. Why did I just leave without talking to her more? Or at least getting her number?"

He knew why and it made him sad, but that couldn't be helped. He had no conscious desire at this point to think of her or any woman that way. Not right now. He couldn't. Yet she felt so good against him for that one moment. The moment he worried about the truck coming too close and pelting her with gravel. The moment he discovered her special tea scent.

It made no sense, but it hounded him, over and over. He needed to quit thinking so much. He just did a pair of good deeds after all. Yet, he couldn't help but be happy that he accomplished a particularly good deed, make that two. For her.

Stop! Just stop thinking about it, about her.

Michael cranked the radio to some classic rock to drown out the noise in his head as he drove home. He simply switched gears. Think about your art, dude. I hope the new web site I post tonight attracts a buyer or two. Otherwise, how on earth can I start selling my paintings? A craft or art fair first? Or should I cold-call some galleries and try to sell myself along with my work?

Liz forced all thoughts of Michael out of her mind long enough to watch the road and finally get home safely. She tossed her keys into the copper bowl on the tiny antique foyer table, and laid her purse next to it. Her empty apartment sat dark in the cool February afternoon. She turned on all the lights to enhance the ambiance of her Old World décor which always soothed and warmed her—the leathers, the dark carved woods, the earth-tones. She could stare at her tapestry and imagine the greyhounds actually running beside their masters on their hunting horses. She would hunt too, but for an artist, not a rabbit or a fox. "It would be nice to have a greyhound beside me, helping me hunt." She talked to herself more and more lately.

Liz changed into some comfy clothes and adjusted the temperature slightly. A glass of crisp Riesling before Morgan arrived would work wonders as well. Then she'd be better company.

Liz answered the door, Morgan's wine glass in hand. "You brought Kung Pao," she said as she sniffed the air.

"Your favorite."

Liz's mouth watered as Morgan spread the spicy goodness from the takeout bag on the glass-top dining table. Liz poured herself another glass of wine as Morgan sat down on one of the lushly upholstered dining chairs. Between mouthfuls, Liz replayed her conversation with Jean-Luc.

"I'm pleased to see that you're hungry," Morgan reached for seconds as well.

"It's wonderful as always. I'm not sure what to do about the slow sales."

"Knowing you, you've conjured a plan already."

"Actually, I may have. I think. I'm going to start with an internet search tonight right after I send you on your way. I know the established artists and they are not selling. So I'm looking for someone new and fresh with lots of inventory. I'll plan a media blitz and an inexpensive, but classy showing. You know the drill. The difference must be who I pull in this time. He, or she, has to be special. Then, I'm going to sleep long enough to be in a decent mood tomorrow when we go to the Renaissance Festival. And, on Sunday, I'll figure out what else to do."

"That's a productive beginning. I'll meditate on the problem as well. You're preoccupied with another matter. What is it?" Morgan's eyes reached into Liz soul and practically willed her to tell the tale.

"You're right, there's more. I met him."

"Met whom?"

"Michael. The man from my dreams and visions—same name even." Liz detailed the day's two encounters. "I swear, I knew him the moment I looked into his eyes."

"Color me surprised," Morgan raised her eyebrows, "not at the awareness of him, but at the timing. I wonder if his presence indicates a diversion or if a larger factor is coming into play."

"I don't see any future in it for more than one reason, particularly since neither of us provided contact information." Liz pushed the remaining food around on her plate.

"Perhaps fate has a larger scheme in mind. Why don't I depart so you can conduct your research? We'll discuss this again tomorrow after you've digested your takeout and your day. I wish you a pleasant dream this evening." Morgan helped pick up the leftovers, hugged Liz, and made her exit.

Liz settled in on her comfy microfiber couch with her laptop, pen, and paper. Several hours of hunting proved futile. Her search found the same old artisans or some new ones that didn't meet the needs of the gallery—not the right genre, not the right skills. Her computer's search engine hid someone. Or perhaps she didn't enter the right search criteria. She'd need to try a different approach. She could check with the local professors and the art framers on Monday. She got leads that way occasionally. Maybe let her subconscious work on it while she slept.

She decided to stay on the couch where she frequently preferred to sleep, hoping to avoid her dreams. Sometimes it worked, sometimes it didn't. She drew up the blanket she kept inside the leather ottoman and fluffed her favorite silk-covered pillow. Oddly, it didn't take her long to doze off.

Liz jolted awake early the next morning when she rolled off her couch and landed in a heap on the cold tile floor. "Ouch," she muttered to herself and rubbed her hip. She cursed both the discomfort and the scene that had played out in her head. Morgan said that Liz's dreams replayed memories of her past lives. But how could either of them truly know? Her dreams repeated periodically, but for all she knew, they could be dreams just like everyone else experienced.

Her nightly dreams didn't have the dizziness, tingling, or heat of her daytime visions. Instead, she shivered for a while, even in summer. So she sat there on the floor for a moment and waited for the chill to pass. Like she always did, Liz closed her eyes and relived every detail of her latest dream...

Two knights jousted, one in red and one in gold. As their lances both found home, the gold knight's had greater purchase and forced the red knight off his horse and into the air. As his helmet flew off, he made eye contact with Liz for one brief moment. Flying through the air, dirt-bound, he yelled her full name, "ELIZZZZZABETH!"

She jumped up from her bench, gathered up her long skirts, and ran into the arena before anyone could stop her. Liz pushed through the gathering crowd and knelt beside him. "Sir Michael!"

He touched her face gently just before his hand fell away with his last breath.

♥♥♥

One last chill shook her core as the memory ended. The knight's kind, light-brown eyes had looked so deeply into hers. Those same eyes teased and tortured her in both her romantic and traumatic dreams alike. The same eyes that looked at her from Michael's handsome face.

Liz longed for those eyes. She had heard that early morning dreams are the truest of all dreams. Perhaps they are. What if her dream Michael existed in this modern-day Michael?

As much as her memories drove her passion, she really didn't want, or need a man at this point, nor did she think she could handle one. Not after Jack, her thieving ex-fiancé! She'd never trust again. Unless her dream Michael became real and trustworthy, then maybe her confidence would return.

She glanced at the greyhound in her tapestry and she thought about the first real greyhound she had ever seen. At the wee age of ten, her parents had watched the neighbor's red-fawn greyhound, Spice, for the weekend. She had never forgotten the dog that snuck into her room, jumped onto her four-poster bed, and joined her in slumber. Liz recalled hugging the affectionate animal all night with a sense of peace and tranquility. The dog had stuck by her side all weekend. Liz didn't want to go out to play with her friends. She had hung out with that dog, and relished his pure love. Spice had licked her face which made it tingle. A strange dizziness had engulfed her momentarily until he cuddled and leaned against her. He had looked into her eyes as if trying to tell her something. Looking back, that dog-kiss could have started the beginning of her life-long vivid and unique dream pattern. She had dreamed her first greyhound dream that very night. The one that must have started it all…

The little-girl Elizabeth ran with Spice through hills of tall green grass, next to a forest of conifer trees. When she ventured too close to the tree line, Spice maneuvered between her and the forest redirecting her away from unknown sounds emanating from within. The dog coaxed her on quickly. He ran circles around her and crowded her, guiding her toward the quaint stone cottage that belonged to her aunt.

Spice stared out the window while Elizabeth and her aunt ate dinner.

Liz, that same little girl, awoke from her dream the next morning in her own bed, to the warmth of a dog chasing away the chill. The girl and her canine friend were inseparable all day. Spice remained by her side that night too, as her dream continued on from the previous night…

After dinner, Liz watched out the window with Spice as two men broke cover from the forest carrying long swords and battle axes. They pounded on her aunt's wooden door. Spice moved to the door as her aunt opened the portal. The big scary men wanted food and lodging and settled for an outbuilding offered by her aunt. They took it gratefully because Spice kept growling. Once again, Spice stood guard over Liz during the night, both in the dream and in her own room at home.

At the end of the weekend, Spice had gone back to her

owners, leaving Liz despondent for weeks. Her parents wouldn't get a dog because of their busy schedule at the restaurant. She understood as best as a child could, but it didn't stop her longing for her large friend.

Liz held a deep love for greyhounds from that day forward. Grown up now, she could, should, and would eventually get one of her own.

Today though, Liz desperately needed caffeine to bring her morning back into reality. Enough dreaming—enough remembering—more action. Donning her fuzzy blue robe and slippers, she limped into her condo's galley kitchen and rubbed her back side along the way. She reached across the white speckled quartz countertop and turned on her waiting coffeemaker.

Through the window over-the-sink, the sun broke free from the mountains in the East Valley and shone inside to highlight the copper and glass tile backsplash on the adjacent wall. The warm and elegant decor made her smile.

Liz generally loved mornings. She could either revel in the afterglow of a sexy dream or escape a more uncomfortable one. After some brooding, caffeine, and ibuprofen, her mind cleared and she finally got excited about the day as she glanced at the time...6:00 AM. She had ample time to shower, dress, and eat something light. Liz wanted to save the calories for some medieval fare as she and her two best friends traveled back in time at the annual Arizona Renaissance Festival.

CHAPTER 2

Liz picked up Katy Wilson first, her other best friend, since Katy lived on the way to the Renaissance Festival. Katy looked like a goddess without even trying—a tall beauty with thick, long blonde hair, sky-blue eyes, and perfect skin. Normally, Katy wore scrubs and a ponytail to her job as a vet tech, but today she wore a pale blue shimmer of a tee shirt with a Swarovski fleur-de-lis emblazoned across her ample chest.

"Hi, Katy, love the tee."

"Ye be too gracious, Milady," Katy said using her best imitation of Middle English and bowing her head slightly for effect. "Hey, guess what. I treated a beautiful greyhound yesterday. A pale fawn. She desperately needed her teeth cleaned." Katy grinned and waved her index finger in front of her teeth as she spoke. "And her nails trimmed," Katy spread out her fingers for effect. "She was so gentle and loving."

Liz loved Katy's best doggie tales and the extra drama that her ever-present hand gestures added to her stories. "Does anyone own her or is she up for adoption?"

"One of our regulars. This is the owner's second rescue." Katy held up two fingers as if Liz needed the extra clarification.

"You're so lucky. You get to see all the cool dogs. I can't wait to have one of my own as soon as I have a bigger place."

"All they need is a couch and a daily walk. Or you could always have a small dog." Katy indicated size with her thumb and forefinger two inches apart.

"Nah, I'll hold out for a greyhound. I love their peaceful

disposition and the fact that they rarely bark."

Liz and Katy stopped to pick up Morgan at her modern condo just off the 101 in Scottsdale.

Morgan's silky black hair swung like fringe just below her ears as she hopped into the SUV. "*Bonjour mes amis*, aren't we gorgeous today?"

"Absolutely, my friend! Liz agreed. "Where'd you get the new duds?"

"My shoes are from *Nordstrom's* and my top and jeans both hail from *Paris, Paris. Très chic, non?*" Morgan asked, gently placing her soft rose-toned, leather espadrille-clad foot on the middle console.

"Quite chic, yes. Pink as always," Katy said.

Liz glanced at Morgan's foot, her eyes returning quickly to the road. "Gorgeous as always. Much cuter than those stuffy suits you wear to work. Honestly, CPAs must have a dress code with only three words—drab and dreary."

"With pleasantries out of the way, I'm anxious to revel in all things Renaissance, particularly since we can avoid the suffering and realities of medieval life. On, James, or should I say, Jane," Morgan commanded Liz. "We wenches require some merriment and mayhem."

"Our very own Damsel's Day!" Katy's hands flew open in front of her. "We'll find you a knight, Liz. One on a white horse."

"Ugh, stop." Liz snapped. She needed to tell Katy she just found one. And it would have been the perfect opportunity, but she worried Katy would play matchmaker, as usual, and not let it go. "You know perfectly well that I don't need a man right now," Liz said through clenched teeth. "Nor do I want one. Do you really believe a knight, or even some dependable guy, is waiting at the Renaissance Festival for me?"

"Liz. Not every dude is Jack-in-the-ASS. You're back on your financial feet now." Katy wiggled her own feet. "It's past time to start living your life again."

Liz winced at the sound of her ex-fiancé's name, but appreciated the reference to Jack being an ass. The shame and pain came flooding back, even after a year. She hated the reminder of how stupid she had been to add him to her bank accounts before they were married, even when he put his own money in them. She would never fall into that trap again.

"I am living my life, and I love it just as it is, thank you very much."

"Okay. Don't bite my head off. I get it. But we can still look, right?" Katy wiggled her eyebrows.

"I don't mind looking, but I don't want to indulge. Ok, enough whining. Between you and Morgan pointing out hot guys everywhere we go, I can't help but look. You just keep your promise to not fix me up," Liz pointed at Katy, "and I'll keep my promise to enjoy the view."

Katy returned the smile Liz offered. "Okay, Liz. I'll try." She crossed her heart like a school-girl. "Let's go eye the knights and knaves."

Katy had been there for Liz more times than she could count, just like Morgan. Liz should go easier on her friend, she reminded herself. Katy was just so damn persistent.

"On a different note," Morgan began, "was the Web hunt successful?"

"So much for jovial topics," Liz said. "No. I filled Katy in on the way to pick you up. I'm not especially excited about any of the artist possibilities. But I feel like there's someone just out of reach. Like a word on the tip of your tongue. I should have looked again this morning."

Liz flashed back to the paintings from those artists. They weren't special. She knew special. One summer as a teenager, she spent a month in France while her dad took some specialized cooking classes. She spent her time in the Louvre and studied each painting, thinking she might be a painter one day. Her actual attempts at painting didn't speak to her any more than those she had found on the internet. She'd decided to leave the brush to others and she'd manage the marketing and sales.

"Perhaps Picasso will surprise you today," Morgan said.

"Hah, funny girl! You certainly have my permission to conjure him up—that is if you have any fairy dust in your pocket."

As they approached the junction to US 60, Morgan said, "I have a birthday request, prematurely if you two don't object."

"You can have anything, anytime," Katy motioned in the air with her hand. "What do you want?"

"To go to a Past Life Regression hypnotist."

Katy frowned. "Okay. Liz and I will pay for it. Right, Liz?"

"Wait, I don't desire funding. My suggestion is that we all participate, so I've arranged tentative appointments. I've located a practitioner who scheduled us for next Saturday, if Liz can finagle another day off."

"I'm not interested," Katy shook her head. "You two can go."

"I know you don't believe in otherworldly interests, but this is for Liz," Morgan said. "The therapist might help her determine if she is experiencing dreams or actual memories."

"Morgan, you know I love you." Katy put her hand on her heart. "But you have so many quirky ideas." Katy counted them off on her fingers. "The Tarot cards, the crystal ball, the palm reading. What makes you think hypnotism will make any difference?"

"That's particularly close minded," Morgan said. "What happened to 'anything, anytime'?"

"I'm sorry," Katy touched her own heart again. "I didn't mean to hurt your feelings. It must be PMS talking."

"Look, Katy, simplistic dreams are scattered, short snippets of random thoughts. Liz experiences what might be coherent extended memories, whether it's her short day time visions or a longer night time dreams. If you were so afflicted, wouldn't you desire a better understanding of the situation?" Morgan waited for Katy to understand.

"Stop!" Liz held up her right hand in an attempt to make peace. "We were having such a good time. I appreciate your concern, Morgan, but let's drop it. Please cancel the appointments for now. Maybe we can go later. Besides, if they are my past lives, it still doesn't change anything."

"As you wish, consider the cancellation a done-deal." Morgan sat back and crossed her arms like a petulant child.

"Hey, look at the desert wild flowers." Liz pointed to the side of the road to change the subject. "They would make a nice painting." She took a quick mental inventory to distract herself as well. The purple lupines stood sentinel like roadside guards, the Mexican gold poppies decorated the wild grasses reminiscent of an antique rug, and the plentiful yellow brittlebush created hedgerows along the highway. Yes, she could definitely see a painting or two.

"Beautiful, indeed," Katy agreed. "Just like in the *Arizona Highways* magazine."

They drove on, in silence, admiring the scenery.

Michael's face and his mesmerizing eyes filled Liz's quiet moments of the hour-long drive to get to the Renaissance Festival. He mirrored her dream-Michael in every possible way. Even though his presence made her nervous, he also stirred some feelings buried long ago, both in her heart and in her nether region. But she couldn't trust the male of the species, and if she were honest, she really couldn't trust herself to determine which, if any, male besides her dad and Jean-Luc could be trustworthy. Still, the tingling in her body wouldn't settle down.

Liz shared the complete details of last night's dream as she frequently did. Katy and Morgan always listened to her out of respect, concern, and for the absolute, sheer entertainment value. This dream held their interest as well.

Liz turned slightly, still keeping her eyes on the road, "What do you think the odds are of seeing a familiar jousting knight, or even someone we know at the Renaissance Festival?"

Morgan's phenomenal brain slipped into her calculation mode. "With an average of 1400 people on any given day I'd calculated the odds at 2 percent."

"She's part computer you know," Katy winked at Liz and tapped her temple. "All intellect and logic, like Spock."

They'd long ago given up trying to fathom how Morgan arrived at her lightning-fast mathematical calculations. "Hey, speaking of numbers. We're clicking along at 30 miles an hour. That's a first. Usually, this last 10 miles is stop-and-go." Katy motioned at the road ahead.

"The poor economy probably explains the reason for the decreased traffic flow," Morgan said, "but let's not scoff at our good fortune."

The ladies arrived about a half-hour before the Renaissance Festival opened. Liz followed parking directions from the attendants who waved flags as seriously as if they guided jets on an aircraft carrier. The parking lot curved in a crescent moon-shape around the front and sides of the festival grounds, which made each row quite long. Liz scanned the parking lot looking for Michael's white Dodge Charger.

"Let's get something to drink as soon as we get inside," Liz said, walking through the dirt lot toward the entrance. "I'm thirsty."

"HUZZAH!" yelled Morgan as they approached the Welcome sign. "HUZZAH!" repeated Katy and Liz in unison.

Just as they joined the gathering crowd at the gate, the Royalty actors sounded horns to part the waiting guests. The

Royal Jester declared in his deep voice, "Make Way! Make Way, for someone of no particular import," and continued on with his foolery throughout their grand entrance. After they passed through the spectators, old and young, costumed and not, the Royalty entourage slipped through the smaller gate, and ascended up to a catwalk over the turnstiles. The actors put on quite a show overhead that kept the guests patient and entertained until the main gates opened at 10:00 AM for the public.

While waiting for the gates to open, Michael and two other men approached Liz in the crowd.

"Hey, Liz."

"Michael?" Liz blushed when she instantly recognized who had tapped her on her shoulder.

Morgan and Katy each gave Liz surprised looks before turning to greet the three men.

"Any more trouble on the way here?" Michael asked.

"Um, no. Thanks again for changing my tire."

"You changed a tire?" Michael's good-looking, but slightly shorter friend said as he pointed at Michael's hands." That's not paint under your nails then, its grime. Very macho."

"My observant friend here is Richard Radu, and the tall guy is Will Griffith." Michael interjected by way of introduction. "At least you didn't get your prissy hands dirty," he said to Richard with a smirk.

"Yes, that's because I must keep mine clean to make money. You don't have to," Richard said.

"True, but at least mine do something," Michael said.

"If you call painting doing something." Richard turned to the ladies. "Seriously though, his strokes are quite something."

Liz listened to their banter while gaining some modicum

of control. She assumed they must be pretty good pals.

"What do you paint, Michael?" Katy jumped in before Liz got a chance to introduce them.

"Contemporary stuff. Mostly oils, but sometimes acrylics."

"Liz!" Katy said. "You should check out his work. Maybe it's what you need for your gallery."

"You own a gallery?" Michael tipped his head slightly.

"No, I just work in a gallery," Liz corrected, recovering her wits. "Is your work any good?"

"I'd like to think so."

"Can I look at your paintings? If you're interested that is." Liz dug out her card. "Do you have a website?"

"Of course," Michael replied and flashed a grin at his buddies, glad he got it finished late last night.

Liz couldn't believe that Katy played at matchmaking again, but at least it was business this time, so she had to appreciate her efforts. Sure, this Michael had helped her, just like her dream guy would have, but he could be anybody. She just couldn't get past the resemblance and the way he made her feel. She couldn't let him slip away this time without more information. "Will you give me your number so we can connect? I didn't find your website last night while I was looking around."

"Sure." Michael fished a card out of his wallet and handed it to her. "I finished my website last night and launched it this morning. The address is on my card."

Liz took the card and rubbed her thumb over the raised text on the card. She glanced quickly at her friends. "I'll call you or you can call me at the shop on Tuesday. We are closed on Mondays."

"Pleased to make your acquaintance," Morgan extended her hand to Michael.

"I'm sorry. You met Katy. This is Morgan."

"Pleased to meet you, too," all three guys said in unison.

"Thank you, but if you'll excuse us, they've opened the

gates." Morgan motioned in that direction.

"Mayhap we will see thee anon," Will looked in Katy's direction and took a bow.

"Mayhap, kind sir." Katy nodded and curtsied in reply with an imaginary skirt. "Be you heading directly into the festivities?"

"We need to rent costumes first." Richard interrupted. "Maybe we'll see you inside."

"Let's go, Lady Katherine." Morgan bowed to Katy, headed off toward the gate, and whispered to Liz, "Oh, she has a taste for Will, doesn't she."

"I heard that." Katy caught up to Morgan. "What's wrong with having a taste for a kindly gent anyway? And what's your hurry?"

"If you snare Will, the hunk, and Liz does business with Michael, that leaves me with Richard, the comedian, and I could skip him altogether. Onward." Morgan pointed ahead with both hands like a flight attendant and began walking again.

"Why?" Liz asked Morgan even though she assumed the answer.

"He's incredibly arrogant."

"Fine!" Katy crinkled her lips together and followed along. "Maybe we'll see them later."

♥♥♥

Michael's graphic art work provided a lucrative contracting career, but he wanted his big break as an artist. Liz's gallery might be a venue to showcase his paintings. What were the odds? If he had just stayed and talked to her yesterday, he might have already had the connection. To think how close he came to missing it all together.

"Such lovely wenches!" Will said, in his usual, jovial manner. "Especially the blonde with the nice assets. She's quite the clever lovely and she speaks 'Ren Fest' What a beauty! I wonder if she's got a bloke?"

Michael flashed a quick grin at his friend as they walked into the costume shop. Most women adored the burly guy, and Katy didn't seem to be an exception, but Will truly looked deeper, which Michael respected.

"You always did like the blondes," Richard said over the musicians who entertained the crowd as they filed in through the turnstiles. "What about the classy one?"

"Which one, Liz?" Will asked.

"No, the one with the bob," Richard answered.

"Who's Bob?"

"No, dumbass. Not who's Bob — what's a bob."

"Okay, I'll bite. What's a bob? And who's on first," Will said in his best Abbot and Costello impersonation.

"Funny guy! Bob is the name of the hairstyle Morgan's wearing."

"Seriously? Did you have to take *Hair 101* to be a jeweler?" Will asked. "Next you'll be talking shoes."

"Follow me, my simple lad, and I'll speak slowly. The more you know about women, the more jewelry you can sell to them. Also, you'd find a baby-maker faster if you took a few lessons in female etiquette. For example, if I told Morgan that her polished exterior reflected a raw brilliance on the inside, she'd fall into my arms in no time."

After a bout of laughter, Will said, "And she'd either barf all over you or frigging laugh in your face. Besides, getting dates isn't the issue. I'm not looking for just a baby-maker. I'm looking for...the one."

"Richard, you make Morgan sound like one of your gemstones," Michael said cutting back into the conversation as they arrived at the costume shop.

"When the carat fits..." Richard wiggled his wrist and flashed Michael with the sunshine that reflected off his diamond-studded Rolex.

"Now look who's the smart-assed comedian." Michael blocked the reflection with his hand.

"I thought about inviting them to join us," Will said. "Put some welly into getting to know them, you know. I'd like to talk to Katy some more; get to know her. Feck, I should have asked for her number."

"I was afraid you were going to, my Welsh friend." Michael frowned at Will as he fingered a velvet costume. "I want to keep this all business."

"Those babes would rock in some Ren-costumes. Could you not see it?" Will asked. "Apart from your raucous time with us, Michael, you really should start having fun again."

"I need my space, thanks. If Liz'll hang my work, I don't want to blow my chances with some lame attempt at small talk and awkward moments."

"You are lame!" Richard said as he pulled out a brocade costume. "However, I agree. It's best to keep business out of the bedroom. She might leave you hanging anyway."

"Not if I wanted her, she wouldn't. Which, I don't by the way. She acted strange, not all there, distracted or something when I first met her." Michael knew heartache well and didn't want another serving, even though Liz pulled at his thoughts somehow. "And how did she know my name before I introduced myself?"

"Who knows?" Will said. "Generic guy, generic name." He poked Michael in the ribs. "Are you more magnetized than you want to let on? I could scan her head and let you know what she's thinking." Will tended to pepper his conversations with medical references on purpose to entertain his friends.

"Shit, never mind, CAT-SCAN man." Michael said to his X-Ray Technician friend.

Tired of that topic of conversation, Michael asked. "How 'bout those A's? We need to decide if we going to see a spring training game soon."

"I spoke with my source and he scored complimentary home-plate seats for us," Richard quickly brushed his thumb back and forth across his fingertips expressing the universal motion for money.

"You have connections for free everything. Why am I not surprised?" Will shook his head.

"I never hear you complain," Richard said with raised eyebrows.

"I'm grateful for the Renaissance Festival tickets, as always, so I'll spring for the first pints," Will offered, as they checked out and headed to the changing stalls to don their personas and store their street clothes. "I'll also buy a second round if we see those babes again!"

"Katy's got a sexy shape," Richard said. "You've been too picky about the women you've dated."

"Perhaps, sparkle-man, but I need the right lovely in my life. I'm not going to be a prat and settle for the wrong one, no offense, Michael. Maybe I should let your golden tongue talk her into it for me?" Will wiggled his tongue at Richard.

"It'll take some long conversations, a gigantic engagement ring, and many kegs of beer to convince her to have your Neanderthal children," Richard said.

"You're just jealous that I'm beefcake and you're cheesecake." Will ruffled Richard's coiffed hair.

"Now children, do I need to call your mothers?" Michael searched for a pocket in his costume. "Speaking of mother types, I need to get these flyers to Adonia first thing."

"I'm thirsty. Let's find a tankard of ale on the way there. It's time for a cool one."

CHAPTER 3

"Spill, Liz!" Katy lightly poked Liz in the arm as they followed the crowd into the Renaissance Festival. "You had a flat tire. The hunk changed it. And you didn't tell us?"

"I had planned to tell you, Katy. You see, Michael has an uncanny resemblance to the man who's been haunting my dreams and visions lately, especially his eyes."

"Positive haunting or negative haunting?" Morgan laughed.

"Positive. He usually rescues me from some dire situation right before I have the chance to kick butt myself. He's always there for me and it almost gives me some hope in the male population, albeit very little."

"It's either kismet or you're projecting a dream image onto that stunning face of his." Morgan grinned.

"Morgan, his *name* is the same." Liz's hands flew up and out. "How can that be possible? I'm not sure about fate, but I don't know how else to explain it." Liz glanced at Katy.

"Don't look at me." Katy put her hands together. "Just pray that the bad guys don't appear, too."

"Oh, they'll be around, sooner or later." Liz waived her hand in a circle.

Katy sniffed the air. "I'm starved. The turkey legs are close by. Let's get some when we find them."

Liz grabbed a map and confirmed that not much had changed other than a few new food vendors and a gigantic rocking horse ride. They could still follow their usual plan to circle right around the winding oval, arriving at the arena in time for the first jousting event.

While waiting for Liz to finish her navigational studies, Katy looked around and squinted. "No guys anywhere. Let's go get food."

"Besides the specialties of the realm: turkey legs, corn on the cob, pizza, and steak on a stick, which are all foods eaten specifically from the hand, I hear they have added stew bowls with spoons to the menu this year," Morgan said. "A vast improvement in sanitary conditions. However, I'm depressed that the theatrics have degraded. The staff once spoke Middle English at every turn. Lately they've resorted to uttering mostly Modern English. It's a shame, but I still adore the atmosphere, all but the dirt." Morgan looked at the layer of dust marring the appearance of her new shoes. "Perhaps we should consider costumes next year."

Keeping to their schedule, they stopped at a stage that showcased bare-chested jugglers. "You gawkers can stay here, but I'm heading over there to see the greyhounds," Liz pointed to the gazebo that held the greyhounds and their costumed keepers. "Meet me there before you go blind."

As Liz approached the dog keep, a short, plump woman with silky black and grey hair quickly glanced up with searching eyes at the same time that her coal-black greyhound jumped up.

"*She's the one,*" the greyhound said telepathically to the woman.

"*Yes, I know,*" she replied mentally. "*I sensed her, too.*"

"Hi, I'm Adonia." The woman extended her hand to Liz.

At the same time, the greyhound pushed against Liz and almost knocked her over as he rubbed his face on her jeans.

"Hi, and what's your name?" Liz stroked the dog with her left hand and extended her right hand to Adonia.

"This grand specimen is Duke."

"And I'm Liz." A comforting sense of well-being enveloped Liz as soon as she shook Adonia's hand. Looking down, Liz noticed a whisper of a reddish birthmark in the shape of a butterfly on Adonia's wrist. It startled her momentarily. "Do you mind if I ask you about your little butterfly? My friend has one just like it. Hers is a birthmark."

"Is it similar or exactly like mine?" Adonia demanded as she held out her arm for Liz to take a second look.

"I think it's exact, but we can check. She's meeting me here in a few minutes. Is something wrong?"

"No, nothing. Sorry. I would just like to see it. Does she like dogs?"

"As a matter of fact, she does. She's a veterinary technician by trade. I think you'd like her. You have a beautiful, but unusual name."

"It's an ancient Phoenician name. It means *ruler*."

"Oh, really? So I bet the greys obey you." Liz chuckled.

Duke nudged Liz again so she bent down to pet him. "*She smells good,*" he mentally sent to Adonia. He kissed Liz on her chin with a delicate tongue—his magic transferred to her skin.

A sharp tingle spread across Liz's face, then down her neck and spine. A strange pull tugged at her heart for this special dog. He reminded her of Spice as he whined softly then rubbed his face on her leg again, as if to pet her in return.

"*It's working,*" Duke sent to Adonia.

"*Good boy,*" Adonia sent back.

Liz shook her head to clear it and when she said, "Wow, Duke, that's some kiss." He whined softly and looked in her eyes as if to tell her something.

"He's one of our most special greys and obviously attracted to you. It's as if he knows you."

"He's so beautiful and his fur is so soft. I can imagine how easy he would be to love."

31

"He's quite the alarm clock, too, if you need one."
Adonia laughed a full belly chuckle. "He gets me up every
morning with a nose-nudge and then a whisper-soft "woof" if
I ignore him. I always wonder how he knows when its 6:00
AM. I think he just wants his turn to sleep on my bed."

Liz laughed with Adonia and kept rubbing Duke's head.
"Is he yours?" He appeared to listen intently to their
conversation, looking back and forth between the two
women.

"I'm his foster mom," Adonia answered. "He's available
for adoption to a Forever Home, and it looks like he's chosen
you. You rub him in his favorite place—the right side of his
neck behind that ear."

"He is beautiful, but he's huge; how much does he
weigh?"

"Duke boasts 90 pounds of graceful stature." Liz noticed
Adonia puff up as if proud of the dog.

"He is all black, but his face is streaked with just a little
silver. Is he getting old?"

"No, that's just his coloring, he's only four. The grey
starts appearing on their faces at about that time. It's a
common trait."

"This collar is amazing." Liz rubbed the texture of the
stitching. "I love the regal golden embroidery against the
Kelly-green color of his collar. Does it come with him?"

"This particular collar is kept for the Renaissance
Festival and used in the royalty procession, but I'm sure we
could find one for you," Adonia explained. "The Martingale
collars are the best collars for greyhounds. See how it draws
closed when you pull it tight." Adonia tugged lightly on the
collar's 'D ring' to demonstrate. "Since their heads are so
small compared to their powerful necks, you can't use a
regular dog collar because it would just slip off if he pulled at
the right angle. Are you interested in adoption? Duke seems
to love you already."

"I am, but I'm in a small place," Liz said. "Although

after seeing Duke, I'd love to find a way to make it work. I'll need to think about it."

Duke gave a soft "Ooof, Ooof" sound on a puff of air as if trying to convince her.

"They're couch potatoes, sleep most of the day, and rarely bark, unless he's trying to tell you something, obviously. He doesn't need room to run particularly, but does need to be walked daily and he loves routine. Think about it. Duke obviously wants you to adopt him. Take this brochure. It was created by a wonderful graphic artist. His name is on the back if you ever need one."

Liz felt strangely compelled to adopt Duke right then and there. Not because Adonia continued to suggest it, but because she did sense a strong connection. She turned as Katy and Morgan approached laughing and pointing. Oh, I can just hear them now. It must be a private joke at my expense — probably something about choosing dogs over men.

As Liz introduced them, Duke sniffed Katy's outstretched hand, but remained by Liz's side as if to say "I'm hers."

Katy instinctively performed a quick visual exam of Duke and he allowed it: teeth, ears, feet, legs, hips, skin, and coat. She couldn't help but check out every dog that caught her attention. "He looks like a healthy one. Do you rescue them locally?"

"Yes," Adonia answered. "Usually from Tucson since the tracks in Phoenix have closed. I hear you have a birthmark like mine. Do you mind if I see it?" Adonia held out her wrist for comparison.

Katy held out her wrist next to Adonia's.

A sharp intake of breath delayed Adonia's response for a moment. "They are identical! I have not seen one of ours for many years."

"One of ours?" Katy asked. "What do you mean? Everyone always asks if it's a Henna tattoo. They think it looks like a butterfly."

"Exactly. Tell me," Adonia asked, "Do you have Roman ancestry?"

"Roman? Do you mean Italian? We have some on my mother's side, but she dismisses it as minimal. We are all blonde, blue-eyed, except my aunt."

"Does your grandmother, mother, or your aunt have the birthmark as well?" Adonia held her arm out to Katy again.

"My aunt does, but I haven't seen her since I was little. She doesn't live here. What does the birthmark have to do with anything? Are we related or something?"

"You are not yet 30 are you?"

"No, not for a few weeks. Why?" Katy furrowed her brow.

"Every few generations, someone in my maternal blood line is born with the butterfly birthmark. They are blessed with a special ability to work with dogs, particularly greyhounds."

"That fits," Liz said. "You should do your genealogy, Katy."

"May I have your phone number," Adonia asked. "I might have a need for a new veterinarian, and we should discuss our similarity further."

"I always carry one," Katy fished a card from her pocket and handed it to Adonia. "You can ask for me at the office. I'm usually there, or hanging with these two." Her thumbs pointed in both directions.

"Katy, I want you to know, if you ever want to talk about the greys, please call me, day or night. Here's my card. My cell number is on the back."

"Um, okay. Thanks, Adonia." Katy looked at Liz with a crinkled brow.

Morgan impatiently whispered to Liz. "Can we move on to the fortune teller now?"

"We need to go now. Thanks, Adonia," Liz said, tearing herself away from Duke and his loving foster mom. She rubbed her cheek as it continued to tingle.

"Let me know what you decide about Duke. I'll hold him for you for a while." Duke tried to leave with Liz, but Adonia held his leash tight preventing his escape. He let out a long whine that tore at Liz's heart.

"I think she'll be back," Duke sent to Adonia.

"I'll follow up with her through Katy if we don't hear from her," Adonia sent back.

"Five more minutes and you would have acquired Duke's birth date, his pedigree, and what time he did his business every day!" Morgan laughed as they walked away.

"Yeah, yeah," Liz said. "You're a funny girl, aren't you?"

"Did you see the tattoos in his ears?" Katy pulled on one of her own ears and pointed to the inside surface. "They give you most of that. And his birth order, too."

"Birth order?" Morgan asked.

"The order he was born in the litter. *BOE, for example,* means fifth of the litter. The 'E' being the fifth letter in the alphabet. The other ear has a code. It's used for racing commission statistics," Katy replied before Morgan could ask about the importance of the tattoos.

"What does *your* tat record indicate?" Morgan reached for Katy's ear only to have her hand slapped as they laughed and moved on to the next entertainment.

"Actually, my birthmark just started itching, almost burning." Katy rubbed the inside of her arm.

"It's probably psychosomatic." Liz said.

"Or you have a strong connection with Adonia." Morgan raised her eyebrows and nodded her head in Adonia's direction. "And maybe your aunt."

"That sounds like something you'd say. I don't have my aunt's number. I can't ask my mother. They don't speak to each other for some reason."

"You could research it and call her." Morgan said. "Perhaps the connection is telling."

"Yeah, maybe someday." Katy walked off.

"We're right behind you." Liz grabbed Morgan's sleeve and pulled her along after Katy.

"I'm anxious to hear what the fortune teller has to say this year." Morgan said as she followed Katy. "Maybe she'll share something exciting."

The three passed a maiden playing a harp. A delicate tune floated from its strings. Only a few people had gathered around to listen. Some conversed near Liz. Instead of their voices blending into background noise like in busier years, she could decipher every word.

Kids laughed and played with their newly purchased, wooden medieval swords and shields. Men ordered beers and watched the buxom wenches draw their draughts.

Liz thought about her friends as they walked along. How different they were, yet they got along like sisters. Morgan focused on future possibilities and all things mystical. Katy lived for the moment with practical sensibilities. And Liz constantly fretted about not repeating her past.

"I'm first," Morgan said like an excited little girl, interrupting Liz's reflections. "You should go next," she added pointing to Katy. "Maybe she'll expound on that muscle-bound guy you fancy." Morgan entered Madame Stephanie's mysterious tent.

Sly; that comment just might eliminate Katy's hesitation to participate. Liz rubbed the tingling in her cheek again.

A lovely young woodland sprite with green wings appeared while they waited for Morgan. Children gathered around to watch the girl mime to them. As she pulled flattened marble-like gems from her leather pouch, bits of fine glittery-fairy dust floated about. After giving them a magic gem, she sprinkled the glitter over their heads which caused a collective giggle.

"Excellent," Morgan said on her way out of the canopy,

pushing aside the gossamer curtains. "Another fine year on the horizon. Oh, sorry, I got ahead of schedule." They had previously agreed to discuss their destinies after completion of all three readings.

"Okay, I'm next," Katy said slipping through the gauzy opening.

"Your psychology worked on her," Liz said. "Finding a nice guy will make her go almost anywhere."

"I hope she's fortunate enough to locate him. In the meantime, I'm thoroughly enjoying the process of helping her shop for him. Speaking of shopping…look at that fine specimen of an executioner over there," Morgan pointed in the direction of the actor on the Boat House Stage. "Who cares if he has a hood as long as he continues to leave his shirt elsewhere? Oh, wouldn't a hood be an interesting scenario? I can imagine that."

"There's plenty to look at on that one." Liz said. "Katy's lucky to have you as her personal shopper."

After a time, Katy came out smiling in spite of herself. "Your turn, Liz."

"Wish me luck." Last year, this same woman had warned Liz that she had a big challenge ahead, but would come out of it in a good place. Half right, last year Jack pushed her almost beyond her limits, but the optimistic side of her still waited for that good place. It had taken her almost a year to replace her funds that Jack stole.

"Please, sit down." Madame Stephanie's table had a beautiful purple shawl draped over it, layered with a horoscope chart and sparkling stones of mixed sizes and shapes.

"I've always wondered what all the stones are for." Liz said.

"The stones help to channel my spiritual thoughts: amethyst for clarity and concentration, amber and hematite to discover the beautiful things in life, rose quartz and malachite for lost love, and garnet for the power of recall."

"I don't remember the shadows in your Crystal ball last year? Shouldn't it be clear?"

"It's new, and it's not glass. Many crystals of this size have occlusions. It's not a problem for my visions. Don't worry."

After shuffling the tarot cards, she asked Liz to cut the cards twice. She then restacked the deck and dealt Liz's cards in a diamond-shaped pattern. "May I hold your hand for a direct link?"

"Sure." Liz placed her fingers in Madame Stephanie's palm.

Madame Stephanie began. "You're always learning. You're also creative and moving more so in that direction. Coming to the end of a difficult time, you still have one obstacle to overcome. Also, you recently met someone essential to your future. He's someone you knew long ago. You will know this person on sight and may already know who I'm talking about."

"Is it someone I met today or yesterday?" Liz asked.

"Only you will know," the oracle advised. Then she added, "Time has run out in your current situation and you must choose another."

"What the hell does that mean?" Liz raised her voice. "It sounds like I'm going to die."

"No, I don't see that, but you will experience a tragic event, and as a result, you must make a choice that will decide your fate."

"And what does that mean? How do I know what choice to make?"

Madam Stephanie released her hand and forced a small smile. She handed Liz a small piece of Onyx. "Keep this in your pocket today. It will give you strength and help keep you safe."

Liz turned the small egg-shaped rock over in her palm and rubbed its smoothness. "Why do I need this rock? What's going to happen?" More confused than ever, Liz became frustrated with this woman and her veiled warnings.

"I'm sorry my dear, I don't see actual events, I only get impressions."

After more probing and getting nowhere, Liz gave up, thanked her, and slapped the tent flap open as she left.

"What's wrong Liz?" Katy approached Liz and touched her arm. "You seem upset."

Liz shook her head. "She said some things I need to think about. We'll talk later. Let's go."

"Just relax. We won't rush you," Morgan said. "We just worried about you."

"She's a frustrating woman, Morgan. Sometimes I think it's better not to have any foresight. At least then I wouldn't have to worry. If her vision of the near future doesn't turn out well, I'm never going back."

Morgan held her tongue on that subject, but said, "The King's Tournament of Champions doesn't begin for a while, so we still have time to eat. Those hand foods tweak my saliva glands."

"I want a beer," Katy said. "And that turkey leg."

"I want roasted corn and a beer." Liz walked on, deep in thought.

Her friends gave her some space until they ordered their food and headed to the arena.

CHAPTER 4

The ladies entered the jousting arena about half an hour before the show started.

"Let's find a good seat," Katy shaded her eyes with her hand. "I don't want to stare into the sun."

"This section is suitable." Morgan said as she started to climb the bleachers. "Liz, have you had time to process your thoughts?"

Liz suggested seats in the sixth row up. "Unlike you, I'm certainly not happy about my reading." She shared, verbatim, what Madame Stephanie predicted. "Just what am I supposed to make of that? It's either a veiled warning or a bunch of bull. If I take this seriously, could Michael be the person she talked about? Look at this rock she gave me." The black stone suddenly looked ominous against the pale skin of her palm.

"That's a great deal to consider. Madam Stephanie has refrained from negativity in the past, so she must believe strongly in an omen to have mentioned it." Morgan's forehead wrinkled almost as much as her tightened lips.

"Look Morgan, I know you believe in all this. Katy, what do you think?"

"You know I'm a big skeptic. I'm trying hard to keep an open mind." Katy shook her head. "I don't like what she told you. It could mean anything. I'm not so sure you should worry about it though."

"It's too much to digest. I'll have an easier time with this corn." Liz stared at her corn-on-the-cob-on-a-stick before turning to Morgan. "What did she tell you?"

"Mine was simple, but promising. I will acquire a large sum of money and become acquainted with two male cousins."

"Lucky girl. What about you Katy?"

As Katy told them about a forthcoming enhanced ability with animals, getting a good raise, and also meeting a handsome guy, her narrative suddenly stopped. She pointed at the set of bleachers to her left. "Hey, look. Your knight in shining armor. Near the bottom. About five rows up from the right." She stood, waved, and smiled.

Liz spotted Michael and his friends. Sure enough, there they were.

Morgan pulled Katy down. "They might see us."

"That's the point." Katy wiggled her eyebrows. "Maybe they're the guys from our readings."

Morgan rolled her eyes.

Katy wrinkled her nose at Morgan.

Liz watched Will talk to the other guys, who then raised their commemorative Renaissance mugs toward the ladies.

"Gotta hand it to them," Morgan said. "They drink and revel in style. Just look at them guffaw and shake their turkey legs at the knights."

"Just like Ye Ol' Days," said Katy. "Eat, Drynk, and be Merrie!"

During the show, the crowd cheered for their respective knights and howled against the other knights. The ladies' section belonged to the green knight from England. The cheerleader at the foot of their bleachers yelled, "HUZZAH!" They yelled at the black knight, "BOO!" enticing a rebuttal from the black knight's section where the guys sat.

Four knights demonstrated their riding skills and lance dexterity. As the black knight caught the golden ring with his lance, Morgan mumbled a risqué remark about his lance piercing her ring, mostly drowned out by the cheering and booing. Liz heard the comment and snickered.

Katy, not so graciously, complained about the horses' costumes. "Just look at all that fabric draping the horses in this hot sun."

Liz liked the shoulder-to-knee caparisons on the horses, each country's emblem emblazoned on the side of the garment, but she agreed about the heat. The temperature made sitting in the crowded stands warm already.

"I can't imagine having a rider with cape and armor riding me on such a warm afternoon...or could I?" Morgan snickered. "The green knight is kind of cute, Liz. He resembles Michael."

Liz imagined the green knight, devoid of his armor, and ready to ride once more in her castle chambers.

After the show, the ladies headed to the outdoor pub next to the arena for a second beer. They arrived early enough to snag a picnic table in the shade, an important commodity in Arizona.

"May we tarry a spell with you damsels?" Michael said as his hand softly touched Liz's back. She looked up, surprised that she flushed so quickly at his touch.

"Please do," Katy said, and moved over to make room for the guys. Michael sat next to Liz, his eyes locked on hers until she couldn't take it and looked away, butterflies tickling her stomach in spite of herself. Will dropped down next to Katy and Richard grabbed an extra chair and sat on the end next to Morgan. Thinking about Michael and the group, Liz mumbled, "What hand fate doth plant?" A little Shakespeare came to mind.

"Your house ale all around, my fair wench." Richard said when the bar maiden arrived. "I assume you ladies drink beer?"

"Do fish swim?" Katy asked which generated a group chuckle. "Do you come here often?"

"We're diehard fans and attend almost every year," Richard said.

"And you always rent costumes, Your Grace?" Liz pointed at Richard's crown.

"We do," Richard said. "That way we can be someone different every year."

"So you're obviously the King," Morgan said, with a roll of her hand.

"Yes, obviously." Richard puffed out his royal chest.

"And Michael's sword makes him a Knight." Katy assumed.

"He should be an Earl," Liz said, and exchanged a knowing look with Michael in reference to their previous Earl Grey tea conversation.

"And you should be Lady Grey," Michael said with a wide grin at their inside joke.

"What ye be, Will?" Katy raised her eyebrows.

"I'm but a lowly commoner, Milady, but I do see that thine eyes are the loveliest in all the land."

Katy blushed and batted her lids. "Tis ale, kind Sir, that blurs thy vision."

"Ohhhhh!" Richard rolled his eyes. "But you are right about this ale. Ah, the aroma of cold barley and hops on a hot day!"

Amid the small talk, Richard took Morgan's right hand and asked, "Is that a Morganite stone?"

Startled, she snatched her hand back in reflex. "How would you know that?"

With a gracious roll of his hand toward Morgan, "I'm a jeweler by trade. May I see it, Your Majesty?"

With a scolding look from Katy, Morgan reluctantly gave her hand back to Richard. As she listened to the conversation, Liz assumed it had to be Richard's delivery that rubbed Morgan the wrong way.

"My highly-trained eye estimates 2.5 karats, brilliant cut, 10-point diamonds surrounding the crown, 18 karat gold, at least 50 years old. Did you buy it because of your name?"

"No. It was a favorite of my grandmother's. My grandfather purchased it for her on their first trip to San Diego; there's a mine near there. Mom named me as a gift to her dad."

"Ah, well, bring it in anytime and I'll give you an appraisal and a free cleaning." Richard handed Morgan his card.

Morgan softened her demeanor slightly. "Thank you for your kind offer, Your Grace."

"So how did you guys discover the Renaissance Festival?" Katy asked.

"Michael's mom adopted a greyhound here many years ago. Now he volunteers with the greyhound adoption group," Will said. "He also takes pictures and creates all the graphics on the adoption website."

Liz pulled the greyhound brochure out of her pocket and flipped it over, noting Michael's name. She then simply stared at him.

"Close your mouth, Liz." Morgan whispered.

"Liz has it bad for one of their black greyhounds," Katy said.

"You mean Duke?" Michael asked.

Stunned, Liz simply nodded her head yes.

"I'll be posting his picture on their website tomorrow," Michael said. "He's completed his foster training and is ready for adoption. I've thought about him for myself and he seems to like me. But if you want him, I'll hold off on the posting and talk to Adonia for you."

"She talked to Adonia forever this morning. Didn't she, Morgan? She'll remember Liz. And Duke really likes her." Katy said.

"I love her name," Liz said. "She told me what it means. It's unique. She's a compelling woman."

"She thinks the dogs bring a special kind of love to certain people." Michael sipped his beer.

"Don't all dogs?" Katy spread her raised hands.

"True, but she's very particular about who gets her dogs. If Duke likes Liz then we should swing by later and talk to Adonia about him." Michael looked at Liz intently.

"Sure, okay." That's twice today that he'd earned big points in her book.

Morgan leaned over and whispered to Liz, "I wonder if he is

Barry White-worthy?"

Liz blushed once more. One of favorite Barry-songs, *Never, Never Gonna Give You Up*, started dripping sex in her mind from that deep velvet voice of his. Now all of her cheeks tingled.

"See those kids pelting the thief with wet sponges?" Will pointed at a man bent over in the fake stocks across the way. "Last year Richard volunteered to go into the stocks for an hour of fund raising for the greyhound group. They got him something good."

"I'd pay to see that," Morgan laughed a bit too energetically.

"Maybe the lady needs a pelting," Richard said.

"Our beers are gone," Katy said before Morgan could retaliate. "Let's go check out the latest medieval duds next door."

Will took that as an invitation to all. "After you, Milady."

"I'll buy the corsets if you ladies wear them," Richard pulled out his wallet and left a big tip.

"Oh, you'd love to see more corset-flesh. Either peeking or heaving as the case may be," Morgan cocked a thumb in the direction of the bar wench and her ample assets.

Michael shrugged as the others chuckled, "He's really a great guy behind that smart mouth," and bowed to Richard who grinned regally.

Continuing on through the village, the guys tried their skill at Jacob's Ladder. Will hunched over and began his angled ascent. He stepped on the first wooden rung, holding onto the ropes on either side. The skilled commoner made it almost to the top before he lost his balance. The ladder, tied at each end with a single pivot connection, spun as designed and sent him to the straw pile below. The thing was damned near impossible to climb.

"Let's wager on these other two," Morgan said to Katy and Liz.

"Two dollars on Michael." Katy dug for the funds.

"I'll bet $20 on myself," boasted Richard, poking Michael in the arm.

"I'll take that bet," Morgan dug in her pocket then fanned an 'Andrew Jackson' in the air.

The other two didn't fare as well as Will. Michael only made it halfway and Richard's cape thwarted his attempt on the second rung.

"Hah, I'll take that $20 please," Morgan stretched her hand out to Richard before he could get up.

"Come here and get it," Richard grabbed Morgan's hand and pulled her onto the hay with him.

Morgan lightly pounded Richard's arm with her fists as he reached for his wallet.

"Make sure he pays you for the tumble in the hay, too," Michael yelled, which sent the watching crowd into hysterical laughter.

Morgan stood up and waived Richard's $20 bill to the crowd, not allowing Richard to get the best of her.

"That's my girl!" Liz yelled, again noting the odd tension between the two.

They stopped at the privies so Morgan could remove bits of hay from her hair, repair her appearance, and rid herself of the beer.

Winding their way along the curvy oval construct of the festival, they gazed into the many boutiques. The facades of the shops varied just like an old medieval village. Hand-crafted products hung in displays around the tops of wooden booths dotting the center of the pathway. Vines, although fake, crawled up wooden window frames. Hand painted signs hung advertising each specialty. Wares spilled out from open doorways and tempted shoppers as they passed by.

"Can we stop here?" Michael asked the group. "I want a flask."

"Sure," Liz answered automatically as if only the two of them existed. She watched Michael shop and noticed how the muscles moved in his arms. His hands closed gently around the vessels as if they were treasures.

"Those are stainless steel, aren't they?" Katy pointed at the hanging flasks.

"Good eye," Michael replied. "The brass plate on the front of each one is stamped with different Celtic designs, like this Tree of Life."

"Those branches signify embracing life and the roots are to keep you grounded," Morgan recited. "The flask Richard selected with the Sword on it represents leadership, power, and protection. Will's flask displays the Ring of Fire which is known for spiritual cleansing and improved health."

All very apropos choices. Liz's friend impressed her.

"And how did you come by this wealth of knowledge?" Richard asked.

"Oh, just something I acquired here and there," Morgan replied, waving her right hand aloft as she walked on.

Along the way, Will stopped. "Milady needs a circlet to bring out her smile."

"Oh, 'tis a grand gesture, to be sure," Katy said, and dropped a curtsey.

Will picked out a white one for Katy, wound with pale blue silk flowers and ribbons to match her outfit. She blushed as he placed it on her head, and touched her hair gently.

"Thou must be a knight in disguise as a knave," Katy said batting her eyelashes.

They caught a fire juggling show at one of the theatres before heading back to the arena for the 5:00 PM final joust, where they found enough seats together. Katy struggled to get around a little boy on the end of the next lower row who waved his sword about to slay an imaginary foe. Liz dodged him trying not to spill her second brew on his head.

Richard watched the busty hand-maiden cheerleader and yelled with enthusiasm after each instruction. His cheers must have helped. The green knight won the joust and received the queen's scarf as a reward.

Beginning their descent from the bleachers after the show, Liz tripped on the little boy's neglected wooden sword. In a flash, she plummeted sideways. Michael grabbed for her, but missed. Her head slammed against the railing. Liz slumped down the stairs. Michael fell to his knee beside her, "Oh, God. Liz."

Morgan cried out and maneuvered her way toward Liz, with Katy close on her heels.

The boy's mother screamed and pulled her son out of the way. "Oh my God, is she okay?"

Nearby spectators crowded in to get a better look.

CHAPTER 5

Blood stained the railing where Liz's head hit and pooled where she lay unconscious.

Michael scooped up Liz before Will could warn him not to move her. He stood there holding her as his heart raced faster than a jouster's horse.

"Don't move her any more, Michael. Let me look." Will quickly discovered the source of her blood. "Katy, press your hand on her head here with this napkin to slow the bleeding. I need to check her pulse. Richard, call Jim. Morgan, handle crowd control."

"Move aside, give us some room," Morgan yelled, quickly following orders.

Richard immediately called Jim Smith, his EMT cousin who worked part-time at the festival's first-aid station. "They'll be here with an ambulance momentarily," he told Michael. "They can drive behind the scenes to get pretty close to the bleachers."

"Make way for the ambulance," Morgan yelled. "Clear the steps." The crowd obeyed fairly well, despite their curiosity.

"I'm so sorry," the boy's mother told Michael. The tiny child cried out, wanting his sword. It had fallen off the bleachers during the fray. Their words and actions barely registered in his mind.

Michael's eyes followed the ambulance that Jim drove through the side gate. Morgan waved her arms to flag him down.

Will hurried down the stairs to meet Jim and the other EMT at the ambulance and told him what happened on the way back up. "She's unconscious, has a steady pulse, and is breathing okay."

"Lay her here," directed Jim, placing a backboard on the bleacher in front of Michael. The remaining crowd silently watched as if holding their collective breath.

Michael also held his breath and carefully laid her on the backboard and Jim quickly began his cursory vital check while his partner radioed his findings to the hospital. "Female, approximately 25-30, unconscious, steady breathing, pulse 75, BP 110 over 75, scalp laceration approximately two inches, applying sterile compress and pressure."

"Let's get her down to the gurney," Jim said to his partner.

"Make way," Morgan yelled. "Move aside people, PLEASE." She followed closely acting as a bodyguard for Liz. Approaching onlookers began murmuring as Morgan waved her arms again, but they retreated despite their curiosity.

Katy just stood there looking at the blood on her hands. Her veterinary training never prepared her for this. She wiped her hands on her shirt while her tears streamed down her face. Michael hugged her briefly, the blood on his clothes mingling with the blood on hers, and then led her down the steps.

Jim gave Richard the location of the nearest hospital.

"Morgan, go with Liz in the ambulance," Will ordered. "Richard, follow us. Katy, Michael, come with me." That took care of all the cars they had arrived in.

"Of course," Michael said as they followed the ambulance out the emergency exit, and ran through the parking lot.

♥♥♥

When the guys and Katy arrived at the hospital, they met Morgan in the emergency waiting room. She had already checked in for Liz and sat alone with her head in her hands.

"Have you heard anything?" Michael half-yelled from across the room as he hurried to Morgan.

Morgan stood and hugged him. She waivered as the dried blood on Michael's shirt crunched against her. "Not yet. I talked to her, but she never woke up. I can't believe this is happening. Jim thought she might be stable, but that doesn't mean she's okay. He mentioned a possible concussion, but they'll have to diagnose that here."

"He's excellent at what he does," Richard assured Michael and Morgan. "He may be an EMT, but he would make a fine doctor. He responded quickly, and in reality, she didn't lose as much blood as it looked. I'm sure she'll be okay soon."

Michael wanted desperately to believe him.

Jim came out after a while. "All I can tell you is that Liz is still unconscious, but her EKG is normal. Her x-ray showed no fractures. The wound itself doesn't look serious unless it gets infected." He lowered his voice, "Don't say anything when they talk to you because I'm not supposed to share any details, HIPPA laws and all. I told them you were here and asked them to let you know something as soon as possible. I need to get back to the festival now." He turned to Richard. "Call me and let me know how she's doing."

"Will do, Cuz. Thanks." Richard shook Jim's hand.

"Michael, call me anytime, day or night, if there's anything I can do. I'll try to check in after my shift."

"Thanks, Bud," Michael said as he watched him leave. He rubbed his right ear as he fidgeted. "This is my fault. I should have caught her. I failed to protect her."

"You know that's not true." Richard clapped his hand on

Michael's shoulder. "It all happened too fast. Liz won't blame you and no one else does either."

"Thank you for calling Jim so quickly, Richard." Morgan said. "You're an angel."

"A diamond-in-the-rough, that's me!" Richard reached out and tucked a stray strand of hair behind Morgan's ear.

"Where would we be without you?" Morgan turned to Will. "You knew the precise procedures to follow."

"I do what I can." He beamed at her compliment and blushed when she hugged him. "I'm going to check for more details. Michael, please stay with Katy for me."

After Will left, Katy asked, "Michael, does Will have access to Liz back there?"

"No, but they may let him in if he presents his X-Ray license, or they might tell him something." At least Michael hoped so.

"I contacted Liz's Mom from the ambulance," Morgan said. "I told her we'll manage everything until they arrive. They were working at their restaurant in Scottsdale and will arrive presently."

Michael worried whether Liz's parents would arrive safely. He imagined their panicked emotions on the drive over and wondered if they'd blame him like he blamed himself.

"We'll keep you company, if that's okay?" Richard asked.

"Of course, thank you." Morgan said.

After a while, Richard went for sodas and water and handed ginger ales to Morgan and Katy.

The solemn group passed the time primarily with tales about Liz. Morgan told the one about Liz reading *Romeo and Juliet* in their college Shakespeare class. "Unbelievably, she forgot Romeo's name precisely at 'Wherefore art thou...' Liz pretended she performed as expected." Her story generated a few nervous chuckles.

A while later, Will arrived with some news. "The good news is that I know someone back there. They've closed her wound and there's minimal swelling at the site so far. She's still unconscious, but they should be out soon with an update on her prognosis. They wouldn't tell me anything else."

Morgan smiled a little smile and called Liz's parents. "They're just pulling into the hospital parking lot now. I'll go meet them," Morgan said. "Katy and Michael, your bloody shirts will send them into hysterics if that's their first impression."

"I hate this damn shirt." Katy looked down once again at the blood on her new t-shirt.

Michael worried about that very thing. How could he make a good first impression this way?

Morgan led Liz's parents to admissions, explaining that she had checked her in, but the hospital needed some authorization on the paperwork because she couldn't admit Liz herself. It didn't take long, because Morgan had given the Admissions person most of Liz's pertinent information. Afterward, she led them both to the waiting room.

Liz's mom, Nancy, cried out when she saw Katy's shirt. Ken, her husband, caught Nancy as her knees buckled and helped her to a chair.

"Here's some water," Will said.

After Nancy regained some composure, Will handled the introductions and explained Liz's current status as he knew it.

They tried to comfort one another while they waited for more news. Time passed slowly, so Michael fetched some snacks from the vending machine for something to do. Katy talked about Duke, the greyhound, to ease their thoughts.

"Liz always talked about adopting a greyhound one day," Nancy said. "Maybe this is the right one."

"Michael informed her he'd arrange it if that's her desire," Morgan said.

"Yes, I can help her." Michael explained his connection

with Duke, hoping to share his concern for Liz.

Nancy smiled slightly. "I think she'd love that."

A doctor finally appeared at the door and called, "Nancy and Ken Nottingham?"

Michael jumped up and prayed it would be good news.

"That's us." Ken and Nancy stood and made their way over to the doctor who introduced herself as a neurologist on staff and said, "Liz is temporarily in the ICU. She is stable in most regards, but is unconscious."

Ken's eyes flew wide open. "Why is she still unconscious?"

"That can happen sometimes with head injuries. We're unsure why trauma can do that, but it usually doesn't last long. Her vitals are good. She has no intracranial bleeding and very little swelling, which is a good sign."

"How long will she be unconscious?" Michael couldn't hold his tongue.

"There's really no way of knowing with head traumas. We'll monitor her closely."

"Can we see her now?" Ken asked.

"Yes, follow me."

Morgan approached and interrupted, "Can we go, too?"

"Are you family?"

"Yes."

"This way, please." Morgan and Katy followed, leaving the guys in the waiting room.

"We'll return soon," Morgan told them. "Please wait if possible."

Morgan's and Katy's tear-stained faces returned to the waiting room a few minutes later with a report for the guys.

Michael's heart sank at the sight of their tears.

"She looks like she's sleeping," Katy closed her eyes. "Except for the bandages. And all the wires and tubes. She's getting oxygen. She doesn't need a ventilator."

"You seem stronger," Will said.

"Better than Liz," Katy answered taking a deep breath.

"Did the doctor say anything else?" Michael hoped for some kind of good news.

"No additional details," Morgan replied. "I detest these hospital smells—all the failed bodily functions covered up by disinfectant cleaners. It's an invisible fog that clings to your clothes and skin!" She turned to hide her tears.

"Morgan?" Richard asked after a few moments and lightly touched her back.

"I'm fine. It's so damned infuriating! We're helpless. We should return to her side now."

"Should we leave or stay?" Richard asked. "We can stay if you need us, of course."

"We'll be fine." Morgan nodded. "Go ahead and go and thanks for your assistance."

"Call me, Katy, if you need anything, no matter how late it is, okay?" Will asked.

Michael handed Morgan his business card before they left. "Please let me know how she's doing."

Liz could hear the people in her room, but she couldn't wake up, couldn't speak, and couldn't move. "It must be one of my memories," Liz said to herself because no one would answer her.

"That Michael seemed rather misty eyed," Nancy said to Katy when they returned to Liz's room. "Didn't you just meet these guys today?"

"Yeah. Weren't they amazing?" Katy said. "Who would come here? And wait with girls they barely knew?"

"They seem decent enough, but I'm not sure about amazing," Ken said. "What do you know about them?"

Katy eagerly provided Liz's parents with a detailed background of each guy while Liz listened.

"Sweetie," Nancy said, "it sounds like you know them pretty well already."

"Somewhat," Katy said. "We're going to stay with you tonight. Okay?"

"Of course," Nancy hugged her for the longest time.

No change in Liz's condition made for a long night. Ken rubbed her hand, he stroked her hair, and he kissed her forehead. Nothing happened.

Liz felt everything, but couldn't move. "*Dad, please, can't you hear me?*"

The neurologist arrived after a time to check on her. "Can I answer any questions?" she asked. Liz had questions, but couldn't ask.

"She hasn't woken up yet. How long will she be out? She won't stay this way, will she?" Ken asked in one long breath.

"There just aren't any standard or specific answers at this point. The good news is that she's breathing on her own and she's strong."

"What else can be done to help her? Is there anything that hasn't been done yet? No offense intended. The waiting is just so difficult." Ken cupped his mouth with his hand.

"Each person reacts differently according to their normal healing patterns, the amount of trauma experienced during the injury, and so on. We're constantly monitoring her and will know if she needs anything else. There's nothing else to do at the moment."

"So we just wait, right? When can we expect to see you again? We're just anxious for some good news."

"I know you are, Mr. Nottingham. The staff will be

monitoring her condition. If there's any change, they'll call me and I'll call you. Otherwise, I'll stop by in a couple of hours."

"Can she hear us?" Ken asked.

"Yes," Liz thought she yelled but no one responded. At least some of her questions got answered. Thanks, Dad.

"There have been a few documented cases where patients claim to remember some of what happens while they're unconscious. I haven't personally experienced that outcome, but you could talk to her just in case."

"Thanks, we will," Ken shook the doctor's hand.

After hours of chatting to Liz and waiting, a nurse finally arrived with extra blankets for the family. "Oh, bless you," Katy said. "It's cold in here."

As the quiet continued, Liz assumed everyone had fallen asleep, even though she hadn't, or thought she hadn't. The constant beeping of her monitors created a low white noise. Liz heard her mom wake up to insist that her dad take a turn sleeping.

The doctor came and went during Nancy's vigil, but Liz didn't learn anything new. Nancy cried silently on and off until Morgan and Katy both stirred, waking Ken as well.

The morning seemed to stretch on and on. All Liz could do was to listen for voices and movement. Katy surfed the Web on her iPhone providing tidbits of information here and there.

An orderly came in to change Liz's bedding. "Why don't ya'll take a walk, it'd do ya some good ta stretch them legs. Get some breakfast. It'll be awhall afore I'm done."

It's good for them to get out of here for a while, Liz thought, but didn't want to be left alone.

The saddened group found the cafeteria one floor below, after a quiet elevator ride. They couldn't think about eating and settled for coffee.

Nancy leaned into Ken and cried against his chest. Ken suggested that the girls should call the guys and provide an update.

♥♥♥

After a short stroll down a well-lit corridor, Katy and Morgan found a small, unoccupied lounge. "Hi, Michael. It's Morgan calling as promised to give you an update."

"Is Liz okay?" He had hoped for good news.

"There's no significant change. She remains unconscious." Her shaky voice unnerved Michael.

"I'm sorry, Morgan. What do the doctors say?"

"The usual. They can't offer a concrete prognosis about her condition or any timelines."

"What can I do? Do you need anything?" There must be something to help the situation.

"We're fine, thanks. I must return, but I'll call again as appropriate."

"Please do. I'll let the other guys know." Michael sat staring at the now silent phone, not sure why he cared as much as he did. It's not as if he needed another woman's problems on his hands at the moment, but she seemed so different. Someone worth caring about.

♥♥♥

When the four returned to the quiet room Liz occupied, she had crisp sheets tucked tightly on her bed. They circled her bed to look for any signs of change.

Liz heard her dad say, "She looks the same, like she is sleeping peacefully."

"I'll go hunt down some magazines or something and

return momentarily," Morgan said as her footfalls echoed out of the room.

As Morgan scouted down a long hall, she ducked inside an empty room, unseen by the staff, and looked up at the plain white ceiling. Morgan prayed to the powers that be and told whoever listened about Liz's good karma. She explained that Liz had done volunteer work, that she was a wonderful friend, and that she had such a good heart. She asked for Liz's blessings to be returned and for her to be healed quickly. After a moment, she ducked back out and began her literature hunt.

After a while, Liz's dad asked, "Katy, will you pray with us? Would you mind?"

"Of course not. I'd be honored." Katy reached for their hands.

Liz listened as Katy led them in prayer asking for a quick and complete recovery.

"Her eyelids are moving," her dad said. "Nancy, look, her eyelids are moving."

Liz recognized her mother's sharp intake of breath.

Morgan returned just then. "I'll find someone." Not waiting for a response to the call button, she threw her collection of reading material on the closest chair and ran out of the room.

The ICU nurse arrived quickly and asked, "What's happening?" Of course, Liz couldn't respond.

"It's only been a couple of minutes," Ken replied, "but her eyelids moved like they do when she's dreaming."

"Let me take a look." The nurse lifted one of Liz's eyelids and shown a penlight back and forth. Liz's eye did not follow the light, but the pupil constricted. "It could be REM sleep."

The pressure on her arm let Liz know that the nurse checked her IV connections and the readings on the various monitors.

"We're monitoring her at the nurses' station, but press the call button if anything new happens. I'll see if the doctor is busy."

The remainder of the day followed like the morning. Medical staff cycled in and out, did what they do best, and provided comforting smiles. Family members traded places and rotated breaks to stretch their legs.

The neurologist stopped by at the end of the day to discuss Liz's condition, which she did with a great deal of patience. "I'm sure you know that she's holding her own. I prescribe some rest for the lot of you. We'll watch her closely through the night, don't worry."

"We can't leave her!" Ken shook his head.

"He's right, Ken," said his sense-of-reason wife. "If we're exhausted, we won't do her any good. We'll come back early tomorrow."

"Fine." Ken nodded and escorted Nancy out of Liz's room.

As they left, Liz began one of her longer dreams, or perhaps it was a memory.

CHAPTER 6

Egypt, 1341 BC

Saturday night, Liz's dream began…

A wet nose tried to nudge Liz awake. She ignored it, too comfy in the cushy bed, and went back to sleep. The soft "Ooof" sound bothered her more; but she ignored that too and rolled over. However, when the dog jumped on her bed, she flew awake, adrenaline primed her into defensive mode, and she pulled at the covers to guard herself.

When nothing happened, she lowered the covers to see Duke staring at her. It was him; she knew it. In addition to looking just like him, she could sense his inner presence. Liz drowsily scratched his ear for a few moments, which soothed them both.

A voice very much like Adonia's boomed. Liz recognized the slight Italian tone in Duke's foster-mom's voice. "Your queen won't wait all day for you to arise." Adonia entered the gossamer curtains and yanked aside the covers, sending Duke bounding for the other side of the bed.

Liz gasped, "Adonia?"

"You were expecting Nefertiti herself to wake you up? Apparently, Duke isn't enough." She stood there with her hands on her hips glaring at Liz. "As you know, this is your first day of training and I'm your instructor."

"I'm excited about it, but I really gotta pee. Where do I go?" Liz rose from the soft linens.

Adonia gave Liz details about the facilities. As Liz got up, Duke sprawled out on the bed as if he owned it.

Upon returning, Liz sat next to Adonia, who waited on a chaise across the room from the bed.

"Your bath is ready and your gown is on your bed." She motioned for Liz to follow her. They proceeded through a long archway into another room with a small bathing pool. Adonia rushed Liz with the sweep of her hand. She chided her to not keep the queen waiting.

Liz disrobed and slid into the warm water. "This smells wonderful. What is that scent?"

"The primary scent is from the Lotus Lily, a most revered smell for royalty. You're entitled to a small portion given your position serving the queen. The cleansing cream is made from lime, oil, and perfume." Adonia handed the cream to Liz.

"What a great way to start the day! What's next, Adonia?"

"To begin with, I hear there is danger lurking about. Remember as the third attendant to the queen you must give your life for her if necessary. Just as each of us must."

"Did they tell you the source of the danger?"

"No, but the rumors are more frequent. Continue to use your expertise to advise Nefertiti on all matters regarding the arts and her funeral items. Remain by her side, but be alert. I'll watch over you and Duke as best as I can from a distance. You must follow the queen into the throne room and sit at her feet on the lowest pillow on the dais. Duke will remain by your side. He is well trained. You will sit at an angle so that you can see Nefertiti's face at all times except when the artisans arrive. When an artisan presents a gift or a commission, you must quickly assess it from your location and then watch your queen. If she needs an opinion, she will look at you and raise her chin. You simply nod or shake your head subtly, yes or no. She might look to you for craftsmanship or authentication, but she will determine if it suits her."

"What if I can't tell from a distance?"

"Simply hold out your hand thusly." Adonia extended her palm upward at waist level. "Nefertiti will instruct the artisan to place the item within your reach for evaluation. You then quickly examine the item and express your approval or denial. DO NOT SPEAK unless spoken to. It could be seen as usurping her judgment. You must take your duties seriously. This is one of the highest honors in the land. Apparently, my life and Duke's life depend on you as well. Your fate is

62

our fate."

Duke watched her from behind the sheer curtains. She moved to go pet him, but Adonia gave her the evil eye again and motioned to the dressing table. "Please hurry."

She sat and closed her eyes as a slave applied Kohl eyeliner. Azurite shadow came next, followed by a peach-colored cheek powder.

"As you know, a new complex is being built north of Karnak at Amarna to further Akhenaten's new religious concept. Some items may be presented today for either that or Nefertiti's burial chamber."

Liz said. "I already know this, but let me make sure I get this straight."

"Morgan verifies the logging of Nefertiti's jewels and other valuables. Her accounts are logged with those that the vizier holds for the pharaoh which Richard handles as first attendant. Katy cares for the royal dogs. The pharaoh's second is Will, his medical adviser, and his third is Michael as artist supervisor. Michael's job is similar to mine, but he also monitors all carvings, paintings, sculptures, and so on in the royal properties. Before this assignment I know he worked as an independent artisan. Is that right?"

"Exactly."

Next came the wrapping of Liz's hair before a black braded wig covered her head. A circlet held the wig in place.

"Liz, your queen awaits," Adonia said and motioned toward another archway. Duke jumped down and stood by her side. Liz smiled, gave him a pet, and followed Adonia. Duke remained by her side without leash or direction. They lined up in the hallway behind Katy and Morgan who turned to look at her and smiled.

"Hey ladies, you look wonderful," Liz said, only to be shushed by everyone at the same time. They turned and progressed down the hallway to Nefertiti's quarters—a room much larger than the one Liz occupied. There, they lined up again and waited while Adonia remained in the hallway. Liz stood in amazement at the opulent nature of Nefertiti's quarters—the spun gold bed curtains that hid the royal blue bed spreads, the stone inlay on her makeup table and stool, and the huge plants that braced the two doorways that led to a long balcony.

Servants bustled about everywhere, preparing the queen for her day.

With an elegant neck, long, thin face, and perfectly placed features, Nefertiti exuded perfection. Almost. Liz thought that her ears were too large or at least not proportional with her other features. Nefertiti's shaved head probably accentuated the dimensions of her ears. Liz took a quick breath, grateful that they hadn't had time to shave her head.

Gold cords and jewels decorated Nefertiti's gown and sandals instead of the silver provided to her attendants. Jewels encrusted her headpiece and the diadem. A gold Uraeus, an asp, the symbol of sovereignty, dominated the front. Jewels encrusted her gold neck bib or collar. Liz wanted to reach out and touch the masterpiece, but feared that they might take her head off if she did.

Nefertiti's white greyhound lounged at her side sporting a similar jewel-encrusted collar. Liz worried about how heavy it must be on the dog's neck. Then she wondered if the pharaoh had a black dog or a matching white dog. She must have been staring because the queen looked directly at her. Liz bowed her head. Nefertiti turned and continued her dressing ritual. She stood, received minor alterations, and then simply said, "Enough."

On cue, her dog stood up, the servants backed off, and Katy and Morgan stood straighter. The queen gracefully headed toward the door to the left. Morgan and Katy fell in line behind her, so Liz did the same. Their dogs, including Duke, were perfectly trained to heel with their respective people. Without Adonia handy, Liz remained on high alert as she had instructed.

They passed several carvings and wall paintings during the long progression from Nefertiti's chambers to the throne room. Many artisans had gathered to alter the carvings to replace the old god AMUN with the new god ATEN. Papyrus columns topped with different capitals held up the ceilings of the huge throne room.

People and goods lined both sides of the entryway. Five large steps spanned the width of the throne platform, the deepest supporting two massively carved, backless seats for the pharaoh and his queen. The royal subjects showed the proper respect for their queen as she floated past. She ascended the dais and scanned the crowd before she lowered herself onto her throne.

Morgan sat down on a pillow waiting on the next step and curled her legs under her to the side. Her dog reclined beside her on his pillow. Katy sat on the next lower step with her dog, so once again, Liz followed their example. Duke reclined on his pillow as well. Constructed of the finest linens with similar silver cording, the pillows made sitting on the stone steps of the dais tolerable. The whole positioning of the scene made Liz think of a wedding procession with the participants positioned in an inverted 'V' at the altar.

Akhenaten, resplendent in spite of his pot-belly, arrived next with a white greyhound. Since he no longer believed in Anubis, the god of embalmment, Liz suspected a black dog would be taboo for him. That dog answered one of her earlier questions.

Richard, Will, and Michael, along with their dogs followed right behind. Their dogs matched those of the ladies, a brindle, a red fawn, and a black. Everyone's eyes met in recognition. She wanted to smile, but sensed that she should not.

"Bring the first treasure," one of the guards commanded.

"I bring you a new collar, Your Majesty," said the first artisan, kneeling in front of the pharaoh as he displayed the treasure. Lapis Lazuli glinted as the light struck it as did the massive gold orb in the center, surrounded by dark green jasper and other stones. The pharaoh nodded his approval, looked to Richard, who then nodded his approval as well.

"Very well," said Akhenaten, and a guard led the artisan to a waiting zone.

As the morning continued, an artisan presented the last item for the pharaoh—a statue of Akhenaten in his kilt seated on a cushion. The head cloth and crown also displayed a rearing Uraeus. His hands held his crook and flail. Carved from dark yellow limestone, his belly looked flabbier than it did in person. Akhenaten looked at Michael without any reference of opinion. Michael took a chance and shook his head "No." Liz's eyes flew open wide and the air stopped dead in Liz's throat.

"Explain." Akhenaten frowned.

"The face and nose are too wide, your majesty, it does you no justice. Thutmosis can alter it to slim the nose and face with no problem," Michael replied. "However, the lips are full and perfect,"

65

Michael added, afraid for Thutmosis, the new sculptor. "I can help him adjust it as necessary."

"Make the change," Akhenaten said to Thutmosis who bowed, turned, smiled at Michael, and took his place on the 'approved' side of the waiting area.

Liz began breathing again. She kept her wondering mind busy by thinking about the statue. Miniatures were often made before carving any grand representation. The proportions must be accurate so that they could be used to scale the larger carvings. The stress of the day wore on Liz and her stomach growled.

The morning's commerce concluded just in time with a grand feast and lively entertainment for the royal entourage and the lucky artisans in an adjacent room.

Liz savored several dishes: fish, grapes, figs, pomegranates, melons, cucumbers, radishes, breads, and beer, as well as some kind of bird. "Gazelle?" a slave offered a serving to Liz. Game to try it, she accepted a small helping.

The attendants sat on either side of Akhenaten and Nefertiti and watched the entertainment. Musicians played lively tunes on a harp, lute, and double flute. A man sang in a language Liz didn't understand while a dancing girl moved sinuously in her costume of ONLY a narrow belt slung low on her hips. Not only did she dance for the pharaoh, she wriggled suggestively for each of the guys in turn. The poor girl didn't seem to mind being ogled. Katy looked shocked. Morgan watched the guys, probably Richard, with an angry look on her face. That's telling, jealousy perhaps?

When the tune ended, Akhenaten and Nefertiti stood, which signaled the conclusion of the feast. Everyone else stood, waited for the royalty to exit, and then filed out of the dining area back down the hallway toward their respective quarters.

Morgan motioned Katy and Liz into her quarters and hugged them.

"Welcome," Katy said to Liz.

"Don't you look sexy," Liz replied. "Did you know that Adonia is here as well?"

"You rang?" Adonia asked. "I've always wanted to say that," she said with a rare moment of laughter. "Come back to your room now. You only have an hour to rest and refresh before you're due back."

Just then, a cloaked figure stuck his head in the archway and whispered, "Are you alone?" Morgan rushed to him and pulled him in out of the doorway. He dropped his hood.

"What are you doing here, Michael?" she asked.

"Why do you dare come here?" Adonia put her hands on her hips.

"No time. Listen," he continued, "we've heard some slaves saying that there may be an uprising against the pharaoh today, so you ladies need to stay especially alert. The old priests of AMUN oppose the pharaoh's new religion and we're afraid it could get ugly. If anything happens, abandon your queen. We think we can get you out safely. Watch each of us for guidance," Michael instructed.

"We have contingency plans for you, too, Adonia. If a short, bald-headed guy grabs you, go with him. He's with us. Be safe. Gotta go." He raised his hood and ducked out.

"Adonia, have you had a whiff of any news?" Morgan asked.

"I heard something a bit ago, and it could be rumor or fact," Adonia waved her hand. "It is a gamble. If you make the wrong choice, it could be deadly. But, heed Michael's advice and be ready just in case. And speaking of that, you all need to freshen up now," Adonia said and gently pushed Liz out of Morgan's quarters. "No more talk."

♥♥♥

The afternoon mirrored the morning, except for a few differences. The pharaoh's vizier stood lower on the royal steps, displaced by additional guards. A subtle change, but one the crowd would notice if they thought to look.

The royal scribe sat off the steps, instead of on the last step below Michael. He had a stack of papyrus by his side.

Liz noticed the additional guards, but they remained at the periphery of the subjects who awaited their moment with Akhenaten or

Nefertiti. The royal offspring appeared in court this afternoon as well. Two young daughters played to the left of Nefertiti and two older ones watched the proceedings on the right of the Akhenaten. Additional protection could be provided by keeping the family together, if anything happened.

After a couple of hours of craftsmen coming and going, near the end of the afternoon, Thutmosis returned with a Quartzite carving of Akhenaten's hand holding Nefertiti's hand. A sample for a future statue as well, Liz assumed.

"Do you approve?" Akhenaten asked his queen.

"It's lovely," she said and gave him an appreciative smile. Then she looked at Liz and said, "What do you think?"

Nervous, but trying to appear objective, Liz studied the statue, then the actual royal hands, and then the carving again. "The proportions are accurate, the hands are in a natural position, and even the fingernails are realistic."

Nefertiti smiled, and then nodded her approval. Liz began breathing again, not realizing she had held her breath.

At that moment, the first of the attackers shoved the scribe off his pillow and lunged toward the royal family. Papyrus scattered and ink ran from his mixing palette, which caused two of the attackers to slide and crash into each other. The scene played out before Liz's eyes in slow-motion.

The older daughters screamed. Akhenaten looked in their direction. The guards encircled them to ensure their safety.

Eight greyhounds jumped up and tried to get out of the way. Not being guard dogs, they only yelped, snapped, and scattered when they were stepped on or shoved in the process. Crowds rushed the doors, seeking an escape. Thutmosis dropped the carved hands, which sent them shattering across the stone floor.

The crying princesses and Nefertiti were rushed out a side door by her personal guards while other guards fought off the intruders.

Michael grabbed Liz's hand and rushed her down a side corridor. Their dogs scrambled closely behind them. He shoved open a secret panel, they plunged into darkness, and ran down a narrow tunnel.

"What about the others?" Liz asked between heavy breaths.

"Quiet," Michael replied and whispered, "They have an escape plan as well."

They came to a small room at the end of the tunnel. Michael looked back to ensure nobody followed them. They ducked their heads and entered the room with their dogs on their heels. Michael quietly closed and barred the door, then listened for a few moments.

The setting sun shone through narrow cracks in the walls of their hiding place. Provisions lined one wall of the dimly lit room while cushions lined the other wall.

Michael reached out to hold Liz and she rushed to him. "We'll be safe here for now," he whispered. "Keep your voice low." He continued to hold her close and stroked her back. Liz trembled slightly, not just from fright, but from Michael's touch as well. His heartbeat raced against her ear. She smelled his Egyptian smell, earthy and vaguely familiar. She looked up at Michael, "You risked your life to protect me."

"And I always will," he replied, "I'm not going to lose you no matter what." And with that came a surprised, desperate kiss that took her breath away.

He continued in a whisper, "My heart has known you for all eternity." He pulled off her wig and head wrappings, loosened her hair, and opened her heart.

She reached up, demanding another passionate kiss.

He tore himself away slightly, looked in her eyes, and murmured, "I'm all for where this is taking us, but we need to remain alert. If you keep kissing me, I can't guarantee your safety, in any sense of the word."

Liz returned a wry smile.

"Let's be ready," Michael continued to whisper. "We wait until

dark. I know a way out of here and we'll rendezvous with the others. Inside that purple cushion is a change of clothes for us." He pointed to the floor pillows. "We can't walk the streets dressed as part of the royal contingent. You'll have to leave your finery here. Let's change while we can." He released her and quietly retrieved his stash from the cushion.

The plain cloth tunic she picked up had a rope belt. "Is this mine?"

"Yes, unless you'd prefer to wear this kilt?" Michael held up the bland tan garment.

"Not hardly. At least we have matching rope sandals." Liz whispered and let out a nervous giggle.

"Women! Be serious and be glad for soft hands instead of calloused ones. We have to dress as working supervisors. If we were plain workers, we'd probably have to go nude."

"Like the naked dancing girl you were eyeing?" Liz performed a seductive dance of her own.

"Oh, just wait for the visions you'll see," he whispered. "Now get changed. I'll try not to peek."

"I could say the same," Liz said with raised eyebrows.

They changed, taking a quick look at each other, and she grinned about getting caught. The golden glow of the late afternoon sun made Michael's tight white buns contrast nicely against his tan, rippled back. Liz liked the view. He looked incredible in his kilt, too. Not tartan plaid, but it produced the same arousing result.

"Let's just sit here for a time. I need to think and listen. When the setting sun disappears through that crack, we need to wait about a half-hour and then leave. I'll do my best to get us out of here."

As they sat down on a cushion, he reached for her and placed his arm around her shoulder. She sat beside him and enjoyed the comfort of his strength. Duke, and Michael's dog, Ebony, had been patiently watching them. Now they whined slightly, got up, and came to rest beside their masters while they waited. Liz rested one hand on Duke, petting him absentmindedly while he stared into her eyes.

Liz tried to ignore Michael's body heat, and the heat that developed within her, so she whispered, "This situation is so weird."

"Absolutely."

"What's been the strangest part for you?"

"Well, since you asked…in a secret meeting, an Egyptian artist named Turin showed Richard and me a papyrus he just finished. So the pharaoh is reborn after rising out of the tombs, right?"

"Yeah, so?"

"Apparently, in addition to all their worldly goods, the Pharaohs are provided with scrolls containing instructions for the next life as detailed by the gods."

"And?"

"This particular scroll depicted instructions and diagrams on twelve sexual positions the pharaoh should know about in the next life. And it wasn't missing any details if you get my drift."

"Oh, that must have been a surprise."

"Exactly." He gave her a crooked grin.

"That certainly tops anything I saw." That description started her imagination going and she zoned out. Michael became so quiet that she fell away from this dream and into a more vivid, Egyptian dream of Michael naked.

CHAPTER 7

A short night's sleep, a shower, and change of clothes, helped to revive Liz's loved ones. Ken and Nancy returned to the hospital on Sunday morning. They found the neurologist examining Liz.

"Hello, Doctor," Liz's dad extended his hand. "How's my girl this morning?"

"She's resting peacefully after an uneventful night and her color is good."

Keep going, Liz said to herself. Tell them why I'm not awake yet.

"What's that smell?" her dad asked.

"We've added something called TPN for nourishment so she continues to remain strong. It's basically a protein/sugar mixture." The doctor pointed to an IV bag filled with a creamy-colored fluid.

"Is she any better?" Ken ran his hand down Liz's cheek, a familiar habit of his.

Her eyes watered slightly, but not enough for Ken to notice.

"There've been no complications overnight, so that's a good sign, but she's still unconscious. We ran an EEG last night, that's an electroencephalograph, to check the electrical activity of her brain."

"She's had EEGs before, during a sleep study. What will that tell us now?"

"Then you know it shows patterns of impulses. In her case, we looked for normal and abnormal sleeping states; we looked for unusual patterns. Liz had mostly Delta impulses as one would expect during sleep; those are the slower ones. We found everything close to normal, but we did see a periodic waking state; those are faster impulses. That is not usual when a person is unconscious; it's not bad, just inconclusive."

"That sounds like her study if I remember correctly, but could that have anything to do with her current state?"

"It's a step toward finding out. We scheduled an MRI for later today which will show more than the CAT scan. I'll check on the schedule and let you know something as soon as we know. We can talk more in detail then. Try to relax."

"I'll try. Thanks."

Liz knew her dad wouldn't relax, not one little bit.

Morgan and Katy padded in just as the doctor left.

"Did something happen? How is she?" Morgan asked.

"She's strong, no complications, but they ran an EEG and found some normal and some interesting patterns. They're going to do an MRI later," Ken said.

"That's a positive step, right?" Morgan rubbed Ken's shoulder.

"That's good," Katy said. "I'm glad they're being aggressive. With the testing, I mean."

"Why didn't they do an MRI first?" Ken asked Katy.

"They're expensive. Her insurance won't pay for it unless it's warranted."

"Oh, glad she has excellent insurance," Ken plopped down in the chair next to Liz's bed.

Liz was glad, too. With her klutzy nature, she knew she always needed the best she could afford.

"Katy, did Liz ever get a new tire?" Ken asked.

"No."

"You drove Liz's SUV home and back on that spare? I'm calling my service guy. He'll bring a new tire here and change it now."

"Yes. Thanks, sorry 'bout that."

"You're safe." Her dad said. "That's all that matters."

Liz always appreciated her dad's get-it-done manner. That's one less thing she'd need to worry about when she did finally wake up.

When the service man answered, Ken made the arrangements. Then they sat and waited some more.

♥♥♥

Mid-morning, a soft knock echoed in the silence. "Michael Donovan would like to visit, do you mind if he comes in?" The now-familiar nurse asked.

"Of course not," Katy said, "that is if you don't mind." Katy turned to Ken and Nancy.

"I can't see that it would do any harm," Ken said.

"Thank you, sir. How's Liz doing?" Michael entered the room at a slow pace. He wished he had a heart monitor on him the way his pulse throbbed.

"Call me Ken and thanks for coming. She's still unconscious, but holding her own. We don't know much more. They're running tests." Ken looked at Katy, then back at Michael. "Are you missing work, son?"

"Oh, no. I can do my volunteer work any time and I usually work a flexible schedule at home for my graphic art work. I hoped you wouldn't mind if I hung around for a little while."

"That would be fine. I hear you've just met our daughter."

"I've only known Liz one day, but I think there's something special about her."

"On that we agree. Come in and sit down." Ken motioned Michael over to one of the extra chairs.

"Thank you, Ken. How are you two holding up?" Nancy smiled, which put Michael more at ease.

"It's been stressful. Hard to watch your little girl just lay there, not knowing anything."

"Did you come alone, Michael?" Katy glanced at the doorway.

"Yes, the other guys are working today."

"Tell me about yourself." Ken said. "I hear you're an artist."

"Of sorts. Yes. I'm currently doing graphic work for three companies as an independent contractor. I enjoy it and it pays the bills. Plus it leaves me some free time to dabble with my painting. I do contemporary abstracts primarily and some animal portraits."

Keeping one eye on Liz, Ken asked, "Where did you go to school?"

"I got my Bachelor's in Fine Arts, with a Minor in Computer Science at Northern Arizona University."

"So you use both sides of your brain then."

"I guess you could say that." Michael smiled and offered a slight nod.

"Do you sell your paintings?"

"I'd like to, but haven't tried yet. Liz and I had talked briefly about showing some in her gallery."

Ken's face turned three shades of red. He stood up with clenched teeth and fists. "So you came for gallery business? Is that why you're here, to check on your future gravy train?"

"Ken!" Nancy snapped, and glared at her husband.

Michael stood, but kept his distance hoping that Ken would do the same. "No. No, Sir! Look, I'm here for personal reasons. Liz and I got along well at the Renaissance Festival. Also, I feel somewhat responsible. That kid left his sword laying right in the way. I tried to catch her." Michael grabbed the air in front of him as he told Ken. "I wasn't fast enough. I blame myself for her being here."

Ken looked up at the acoustic tiles in the metal ceiling grid and took a deep breath. An uneasy silence filled the room until Ken processed what Michael said.

"I'm sorry. I didn't mean to jump down your throat like that. This is just so damn difficult." Ken unclenched his fists, fell back onto the hard chair, and wiped his hand down his face.

"Sir, uh, Ken. That's understandable. I can't blame you for being protective."

"I suggested the gallery," Katy said on Michael's behalf. "We talked about it at the Renaissance Festival."

"I would never do anything to hurt Liz, at least not on purpose, but you'll just have to take my word for it at this point." Michael offered a half-smile and he sat down again.

"I see. Are you planning on staying long?"

"Ken, what's wrong with you?" Nancy grabbed Ken's arm.

Michael caught the scolding look that only wives can manage.

"Oh, I didn't mean it the way it sounded, Nancy. Let me rephrase that...Michael, can you stay a while so we can get to know each other. Is that better?" Ken looked at Nancy with raised eyebrows.

"I'd like to if you don't mind. Will you tell me about Liz?" Michael struggled to refocus the conversation.

"The apple of my eye, as they say," Ken replied. "A darling little lady one minute and a tomboy the next. Lots of bumps and bruises. This is not our first hospital visit. Her eyebrow scar is from falling off a block wall, a bloody scene that one. The small scar on her chin is from a bike wreck that included broken front teeth and several trips to the dentist. Fortunately, there's been nothing major, until now." Ken paused, pressing his eyes shut.

He resumed, "She liked to draw, color, and paint. To this day, she still traces shapes with her finger no matter where she is. She loved the art museums from a very young age."

"It sounds like we had some of the same hobbies," Michael smiled an easy smile.

"Her eyes are moving again," Morgan pointed at Liz's face. "Look, she has to be dreaming. I think that's a good sign." Everyone hurried to her side. Michael remained toward the back of the group, but tried to see through the small crowd.

"I'll get someone," Katy ran out. She returned quickly with the ICU nurse who examined Liz.

"There's still no change in response, but I'll let the doctor know what's happening. You can all stay for now, but no one else unless someone leaves."

Ken held Nancy while they waited. "I know she's going to

be alright. If she's dreaming, she's fine."

Ken turned to Michael. "Liz has a long history of both daydreams and regular nighttime dreams. The majority of them are good, but some are nightmares. We've heard her frequent dreaming is nothing to worry about and she deals with it just fine."

Liz's eyes stilled after a while and the group watched in silence for quite some time.

Katy laid her hand on her stomach. "We should go get some lunch. Take a break. Anyone hungry?"

"Always thinking of others." Nancy hugged Katy.

"I should be going," Michael said. "Sir, do you mind if I come back tomorrow?"

"It's Ken, remember. That's fine. Sorry again about earlier." Ken actually blushed.

"No problem." Michael turned to Morgan. "Will you call me later?"

"Of course," Morgan said. "It was kind of you to visit. Katy and I will escort you out."

"How good to see you, Jean-Luc." Nancy hugged him when he arrived at the hospital shortly after their lunch.

Liz smiled inwardly comforted by the presence of everyone she loved.

"The pleasure is mine, except under this sad situation. Our girl, how is she?" Jean-Luc turned toward Liz.

Nancy described her condition then Ken explained how it happened.

"That girl, she can trip on a leaf. You have my whole heart for her to be better soon. Can I hold her hand and talk with her?" Jean-Luc asked Nancy.

Nancy nodded. "Of course."

"Hurry with your nap, *ma chère,* I am bored without you. I need you back at the shop. You look pretty while you sleep, but it's time to wake up." Jean-Luc pressed a kiss on the back of her hand.

He looked at the noisy machines, took a deep breath, and then addressed her parents. "Her timing is good with her day off. Can I do anything for her or you both?"

"Just come back and visit when you can." Ken shook his hand. "We'll keep you abreast of her status."

"*Oui, s'il vous plaît.*" Jean-Luc shuffled out even more slowly than normal.

Liz hated to hear him go.

"How old is Jean-Luc?," Nancy asked Ken after Jean-Luc left.

"I think Liz said he was seventy-something, but he seems much older than that."

"I'm worried about him." Nancy clasped her hands together. "He looks so tired."

Now Liz worried more. She thought he looked exhausted, too.

"I'll check on him later, or we can ask Morgan to look in on him. She sees him more often than we do. She'll know if he's just missing a night's sleep or what."

Liz knew Morgan would go and continue to watch him, which gave her a little peace.

Early afternoon moved slowly into late afternoon with the tire repair providing the only diversion for the group.

Finally, someone wheeled Liz away for her MRI, leaving four sets of eyes to watch her go.

The doctor finally arrived later that evening. "Fortunately or unfortunately, the MRI didn't show anything out of the ordinary."

Oh great, Liz thought. My parents were going to go nuts.

"So what's next?" Ken asked. "Aren't there other tests that can be done?"

"Not at this point. All her tests show no specific issues that can be treated. We'll let her rest for now and we'll monitor her closely."

Ken placed his hands on his hips. "We need to know what's wrong."

"There's nothing that we can isolate at the moment. Why don't you folks get some rest tonight? We'll talk tomorrow and, of course, call you if there's any change at all."

"We'll stay for a while, then go," Nancy said. "Why don't you girls go home now?"

"Okay. We'll be back again tomorrow." Katy nodded.

Liz felt Katy's presence before she even touched her. Katy petted her arm as if she were a puppy.

Morgan added, "Don't stay too long, you need some sleep, too. See you tomorrow." She and Katy both looked back as they passed through the door frame.

Ken turned to Nancy once they were alone. "I'm not proud of my outburst today."

"Shush." Nancy picked up Ken's hand and held it to her chest. "Don't be so hard on yourself. That's my job." She gave a tiny laugh.

Liz laughed inside, too. She loved that her parents still cared for each other to the extent they did and wondered if she'd ever have that same luck with love. She fell asleep inside her coma, both happy and sad at the same time.

After work that night, Will called Michael. "Any word on Liz?"

"Actually, I stopped by the hospital and she's still unconscious, but holding her own."

"Are her vitals within normal range or what's her situation?"

"I assume so, DOC. Her dad didn't say otherwise."

"Oh man, you met the dad?" Will asked. "Bugger, did he think you daft?"

"It went fine until I mentioned the gallery. He lost it then, assuming I wanted to use Liz."

"At least you're not in an adjoining ICU room!" Will snickered on the other end of the line.

"Katy came to my rescue telling him it was her suggestion."

"Hum, nice lass. Is she well?"

"Seems to be. She and Morgan took the day off to be there with Liz. They're pretty worried. Hold on Will, I've got another call." Michael clicked back and forth between calls. "Will, its Adonia. Let me call you right back."

"I'll keep my trousers on and tug on my beer while I wait."

"Hey, Adonia, what's up?"

"You know that lady named Liz that we talked about? I wondered if she is seriously interested in Duke. He's been whining for days. Do you have any way to contact her? I've tried her friend, Katy, but no answer. Another couple left a message that they're interested in him, but he really belongs with Liz, as you may know."

Michael told Adonia about the fall and the hospital.

"That's so sad. Is she going to be okay?"

"Who knows at this point? At any rate, I want Duke, okay?" Michael questioned his request as soon as he said it, but went on gut instinct.

"What about Liz? She's meant to have Duke, not you, or anyone else. He kissed *her*."

"I'll worry about that later. Maybe he'll kiss me, too. Dogs love me."

"You know if you take him, you have to keep him or return him. Are you sure you are ready for another dog? This one is gifted."

"Yes, Adonia, I know the adoption rules." Michael rubbed his ear as he often did when frustrated, nervous, or otherwise unhappy. "And I understand what you mean about him being meant for *her*. I'll do my best to get Liz to visit him. If it's truly meant to be, it will be."

"Will you make sure Liz knows about it when she's better? She should really get to know him."

"Yes, of course"

"Then he's yours. I'll get the paperwork ready for you and tell the other couple. When do you want him?"

"Can you give me a couple of days?"

"Anything for my artist. He is due to be neutered tomorrow so the timing is good?"

"Ouch." Michael instinctively grabbed himself. "Thanks. I'll call you soon."

"Hey, Will." Michael returned his call.

"That was fast. You usually take longer when you talk to Adonia."

"We didn't have much business to cover this time. Hey, I just adopted Duke."

"Come again?" Will asked.

"You heard me. Another couple wanted him and I couldn't let him get away."

"You wanker. Liz is gonna tell you to sod off if she ever wakes up."

"*When* she wakes up, asshole. Besides, I'll think of a way to let her have him if she still wants him. If not, I don't mind keeping him."

"Touché. You're always too kind for your own good, man."

"You know I might not get to keep Pricilla, depending on how things go."

"Yeah, sorry, man. Duke is a better guy's dog anyway."

CHAPTER 8

Florida, 1922

Liz remained unconscious, her eyes darting to and fro under their heavy lids. Another dream began on Sunday night…

Once again Duke stuck his nose into Liz's face to wake her. She pulled away.

"Yuck, Duke, what did you eat?" He waged his tail and nudged closer, wanting attention.

"Ok, buddy, come here" Liz rubbed his right ear. "It must be 6:00 AM, right? I guess I'd better get up."

The sun peaked through the lace curtains, softly illuminating the floral rug strewn across the wood plank flooring. Liz took in the old-fashioned décor and told Duke, "It is so peaceful here." The antique dresser and armoire, the saddle-back chair with cane seat, and the metal headboard added to the ambience of the room.

Katy stood in the doorway laughing. "Yes, it's 6:00, so get outta those covers. We need to get to the track early."

"Okay," Liz said as Katy turned to leave.

Katy's fawn greyhound entered the room and dropped her front legs with her butt in the air in a cute 'play bow', wanting Duke to run with her.

Liz looked at Duke and said, "Go play." He kissed Liz and ran after Katy's dog.

Liz sighed just as Katy popped back into the doorway and gave Liz the look. "Jim's giving us a ride today. Morgan left early. She had paperwork to do."

"What paperwork?"

"To double-check the take. You know, yesterday's race. She thinks someone is skimming."

"Oh, that paperwork."

"So get a wiggle on!" Katy chided, turned, and left the room.

Liz rose and crossed the room. She thumbed through her dresses in the carved-wood armoire and drew out two of her favorites—a long, pale blue sheath ribboned at the hips and a pale grey one with lots of lace.

When Liz appeared in the kitchen, Katy looked wistful standing at the Hoosier cupboard next to the farm-style sink. The checkerboard floor added a modern 1920's feel to the room. "Liz, that lacy style is the latest rage. You're so lucky to be able to get dolled up for your nice job at the track's gallery."

Katy looked stodgy, in her long dark skirt and high-necked white blouse and her lace-up shoes. "Why aren't you all decked-out?"

"In a kennel full of dogs? I'd step in something and ruin my best shoes in no time. Oh, I have good news; I missed talking to you last night. I've been promoted." Katy performed a wiggle dance. "I'm the new assistant kennel manager. As of yesterday. That's unheard of! Imagine, me, a woman. In that position."

"Congratulations!" Liz gave Katy a big hug. "I'm so happy for you."

Jim knocked on the screen door and yelled, "Good morning, ladies. Your chariot awaits."

They walked outside to Jim's White Motor Company ambulance, a Model T delivery van with a cross painted on the side and Liz pointed, "Whoa, where'd you get this jalopy?"

"Jalopy," Jim parroted with his brows crinkled. "Liz, it's only four years old. Although 1918 is the last year that they made this ambulance, she still runs like a champ, four cylinders, and she goes 40 miles per hour." Jim beamed, defending his mode of transportation.

"No offense intended."

"Okay, none taken." Along the way, Jim made small talk. "This land boom is sure bringing lots of money to the area. Between us, I think some big cheese is getting his pockets lined."

"Just between us as well," said Katy, "Morgan thinks there is a money leak at the track." Katy rubbed her thumb and fingertips together, the international sign for money." She hasn't found anything yet. But I'm concerned. She might get in the middle of something. Dangerous even."

"Who knows?" Jim replied. "There's bound to be someone on the take somewhere. It is a gambling spot after all."

"Do the owners know what Morgan is doing?" Liz asked.

"Yeah. It's all very hush-hush. They told Morgan to be very careful. They don't want her bumped off." Katy imitated a gun discharging.

"She'd better be careful," Jim said. "Tell her I'll escort her in my off-time so she's not alone any more than necessary."

Jim dropped them off by the kennels.

"Let me check in first," Katy said. "We can go up to the gallery afterward."

Liz watched Katy do a quick, 10-minute sprint to finish her morning dog rounds. Liz noticed how organized and clean the kennels looked. The dogs—Liz counted 21— seemed well cared for.

"Let's go on up now," Katy said as she finished washing her hands at the kennel sink.

"It still seems so strange to have a gallery at the race track," Liz commented as she put her purse in her desk when they arrived.

"You should be grateful for your job! I really like the paintings Michael hangs here. Some of the others though," Katy waved her hand in the air, "they look like kids painted them." Katy continued. "I see how you encourage shoppers to buy. Like it was their idea. Ralph must be

happy with your sales."

"Ralph!" Liz made a gagging sound. "How'd he get to be the Gallery and Tea House manager anyway? He's short, has a portly belly, and slicked-back hair. That's not particularly attractive for a customer service position."

Katy frowned. "I think he's a torpedo."

"Why do you think he's a hired gun?"

"Because, Ralph is not here that often. When he is, he's always looking around like he's scheming. I've seen him with strangers at the gate. Someone gave him a wad of cash."

"Oh, that's interesting!" Liz said as Katy waved her leave.

"Okay, see you later. Watch yourself. You know he doesn't think a woman should be working the gallery. Or doing the accounting. Or working with the dogs. No one thinks as progressively as the track owners do."

Liz took a quick walk through the gallery, then the adjoining tea room, stopping at the large wall of glass that overlooked the track. The stands were empty except for two men wearing striped suits and straw boater hats. They seemed deep in conversation. Looking back at the Victorian-style tea room, Liz imagined how easily it could be turned in to a speakeasy late at night or some gin mill if prohibition ever ended. No more tea and paintings.

Ralph's pungent hair oil breezed past her just before he did. "Have you spotted today's winners yet?"

"No," Liz replied, saying as little as possible.

"I'd bet on Turner's Hooch," said Ralph. "I hear he's a shoo-in today." Ralph winked. Liz didn't ask him where he got his information, but wondered if dog racing could be fixed like other contests.

"Are you ready to put on the Ritz for today's crowd?" Ralph pressed. "I got wind that some important people plan to grace our humble establishment today. Move some of those expensive pieces and I'll give you an extra two percent. So put a big smile on that kisser and flirt with any dandies that come in or compliment their wives."

"Yes, sir," Liz said as he walked away whistling. She made a face behind his back.

Time flew as quickly as a turn around the track. Before long, Katy walked through the gallery door for lunch. She looked wilted.

"Oh, it's so good to get out of the sun," Katy fanned herself while enjoying the cross-breezes that flowed through the open windows of the gallery and adjoining tea room. She and Liz moved to the tea room and sat at a table with a pretty linen tablecloth and Black-eyed Susan bouquet. The waiter brought them cool water.

Liz brushed away a fly. "I saw Ralph this morning and he acted like I couldn't sell a glass of water to a man dying of thirst."

"Sounds like Ralph."

"Can I take your order?" The waiter appeared with a note pad and a pencil.

They both ordered the daily special and an extra one for Morgan who would be there any moment.

"I wonder which of my clientele will show up today." Liz looked at the empty tables.

"Probably that older lady. Heavy-set. Silver hair. Large hats. Expensive suits. Lots of jewelry—Richard's, of course. Her husband spoils her."

"Probably. Do you know her husband's first name?" Liz had remembered reading her first name on several invoices, but not his.

"Hines Hildebraun. The wealthy real estate mogul. Is she Gabrielle, Gretchen, Geraldine, something like that?"

"Yes, Gretchen. She has purchased some nice pieces in here before."

"Hel-lo, Ladies," Morgan sang as she glided in on pointy new heels and sat down. "I see we're ahead of the lunch crowd as usual; best to eat well before the races begin and the women descend to lunch and gossip." She glanced around the floral-clad room. "No handsome men to grace our eyes. Oh, I retract that statement, here comes one now."

The waiter came out with their Crabmeat Croquettes and set Katy's lunch down as Morgan greeted him. "Hello, you handsome man," Morgan said as she reached to touch his cheek. Trying to duck her touch, the waiter bumped Liz's water glass with her lunch plate, sending the cool liquid down the front of Liz's dress.

His face flushed red. "Oh my gosh! Oh my gosh! I'm so sorry.
Katy jumped up to give her napkin to Liz.
"Lucky me," Richard crooned as he magically appeared. "I do like
a lady in a thin, wet dress!"
"Gad zukes," Morgan threw up her hands.
"And good day to you too, Miss Morgan." Richard bowed.
"Come on," Katy directed. "Let's go to the john. We'll get you
dry."

"My you look spiffy in your black suit and pretty pink silk
blouse," Richard wiggled his eyebrows. "A lady who knows how to dress!
So did you flirt with the waiter and cause this ruckus?"
"Oh dry up. Why do you assume I'm to blame?" Morgan's hand
touched her chest.
"Because my dear, timing is everything. I walked in just in time to
win, place, and watch the whole show."
"Ah, Richard, so good of you to come in early today," Ralph
approached from the prep area, ruining Morgan's chance at a retort.
"May I take you away from this lovely lady and discuss a matter of
utmost importance?"
"He's all yours," Morgan stood up to leave. Richard matched
Morgan's glare with a burning smile of his own.

Morgan joined the women in the ladies room. They held Liz's dress
up to the breeze that drifted in through the window slats. "This will be
dry in no time," she told Morgan on her way in.
"Can you believe that cad? He blamed me for this." Morgan
motioned to the dress and leaned back against a sink. "You don't hold
me responsible, do you Liz?"
"Sweetie, you did scare the poor man, but I'm not mad. There's no
harm done." Liz stood in a silky slip, still fanning her dress in the slight
breeze.

Morgan paced and continued to rag on about Richard.

"The lady doth protest too much." Liz pointed at Morgan. "One might assume he's gotten under your skin."

Morgan laughed and pointed at Liz. "Are you dry yet?"

"Dry enough."

"Then let's go back out and eat." Katy motioned to the door.

The daily special awaited them on their newly dressed table. They ate quickly while watching the scene play out in the now busy tea room. Women evaluated and complimented each other on their fashions. The more matronly still wore Victorian styles, while the younger ladies wore the more risqué flapper dresses. After lunch, Katy and Morgan went back to work so Liz made the rounds greeting the guests. She spotted some elderly women and altered her course. "Mrs. Hildebraun." Liz addressed her with a tip of her head.

"Good afternoon, Miss Elizabeth."

"I adore your hat."

"Oh, thank you, darling. My milliner says it's the latest rage."

Yeah, right. Liz held a snicker. Has she looked around the room? Hello? The close-fitting cloche hats are the latest rage. "You're always the most elegant woman in the room—these other lovely ladies included, of course." Liz smiled at the other women sitting at the same table.

"Do you have any new pieces to show me, darling? I'm afraid Mr. Hildebraun is tired of my Impressionists and wants to see some new artists. Something with more feeling, he says."

"Why, yes I do. Please come see me after your lunch."

"Where are my manners? Let me introduce you to Mrs. Cabrini from Chicago. She and her husband are here on vacation."

"A pleasure, Miss Elizabeth," said the pert Italian woman with a nod. "Here's my husband's calling card should you ever need some new transportation."

Liz read the card:

Angelo Cabrini
New and Used Cars
Chicago, Illinois

She looked up, wondering why she would go to Chicago to get a car. "We do so adore it here. Angelo says we may even look for a home here."

"Welcome, Mrs. Cabrini. Thanks for the calling card." What else could Liz say? "I have some newer Expressionist pieces that may catch your interest, or at least your husband's, Mrs. Hildebraun. Please excuse me for now. I must greet the other guests before the gallery officially opens."

With Katy and Morgan gone, Liz readied a stack of sales receipts for the afternoon showing. She greeted the first of the hopeful collectors, and showed her a work entitled Amadeo Modigliani by Diego Rivera, 1914.

"How can one paint the likeness of a man with only four colors," the woman scoffed and walked away as Mrs. Hildebraun and Mrs. Cabrini approached.

"It seems as though she didn't appreciate that piece," Mrs. Cabrini bent closer to appraise the painting.

"Apparently not," Liz agreed. "It does take an understanding of the artist to truly appreciate the message."

"Miss Elizabeth," started Mrs. Hildebraun, "do show me the new Expressionist paintings you mentioned."

"Of course, Mrs. Hildebraun, please follow me." Liz led the ladies 15 feet to the other end of the gallery. Also painted in 1914, this one is called Fighting Forms, by Franz Mark from Germany."

"Oh, it's dreadful. It looks like a red dragon fighting a black gorilla," Mrs. Hildebraun wrinkled her long nose.

"You have a creative eye," Liz replied. "Unlike the soft, blended impression of a subject, as you're used to, Expressionism portrays intense

emotion and many times, angst. Franz Mark is quite a skilled painter in his genre. See how he used the brighter colors and sharper lines as well as distorted two-dimensional forms."

"Yes, I have heard something of this new fad, some of it not so pleasant, like this monstrosity," Mrs. Hildebraun flipped her hand at the painting. "But, it's what Mr. Hildebraun desires after all. Wrap up the gorilla for me will you, Dearie?"

"Of course."

"Shall we get the paperwork out of the way?" Mrs. Hildebraun circled her hand. "Mrs. Cabrini and I are dining out this evening at that new Italian restaurant, after some shopping of course, so we must be on our way."

"Yes, our husbands have a dinner meeting with some customers," Mrs. Cabrini added.

"I hope you enjoy your meal," Liz provided the sales slip for Mrs. Hildebraun to sign. "I'll have your painting delivered by tomorrow afternoon as usual, Mrs. Hildebraun. Please let me know how your husband likes it."

Liz watched the ladies walk away as Ralph caught her eye from across the tea room. He grinned, tipping his head in approval.

"Slimeball," Liz said under her breath.

After a successful afternoon of sales, Liz watched from the expanse of windows as the tea ladies greeted their husbands in the stands after the race.

"Have you tallied your receipts?" Ralph appeared behind Liz and made her jump.

"Yes sir. I think you will be happy with the total."

"If I have no beef with it, your extra two percent will come in handy for a haircut. Why don't you get your tresses bobbed like Morgan's? That doll's the cat's meow."

"Thank you, Ralph," Liz gritted her teeth and gave him a fake smile. She would have preferred to pop him one right in the kisser.

Just then, Liz watched Richard stroll into the tea room followed by

Michael with a moll in tow. The sight of the woman disturbed Liz so she turned her back on them as Ralph abandoned her there. Why should I care? The woman did nothing wrong other than exist. I'm jealous of some floozy who has nothing to do with Michael other than using him.

"Oh, Richard," Ralph sang in his sickeningly sweet tone. "Did you wager today? Turner's Hooch won by a nose." Liz turned slightly in time to see him wink. "I'm a rich man. Tonight is on me."

"As a matter of fact, I did just fine myself; pulled in a few clams." Richard patted Ralph's shoulder.

"And who is this doll with the shapely gams?" Ralph asked Michael.

"She's a friend of Angelo's. I'm escorting her this evening. Ralph, this is Mona. Mona, Ralph."

"Excellent. Hi, Doll. If you arrive sometime between 7:00 and 9:00 PM, I'll be at the door to admit you. Don't be late," Ralph whistled while he walked back into the kitchen.

"Hello, Liz." Her heart raced at the sound of his voice behind her.

She glared at him over her shoulder. Mona had stayed with Richard. "Hello, Michael," she answered flatly.

"Are you coming tonight?"

"To where are you referring?" she sniped as she turned toward him.

"Didn't Richard tell you? We're going to a new speakeasy."

"No, he didn't extend an invitation. And it looks like there will be enough ladies going."

"Come on, Liz, you know Mona's just another one of Angelo's girls I have to escort. Please come."

"I know, but I don't have to like it. Are Katy and Morgan invited as well?"

"Uh, sure. We can pick you up at 7:00."

"Who knows, it might be fun."

"Wear your glad rags." He reached out and touched the lace at the hip of her dress.

The touch of his hand on her hip bone sent a fire straight to her nearby soft zone. How could this man make her hot and moist in an instant? Maybe she couldn't trust in forever, but she had to admit, a few stolen moments with this man wouldn't be half bad. A vibrant, young woman has needs after all.

"Liz?" Michael touched her cheek with his warm, sensual hand which brought her back into the moment with a flush to her face.

"Yes, I will. Glad rags."

"See you then," Michael said and turned to go.

She watched the strained look on Richard's face as Michael told him that the ladies were coming along. He quickly recovered, smiled at Liz, and waved goodbye. Richard held the door as Katy and Morgan entered, exchanging greetings.

"Hi, Liz. Jim's here. Let's go," Katy announced by way of hello.

"It's nice of him to haul us around," Liz replied on the way down to the ambulance.

"We're right on his way home and he is off duty. Besides, I think he likes Morgan."

"Jim's a nice enough gent," Morgan replied, with barely any enthusiasm.

"Richard and Michael came in to talk to Ralph. It seems like Ralph's dog-of-choice won today. They all made big money today on their wagers."

"Speaking of Ralph and money," Morgan said, "he's obtained a new food purveyor. What's not copacetic is that he pays them almost the same amount every month, and more than the previous vendor, which is suspicious. I'm investigating that purveyor and anticipate finding a front. Ralph might be the one who's skimming from the till."

"Oh, I watched the race as usual," Katy said. "I think he cheated, but I can't figure out how. He has to have help from one of the guys that set the track."

"This guy is bad news," Liz shook her head. "He invited the guys to a new speakeasy behind a new Italian Restaurant tonight, but through the back door. Michael invited us to go as well."

"How exciting! I haven't danced in an eon," Morgan danced an abbreviated Charleston right then and there.

"What about the Volstead Act?" Katy lost her balance

momentarily as they descended the steps to the parking lot. "You know...prohibition?"

"Relax," Liz said to her worry-wart friend.

"Yeah, relax." Morgan threaded her arm through Katy's to steady her. "This might be my opportunity to get the goods on Ralph."

"On the level, Morgan," Katy said. "What can we find out in one night?"

"Perhaps plenty— at least it's worth the effort to investigate."

"Then it's settled," Liz said. "Let's go home and get spiffed up. I'll let you borrow any one of my dresses you want, Katy. Maybe that blue one with the fringe?"

"Fine," Katy threw up her hands.

Liz laughed as Morgan rolled her eyes. "Just enjoy the adventure, alright?"

CHAPTER 9

Sunday night's dream continued…

Richard knocked on the door of the small rental house the women shared at precisely 7:00 PM. Morgan opened it and watched his jaw drop and his eyes bulge. "What's the matter, haven't you ever spied a spiffed lady?" she teased, batting her heavily made-up eyes. "Come in." Morgan stepped backward into the small living room.

"Doll, you look like a million bucks. If the other two look half as good, I'll be the envy of every man in the joint." Richard bumped the console next to the door as he entered.

"Aren't you the charmer this evening? You look quite elegant. Your black bow tie and black silk suit may just start a fashion trend. Where are the other gents?"

"Michael had to make an early delivery so they went with him. We'll meet them inside."

"I'll wager it's a-who, not a-what, that he's delivering," Liz walked into the living room and caught the tail end of the conversation.

"You know it's just business, doll." Richard said to Liz.

"Since when did you start doing business with the big cheese? You better be careful you don't end up as his fall guy."

"Liz. I'm no pushover—you should know that by now. I always come out on top. Let's get moving. Got any of that Beech Nut gum in your bag?"

Richard dropped the ladies off in front of Tuchello's Ristaurante,

the newest Italian restaurant in town, to look for nearby parking.

While waiting, Morgan scanned the surrounding area. "Watch for Revenuers."

Bright lights across the façade also shone across the street on a couple of simple brick buildings. Tuchello's sat like a rose among weeds. Brass chevrons adorned the glass front doors to the restaurant. Liz hoped to eat there one day soon.

When Richard returned, Morgan gave him an all-clear-nod.

"Let's go around back." Richard had explained the entry process in the car on the way there. When he knocked on the portal, it opened a smidge. He whispered, "Waterfront" and at once, Ralph opened the small window all the way. A muffled jazz tune met Richard as he handed Ralph the calling card.

"Is everyone here?" Ralph eyed the group and frowned at the ladies.

"Yes," Richard nodded. "Everything is copacetic."

"Then come in, quickly," Ralph opened the door just enough to allow them entry.

A tiny poker table and two chairs occupied the dimly lit antechamber. A burley gent stood silently near Ralph, ready for action if need be.

"Glad to see you finally did something with your hair, Liz. Now you look almost as classy as this chippy," Ralph shoved his thumb in Morgan's direction.

Richard put a hand on each lady's shoulder. Liz supposed it meant to still them so they'd give Ralph no reason to deny them entry.

"Right this way," Ralph passed through the interior door that his muscle guarded. He led them past the jazz band, the busy bar, the dance floor surrounded by tables and chairs, and on toward the thick wall framing a wooden door. "Your other gents are already seated," Ralph said to Richard.

"This sure is a gem of a place," Morgan looked around. "Lots of bright colors and sleek metal finishes. A real class act."

"Only the best," Ralph raised his arms toward the decor. "Art Deco, they call it. All the rage."

"Here's your table, Richard." He gestured Richard toward a glossy, veneered table located next to a table occupied by a tough-looking

Italian man and his entourage, including Mona, the floozy.

"That's the restaurant." Ralph pointed to the wooden door behind Mona's dapper gents.

"This is swell. Who's the band tonight?" Richard asked.

"That's Bix and the Wolverines; paid big money to get 'em here."

"Thanks, Ralph," Richard palmed a bill into Ralph's hand before he left, and selected a chair facing the front door. *"Hello, gentlemen."* Richard saluted Michael, Will, and Jim who had arrived earlier. The men stood to help the ladies with their chairs, and provided warm greetings.

"That's Angelo Cabrini with Mona," Liz whispered.

"How do you know?" Richard frowned.

"Oh, um, I must have seen him at the track. I met his wife today with Mrs. Hildebraun."

"Let's order," Richard motioned to the waiter.

"Whadda have? I got wine, champagne, beer, whisky, gin, and Puerto Rican Rum. If you want a Gimlet or a Whisky Smash, I can get that too." The waiter took their orders.

"Can I have a grapefruit juice?" Katy smiled sweetly.

"One Whisky Smash, coming up," the waiter repeated.

Katy grimaced. *"No, just a plain juice."*

"I'll take care of you doll, don't worry," winked the waiter as he left to fill their orders.

Richard laughed. *"The waiter must have thought you were speaking in code. Remember, if anything happens, get through the restaurant door as fast as possible, but only after the gentlemen at that table,"* he tipped his head at the gents in the shiny suits. *"There're a few tables kept open in the back saved for us. If we have to go in, just sit down and pretend you're eating. They keep food on those tables just in case. With any luck it will look like we were always in there instead of in here."*

Katy whined. *"A raid? How can we pull that off? There'll be no time. Why are we in here if it's dangerous?"*

"Because it's fun!" Morgan answered.

"And how!" Michael seconded as he put his arm around the back of Liz's chair. She leaned a little closer toward him hoping for more

96

attention.

"And the odds of a raid are slim-to-none because this is a new place. Right, Richard?" Morgan whispered. "And because we'll know in advance because someone got paid off."

"You got it. You're one smart cookie."

"Like he says, Katy," Morgan nodded toward Ralph. "As the owner, Ralph will protect his interests and those of his best customers."

"Half-owner." Richard corrected Morgan.

Morgan nodded. "I need a ciggy."

Richard signaled one of the cigarette girls and watched her long, shapely legs make their way over to him, her cigarette tray a nice shelf for her other assets. "Give us a pack of Marlboros and one of those long holders, doll, and keep the change." He handed her $5. In turn, he handed Morgan a loaded cigarette holder and lit her cigarette. Morgan suppressed a light cough.

"Please don't smoke," Katy whispered.

Morgan snickered and kept smoking even though she didn't inhale much. "I adore those pill-box hats they wear. I could don that short skirt. Perhaps I'll see Ralph about a part-time job here."

"Morgan," Liz scolded while laughing, "That outfit is scandalous, but if anyone could wear it, you could."

"I can arrange that." Richard wiggled his eyebrows.

"Come on, ladies. The hoofers are on the floor already. Listen to that cornet." Morgan pulled her friends to their feet and onto the dance floor. Morgan's long string of pearls jiggled as she moved.

After the song ended, Katy panted on the way back to the table. "Hey, we have tea."

"You are naïve, doll," Richard blurted out. "The teacups just help to hide the booze." He looked at Will just in time to catch a scolding glance.

"Do you ever think about what you're saying?" Morgan sat down next to Richard.

"Much like you, doll, I say what I think. No games. How 'bout we go out to my car and neck?"

"Uh, I'd need to be snockered first, and then I could show you how it's done."

"Back so soon?" Richard looked up at Michael as he turned around and interrupted the conversation.

"It looks like Ralph is closing up shop. The bartender is pulling the false wall to hide the bar and Ralph is coming this way." Michael whispered.

The occupants at Mona's table stood and headed through the restaurant door shortly after Ralph stopped at their table.

"Your dinner table is ready, now," Ralph told Richard, stopping at their table briefly before moving on.

"You heard the man. Quickly, our table is ready," Richard whispered and ushered the group through the same door.

As Richard closed the door behind them, the music stopped. Liz heard Ralph starting to make an announcement, but couldn't hear the details through the thick wall. As they sat at the other empty table in the back, Richard suggested, "Take a bite. Get some of that delicious garlic on your breath, now."

Everyone did as instructed. Angelo Cabrini and an older gentleman joined his wife and Mrs. Hildebraun at their table in the front of the restaurant. "Bet they're surprised to see their husbands at the same restaurant. Wonder how they'll explain where they came from," Liz whispered to Morgan, pointing discreetly at the women.

Morgan just smiled. "Look how efficiently his people are trained. That skinny guy is draped over the moll like she belongs to him instead of Mr. Cabrini. His wife should miss the deception entirely."

Ralph entered the restaurant, locked the door behind him, and sat at the Cabrini table.

Just then a ruckus broke out in the speakeasy, barely audible to Liz in the restaurant. She could hear some women scream, and a man yell. Someone kicked down the locked door to the restaurant. Diners at the back tables ducked to avoid wood splinters flying off the door jam. Two burly cops walked through the broken entry, guns drawn.

Women in the restaurant screamed at the sound of the broken door while their men jumped up to defend them. "Stay where you are,"

98

shouted a cop with a mustache. "Everyone, sit down now."

The two men walked from table to table and smelled the patrons' drinks. "Hey, don't I know you?" the chubby cop asked Angelo Cabrini.

"Now, see here," Mr. Hildebraun said. "What's the meaning of this?" These fine folks are visiting our lovely city from Chicago and this is no way to treat our honored guests."

"Oh, Mr. Hildebraun. Forgive me, Sir," the cop said after he recognized him. "We must have gotten a bad tip about this restaurant. Please excuse the interruption and the confusion. We'll leave you to your dinner."

The two cops turned and walked back into the speakeasy, propping up the broken door on their way out.

"Now wasn't that fun," Morgan said to her friends. "What's next?"

CHAPTER 10

Katy snuck into Liz's hospital room early Monday morning and surprised the nurse who dropped an IV bag on Liz's hand. Liz didn't move. Katy didn't move. The nurse finally did. She retrieved the bag, checked Liz's hand, and then hung the bag.

"I am so sorry. I didn't mean to scare you."

Liz imagined the crimson as it flooded Katy's cheeks.

"That's okay. No harm done; it's not that heavy. I wasn't expecting anyone this early."

"I know. I shouldn't be here. I couldn't sleep and I wanted to beat rush hour. Anything new?"

"Not really. We're still waiting on results from the MRI. Go ahead and visit with her, I need to take care of a few things. You might want to rub her hand."

"I will," Katy said to the retreating nurse.

Katy held Liz's hand as she talked. "Are you okay, Liz? Sorry about the hand. My heart leapt into my throat. I'm sure I surprised you, too."

Liz appreciated the physical contact with her friend and knew it gave Katy a momentary sense of purpose, since she could do nothing else.

"I've been thinking about the guys, Liz. Hah...you have to listen to me for once. You can't bite my head off. Did you hear Michael the other day? He seemed genuinely concerned about you. Did *Mr. Sandman* bring him to you last night? Dreaming of Michael as your rescuer should tell you something. You *are* ready for a man—one that you can trust. Maybe he's that man. We could run a background check on him. There are people who do that. What, no snide retort? Come on Liz, it's time to wake up."

"A clever attempt, Katy. If that doesn't goad her into waking up, I don't know what will." Morgan appeared right behind Katy which made her jump.

"Crap! Quit sneaking up on a soul."

"Never expose your back to the door. If you are going to talk about background checks and spy stuff, you should consider that your first lesson."

"It serves me right. I did the same thing to the nurse this morning." Katy explained the incident to Morgan while Liz listened.

"I bet Liz is in stitches right about now. Aren't you, Liz? It's entirely possible that you can hear us." Morgan rounded the bed and rubbed Liz's other hand.

"What would she be laughing about?" Nancy entered the room while Morgan wasn't looking.

"Oh, shit." Morgan jumped, too. "Everyone seems to be sneaking up on everyone else in here this morning. I'm sure Liz is finding this great fun."

Tiny laughing tears slid out the sides of Liz's eyes, but no one noticed. She wished she could give a full belly laugh.

"She would find that amusing," Nancy crossed the room to hug the girls. "Have you been here long? How's she doing?"

"She's doing very well," the doctor said behind Nancy which gave her a start.

"Oh, this is too much!" Katy hugged her stomach, blurting out hysterical laughter. "We're all a bunch of raw nerves."

"Can you qualify *very well?*" Nancy turned to the doctor.

"Yes, results of the MRI are in and there are no anomalies."

"And?" Nancy rolled her hand to ask for more info.

"That means there were no tumors, no masses, no subdural hematomas, no aneurisms, no swelling, nothing."

"So, that means?" Nancy pushed the doctor for more information.

"It means that no internal intervention is necessary at this time, ah, no surgery is required at the moment. We will continue monitoring her and keep her as healthy as possible while we wait."

"So, if there's no cause, why's she still asleep?" Nancy crossed her arms over her chest.

"There's always a cause. Sometimes it's just the trauma of the accident. There's nothing else to attribute it to at the moment, which is a good thing."

"If it's just trauma, then she'll wake up, right? She's certainly had enough of that in her lifetime. She's quite accident prone."

"It's entirely possible at some point. I'll be back later to check on her." The doctor turned with a thud. He ran straight into Ken who had just entered the room after parking the car.

"Careful, Doc, or we'll have you in a bed beside Liz." Ken snickered.

"I have to sit." Katy held her stomach. "I'm going to pee myself laughing so hard."

"Go ahead, Doctor, I'll fill him in." Nancy reached for Ken's hand.

"Fill me in on what?" Ken asked.

They sat down and the three ladies took turns filling him in on the 'what' of the morning surprises thus far.

Liz took in the retelling. She couldn't have been more pleased for the break in the stress.

"Can Will come visit tonight?" Katy whispered. "He'd like to see Liz. I'd like you to meet him."

"Why are you whispering?" Nancy whispered back.

"In case Liz can hear us, I don't want to upset her if the answer is no."

The whispering did reach Liz's ears and she waited for the answer, too.

"Are you sure it's not *you* who would be upset if we said

no? Have you seen him since the Renaissance Festival?"

"No. It would be nice to see him again. But it's no big deal if it's a problem."

"So you talked to him?" Morgan asked.

"Yes, last night."

"See if he wants to bring Michael as well," Nancy gave Ken a stern look. "That is if he'll come back."

"Thanks! I have to get to work. I'll be back tonight," Katy wiggled her fingers in goodbye.

"I'll escort you to your transportation, my good woman." Morgan said in her best Middle English. "I must toil as well, and I want the juicy details of your conversation with Will."

Liz wished she were the proverbial fly on the wall to hear those details as well.

After the girls left, Nancy and Ken held each other and stared at Liz, rubbing her hands and willing her well.

"Her hand just twitched, Ken, did you see it?" Nancy picked up her hand and held it aloft. No movement. Nancy stared. She shook the lifeless hand hoping it would do anything.

At that same moment, the heart monitor to her right, flat-lined. Alarms went off. Nancy screamed. "NO!"

Hospital staff came running in, a crash cart close behind. "Step back," someone yelled.

Before they finished charging the defibrillator, Liz's sinus rhythm began again. By itself. All movement stopped. Liz wondered what was happening in the room.

"What just happened?" Ken turned around to ask anyone and everyone. "How can that happen?"

"I've only ever seen that one other time," one nurse said. "Keep the cart here for a while," she told the guy holding the paddles.

"Why?" Ken demanded.

"It's just a precaution. We need to watch her closely. It's hard to know what might happen."

"Ugh," Nancy expelled a growl. "I'll scream if I hear that one more time."

"It appears she's back to normal," the crash-cart guy said.

"This isn't normal," Nancy said through gritted teeth.

"Sorry, Ma'am; I meant her heart rate."

After a time, with nothing happening, the hospital staff left, leaving the overly-stressed family alone and in for a long and otherwise uneventful day before they left for something to eat.

The blip, blip, blip echoed in Liz's head, louder than if she had been standing in the tower of Big Ben.

CHAPTER 11

Paris, 1572

Monday night, Liz's third dream began…

Elizabeth smelled a hearty stew simmering in a pot hanging in the hearth. Women chopped vegetables and sliced cheese on a block to her left. Leaning against a sturdy table, Elizabeth looked around for Duke to no avail.

Hearing a strange sound, she turned to locate the desperate, honking noise. Through a small window, she noticed a red-headed man standing beside an outbuilding, butchering what seemed to be a large goose.

"Where am I?" she asked a sturdy woman kneading bread for trenchers next to her.

"In the kitchen, mademoiselle."

"Oui, but whose kitchen?"

"Yours. Or rather Queen Catherine's, but you're Chef du Cuisine, of course. Are ye not well, ma chère?"

"A bit of dizziness, I am afraid." Elizabeth headed to a bench next to a trestle table to sit down.

"We had best get you to your chambers." The baker woman said. Taking Elizabeth's arm, the woman led her down a back hallway toward the sleeping wing of the keep.

"I shall see to the midday meal. Ne vous inquiétez pas."

"Thank ye. What date be it?"

"Tis Friday, 23 August in the year of Our Lord, 1572. I best summon the apothecary. Ye toils toward the royal wedding festivities have left you weak."

Elizabeth followed the nice lady through the hallways of the Paleis

Louvre.

"*Cousin. Thank God,*" *Katherine rushed to help with Elizabeth, Morgan close on her heels. "How fare thee?" Katherine relieved the old woman of her burden and settled Elizabeth on her cot.*

"*Bless thee, Sister Katherine. She is a might spent s'all,*" *the cook backed up slightly. "She best rest. I shall prepare some sustenance for her. By your leave." The woman bowed slightly and glared at Morgan on her way out.*

"*Bless thee, Elise,*" *Katherine nodded.*

"*Why serveth me the evil eye?*" *Morgan's face scrunched up.*

"*Tis thy chosen profession that offends her,*" *Katherine replied for the cook who ignored Morgan.*

"*The service I perform for this kingdom tis a noble one.*" *Intrigued, Elizabeth listened to Morgan as she defended her membership in the Flying Squadron, a group of high-placed, ladies-in-waiting who spied for Queen Catherine de Medici using whatever methods they had available.*

"*Methinks it tis thy loose ways, not the results of such, to which she objects.*"

"*Spoken as a true woman of God. Tis value in judge thee not, Sister Katherine.*"

"*I judge not. I simply addressed thy concern.*"

"*What be ye whispering about my loose and obedient ones?*" *Elizabeth asked.*

"*I be unsure of saving thy life after such insult,*" *Morgan said with a glare of her own. "At thy moment of intrusion, I had informed our blessed Sister Katherine about the attempted assassination of Gaspard de Coligny. Tis not a conversation for busy ears. Let us away, Elizabeth." Morgan pulled the covers off Elizabeth and helped her to her feet.*

"*Why?*"

"*We must hide thee for thy safety—this way.*"

"*Where? What has happened?*"

"*Shush, we mustn't tarry, cousin.*" *Sandwiched between her two cousins, Elizabeth scrunched through a secret door behind a tapestry only to find darkness. Morgan lit a torch and silently navigated her way through a shadowed, musty tunnel.*

Ducking through another portal, Elizabeth entered a small room with a tiny wooden desk and what looked like a straw bed. After the muggy August temps in the kitchen, the coolness of the stone room touched her skin like the cool water of a dip in the pond on a hot day. A slight draft tickled the flame of Morgan's torch.

"Sit thee hither and harken," Morgan instructed her cousins, motioning to the cot. She told them about providing the queen with word of plans of a raid to kill all Huguenots, both here, in Paris and in other nearby cities. "Her son, Henry of Navarre, ordered it to start this night at matins."

"They be Heretics!" Sister Katherine said with venom in her voice. "But why now? Tis St. Bartholomew's Eve."

"Because of the vast numbers in attendance at the interfaith wedding today. How simple 'twill be to slaughter them as animals in a pen," Morgan splayed her open hands. "Tis worse...he shalt lay blame on the very woman who birthed him."

"Art thou quite sure of this?" Katherine frowned.

"Believeth me, I enticed enough details from a wittold Duke to understandth the puzzle."

"Ye must mind thy ways." Katherine shook her finger at Morgan. "How will thou enter heaven?"

"Ye durst to support the pending inquisition, Katherine? I side with the queen. I beseech thee for religious tolerance."

"But thee be a Catholic, Morgan. How can thy so believe?"

"Tis one of the many religions I practice. With thy own ears ye heard what Nostradamus told the queen regarding the coming revolution."

"Enough," Elizabeth slapped the mattress. "If I am of the court, am I not safe?"

"Being the Master of French Cooking will not save thee. Ye must reconsider converting to the true religion," Katherine's hands prayed.

"Elizabeth, we must go. Sister Katherine and I shalt bring you food and water soon. If we don't come for thee, I'll send a friend. If he speaks of 'eyes', ye shalt know to go hence. Be safe."

"Bless you," added Sister Katherine as they closed the door behind them, plunging Elizabeth into semi-darkness.

Adjusting to the lack of light, Elizabeth studied the musty, damp room. Carved partly from a hill, two walls looked much like a cave with a packed earthen floor. The remaining two walls were stacked stone. The semi-rectangle room housed not only the cot on which she sat and a desk that she had nearly bumped when she first entered, but a stool and a chamber pot as well.

A chamber pot. Oh, I hope I'm not here long. What is it about those smells anyway? You can almost stand your own, but someone else's makes you want to barf.

And why do dogs smell everything, especially butts. They don't differentiate between good smell/bad smell.

Oh to have a book and some light. I am beyond anxious.

Elizabeth lay on the straw mattress to wait. Just before they had entered this room, she had noticed a painting of a richly dressed couple, a Huguenot with a lady in his arms. A recent wedding present from Millias, the painter, she remembered. The lady had tied a white scarf on the man's bicep, the sign of a Catholic. I wonder if that's a sign to spare him during the massacre? Boredom lulled Elizabeth and she fell into a light slumber.

Sometime later, a loud clank of the iron door latch awakened Elizabeth. Flames dancing from a torch obscured its carrier. Elizabeth readied her dagger as she feigned sleep.

A slight draft from the open door brought the smell of stew in with it as Morgan announced herself and sat a tray on the desk.

"Thank ye, Morgan. What be the hour?"

"The hour grows late. I have but a moment. Sister Katherine took a tray to thy room for thee to deceive any prying eyes. This tray 'twas mine. Prithee eat whilst thou have a chance and ready thyself to be spirited away before Matins." Morgan gave Elizabeth a desperate hug then turned to leave. "We shall rendezvous anon."

Elizabeth used the candle on the desk sparingly while she ate. Her mouth watered for the boeuf bourguignon. A small plate of mixed vegetables rounded out her feast along with the freshly baked trencher bread.

Once satiated, Elizabeth felt the need to visit the chamber pot. She had put it off thus far.

Afterward, Elizabeth paced for what seemed like hours. Katherine would have advised her to say some Hail Marys while Morgan would have wanted her to dream of bustiers and handsome knights.

Elizabeth hoped for a handsome man to open the door. And that's precisely what she got. The now-familiar clanking sound gave way to a small torch preceding a bulkier form. "Lady Nottingham?"

"Who is inquiring?" As if Elizabeth needed to ask. Even in the faint glow, she recognized his face. She knew the tenor of his voice.

"Harken, the comely maiden with 'green eyes' sent me."

"And thy name?"

"Tho 'tis of no import, Michael be my given name, of the Donovan clan. I'm honoured to escort thee to safety. We must away at once."

The black dog beside Michael ran to her, leaned into her, and looked up at Elizabeth.

"Tis a beautiful dog."

"Duke is a faithful hound. He taketh to you heartily."

"Let's hence," Elizabeth followed Michael and Duke through the door and down a musty corridor in the opposite direction from where she originally came. He carried the torch so they could see where they were going.

Arriving at a dead end, Michael whispered, "Prithee hold this torch whilst I open this portal."

She strained her eyes to find a portal, but took the light from him holding it up so he could locate his invisible door. He knelt down, tapped the lower wall with his knuckles, and listened to its report. When he located a spot to his liking, he unsheathed his dagger and began scraping away a clay-plastered disguise. When the crumbled clay fell away, he pushed a stone and a half-door clicked open.

Michael placed his ear against the slight opening and listened a moment, smiled at Elizabeth, then whispered, "Prithee hold thy tongue and thy breath whilst I try our escape."

She nodded and watched as he pushed slightly and listened again. Apparently content with their safety, he pushed harder, meeting some resistance from the heavy stone door. Dirt and brush from outside rained down as Michael pushed against the stone door hidden in the wall at the base of the castle. The snapping of brittle branches and the rustling of leaves that hid the door from exterior view fell away, none too quietly. He took the torch from her and snubbed out the small flame against the dirt floor.

"Follow, kind maiden." Michael wedged his bulk through the half-open space, peered through the brambles, forced branches aside, and then reached back for Elizabeth. Her skirts hampered her agility as she crawled through the small opening. She ripped her shoulder seam on the brittle branches which left her skin exposed. Michael smiled at the sudden glimpse of her pale skin in the half-moonlight. He pressed a quick kiss on her lips. "Forgiveth me, maiden. Thou are beyond resistance." He turned away and whispered "Merde."

She inhaled deeply after the surprise kiss and then wrinkled her nose against the smell as she righted herself. They had emerged near the outlet to the cesspit. No wonder the guards had no interest in patrolling this area. They would have been found out otherwise because of the rustling. Duke anxiously pushed against Liz to accompany her through the opening.

As Michael scanned their surroundings, the half-moon overhead cast a play of light and shadow. He reached for her hand, raised her close to him, and hesitated. He shook his head, pulled away, closed the stone portal with a click, and pushed back the bushes as much as possible. He then led her and Duke, skirting the stinking pit, through the unoccupied open space. "We must pretend we be lovers out for an early evening tryst. The stable guard has received handsome compensation to pay us no mind. In the stables, mounts await for our escape."

The bells for tocsin began to ring. "That's Matins. We must make haste and gain distance before the massacre doth begin."

Michael motioned for her to stop. Elizabeth could make out two guards ambling before the stables by the glint of their swords.

As the intruding men reached them, they sensed strangers. Michael waited until one of the guards approached the other with his back to them, before he bound from the cover of the shadows, drew his sword, and quickly closed the short distance to the first guard. At the same time as their swords clashed, Duke charged and circled the other guard. The horses neighed in the stables and danced in their stalls.

Elizabeth held her breath. Michael dispatched the guard after one close parry and a final decisive thrust. As the guard dropped his sword, Elizabeth ran forward, grabbed it and yelled, "Michael."

Raising her sword, she attacked, surprising the younger guard who had approached Michael's blind spot. Her first blow sliced through his sleeve and into his sword arm. He wore no armour so then she easily plunged the sword into his chest just as he did the same to her.

CHAPTER 12

Liz awoke in a darkened room on Monday evening, gasping for air, and choking on something. *Breathe, just breathe.* She realized she could and wasn't dying. One hand flew to her nose to feel a tube clogging one side.

Shit, where am I now? Her other hand grasped something cold and plastic. She raised her arm and felt the pinch of the IV in the back of her hand. Hospital memories came flooding back to her. Both the sensations and the sterile odor she thought she'd never forget, and knew she never wanted to remember. Not again!

She realized she had a buzzer in her hand, so she pressed it, and kept pressing it, hoping for attention.

"Call the doctor." A nurse yelled as she came rushing into the room. "Liz, you're awake. Don't sit up, just relax. I'm Julie, your ICU nurse. You're in the hospital." Her hand hovered over Liz's eyes. "I'm turning up the light. Don't try to talk just yet. You have a tube down your nose and throat. We'll take that out very soon. Are you in any pain? Just nod your head yes or no."

Liz shook her head no. She lifted her hands and spread them apart in an attempt to ask what happened.

"Just relax, Liz. You're in St. Catherine's Hospital. It's Monday night. You had a nasty fall and bumped your head on Saturday. The doctor will come to see you soon. Just breathe and relax." Julie turned as footfalls echoed on the tile floor behind her.

"Liz just woke up." The nurse's smile beamed and she

stepped aside as Ken and Nancy entered Liz's room. They had wanted one last look before leaving for the evening, and what a look they got!

"Oh, my baby." Nancy stumbled slightly as she rushed to Liz. Ken reached to steady her as they hurried to their daughter.

"You're awake." Nancy bent and laid a kiss on Liz's forehead. A tear dripped to join the kiss. "Are you okay? Are you hurting?"

Liz tried to smile and shook her head slightly. Her eyes lit up when her dad's warm, rough hand grabbed her cold, soft one.

"Hi, doodle. We're here. Don't worry; everything is going to be fine." He turned to Julie, the nurse. "How long has she been awake? No one called us."

"No more than two or three minutes. She pressed the buzzer and I ran right in. She seems good. I'll go check on the doctor's status; I'd like him to see her soon. Just keep talking to her."

Ken turned back to Liz just as Julie nearly bumped into the doctor. Ken turned again at the noise. "She's awake, Doc, she's awake." Ken smiled from ear to ear.

"Very good," the doctor replied, separating himself from Julie with a chuckle. "Let's take a look."

Ken and Nancy moved out of the way. Ken sat down hard in a soft chair, and took a deep breath of relief while the doctor checked Liz's pupil reactions, her reflexes, and so on.

"All of your reactions are fine, Liz. We can go ahead and remove that tube momentarily. It's not going to be comfortable, but it shouldn't hurt. You might gag. Breathe deeply and it will be over in no time. You won't like the sour smell, but it's normal. Ken, why don't you both come over and tell Liz what's been going on while we take care of this. You can stand at the foot of the bed and talk to her."

Ken and Nancy positioned themselves as instructed and put on their happy faces. "Doodle, do you remember being at the Renaissance Festival?"

She nodded while watching the medical staff make preparations for the extraction.

"Do you remember falling?"

She closed her eyes and pulled her eyebrows together.

"Well, I'm sure you don't remember the next part." Ken continued to tell Liz the story of her latest accident while the doctor removed Liz's oxygen tube, and then began extracting the feeding tube.

Liz gagged as expected, and Ken flinched, halting his history lesson in mid-stream. And then it was over, except the cleanup. Liz coughed a couple of times as they cleaned her face and neck.

"Can you swallow?" the doctor asked.

Liz nodded.

"We're going to give you some water, Liz. Sip slowly. Let me know if you have any trouble swallowing. Your throat may be sore for a short time, but that will go away in a day or so." Julie handed Liz a cup with a straw sticking out. Liz managed to drink with a fair amount of ease.

"Water never tasted so good. My mouth is so dry and icky." Her words were barely audible over the beeping monitors, the announcements, and other hospital clamor.

"How do you feel?" Julie took the cup away.

"I'm hungry."

"Let everything settle down and then we can bring you some Jell-O to start with, okay?"

"Thanks, Julie."

"Are you in any pain?" the doctor asked.

"My head hurts some." Liz touched her injury. "Here and everywhere really. My shoulder hurts, too."

"From one-to-ten, where ten is your worst pain ever, how bad is it?"

"Three."

"That's good. It shows you are getting back to normal. No pain or extreme pain would worry me. Can you stand the pain temporarily? We want you to stay awake for a while, so I don't want to prescribe anything yet."

"I can wait."

"Let's check your reflexes again." The doctor performed that task as well as some motion movements with all her extremities.

Liz watched the doctor's face for any tell-tale frowning. She saw none. The doctor continued to question her for a while until he seemed satisfied with her condition. Liz glanced at her arm.

"Don't worry about those bruises. They are coming along just fine. I'll come back and check on you later." The doctor turned to Ken and Nancy. "In the meantime, Julie will stay here and keep tabs on her. She'll let me know if anything comes up. Keep talking to her; keep her mind active. She'll probably be awake for quite a while." The doctor took a last look at Liz. "You let me know if you need anything or don't feel well. I'll come back as soon as I possibly can."

Liz nodded. "Thanks."

Ken finished his story about her latest accident to keep her mind active.

"We'll have a party as soon as you feel up to it, Liz." Nancy grinned from ear to ear. "The girls can help me plan it. A luau would be fabulous. Or a fiesta. Or whatever you want. Morgan and Katy have been here every day. They love you like a sister, but you already know that. Oh, and your friend Michael also came to visit. He's a nice young man and blamed himself for not catching you. Imagine that. Katy assured him that it wasn't his fault. We had some nice conversations and got to know him a bit."

Nancy rattled on. Liz remained alert and followed along as her mom's conversation meandered through the events of the last few days.

"I know we should call the girls. They should be home by now." Nancy tried her cell phone, forgetting it wouldn't work in the room. She laughed and used the room's land line instead. Nancy suddenly held the phone away from her ear laughing and handed it to Liz, who smiled at Katy's overly vocal congratulations.

Liz didn't have to strain her voice much for the next ten minutes as Katy rambled on. Nancy retrieved the phone and tried Morgan next. "That's odd, Morgan isn't answering her phone."

Morgan found herself sleeping on a pew in St. Catherine's chapel in the hospital. Morning light shined through the small stained glass window in brilliant tones and hues. The light draped Morgan in a dappled glow. "Is this a sign? Can you possibly be answering my prayers this time?" She stared at the glass eyes that stared back at her from the figure in the window. She wanted to touch the transparent hand that reached out to her from the holy figure.

Even with her arm asleep and her back stiff, an unusual kind of warmth filled her. She should have been chilled. The air-conditioner kept the room quite cool, but she didn't notice the temperature. She stood, crossed herself from a long-ago habit, and as she turned to leave, she wondered about the new sense of peace that filled her.

Morgan had arrived at the hospital just after visiting hours last night and had almost passed the chapel. To her surprise, she didn't. She had not set foot inside a religious institution of any kind since her parents died. She saw no purpose; she had no faith left. She didn't understand why she had entered, and particularly, why she had stayed all night long.

Making a quick stop in the ladies room to freshen up, Morgan headed toward another lady's room. The Lady Liz.

Morgan entered Liz's room to the sight of Ken and Nancy sitting in chairs on either side of Liz's bed, asleep, with their heads resting on her bed. Another note of peace. Liz's hands rested on their heads and she nodded a happy greeting to Morgan.

"Oh my God." Morgan made no attempt to temper the volume of her voice.

Ken cursed and Nancy said "Aaaaaah" as they jolted awake from their night's rest.

"I'm sorry," Morgan said and ran to hug Liz. "When, how?"

"Late last night," Liz said in her new scratchy voice.

"Oh, thank God, welcome back, Sis. Where did you go? We were so worried. Are you okay?"

"Other than a mild headache and some soreness in my shoulder, I'm just fine." Liz lifted her messy hair. "I could use a shower and a shampoo."

"That's my girl," Ken said. "I'm a little stiff myself. Morgan, will you stay with her for a minute. I need to stretch my legs. Come on Nancy. Let's take a walk."

"Where were you last night?" Nancy asked Morgan as she hugged her. "We tried to call you about Liz."

"It's a long story, but I had turned off my cell phone and forgot about it. I'll remain and cancel my work schedule for today. Go stretch. We'll talk later."

"Liz, I can't believe you are awake. I'm so thrilled. So tell me what happened."

"Wait for me." Katy said entering behind Morgan and pointing at her. "And where were you last night, Missy? We had to worry about you, too."

"Sorry, my phone was off," Morgan said. "Forgive me later, please. Right now Liz needs to share. So, do you have a frequent patient card with the hospital system or what?"

"Good one. I'll have to see if they're available," Liz said.

"Yep, she's okay," Katy stuck her hands in her pockets. "She has her sense of humor back. Now tell us."

"I panicked at first, I'll have to admit. You'd be amazed at the dreams or memories, I had, but we'll cover that ground over drinks soon. In the meantime, I'm being transferred out of here in a while to a regular room. They want to observe me for 24 hours before they'll release me. My parents insist that I stay with them for a while after that. Honestly, I don't mind. They will spoil me rotten plus I would feel more secure not being by myself."

"Like we'd let that happen," Katy reached for Liz's hand.

"I'm a lucky girl." Liz reached to hug her two best friends who immediately complied.

"And I'd be a lucky guy if you're still speaking to me. Can I come in?" Michael stood in the doorway with his hands in his pockets. Visiting hours had just started for the day. "I would have brought flowers, but they won't let them in ICU."

"She'll be in a regular room later today." Katy winked at Michael. "In case you wanted to deliver flowers there."

"Katy!" Liz scolded. "I'm a mess, but sure, come in."

"Your parents told the nurse it was okay. I saw them out in the hallway. It's great that you're awake."

"Why do you think I wouldn't be speaking to you?"

"I should have caught you when you fell. It's been eating at me."

"We'll just wait outside." Morgan motioned to Katy to come with her.

"No, stay." Liz didn't want to be alone with Michael. Her stomach turned over on itself. "Michael, there's nothing to forgive. It wasn't your fault that I fell, and it wasn't your responsibility to catch me. I've heard that you tried and all that you did since. Thank you for that and for coming to meet my parents. Oh, and sorry about my dad—only daughter and all that."

"No worries, you have great parents and great friends."

"Don't I know it. Speaking of which, how are your friends? Please be sure to tell them thanks for me."

"They're good. I'll be sure to tell them. I hear Will and Katy have been talking on the phone." Michael turned to look at Katy.

"Do tell?" Liz turned to Katy.

"Just a little," Katy's forefinger and thumb made the universal 'small' indicator. "We'll talk later." She blushed.

"Yes, we will. Michael, would you mind doing me a favor? If it's not too much trouble?"

"Sure, whatever I can do." He seemed to light up at the thought.

"Can you reach Adonia for me? I'd like to talk to her about adopting Duke after I get out of here. Do you know if he's still available?"

"Ah, no."

"No you don't know, or no he's not available?" Liz tried to push herself up to a sitting position.

"Um, he's not available for adoption. I, um, already adopted him. I thought…"

"What the hell!" Liz interrupted him. "You knew I was interested in him. Get out of here, NOW." Liz pointed to the door with all the energy she had in her arm and in her voice.

"But you don't understand." Michael took one step forward.

"I understand all I need to understand. GET OUT!"

"You better leave," Morgan told him. She grabbed his arm and led him out. "She's not herself yet. I'll explain everything to her. We need to quiet her quickly. Now go, please. I'll call you." Morgan left him in the escort of one agitated nurse and ran back in with Nurse Julie on her heels.

CHAPTER 13

"What's going on in here?" Nurse Julie demanded after a quick glance at Liz, then at the elevated heart rate on her monitors, then back at Liz again.

"Oh, nothing." Liz growled, and then grimaced as she threw up her hands and the IV needle bit into the back of one hand. "It's just men. You can't trust them with anything that belongs to you or that you even think you want to belong to you."

Morgan smiled and shook her head at Julie as if this event rated no merit.

"I see." Julie said. "We'll keep those men types out of here except your dad." She patted Liz's good hand and went back out to her station in the hall.

"Come on, Liz, it wasn't his fault that you are upset, it's yours." Morgan put her hands on her slim hips and glared at Liz. "It's usually Katy defending the male population to you, but this time it falls to me, so shut up, calm down, and listen." She liked that Liz dropped her jaw and remained speechless. Morgan loved to banter, but rarely ever raised her voice—certainly not in her current tone, but Liz was out of control.

"That's better. Now, here's what really happened. Adopting Duke was Michael's only remedy to prevent another couple from adopting that pooch. His noble act was for your benefit, not his. And if you weren't so mulish in your attitudes, you'd see that you just drove away the most honorable prospect that's been along in ages."

"I…" Liz had no retort.

"That's right. You…" Morgan waived her finger at Liz.

"I…I trust you guys. I trust my parents. I don't know how to trust anyone else. I can't trust anyone else, even if he seems wonderful, even if I've known him in another life." Liz whined.

Morgan knew the sorrowful expression on Liz's face came from the emotional pain, rather than anything physical. Silent tears rolled down Liz's cheeks. Morgan walked over to stare out the window. She desperately hated to blast her friend, particularly in her condition, but Liz needed a serious jump-start out of her rut. On that point Katy was right. Morgan ignored her, allowing Liz time to fully process the situation.

"Here now, what's with all the tears; are you in pain?" Ken asked as he and Nancy strolled into the room.

"She just torpedoed Michael for adopting Duke and he hadn't been in the room more than three minutes. Her full-blown tirade didn't even allow him to state his case." Morgan's Irish-Italian ancestry leapt out undeterred by the lid she normally kept on her temper.

"Like father, like daughter." Nancy shook her head. "I'd be very surprised if we ever see that young man again."

Shame came over Liz, not only for her behavior toward Michael, but also for upsetting the people she loved the most. They were right. They were *all* right. Michael had shown her nothing but kindness. He changed her flat tire. He helped her enjoy the Renaissance Festival. He helped get her to the hospital. He even came back and visited with her family. How could she have been so utterly cruel to such a nice guy? Because she *couldn't* trust. No, because she *wouldn't* trust. How could she? Could she ever find it in her heart to trust again? Let alone love again. She needed to work through this dilemma, just not right now. First, she needed to see to those in the room with her at this very moment. She pulled the covers up and tucked them under her arms as if to give her strength.

"You're right. You're all right. I couldn't see through the disgrace I've felt this last year to think that anyone, other than you all, any man, could be, or would be kind to me without an ulterior motive. What do I do now?"

"You just get better for now," Nancy said. "You can deal with this situation later. Michael's character will determine whether he accepts your apology or not. That may help you with the answer you need."

"There, you see why I married her." Ken hugged his wife. "Besides her unending beauty, she is the wisest, calmest woman I've ever met."

"Son of a bitch!" Michael spat into the phone when Richard answered. He paced outside the hospital in the shade of a large Chilean Mesquite tree near the parking lot. Driving at the moment was not an option. He'd probably be arrested for Road Rage if he tried.

"What'd I do?" Richard asked.

"Nothing. It's what I did. Or didn't do. Or what Liz did. I don't know—what the hell. That chick has issues. I'm not sure I want anything to do with her. Personally or professionally."

"As if you don't have issues." Richard said.

"That's true. I do have one major pain-in-the-ass issue, but at least I don't act crazy because of her."

"Who are you trying to bullshit, Michael? Can you honestly say that you are yourself right now? Besides, you have more important issues to deal with now."

"Maybe I'm grumpy now and then, but I don't blow up at people who try to help me…shit! I just did. Damn it, don't say it. Point made. Yes, I've been less than cordial a time or two, sorry." Michael kicked at a root breaking through the grass.

"What happened?"

Michael told Richard—his version anyway. All three minutes of it. "Guys don't whine, we grumble, we vent, we yell. So why do I feel whiny? Do I have, 'Kick Me' tattooed somewhere that only women see?"

"Okay, so let me get this straight," Richard began. "She's out of a coma for less than a day and you went to her, told her the minute you walk in the door, that you stole her dog. Is that right?"

"Yeah, sort of." Michael let out a heavy sigh. "But she didn't give me a chance to explain. Not one word."

"They say that timing is everything."

"Oh shit..." He let out yet another big sigh.

"What now?" Richard asked.

"Morgan is calling, hang on, I'll switch over."

"I'd hate to be in your shoes with her on the line. Better go do her bidding."

♥♥♥

"Hey, Morgan." Michael wiped the sweat from his brow. The filtered shade barely cut the Arizona sun, a warm day, already the first day of March.

"Hello, Michael."

"Before you start in on me too, I know I probably could have handled that better."

"And Liz could have as well," Morgan interrupted. "We explained your reasoning and she wants to talk to you now. Is that okay?" She waited a moment. He was silent, but he didn't refuse. She handed the phone to Liz.

"I guess so." Michael finally replied. "She won't bite my head off again will she?"

"No, Michael, I won't," Liz said. "And I'm very sorry I did the first time."

Oh man, it's Liz. He had no idea what to say.

"I realize what a kind gesture you made and I feel just terrible for what I said," Liz continued. "I have an excuse, but in reality, there is no excuse for my behavior. Can we start over?"

"Um, sure. I suppose I could have done a better job explaining in the first place."

"Seriously, Michael, thank you for rescuing Duke for me. I understand we need to share him. It's actually a good thing since I'll need time to get back to normal. We can figure out some long-term arrangements later."

Silence.

"Michael, are you there?"

"Um, yes. I'm here. Just get well for now, okay?"

"Yes, thanks again for understanding and for saving Duke. I'll talk to you soon."

"Yeah, sure. Bye." Michael clicked back over to Richard. "You still there?"

"Yep, how's Morgan?"

"I talked to Liz, Morgan put her on right away. Remind me not to be Mr. Nice Guy next time I do something like this. I have no idea how I'm going to straighten out this dog-sharing thing. She thinks she'll get him full-time later. I'm hosed. Anyway, Adonia said Duke is ready. She got him neutered and I need to go pick him up now."

"Tread lightly my friend, or Morgan just might help Liz neuter you."

"Bite me, Richard! Later." After venting and the apology, Michael felt capable of driving without killing everyone on the road. He jumped back into his second vehicle, a dog-friendly Jeep, and headed over to Adonia's.

As Michael knocked on Adonia's front door, and waited for her to answer, he scanned her large home. The column work on the outside gave it the slight flavor of a Roman coliseum. It suited her, he thought.

Adonia answered, "Angel boy, come in." Her ancient, but strong legs blocked the escape of several greyhounds. If they got out, they'd run 40 miles-an-hour after whatever they saw until they tired, then they would wonder where they were.

Michael squeezed through the blocked opening and into the elegant foyer, and rubbed several excited dog-heads vying for attention, including Duke's. They slipped and slid on the marble floor as they danced around Michael wanting attention. "Duke doesn't look any worse for his ordeal."

"True, after a few long nights of sleep, he acts like nothing ever happened. He's just a might slower than normal. Not being the alpha-dog in his litter, he won't miss his parts as much. I have your paperwork in the kitchen. Come on. You know the drill." Duke pressed his head against Michael's leg, herding him into the kitchen as if he wanted to hurry the process.

"Adonia, any man's going to miss his parts. You women will never understand." Michael signed the adoption papers and left them on the desk in the kitchen's office space.

"Don't be so sensitive. What's bothering you?"

"It's just been a challenging day already. Duke can maneuver the doggie door, right? It took Pricilla a little while."

"He had his aggressive man-parts long enough, you know. He didn't fear the portal to the grass any more than he did the vet. Little did he know." Adonia snickered.

"Alright, Adonia. Enough with the parts, okay? I'm getting queasy just thinking about it."

"Are you ready to take him home?" By signing the adoption papers, Michael had agreed to return Duke to the rescue group if he couldn't keep him for any reason, and he flinched at the reminder.

Michael looked at Adonia with a slight pang of guilt. He couldn't tell her what he was doing. Hell, he didn't even know what he was doing, or how it would turn out. He may even keep Duke. Maybe he could return Duke when Liz was ready, and then Liz could adopt him. But would that prevent him from adopting later?

"I got him a square dog bed at Costco. I got Pricilla a new one, too so she wouldn't get jealous. Duke seems to get along with your two and your other fosters."

"Yes, they all socialize well. Once in a while we get a loner, but that's rare. They follow each other everywhere."

"You certainly have enough space for all of them so they don't feel crowded."

"After Raphael died, I needed something to fill the house. My two weren't enough. These creatures don't keep me warm in bed, but they do warm my heart. And the group fills the time."

"I didn't mean…"

"Ah, well, it's just the way it is for now. Don't fret. How is Liz? You've checked in on her, haven't you?"

"You always know everything, Adonia. She finally woke up. I suppose she's going to be okay. I met her parents there, and of course, saw her friends."

"You've the eyes of a sad pup. If you are patient, everything will work out." Adonia stroked his face, and then patted his shoulder. "You'll promise me that Duke gets to spend some time with her. He was destined to be hers, but he'll be thrilled with you if he can see her too."

"There's nothing to work out, Adonia. I just need her to hang my paintings. Then I won't be sad." Michael almost cracked under Adonia's I-see-everything eyes that were staring into his heart. "I do promise to connect the two somehow." This might be okay after all. "So what do I owe you? I have some cash with me, but I can bring more money later if it's not enough."

"Nothing, Michelangelo." She pushed against the wallet he had extracted from his pocket. "I owe you more than I could repay. What would I do without your technical skills?"

She handed Duke's leash to Michael.

"Then we'll call it even, and thanks. Come on Duke. Let's go introduce you to Pricilla."

"I have to work tomorrow so I'll see you tomorrow night," Morgan said tugging up the hospital sheets and hugging Liz. She would apologize later, after the emotional thrashing she gave Liz. She needed time to help heal her soul as Morgan hoped she would.

"Ok." Liz barely responded as Morgan walked out the door. Thank goodness Katy was working. She didn't have to deal with her as well. Liz wanted the afternoon to rest and to reflect on her behavior and her future. She wouldn't have a moment's peace tomorrow since she agreed to go home with her parents for the weekend. Provided nothing happened, the insurance company wouldn't let her stay longer than tomorrow, particularly since there were no after-effects from the accident.

"...and we'll plan a nice dinner on Saturday night. Anything you want Liz. How about your favorite Artichoke Fettuccine?"

Liz hadn't been listening to a word her mother said after she arrived, but the mention of good food brought her around. She could almost taste the salty capers floating in the creamy parmesan sauce. "Thanks, Mom. Would it be too much trouble to invite Michael and his friends? I'd like to make up for yelling at him, and they would love your cooking."

Nancy gave Liz the knowing smile Liz was used to. Her mom could always see what she was thinking, as most moms could. "Of course," Nancy said as if it were any normal request. "I'm sure Katy and Morgan will be happy to see the guys as well. And you will behave, Ken. Liz may need those paintings and if so, we must help her get them any way we can."

"Oh, and now I'm the ogre, just because I was concerned for my daughter's well-being?" He reached for Nancy and planted a loving kiss on her neck and tickled her back.

A pang of sorrow stabbed Liz in the stomach, as she witnessed the moment of affectionate joy her parents openly shared. Would she ever have the comfort of a soul-mate? Her parents were more in love than the day they married, as she heard and witnessed on so many occasions. She was incredibly happy for them, and for herself as part of that joy, but she couldn't help wonder if that bliss was free to all who were open to it.

"Go get a room," Liz said with a grin, "And not in this establishment. I need my rest."

"You've had quite enough sleep, young lady, but I agree you do need the rest. We'll be here bright and early tomorrow to take you home, but call us if you need anything and we'll come right back."

"Thanks for bring me some magazines, Mom. I'll have to look for a hair-do to hide my bald spot."

"I'll bring you a ball-cap," Ken said, ruffling Liz's bangs.

"That'll be easier. Thanks, Dad. See you both in the morning."

"Finally," Liz said to herself out loud.

Now if the nurses would just leave her alone. She kept that thought to herself because of the proximity to the nurses' station.

What did she do now? She needed to come up with a plan. Did Michael need her to sell his paintings more than she needed his paintings? Or was it the other way around?

CHAPTER 14

The warm water rained down on Liz like tiny hands massaging her overly stiff muscles. She could never remember a shower feeling so good. Unless Michael had been in the shower with her. Hmm, another memory?

Her dirty hair disgusted her, so she shampooed one side and as close as she dared get to her stitches on the other. That would hold her for a couple more days. Maybe she'd get some of that dry shampoo and give that a try.

Forcing herself out of the shower, Liz stretched her achy muscles after drying off. The simple act of movement gave her a profound appreciation of being awake and alive and she realized that no matter what came before, she could count herself as being truly blessed. She'd leave that all behind and move on now.

Leaving the hospital had been uneventful; her arrival at her parents' house—not so much. Liz inhaled the heady scent of what must have been a thousand flowers. Bouquets decorated not only the family room, but also fragranced her old bedroom, welcoming her home to a place where she was always wanted. To a place where spare clothes, extra makeup, and more awaited her anytime she visited, in case she stayed over. It would all come in handy.

Liz donned comfy sweats and fuzzy socks and headed out to the family room. A cinnamon roll and apple juice awaited her on the coffee table. Liz appreciated that her parents never missed the details.

"Good morning, Dad. Still doing the crossword puzzles I see."

Ken sat in his brown leather recliner with a section of the daily paper folded in one hand, a pen in another. He rose to greet Liz, careful to hug one side.

"It keeps the ol' brain sharp. Good morning. How's the headache, and how'd your hair get wet?"

"Almost gone. Quit worrying, it's only partially wet. By the way, I didn't have a single dream last night."

"That's a first. I'm surprised, but happy for you, honey."

"Thanks. Personally, I'm shocked. Where's Mom?"

"In the kitchen, fretting over special meal plans for the next few days. Go tell her your good news, then come back in here and relax."

Liz found her mom seated at the breakfast nook hunched over her collection of favorite recipes. Liz had assembled them into a recipe scrapbook for Christmas a few months back. Ken taught at the Scottsdale Culinary Institute before they opened their own white-linen restaurant, *Two for Dinner*, so these special recipes rated special treatment.

"You use the book?" Liz asked as she kissed her mom and then sat on a yellow leather Parsons chair next to her.

"Oh, of course I do. You know I almost cried when I opened it. You spent so much time, retyping the recipes and making it beautiful. I love it. I didn't hear a peep from you all night. Did you rest well?" Nancy covered Liz's hand with her own.

"You'd think I wouldn't need any sleep, but I slept through the night. Thanks for checking on me. No dreams, Mom."

"No dreams? That's a good sign."

"Yeah, maybe I should have taken a blow to the head years ago." Liz grinned at the scolding expression on her mom's face. "I crashed hard and woke up stiff. I could have stayed in the shower all day."

"Oh, before I forget, Morgan called. Did you know she covered for you some this week? She's having a blast with Jean-Luc and keeping him updated on your progress as well."

"I didn't know, but I'm not too surprised. I'll go call her. I need to call Jean-Luc later as well."

"Your cell is on the charger by the couch."

"Have I ever told you I love you, Mom?" Liz hugged Nancy before heading to her phone.

"Once or twice, I think. Before you go, the girls will be over for dinner tonight. And if you are up for it, we'll host that small party on Saturday night. Do you have any requests?

"If you wouldn't mind, I'd like to invite Michael and his friends on Saturday. I should keep this business with Michael, just business, but with Duke involved, we should become friends as well. Besides, Katy would love to see Will."

"The more the merrier."

"I don't know how I can ever repay you for all you have done. And always do. You are taking so much time away from the restaurant. Is everything okay over there?"

"Yes, that's one reason we have a manager. Besides, it's nice to be away from there now and then. Just not for this reason." Nancy shook her finger at Liz, like moms often do. "Your dad brought your laptop over as well. He thought you'd like to check your email. I think he even remembered the cord."

"Good, I'd better check them. Do you need help with anything?"

"No, go relax."

Back in the family room, Liz snuck up on her dad, bent over the back of the recliner, and put her arms around her dad's neck. "Have I told you how much your little girl still needs her dad, even at 28? I can't begin to thank you for everything. You even remembered my laptop."

"Yep, it's waiting for you on the couch. And you are welcome. You can't imagine how happy we are to have you back safe and sound, even though your hair looks funny."

"Yeah, keep it up and I'll shave it off." Liz ruffled Ken's hair, kissed his head, and went to check her email. She had one from *artnsoul@gmail.com*. Her pulse quickened when she confirmed Michael's email address. He had sent her thumbnail pictures of some of his paintings, and provided the URL to his website. After unzipping the file and viewing each picture, she accessed his website to get a better understanding of Michael the artist. In his sales photo, he stood on the hearth of a grand, stone fireplace next to an abstract painting. This site catered only to his paintings. Liz wondered if he had another site for his graphics business. She searched the internet and, sure enough, there he was. Not him personally, no photo, but a listing of satisfied clients, capabilities, and contact information. Not to mention samples of logos, ads, and websites he had built. So he hadn't fed her a line, but a list of questions remained. Did he have a good head for business? Was he amiable? Was he personally reliable? And how often did he think of her? Whoa, where'd that come from? It, too, was a legitimate question. After all, if she didn't cross his mind frequently, then he wasn't serious about showing his work. She had to admit, she thought about Michael, the man, more than she expected to.

Liz showed his information to her dad. "You have a good head for business—what do you think of him?"

"I think I need a better website for the restaurant. Maybe he could give me some tips. If he's half as impressive as his presentation, he should do well. Someone has money to buy art, even in these tight economic times."

"We just need to get buyer and seller together. That's my job." Liz finished responding to her emails and completed some strategic searches on the internet. She made lists. She made plans. She made herself hopeful that her plans just might work.

♥♥♥

Later that day, she called Jean-Luc.

"*Ma chère*, thank God. I was much worried."

"I'm fine now, Jean-Luc. You can quit worrying. How are you and how's business?"

"I am still as handsome as ever, and two times as charming. I miss you, but our lovely accountant kept me company and charmed our customers. We sold one *tableau*—the *Forest Rain*. It's minimal *oui*, but every sale is important."

"I may have a possibility for us. It's a contemporary artist you might like. I'll email you his website link. Tomorrow will be a good day to go see his work, and then I'll stop by to talk to you about it."

"Do not push too hard. You must be well soon."

"No worries, I told you. I mend quickly. My check-up is tomorrow morning. If all's well, I'll be released to drive and will come back to work on Friday."

"Call me with updates, *ma chère*. Philip Durand just arrived. I must attend him now. Be well."

"Michael. Hi, this is Liz. Do you have time to talk about the gallery?" Her stomach flip-flopped like a fish on shore, but her determination took control. She paced her bedroom, but making the call right after talking to Jean-Luc gave her the drive she needed.

"Yes, Morgan told me that you were home; what a relief. Are you stronger now?"

"I'm at my parents' now and doing well. I've been reviewing both of your websites and I'd like to see your paintings in person. Is that possible?"

"Of course, anytime. I'll be at my studio tomorrow and Saturday. I have some meetings on Friday. When did you want to come? Or do you want me to bring them to you?"

"That's thoughtful. I'd love to see your studio, if that's okay? How about tomorrow afternoon? I have a doctor's appointment in the morning." She held her breath hoping their schedules would mesh.

"Perfect. Does 2:00 work for you?"

"Where are you located?"

He provided her with the address, directions, and description of his studio.

"Ah, you're in Catlin Court in Glendale. I know exactly where you're located. I should be there around 2:00."

"Then I'll see you tomorrow."

"I'll be there. Bye." That went easier than expected. She didn't know why she was so nervous. He seemed relaxed enough. His paintings will be great. It'll be fine. This can work.

With business over, Liz forced herself to relax with a couple of movies until dinner. Her parents puttered around the house and made a few business calls of their own. Liz knew how fortunate she was to have them.

Katy arrived for dinner, still in her work scrubs, spreading hugs and happy feelings all around. "Hey, lazy girl. Did you get spoiled today?" Katy motioned to Liz's total domination of the couch area.

"What else are parents for?" Ken asked. "You should come spend the day for your share of the same. It'll be just like when you were in college."

"Careful. I may just do that." Katy hugged Ken.

The doorbell announced Morgan, moments after Katy arrived. "You look marvelous, Liz. And you'll be pleased to know we made another sale. Mr. Durand almost drooled over *Tahitian Hut* and bought it on the spot for his daughter's engagement. Tahiti is her honeymoon destination. The sale finally provided a profit for the month."

"I'm not sure which of us appreciates it more." Liz's eyes welled up. "I'll return the favor one day. What can I do for you?"

"We should all go to Tahiti," Morgan said.

"Hah, maybe we'll get rich off Michael's art." Liz had told herself to practice positive thinking, and the vibes in the air started her believing.

"How about dinner first?" Nancy offered. "*Chicken in Lemon Beurre Blanc* will be ready in ten minutes."

"Forget Tahiti." Katy headed straight for the kitchen and called back over her shoulder, "I'm vacationing here."

Dinner conversation included group vacations, favorite dinners cooked by Nancy and Ken, and twenty questions about Will.

"Yes, we talked twice this week." Katy blushed. "He called to check on Liz. He asked about my work. My hobbies. Oh, and my food preferences. Of course, I said anything from your restaurant. His parents were born in Wales. Thus, his British/Celtic accent. He was born here, though. He loves Mexican food. And he loves dogs. Isn't that great?"

"Sounds like you like him. Are you going out?" Liz couldn't be happier for her friend. She found a nice guy and was on her way to finding out if it would go anywhere.

"He hasn't asked me yet."

"Can't women ask men these days?" Nancy asked.

"He's the x-ray guy, right?" Ken asked.

"Yes, to both. Also, he invests. He has a house in Cave Creek. A half-acre, I think he said. No horses. No dogs yet, but eventually. That's the highlights."

"Do you want me to ask Michael about him?" Liz asked. "I'm going over to his studio tomorrow afternoon."

"Really? Hmm. Let me think about it…duh, yes. Thanks."

"Why don't you girls go watch a movie? Dad and I will do dishes." Nancy started collecting the square white plates.

"I'd prefer the more juicy details." Morgan whispered once out of ear shot from the kitchen.

"No juice for you." Katy pointed to Morgan.

"We're here, Duke. Let's see how you like my gallery. Pricilla, let's show him the ropes. Come on, boy." Michael lifted Duke out of his Jeep instead of letting him jump. He wanted to make sure Duke didn't tear his stitches. Duke groaned slightly, but was good mannered about the movement.

Once inside, Michael walked his new buddy around, showing him the locations of the stuff important to dogs: his bed, the food bowls, and the doggie door to the small enclosed back yard, all of which he smelled with passing interest. However, the water bowl captured his attention until his thirst was quenched.

Duke settled in as if he belonged there, which he did. He allowed Pricilla her alpha-dog status, and followed her lead, keenly aware of her every move.

Later, as Michael re-arranged paintings in his mini-gallery, Duke followed, seeming to stare intently at each piece. "Do you like me or my work?" Michael bent down to ruffle Duke's ears and received a big dog-kiss that tingled in a strange way all over his head and neck. "Thanks, boy, I'll take that as a 'both'."

Pricilla watched, half-interested, from a distance, having lived through Michael's routine many times. As Michael hung the third piece of a triptych painting, Duke barked one loud bark, startling Michael which caused him to bump the upper pieces askew. "What is it, boy, do you hate it?"

No response.

"Do you love it?"

"Woof." Duke said, a little louder than his usual Ooof.

"Thanks, Duke. That's your first bark. Do you think Liz will like it?"

"Woof, woof."

"Good. She's coming this afternoon, so we'll see what she has to say."

Michael hung others while Duke simply watched.

"Woof, woof." Duke said as Michael hung the last painting.

"Ah, this one is named *Heart Storm*. Think it will sell?"

Duke rubbed his face on Michael's leg so he knelt down and gave Duke a thorough, but gentle rubbing. "Thanks, boy. Maybe this one will be my *pièce de résistance*."

Duke kissed Michael non-stop.

"What's in your saliva boy? You keep making me tingle."

Duke gave him a little "Ooof," and seemed to smile.

"We'll see if it sells. If it does, I'll have you critique all my work." Michael stood back eyeing his choices. "I guess that will do. Hard to say what she'll like. Come on, let's get some lunch. Want a doggie treat?"

Duke and Pricilla stood patiently by, sniffing the air, hoping for a handout of cheese or meat while Michael made a sandwich in the kitchenette he designed when he had remodeled the house into a studio. A man has to eat during a busy day, and fast food usually didn't fit into Michael's gourmet tastes. A burger just wouldn't provide the proper inspiration. He preferred cracked-wheat bread, brie, avocado, Dijon, and organic sliced beef, a sliver of which he gave to each dog. An Asian pear followed for dessert.

As he ate, his mind drifted to Liz. He didn't know all that transpired, but he could sense that she must have been through a lot of injuries. He opened his mind to try to understand her and his comfort level increased a great deal. In fact, he suddenly thought, she might belong in his life. He just didn't know where she fit. It had to be business only, given his current personal and work situation, but it seemed like there should be more. Like there already was more.

He stared at the partially eaten sandwich waiting in front of him on the tiny bistro table. He pictured Paris and croissants with Liz on a sunny April morning. Whoa, dude. Where'd that vision come from? His imagination went way off in a foreign direction, so to speak. Perhaps he thought of another painting. Yeah, that must be it.

No longer hungry, he put the remaining food away in his tiny refrigerator, got the dogs each a dog biscuit, and went back to work.

"I want to draw you," he said to Duke.

Michael set up his drawing easel and began sketching while Duke kept Pricilla company. Michael managed to settle into his creative mode. Before he realized it, he had drawn Duke standing in front of a seated woman, her long brown hair fashioned partly in an old-style braided crown. The woman's hand rested on the dog, who looked up at her with affection. He hadn't drawn the woman's face completely, but he knew he had started to draw Liz.

"Duke, have you put some sort of spell on me? Just look at this." To his surprise, Duke came to him, looked at the drawing and rubbed his face on Michael's leg. "I'll be damned. You are one unusual dog. I need to run you two home before Liz gets here."

Duke ran to where Pricilla slept. He crouched with his front legs down and his butt in the air, in a playbow position. He danced and played until Pricilla rose, then led her to the front door.

Michael busted out laughing. "You are going to be one fun dog to have around, Duke. Let's go."

CHAPTER 15

Raising a hesitant finger, Liz rang the bell at Michael's downtown Glendale studio on Thursday. She loved the quaint, Craftsman Bungalow houses in the old neighborhood. The variety of homes—many of which had been converted into lovely antique shops, tea houses, and craft establishments—portrayed an ambiance of creativity, a perfect place to have a studio.

Liz expected to be kept waiting, imagining the halted process of a temperamental artist interrupted during a masterpiece in progress. She wanted to turn and run. If only she didn't need what Michael had to offer. On one hand, the thrill of discovering a new artist made her pulse race more than the quintessential new bike at Christmas, one of her favorite presents as a child. On the other hand, what if she had put more hope into the situation than it warranted? What would she do if...

"Oh, hi." Liz visibly jumped as Michael opened the door wide.

"Hey, Liz. Thanks for coming. Welcome to my mess." Michael reached for her hand and guided her inside. Once more, a warmth spread from her hand to his, and up his arm to his heart. It wasn't a spark. It was a feeling of comfort. A feeling of belonging, as if it were natural for her to be here with him.

"Um, did I interrupt anything?"

"Just finishing a sketch of Duke. He needs to be in my doggy hall of fame." Aware that he still held her hand, Michael reluctantly let go and pointed to his drawing area.

"Hall of Fame?"

"Each dog that tugs at my world gets one. Like a photo, the memory lingers, long after the mind forgets. Corny, huh?"

"Not at all. One does what one feels, right?"

"You have the soul of a painter as well as a critic."

"No, I'm not a critic, I'm an aficionado."

"Perdón." Michael bowed slightly.

"De nada. You're excused. May I see your sketch?"

"Later. I'm not finished."

"Where is that black beauty?" Liz scanned what she could see of his gallery.

"He's at home with Pricilla, my other dog. I felt it best for us to be undisturbed today." Michael grinned like a sly dog. A twinge of unexpected anticipation surged through him that went well beyond business. He couldn't help but have feelings for her, romantic or otherwise.

"Oh yeah? And what might he be disturbing?"

That comment took his warm glow into a hotter direction. "Just wherever this takes us."

"Well, then. Let's get started." Her smile grew.

Michael stepped closer and gently cupped her elbow. Her cheeks reddened as his room grew smaller, warmer.

When she hesitated, he reluctantly stepped back. As right as their synergy seemed, he wasn't quite ready or able to explore it and guessed she wasn't either.

"What do you think of my studio and gallery?" He waved his arm to display his space and to change the direction of their conversation. "I've just renovated the place." He walked to his left, placing a hand on a wall partition. "I removed a couple of walls to open up the house, and installed several four-foot-wide divider sections for more hanging space in most of the now open room. They can be moved around." Michael pointed to the industrial wheels supporting the mini-walls. "It's like a small maze, but gives me loads of display space. Behind me is my work center." He motioned over his shoulder with his thumb.

"It's wonderful. Efficient and quite similar to the layout of our gallery."

"Where do you think I got the idea?" Michael grinned and spread his arms wide.

"You've been to our gallery?" She turned to him with wide eyes.

"Liz, I've been in just about every gallery in Scottsdale, Phoenix, and throughout the Valley of the Sun. I wanted some fresh ideas to change my location. I don't plan to be here forever, but it suits me for now."

"Tell me about these?" Liz scanned the walls to her right.

"They're my newer pieces. Some of which I hope you'll find adequate to hang in your gallery. Why don't I leave you alone to view them at your leisure? Take your time and look around. I'll be right over here until you have some questions." Michael returned to his drawing.

Liz watched his retreating form, and participated in a little art appreciation of a different sort. She scolded herself for her mixed emotions, and then mentally tucked them away to handle the job at hand.

She took a deep breath. The scent of paint, gesso, and thinner put her at ease as she analyzed the various-sized paintings, diptychs, and triptychs. One particular triptych caught her eye and spoke to her immediately. The representation split vertically, one on top of the other, instead of horizontally, the normal configuration. She could imagine the trio hanging against a tall stone fireplace like the one she had seen on Michael's website.

The three paintings displayed graduated red, purple, and

blue swirls lit by yellow and white bringing an internal illumination, mostly on the upper canvas. Very much like a storm stirring inside the clouds. This one will do nicely.

"Do you like that one?" Michael called out bringing Liz out of her reverie.

"It feels like a storm, but there's no brooding or angst. It's alive and compelling."

"I call that one *Heart Storm*." He smiled, and then turned back to his drawing.

Across the short distance, she watched as a blush come to his face. His arm continued to dance behind the easel.

"It's a perfect name! That one will sell, I know it."

Moving on to a juxtaposed diptych, she said, "This set is a good commercial piece, sellable because the perception of color is altered by the colors you've used against each other."

"You have a discerning eye. I emulated Josef Alber's color theory when I painted that one. Notice how the rich browns make the creams more golden."

Having moved on to the next one, Liz asked, "Are all your pieces this good or did you just hang the best for my viewing?"

"I hung what I hoped you'd like. I try to keep track of what seems to be selling at the other galleries. I thought something similar, but different, fresher, might sell well. Something bright, but not the usual primary colors in the usual way. One needs to do a little recon to be marketable."

"So you have a head for business as well? That's good. Oh, this one is quite different." Two entities surrounded by pale light and colors drew her into the painting. Not only did this one speak to her esthetics, but it called out to her soul.

"I call that one *The Guardian*. It represents Adonia and one of her dogs. That's what she calls herself, *The Guardian*."

"Why is that?" When he didn't respond right away, Liz turned to Michael.

"Because of her special relationship with the greyhounds." He finally raised his eyes to hers, but displayed an odd expression on his face. It seemed like he had more to say, but didn't say it.

"It must take a special lady to run a rescue group, to foster and adopt as well. She sounds Italian—where was she born?"

"In Rome. She won't say how long she's been here, but she does say she's a lot older than she looks. I've only known her a couple of years, but she hasn't aged at all."

"I hope I'm that lucky." Liz touched her face, feeling older than her 28 years. An ethereal painting on an opposing wall called to her and she felt compelled to study it.

After a time, she realized that Michael was watching her.

"Are you ignoring me or should I take it as a good sign that you like that one as well?" His eyebrows raised in question.

Man, is he handsome. "I'm sorry, did you say something? I'm enthralled with this painting and I don't know why. It looks like a winged man and a reclining female, but there is no definition. How can that be? Tell me about this one." She reached out to feel it, following the brushstrokes with her fingers, and then suddenly removed her hand. "I'm sorry, I know better than to touch a painting, finger oils and all that, but I couldn't help myself."

"That one's *Love and the Maiden Too*. It's an homage to Stanhope's painting of the angel, *Soqed Hozi*, the angel of partnerships. I'm surprised and thrilled that you sense the gist of it."

Liz first thought her imagination created the figures, but was relieved to hear Michael confirm what she had envisioned. The angel-person and the woman seemed to have a strange energy between them that changed with the angle and the lighting. She liked it, but it unsettled her at the same time. It energized her.

"I want this one, *The Guardian*, the storm one, the color theory, all of these. Do you have what you need to get them packed for shipment? I can have a truck pick them up. How soon can they be ready? I'd like them right away."

Michael crossed the room and hugged Liz, a grateful hug, not a romantic one. "I don't know what to say. I can prepare them in the morning and bring them over myself in the afternoon if you like." The excitement that sparked off his body aroused Liz in places she had long ago consciously ignored. It also opened her mind to other possibilities she had deliberately ignored. Passion radiated in his face as he released her, bathing her with pleasure from head to toe, especially everywhere in between. Liz suddenly hoped his passion extended to her personally as well as professionally. She had awakened in more ways than one and decided to fully open up and enjoy the moment.

But...Liz had to force herself back to business. "I'll need another day. You'll need to come in and go over your contract, I need to prep the space, and we need to talk about advertising, promotion, and pricing. Can you come in tomorrow and meet Jean-Luc? He's my boss."

"Sure, what time?"

"How about 10:00? We open at 11:00 tomorrow."

"I have another appointment at 2:30, so that'll work. I'm glad you came by."

He piqued her interest, professionally and personally. Maybe her friends were right. It doesn't hurt to look, and maybe have a little fun. It wasn't like she was in a situation where she had to trust him financially. Other than in business, anyway.

"Would you like me to bring Duke by this weekend? He's almost healed."

"That was quick. Yes, please. I can't wait to see him." He surprised her at every turn.

"Can do. I dreamed about you last night. I took it as a positive sign about our doing business together."

Liz searched his eyes, hunting for more meaning. "Oh...really? What happened in the dream?"

"It was a medieval kind of thing. I fell while jousting and

you ran to the arena to check on me. And then I suddenly woke up."

Liz paled. She couldn't believe what she heard. What he said registered, but what could it mean; the same dream? "Um, I have to run. I'll see you tomorrow."

Liz couldn't breathe. She needed air and time to think. She hurried for the door and didn't look back.

"Morgan, call me as soon as you get this message." Morgan would recognize Liz's soft voice.

Liz sat in her car in a nearby parking lot, a burger place, her mood vastly unsettled, shivering despite the warm March sun shining through the windshield. She watched the smoke that billowed out of the restaurant's chimney.

Her pulse still throbbed, as much as it had when she made her quick exit. Had he dreamed the same dream? How is that possible? She had wanted to ask a million questions, but fear had dried her mouth and stilled her tongue.

She focused on each detail of her conversations with Michael. Had he really flirted with her, or had she mentally twisted his words and actions? Did she flirt back? It must have been her dream history that loosened her demeanor with him. He was both comforting and exciting to be around, like they belonged together. And what about that dream? Their connections kept increasing.

The Rolling Stone's *Satisfaction* ring tone on her cell suddenly jerked Liz out of her mental replay. "Hey, Morgan."

"Hello, Liz. Is everything okay? I have a moment between clients."

"Yeah, I'll make it quick. Just left Michael's, great paintings, we flirted, and *he* dreamed the *same* jousting dream."

"I'm not sure which to address first. Paintings later; not surprised. Flirting; good. Give me the abbreviated dream interaction."

"I'm not sure I can, Morgan. I was near the door getting ready to leave, arrangements made for the art and to have Duke for the weekend, and he said he dreamed about me. I remember smiling until he shared the details. His dream seemed to mirror the one I had the night before the Renaissance Festival. How can that be?"

"Hmm, that's fascinating. How did you reply?"

"That's the thing. I don't know. I only remembered saying 'See you tomorrow,' before I dashed back to my car. He must think I'm nuts."

"Liz, consider that he might be thinking that he crossed the business line and shouldn't have shared his dream. He could be kicking himself about now."

"I hadn't thought of that."

"Don't concern yourself. He needs the gallery situation as much as you do. You'll resolve it. I have another meeting now, but I'll remain if you need me."

"No, go, I'll be fine. I just wanted a second perspective."

"We'll talk more, later."

Liz sat in her car for what seemed like hours until she had settled down. What's done is done. She couldn't imagine how he would react tomorrow.

"Adonia, I need to talk now and I have a question." Michael found her at home, as usual, as long as she didn't have a dog matter to handle. He wanted this discussion to take place in person. He angled past her through the door so the dogs didn't get out, skipped their usual hug, and stormed into the great room.

"Michelangelo, what's on your mind? Can I get you something?"

"Just an answer. Are you using your doggie gift on Liz and me?"

"Come sit down. Let's talk." She waved him on over her shoulder.

He followed her back to her formal sitting room that overlooked the bouldered desert vista beyond her wall of glass. Her Carefree home had been in *Phoenix Home and Gardens* a few years ago. Despite its beauty, the view did nothing to calm his edginess.

"Exactly what's bothering you, Michael?" She sat with ease and grace, but he paced, while multiple pairs of dog eyes followed his movements.

"I know Duke is one of your gifted dogs. That's why you are so anxious for Liz to be part of his life as well. I just didn't know that I was going to be on the receiving end of your playing Cupid."

"Michael. I. Don't. PLAY." Adonia's voice boomed off the walls and the ceiling of the great room. Michael felt the vibration to his core. Sparks flew from the outlets. A light bulb burst. Michael's hair stood on end. And his face tingled like Novocain after a dental visit.

Adonia's own two dogs and her foster dog took a protective stance at her side. She leaned back in her floral wing chair and glared at Michael, a look he had never seen before and hoped to never see again. Did the wrath of the gods truly pass down through future generations as well as their other gifts? He didn't remember reading that Cupid and Psyche, Adonia's ancestors, had any anger management issues.

"I didn't mean to insult you. I just need some answers." Michael bowed his head slightly, just in case. In—case— what, he didn't know, but it felt like the right thing to do. Yes, he was angry, but there were other, maybe better ways to get his answers.

"You have known about our gifts for some time now. Seen them in action. You should already know all the answers. But, calm down and explain what happened to infuriate you so."

Michael sat on the edge of the chair that faced Adonia's chair. He stared out the windows for a moment, not seeing the view, and then told her about his meeting with Liz, finally getting to the dream.

"When I shared my dream with her, she went pale. I was afraid she'd faint. Then she said, 'That was the same dream I had the night you changed my tire.'"

"Good."

"Good? How can that be? How can we have the same dream? Are we on your list? Are you using your powers on our lives?"

"In a word, yes, but in your heart, you already knew that."

He couldn't have been more surprised. He combed his fingers through his hair as if to better understand that simple word and what it meant.

"Duke recognized Liz immediately at the Renaissance Festival and kissed her then. I've told you how they find and awaken the female first. It was only after that event, not before, that he recognized you as her soulmate. Dogs have more genetic memories than people, particularly the descendants of the dogs the Goddess Diana gave me. You and Liz both have the same memories of each other thus your attraction, and the same dreams, but logic won't let Liz, or you, consciously remember your past lives. You have been lovers more than once and are destined to be together in this life as well."

"But Adonia, this is me! You don't have the right to play matchmaker with my life."

"I told you once, boy, I don't play." Adonia's voice boomed again. "I am the descendant of Cupid and Psyche and it is not only my right, it is my destiny, my duty. Someone has to intervene to help bring eternal lovers together again when they are too busy or stubborn to open their hearts. Now that you all have *free will*, we can no longer force it to happen. Since fate has brought you to the same location, it's now our job to help you *sense* the eternal attraction. You can fight it if you like, but you'll never be happy in this life until you accept your fate."

Michael was speechless. And a little scared. He had never seen Adonia in a rage and had *never* seen greyhounds display an aggressive stance. They rarely get upset. They are one of the most tolerant breeds around. It was his turn to be truly submissive.

"I'm…just…having a hard time with this." Michael knew he had offended her without meaning to do so. It was he who leaned back into his chair this time.

"It's okay, babies." Adonia rubbed her dogs. They immediately accepted her command and reclined, but kept Michael in their sights. "I realize this is hard to accept. You have the disadvantage of knowing what the dogs and I do. You are one of the very few I have taken to heart over the years. You are the proverbial son I never had, which is why you have this knowledge. My *interference* has never bothered you before, but I understand your distress when the gift happens to you. You see, even possessing the gift, it happened to me. That's why you have the perception that I got over Raphael's death so easily. I didn't have to, because I also know that we will be together again in the next life. Our love is eternal."

"I don't know what to say. I once thought I had found the love of my life and was wrong. Am I to accept that Liz is the one? And the timing is so wrong."

"That first one was not meant for you. Bethany could not be the love of your life, because she is not Liz. And Liz is fumbling about because she is fighting what her heart knows, but her mind refuses to accept, because of free will. You also have the option to live a happy, love-filled life. You simply need to make a choice."

"How can I deal with this? Knowing what I know."

"You turn down the noise in your mind, and listen to your heart."

"I know it works. I've seen it happen many times. But I'm not blinded like the others. I'll need to think about it."

"Don't think, Michael. Feel. Leave yourself open. Liz needs to accept it as well. This gift is not a guarantee. It's only an opportunity. Your dreams…Liz's dreams and visions, they are memories, not dreams. That's why they are the same."

"I've had dreams of a woman this past week in different places, different times, but I could never see her face, until this last dream."

"That's the way it happens. Liz would have seen your face long before you ever saw hers."

"Perhaps that explains some of her odd behavior."

Adonia rose, moved to Michael, raised his hands so he would stand, and hugged him. White energy circled them both with a swirling power that calmed his temper. He saw it and looked questioningly at Adonia when she released him. The dogs circled the two, wagging their tails as if nothing stressful ever happened.

"Not to worry. You can see my love for you. Have you never seen me hug my dogs?"

"Yes, but I've never seen the energy."

"Then you have finally opened your heart to truly believe in the gift of love."

"People would never believe this, even if I took pictures."

"It is not for others to see. Love this deep only shows in people's eyes, sometimes on their faces, but never in full."

"I've bothered you enough. I should go. Sorry for snapping at you." Michael hugged Adonia this time and finally rubbed her greyhounds, albeit cautiously. They had relaxed to their normal, calm selves. He headed toward the door, and then turned when his hand reached the carved ornate knob. "Thanks for the explanation. I still don't know what to do about Liz."

"What happens will happen. Be open to her. She is yours if you both accept your destiny."

"You know I can't have her. Not yet anyway."

"Time will take care of your other problem, Michael."

CHAPTER 16

Liz slept dream-free once again and rose to ready herself for her first day back at the gallery on Friday morning. What to wear? One of her gallery staples? Or something with a little more flash to brighten her mood? A mix, that's it. Hunting through her closet, she found a black skirt, short, but not too short. Modest, but enough leg displayed to be attractive. A red cropped jacket with a lightly ruffled cami underneath. Red heels, the silver Fleur-de-lis jewelry that Jean-Luc gave her last Christmas. The same jewelry that she wore to the Renaissance Festival. That would do. And a beret to cover her shaved spot instead of a baseball cap.

Jean-Luc had arrived early and had already started checking the stock. He loved mornings. He usually took his *café* on the back patio of the gallery, listening to the birds sing just for him. They told him of the old tales, songs of his own life, and stories of the future. So he said.

Birds were a pooping irritant as far as Liz was concerned, even though she respected nature's necessary tool to spread seeds and be an early-warning-system of approaching danger. Blah, blah, and more blah. On that one thing, her affections differed from Jean-Luc's.

Liz tugged opened the heavy, back door of the gallery with a little trepidation. Could she pull this off? Could she help save the gallery from the waning economy?

Once again, the familiar smell of oils and acrylics

immediately calmed her. Her second home.

"*Bonjour, ma chère.* I am pleased to have you back. Are you well?" When Jean-Luc's craggy face broke into a smile, the atmosphere in the room changed and Liz couldn't help but feel more positive.

"*Bonjour,* Jean-Luc. I am well and happy to be back at work. I see your birds followed you to work, as always. They are perched in the shade tree above my car, ready to remind me of their grandeur."

"Ah, more respect, *ma chère,* and perhaps reminders would not be necessary. *Préférez-vous* a car wash instead of jewelry for your bonus *annuel?*" Jean-Luc touched the necklace she wore. His booming laugh cheered her spirits as did his usual kiss to each cheek.

"I have missed you. How have you survived without me?"

"With difficulty, *ma chère.* But you are back. Where is your promising gentleman?"

A promising gentleman? What a strange turn of phrase. Would Michael truly fulfill a promised need? Her thoughts took her elsewhere for a moment. "He will arrive about 10:00 today. I wanted time to settle in and tell you about him first. Do you have time before we open?"

"I have time always *pour ce qui est important.*"

French in college made more sense with her art studies, even though she considered Spanish. Liz was pleased that she could practice all these years with Jean-Luc and become fairly fluent. His mixed speech patterns never fazed her one bit. It was one more endearing mannerism that made her love her mentor like a second father.

She explained the paintings she had seen at Michael's studio, described which ones she requested for the gallery, and shared why she thought each one would sell. "I asked him to bring a small one in person to show you and he'll bring his others on a thumb drive. If you agree, he can deliver some paintings later today. I thought we could place him front and center. We can do the usual cocktail hour for select invitees and…"

"Liz…" Jean-Luc shook his head briefly.

She knew something was amiss when he interrupted her and used her given name.

"I'm saddened to say, but the usual hors d'oeuvres and Champagne cannot fit in my wallet. Plus, the turnout was negligible for the last two shows."

"I think I have a solution for both of those issues," Liz said. "I'm hoping we could talk Michael into donating some paintings for charity. Maybe we could hold a raffle or something with the proceeds going to the winners' favorite charities, in their names.

"Mom and Dad can provide the food, and deduct the event for charity. We have some wine left from last time. We could serve bubbly water adorned with fruit, too, as a healthy alternative. We still have a small credit with the printer, and can ask them to donate the remainder for the fliers and give them free advertising in exchange.

"Since its short notice, we can personally call select guests inviting them to let us know about their charity of choice and follow up with invitations using a free email application. Either Morgan or I could do that part.

"We already have tables and cloths, napkins, and the like. Mom and Dad have whatever else we need. We could do it with very minimal expense. I know, we could hold a silent auction in the gallery, I'm sure everyone would help."

"*Bon.* You have thought much on this and figured it out on a string from your shoe."

"Yes, it is good. It's important to us. Maybe some of the other artists will sell as well. I think it's worth a try. Here's the budget." Liz handed him a copy of her spreadsheet. "I can supplement it some as well. I've been saving."

"*Ma chère,* will he sell?"

"There's never a guarantee, but I have a good feeling about this one. What do we have to lose at this point, but a small outlay and some time?"

"*Bon.* Hope is King, *ma chère.* We shall charge onward. All this…" Jean-Luc waved his arm around the gallery, "is yours as much as it is mine."

Her eyes followed his arm and trailed back to his pale grey eyes to find unshed tears there. What could she say now? Was he happy or sad? She needed a clue. A rap on the front window made her heart jump and her hope soar. This had to work.

"That's him. Come, let me introduce you." Liz unlocked the front door to let Michael in and made the introductions.

"I know your face," Jean-Luc said as he shook Michael's hand.

"I've been in before. I've modeled the small gallery in my personal studio after your shop. You set your displays so well."

"*Oui, merci.* But somewhere else? Ah, university. I do not forget faces."

"Yes, you gave a talk on perspective of light and depth."

"And you showed promise."

"But you said I had much work to do."

"*Oui*, and let us look to your progress. What have you there?"

Without a word, Michael removed a 12x20 inch painting from his portfolio and held it for Jean-Luc to see.

"May I?" Jean-Luc reached for the paining and carried it away.

Michael's wrinkled brow turned to Liz, and then turned back to Jean-Luc.

"Just wait," she whispered. "Watch him."

Jean-Luc carried the painting around exposing it to the light at different angles. He touched the brushstrokes. He took a painting down and hung Michael's underneath the spot light there. He walked back and stared. He moved left, then right. "*Bon*. Much progress. You learned well that lesson. I want to see more."

"The computer's over here. Hand me your thumb drive, Michael." Liz sat behind a Louie XV desk in the middle of the gallery and inserted the thumb drive in the booted up laptop.

"I know you can't really see the full detail in these pictures, but perhaps you can get enough of an idea of my work. May I?" Michael pulled a chair to the left side of the desk.

Liz got up and moved her chair to the right so that Jean-Luc sat between them. She held her breath while he paged through the files, looking at one painting after another without comment. Then he paged backward again. Finally, she let her breath escape. Jean-Luc was interested.

"Have you art in other galleries?" Jean-Luc leaned back in the ornate desk chair and steepled his fingers against his lips.

"No, only my own. I don't have any contracts or any commitments that would prohibit me signing with your gallery."

Jean-Luc removed his fingers from the mouse and reached for Liz's hand. "He understands business!"

Liz nodded and Jean-Luc kissed the back of her hand.

"Oui, you have progressed well, Michael. You could paint here in this shop just over there. The light is good in the second half of the day." Jean-Luc pointed to an empty space close to the front window. "Wednesday nights as well as Saturday afternoon, *oui*? It would create interest in your work, your methods."

"Yes, an Artist-in-Residence. What a good idea, Jean-Luc." He never ceased to amaze Liz, even after all her years working with him.

"That would work with my schedule, but I've never painted in front of an audience."

"The tricks I'll show you. You do this and I would be honored to debut your work. Liz, some champagne, *s'il vous plait.*"

Liz returned Jean-Luc's grin. "We still have one bottle. And the paperwork?"

"*Oui.*" Jean-Luc stood to shake Michael's hand. "First Champagne. Then paperwork. The way of France."

"It would truly be my honor to be part of your gallery." Michael shook his hand as Liz returned with the *Perrier-Jouet Fleur de Champagne Rose* and three tall flute glasses.

"Ah, only the finest and Liz's most favorite." Jean-Luc popped the cork and Liz poured. "To progress and success."

"And to a master of his trade, to the *fleur* of his shop, and to future success." Michael nodded to Jean-Luc, then to Liz, and then sipped his bubbly. "Outstanding finish. I taste cherry and ginger notes. No wonder this is your favorite, Liz. The wild roses on the bottle are nearly as beautiful as you." He blushed the color of the bubbly. "Just a bit of art appreciation."

"*Oui*, progress indeed!" Jean-Luc let out a full belly-laugh.

"How about that paperwork now?" Liz dug in the file drawer to hide her embarrassment and pleasure. After the contract was read and signed, Liz went to her office to make copies. When she returned, she noticed that Michael's cheeks remained flushed, and the two men were laughing, while Jean-Luc poured another short round.

"To a relationship destined to be." Jean-Luc raised his glass with his next toast.

Liz wondered about the momentary shock on Michael's face before he recovered and then joined in the toast. "This is now my new favorite champagne. To Liz for the dual introductions, bubbly and master. And to Jean-Luc for this opportunity."

"It's 11:00; we must open now. Do you two want to take this back to your office, Jean-Luc? I'll watch the floor."

"No, *ma chère*. We are now finished. Michael, take Liz to lunch to finalize the details. Liz, plan his opening as you suggested. I feel the need to walk the floor this day. I am content."

"Then shall we?" Michael extended his hand to Liz.

"Are you sure Jean-Luc? I've been out so much. You look a little pale this morning, are you okay?"

"*Oui*, I have a rendevous with Morgan. She's covering for you this afternoon so I shall not be alone long." He wiggled his eyebrows at Liz. He loved to tease her, using her friend as the source of his material. "Off with you." He waved his hands at her to shush her away.

"If you insist." Liz kissed both of his cheeks as only the French do so well, and turned to go.

"Thank you again, Jean-Luc, for this opportunity." Michael shook his hand once more.

"I shall be proud of your first sale. Now go." Jean-Luc handed Michael his thumb drive and sat down behind the desk.

"I'll get my purse." Liz said as she removed the bottle and the glasses and headed to the back. When she returned, both men wore frowns instead of smiles.

"All set?" Michael asked her. When she nodded, he nodded at Jean-Luc, shook hands, and turned to go.

Liz stopped in the parking lot under a shade tree. "What was that all about?"

"What was what about?"

"Come on, Michael. You two were way too sober when I entered the room, considering the happy event that happened previously. We all got what we wanted so why the faces?"

"You are too observant, Liz. Your boss was just protecting your interests. He wanted to make sure I treated you fairly."

"Wow, thanks for your honesty. We've known each other many years and he thinks of me as a daughter. He has no family left so he's protective. I'm sure he didn't mean it personally."

"I don't mind, Liz. You should be treated fairly and I respect him for caring about you. Don't worry about it. Should we take your car? I'm afraid there may be dog hair in my Jeep and you're wearing black."

"Why don't we drive separately. I'll probably head home afterward. Let's meet at the Cheesecake Factory at Kierland Commons. Their booths are tall and padded so we should be able to hear each other, plus it's still too early to be crowded. I brought my laptop and we can finalize the plans for your showing."

"That's fine."

"See you there." She suddenly wanted to hug him, jump in his Jeep, and go wherever he took her. It was a strange sensation, considering this was just business, but with Michael, it felt like so much more. Her nerves were on edge, more than she had anticipated. Perhaps that was it. Perhaps she wanted everything to go well and she transferred those positive thoughts onto the situation making it seem like more than business. His polite demeanor might be just that, polite demeanor and nothing more. But she sensed his *café au lait* eyes reaching for her, wanting something more as well. Just listen to me—he is like fine coffee. There's no getting around it. Liz wondered if she'd have the opportunity to satisfy her caffiene craving. She headed for her car without looking back.

Michael waited outside the restaurant and watched Liz park. She had a new tire in place of the one he had changed. That seemed so long ago. Her days in the hospital seemed like weeks. He didn't know why at the time, but he did now. He watched her walk toward him. She is beautiful. Not in the traditional, classic red-rose kind of way, but more like the pretty wild-pink rose that adorned the champagne bottle she liked so well. "Is it okay if I tell you that you look very pretty in crimson?"

"You may, and thank you. You would know it's not just red, wouldn't you? Hey, sorry about running out so quickly the other day. I, ugh..."

"Don't worry. We're good." Michael waved his hand in the air to shoo away the issue.

After they ordered—he a burger, she a salad—Liz itemized the ideas she had for the showing, leaving out the budgetary details. Michael admired her organizational skills and her imagination. He listened to the soft melody of her voice, and wondered if he sounded as familiar to her as she did to him. Damn, Adonia might be right. Conversation with Liz just seems so natural.

"I like the charity idea for two reasons. Besides helping others, it might draw a crowd who wants to see and be seen. Oh, and a third. It allows me to donate a painting, good for my soul and a minor tax deduction, but mostly because it should bring in a large sum for the selected charity. Also, your idea of an auction could draw more money than just a showing."

"That's exactly what I thought."

Sensible and agreeable. The attraction truly more than physical He had certainly started to change his opinion of Liz. However, he needed to remember to keep this under control. Friends and business partners, at least for the present.

"Now, about the advertising. I thought I could use one of those free online invitation sites to send invitations to our list, and of course, anyone you want to invite. I can handle the text, but if you have any thoughts on designs, let me know, or I could just use one of their templates."

"I'll look at their designs, but I can upload my own graphics. I'm sure I could setup something to draw attention quickly."

"Good, and I'll hit up a couple of charities for their brochures for the tables. We'll need a good picture of you for promo materials. If you don't have one..."

"Yes, I have a recent one." He interrupted. "I'll send it to you to see if you like it. If that doesn't work, Richard can take another one. He's into photography as well."

Their meals arrived, pretty as the pictures on the menu, and just as huge. They took a minute to eat and think. And occasionally stare at each other.

Liz started picking at her greens. "My parents can make the food if you don't mind. My mom suggested that you and the guys attend a little dinner gathering tomorrow night. If you are free, that is. They want to celebrate this lovely hat I'm wearing." Liz giggled. "You could sample some of their specialty party foods. Mom said she won't take no for an answer. Are you available?"

"I don't have any plans and your parents are great," Michael answered. "I'll check with Will and Richard. I'm sure Will would jump at the chance to see Katy."

"I think she's pretty interested in him as well. Funny how connections happen, isn't it?" As Liz smiled, her eyes glistened ever so slightly.

Adonia would love the irony in that comment! Michael's mind switched gears quickly. "Would you be interested in coming over to my gallery and working on the invitations? That is if you are up for it. We should probably give the guests the weekend to make plans."

"You do have a good head for business. If you know what you want for graphics, we could finish in no time. I know the boiler-plate language by heart. I'd just need to tweak it for the auction."

"Then it's a date—businesswise, that is. I'll take care of this bill and meet you there. Do you remember the way?"

"I can deduct the bill, Michael. I'll get it. And I do remember how to get there."

"I can deduct it too, now let me be a gentleman." He stood and dropped some bills next to his plate. "Walk away from the table, Boss."

"Oooh, Boss...I like the sound of that. So you'll

immediately do everything I tell you to do?"

Something inside him stirred when she wiggled her eyebrows. She's definitely flirting with me. He stuffed his wallet away to gain a moment to create a come-back. "Only if it's in my best interest. Or yours."

She grinned, not smiled, but grinned, turned on her pretty red pumps and headed for the door.

Man, I'd follow those shapely legs just about anywhere. So he followed her out the door.

Liz maneuvered her SUV through traffic on the 101 freeway like a race car driver, as usual, but in a more careful sort of way. She was anxious to see how well she and Michael might work together, yet her tension had eased somewhat. She no longer let her vulnerability control her emotions. She could be herself, handle business, and even enjoy Michael's company. After all, his mannerisms mimicked those in her dreams, as did his sense of humor, and even his gallantry. His intelligence impressed her as much as his skill with a paint brush. And the fact that he was H-O-T made the time they spent together all the more pleasurable.

Michael pulled up seconds after she did. "And I thought I drove fast." Michael held her car door as she opened it. "Hand me your briefcase-purse thing."

Liz obeyed. Her skirt slid up as she exited her vehicle. She quickly tugged it down as she stood.

Michael's heart leapt up into his throat and his loins tingled and tightened. This is going to be harder than I thought. How can I stay objective and professional when I react so strongly to her?

"Right this way." He had to turn away at that moment to

hide his obvious physical reaction. He thought about graphics to get himself somewhat under control by the time he unlocked the bungalow door and held it open for her. Crossing the gallery space to his work space, he grabbed his laptop and an extra thumb drive and then moved over to the kitchen area. "There's more room at the table than in my little office alcove." He pulled out her chair.

"Funny, I never noticed your office area the last time I was here."

"It's really not much more than shelving in an unused alcove, but it meets my needs. I have a more extensive office at home."

"Your kitchen is nice. You've even given thought to lush colors in here. Golden stained concrete floors, stainless appliances, green glass tile backsplash, even black granite countertops. I'm impressed."

"I know a kitchen guy. I got the counters from a demo and had them recut. I like to recycle and reuse when and where I can." Liz stared at him without comment, her head slightly bent to one side. He didn't know what she was thinking. "Shall we get started?"

They spent the next 25 minutes working through the graphics, text, and overall concept of the invitations before finalizing them.

"I'll send them to our usual mailing list when I get home. Who would you like to add?"

"I'll email the list to you after you leave if that's okay. You should have it by the time you get home."

"Yes, and I wanted to remind you about donating a painting. It would be really good publicity." Michael could have sworn she held her breath awaiting his response.

"Did you have something specific in mind?"

"Oh, probably almost anything. Everything you've shown me is in good taste. Maybe have two options, just in case Jean-Luc has any preferences. Would that be okay?"

"You are a conscientious one aren't you? That's fine.

What's next?" Michael could think of all kinds of things that could be next. He couldn't help himself, being a man and all. He was seriously drawn to her. Lately, she intruded on his thoughts when he least expected. He found that he would frequently turn to talk to her, but she wasn't there. He had even thought of her in the shower, which was an image best saved for later.

"Hellooooo, Michael." Liz waved her hand in front of his face. "Are you there?"

"Sorry, lost in thought."

"Well, I'll take care of all the remaining details, the food and beverages, setting, advertising, and so on. I just need some background info on you for an advertising piece. Your 'bio' needs to reach the publishers on Monday for Wednesday's paper and the printers for the other publications. Can you send that info to me as well as your list?"

"Yeah, that would be great." She's great.

"I should go."

He noticed the circles under her eyes and thought her color might be a little pale. "Are you okay?"

"Yeah. Just a little tired."

"Let me walk you to your car." He followed her to the door where her stiletto heel caught on a small crack in the polished concrete floor and she tripped. Michael caught her in his arms this time with her back pressed against the door, and Michael pinning her there accidently. A convenient accident. No words were necessary. Michael knew that the gift of the gods played him like a puppet. He had no choice in the matter. His arms had encircled her already, so dipped his head to meet her parted lips. She didn't fight him. In fact, she cooperated as well. Very well. Her hands went from his arms to the back of his neck, pulling him deeper into the kiss. He took that as permission and explored her mouth with his tongue. She returned the favor as he pressed her tighter to the door.

A car horn honked and a car door closed which pulled him out of the moment. "That's Will. He always honks." Michael stepped back and helped Liz right herself, knowing that this moment was over, but not knowing what it meant. Other than he hated that it ended so soon.

Liz stepped away and straightened her snug clothing that had ridden up when she was sandwiched between the door and the man, but he would have preferred an alternate movement of that clothing. Just as she moved away from the door, Will knocked and entered without awaiting a response as was his habit at Michael's gallery.

"Hello, Lad. I saw your car and…oh, I'm interrupting something." Will stood with his hand still on the outside door knob, looking first at Michael, then Liz, then Michael again.

"No, not at all." Liz adjusted the tote on her arm. "I was just leaving. It's good to see you Will. I was just telling Michael about a dinner at my parents' house tomorrow night. We were hoping you guys would join us. Michael can give you all the details. Oh, and thanks again for all you did to help me." She gave him a friendly hug and then started for her car. "Thanks, Michael, I'll be in touch."

"Yes, Lad, give me all the details." Will grinned, slapped Michael on the shoulder, and closed the door blocking Michael's view of those retreating legs.

"*Hen ddyn*, keep your nose where it belongs. We were creating an invitation to my showing." He liked calling Will an old man. Michael had learned some Gaelic language from Will and his family, and practiced it whenever possible. The sound was as beautiful as art, much like his paintings.

"Aye, an invitation…I'm sure. I know a mussed lovely when I see one." He gave Michael a little shove. "What's this about a showing?"

Michael filled him in on the details of the last day or so

over beers that he pulled from the mini-fridge. They sat in teak lounge chairs on the back porch staring at the mature orange and grapefruit trees in the little back yard.

"I missed a lot, pulling a double-shift yesterday. You have too much drama. Be careful with this one, she's a nice lovely."

"That, she is. Shit, it's so complicated. I don't want to blow my big chance, I don't want to hurt her, and the two are inseparable."

"You'll do the right thing. You always have. So what's this about dinner?"

"The three of us are invited to Liz's parents' house for a celebration and to sample food for the showing. And Jim if he can make it. I take it that Katy might be interested in you, you big oaf." Michael clanked bottles with Will.

"Ah, now there's a fine lass. We've talked on the phone some."

"Then I take it you're willing to go?"

"Hell, yeah. What time? I'm off tomorrow night, although I might be late."

Liz should have started the car, but needed a moment. Licking her lips, she enjoyed the afterglow of that surprise kiss. Her lips weren't the only thing tingling. She closed her eyes leaning her head against the headrest.

After her moment passed and she could breathe normally again, she headed home. She did not want to analyze this, or fret about it, but simply enjoy it.

Liz considered taking a nap when she got home, but there'd be no sleeping today. She needed to get busy. Suddenly she had lots of energy. She had Michael's thumb drive so she'd send out the invitations on her list and send his as soon as she got those names. She'd meet with her mother to discuss the menu, now that the party was set. She should make a preliminary stop at the printer before going home, even though she was tired.

Juan, the printer, was thrilled with the extra work in the slow economy and was equally happy to provide some additions in exchange for some advertising. Another happy stop for today.

An emerald green silk blouse caught her eye at the boutique next door to the printer. She had to go in. And then she had to buy it. It would be perfect to brighten up her new grey suit. Another happy stop!

Ken's ever-present crossword puzzle occupied his hands when Liz walked through her door. "What are you doing here, Dad? Is everything okay?"

"Hi Sweetie, yes, everything is fine. Your mother thought you might like some dinner so we came over. She's in the kitchen tinkering. How are you feeling? You look tired but happy."

"I'm both. It's been a day full of nice surprises. I found a new blouse without even looking." Liz held up her shopping bag.

"I could use a new blouse, too." Nancy overheard the conversation as she walked into the living room. "I hope you don't mind us stopping by. If you have plans, we can just leave the food and go."

"No, please, it's perfect timing. I wanted to go over a few things with you."

"Well, you have perfect timing as well. Dinner is ready." Nancy hummed her way back to the kitchen and spoke over her shoulder. "If you'll set the table, I'll get the food."

Liz itemized the success of all the arrangements thus far before asking about the appetizers. "I wondered what you were thinking about serving. I have some red wine we can use, not that it really makes a difference, and believe me, I'm grateful for anything."

"We thought of several options. You know my garlic chile-glazed shrimp and Dad's chicken stickers with ancho mole sauce. If we continued with a Mexican theme, we'd also do our chile cornbread circles with the lime cream cheese topping and for dessert, our margarita flan and spicy chocolate mousse."

"Yum."

"Or," Ken continued, "We could go a little more elegant with Marsala Chicken Skewers and Tenderloin Pockets, Bruchetta Polenta Patties, Balsamic Roasted Veggies, Tiramisu in Glass, and Cappuccino Brownies. We have new recipes."

"Oh, I'm here eating this delicious dinner and my mouth is watering not only from this Pesto Alfredo, but the list of appetizers as well. I'm one lucky daughter. Anything would be fine, really. I'll have a rough head count for you tomorrow and then closer when I get the RSVPs. I'm thinking maybe 50 people tops. Is that okay? And you could advertise of course."

"Of course," Nancy gently squeezed her daughter's hand while her dad chuckled.

"What's for dinner tomorrow?" Liz was ever hopeful about new and delightful creations from her folks. "The guys will probably come."

Ken reached across the table, and stole a bite of Liz's Lemon Meringue Pie as Nancy lightly slapped his hand. "We need to practice creating those new elegant appetizers so you'll all be our taste testers. We thought a buffet might be a little more comfortable for the first time the guys are over."

"Again, a perfect event." Liz stood in response to her mom starting to clear the table. "Just leave the dishes, Mom. I'll get them later. It will help me think things through with a mindless task to do. You'll leave the leftovers, won't you?"

♥♥♥

"Michael, this is Liz. Is it okay to call this late? My parents were here and I didn't hear my phone ring when you called earlier." She held her breath wondering what he wanted to discuss.

"Sure. I wanted to see if you were okay after you left. I would prefer to stop by to talk to you in person, but, look, I'm sorry I kissed you…"

"You're SORRY you kissed me?" Liz couldn't believe he said that. Why would he say such a thing? Was she that bad of a kisser?

"Yes, it was just that you were so close, and you smelled so good. It was not intentional, I just reacted. I hope you aren't offended and I want you to know I have no intention of taking advantage of you or our situation. I know we are just business associates, and I hope friends."

Liz took a deep breath. "We are associates, and one can never have too many friends. And, no, I wasn't offended."

"Great. Thanks for understanding. I'll see you tomorrow, okay?"

"Yep. Goodnight." Liz stared at her phone. That had to be one of the strangest conversations she'd ever had. She hadn't been offended in the least about the kiss, but for a moment, she had been offended by his remorse. Now that she replayed the exchange, perhaps his concern wasn't for himself, but rather for her and how she felt about it. That was thoughtful. Odd, but thoughtful. And probably more fodder for dreamland.

CHAPTER 17

"Did you clean my chair already?" Liz had agreed to
meet Jean-Luc in his small courtyard outside of the gallery
early Saturday morning for a *café* and a croissant.

"No, *ma chère*. The birds have no need for disrespect in
my presence." He grinned like the proverbial Cheshire Cat.

"I know, I know. They love you just as you love them
and I would do well to learn that lesson, as you've instructed
over the years. Ain't gonna happen." Liz shook her head and
chuckled as she sat down on a poop-free chair.

"*Merci* for the croissant. My feathered friends have been
waiting for their share." Jean-Luc had the little table set and
had included his French Press. "Your timing is impeccable,
ma chère. My four-minute steep is complete. He pressed his
coffee, opened the bag Liz brought, placed the pastries on
small white plates, folded the bag, and placed it on the table.
He threw some crumbs to the birds, and then poured a *petit
café* for Liz and himself. "Tell me of your afternoon
yesterday."

She did and guessed his agreement from his sideways
grin. "What shall I do?"

"Nothing. You can be your usual, charming self. I have it
all in hand. Do you have concerns? Is that why you wanted
me to come in early today?"

"I shall speak about running the gallery. I have shared
adequately my knowledge with you, *non*?"

"Yes, you have Jean-Luc. Why do you ask?" Liz set her
croissant back on her plate. She couldn't eat, sensing he had a
concern.

"*Ma chère.* I am tired and I am old. I want to see, to feel *ma douce France* again. If your Michael is successful, we also will be, and I can go home for a time. I hope you will run this when I'm gone?" His arm waved to the gallery as it always did when he talked about his treasure.

"Of course I will, and you are not that old, but I understand the tired part. It's been rough lately. Have you seen a doctor? Maybe you need some vitamins before you go. When do you plan to go and how long will you be gone? Do you have your passport?" Jean-Luc did look tired, and had quite often lately. She wondered why he hadn't taken a trip long before this. He'd mentioned it several times.

"Time is elusive. Soon. And vitamins are a good idea. Can you drive me to the bank now? I want you to sign on two other accounts. One is for emergencies."

"What kind of emergencies?"

"If you need other cash while I'm gone. If a big bill arrives. Something unexpected."

"Okay, I would need to know specifically when you want me to use it or not."

"You would know. You are good with the gallery, Liz. I know it is good with you. Also, I would ask another favor. Would you handle my personal bills too? You will need that account as well."

"Of course. Whatever you need."

"*Merci, ma chère.* Shall we go after you eat your croissant?"

"Let's go now. I'll eat later." Liz re-bagged her bread while Jean-Luc divided the remainder of his for the birds.

The gallery sat quiet for the first hour after opening for the day. Liz had presented her news article to Jean-Luc for his review before submitting it for Wednesday's publication. He tweaked only a few words, always pleased with her writing ability.

Jean-Luc watched Liz roam the gallery checking for dust and the various things she did to keep it perfect. She couldn't bring more pleasure even if she had begun from his loins. He remembered wanting children, many of them. That dream died inside him when his wife had died of cancer, early and barren. Elise was his soul-mate. He could never think of another, never remarry. He had friends, drinking buddies, and his chess club. Otherwise, he was alone; his older sister and brother—now gone. Liz had proven to be the daughter he never had. She had become the highlight of his life.

Later, Liz watched Jean-Luc make a sale to one of his regular collectors. He had a style about him, like no other. He could easily determine what brought pleasure to the eyes and to the heart. She had her own style, yes, but as his protégé, she mimicked his style in many respects. He had mentored her with a skill that transcended mere tutoring. Jean-Luc inspired the best from her. Liz brought another set of skills which had helped keep the gallery alive. She brought in music to add ambiance. She enticed sculptors and furniture artists which added sales to the bottom line. Technology lived for Liz as it had not with Jean-Luc, and it had made his life easier with her help. They made a great team. She would miss him during his stay in France and worried that the gallery would suffer without his touch. She could keep it going and make a sale here and there, but the heart of the gallery would always be him.

"Emilio, hola. What have you brought today?" Liz answered the receiving bell that chimed from the back of the store and reached out and gave a one-armed hug to her friend as he hauled boxes on a dolly through the back door. She

172

hadn't seen any new work from Emilio, her favorite metal sculptor, for over two months.

"*Hola, Bonita*! You grow prettier every time I see you."

"Oh, stop. How's *la familia?*"

"Carmen is due any day now. She is happy one minute and yelling at me the next. She ordered me to get these boxes out of the house before the baby comes, so here I am." Emilio unloaded the boxes and started to open the top one. "I call this one *Crone*. She's black, but made of 100% recycled steel."

"Look at the talons on that thing. You know I hate birds, but this is so unusual I almost like it. You've done so well to make the feathers droopy, and tired looking." Poor old bird, she looks like Jean-Luc must feel right now. "I know right where I'll display her. What else do you have?"

Emilio pulled out two matching bells on stands, one over a foot tall and one twice its size. The arms curled up and out from the base to hold the cylindrical bell in a curled handle. The arms also held a removable striker on the opposing side, all done in milk chocolate-colored reclaimed metal. These shone in the light, where in contrast, the bird absorbed the light with its matte finish.

"I don't know who would buy the damn bird, but I'd love to have this small bell for my patio garden. These will go fast. What's in the small box?"

Emilio pulled out a sculpture with three wild-roses winding around a blown-glass vase. "This is your early birthday present. Like the champagne you gave us for Christmas. My friend in the auto-paint business painted the metal flowers rose pink. My brother owns a glass business and made the vase. I hope you like it."

Tears danced in her eyes as she examined her gift. "I've never received anything so creative and so beautiful. I love it. *Muchas gracias, mi amigo!*" Liz hugged her friend and he wiped a single tear from her face.

"Shall we show Jean-Luc the new treasures?" Emilio

picked up the small bell and the bird, ready to enter the gallery from the receiving area.

"Absolutely. I'm sure he'll be happy to see you." She led the way, finding Jean-Luc staring out the front window. "Look who's here."

"Ah, *bonjour* Emilio. Your hands are full. Here, hand me that crow." They shook hands because French-cheek kisses made Emilio uncomfortable. "This bird, she looks waterlogged and tired. Her head is drooping. What is her story?"

"The real story is that my mother-in-law visited us in January and I saw a black bird outside hiding from that big rain we had. I melded the two and came out with the *Crone*. But I'll create a better sales story for you if you need one."

The two of them laughing warmed Liz all the way through to her heart. Emilio always had that effect on Jean-Luc. Liz counted it a lucky day a few years back when her neighbor Carmen introduced her then-boyfriend.

"Come. Let me write you a check for your last sale. Your *Holey Chalice* sold yesterday. My collector said that's how he feels when his wine glass runs empty." The two departed for the office in stitches and Liz happily manned the floor.

A few tourists filed in and out during the remainder of the afternoon with no sales and Liz had time to think about life. So many aspects flooded her mind, all competing for her undivided attention. Family and friends would push those thoughts aside tonight and she couldn't wait to try her parents' newest recipes.

"*Ma chère*, go to help your mother. Get ready to enjoy your party."

Her head flew up to face him. "I didn't hear you coming, Jean-Luc. You are coming tonight, aren't you?"

"*Oui*, I may nap first then arrive. It's been so quiet today I've grown sleepy."

"Then why don't you leave now and I'll close up. There's only a half-hour left. And don't give me that, 'Oh, *ma chère*,' business. My mom has my dad to help and there's two hours before the party starts. You go. I insist." Jean-Luc looked pale again. He either needed the rest or some sun.

"*Oui, mademoiselle.* If you insist." He blew her a kiss and trudged away toward the back door.

His leaving filled her with an uneasy feeling deep in her chest. She'd press him to see his doctor before his trip. That way, she wouldn't worry. With one concern solved, she finished some paperwork, and then closed up to go home.

"You look beautiful as always, Liz, and we could use a little help in the kitchen if you're up for it." Moms always boosted the ego. Liz had changed into a haltered maxi dress in a turquoise and green print, anxious for spring to arrive. She left her hair in the same chignon she wore to work, but refreshed it with a flowered comb to catch the strays and help hide her wound. She added a knit shrug to finish her look and to keep her arms warm.

"You shouldn't wear your fine linen when you cook, Mom."

Nancy paced the kitchen and continued to prep. "I didn't, honey. I changed just before you arrived. The dessert is done of course, the veggies and tenderloin are in the oven, and Dad is out grilling the skewers. You should go say hello. Then what I need help with is assembling the polenta patties. If you wouldn't mind doing that, I can go check on finishing touches. The girls called and they'll be here any minute. Oh, and the boys will be late, they are waiting on Will; Michael said Will's work ran over as usual."

"Relax, Mom. Everything looks lovely, as always."

"I'll assume doorman duty and leave you ladies to finish plating and saucing the skewers," Ken said.

175

Liz listened from the kitchen as her friends arrived.

"Morgan, Katy, my other favorite women, come in." Ken spread his arms in welcome.

"We know you love us, Ken. We love you, too," Morgan replied.

Katy followed Morgan's example but tickled Ken into laughing as they parted their hug.

"The women are fretting in the kitchen, you know the way. Here come our dear friends, Bonnie and Jerry right behind you. I'll catch you later."

Morgan chose bartending duty and simply waved when the guys arrived. Liz and Katy extended greetings and introduced them around.

"Come on, Will. Let's get some snacks." Katy motioned to him, then toward the food table.

"I'm starving. I haven't had time to eat all afternoon." Will followed Katy without a word to the others.

"I guess I'm thirsty." Richard motioned his thumb toward the bar and winked at Michael before walking away, dragging Jim along for moral support.

"Can I taste the spread as well?" Michael's smile radiated as if Liz and no one else existed in the room.

"If you can crowd Katy and Will out of the way, you can. Katy has a monster appetite when it comes to my parents' food, so there may not be anything left."

With food finally in hand, they headed to a tall linen-draped table to eat.

Liz pointed at Michael with a chicken skewer. "Thanks for sending your list of names. The invitations are all out and I've received a couple RSVP emails already. People are curious when there's something new. Michael, *you* are something new."

Or something old that feels new again. Michael could

sense her losing some of her reticence. Maybe Adonia is right. Could something work out for them long term? Should he, how could he, even be thinking about romance at this point? Did he have a choice or are the gods truly playing him like a puppet?

"You could be the next breakout artist." Her voice pulled him from his meandering.

"I appreciate your confidence. It would be good for both of us if it works out. Your gallery would do well and I could continue to do what I enjoy most."

"I'll second that!" Ken walked up beside them and put his arm around Liz. "She always did have a good eye for talent. If anyone can sell you, my Liz can." He kissed her temple. "So what will you do with your new found wealth, Michael?"

"Probably buy more of these amazing appetizers."

"Hah, and I doubted this boy at our first meeting." Ken reached to shake Michael's hand. "Good to see you, son."

"Don't make his head swell so, Michael. I won't be able to live with him." Liz poked her dad in the ribs.

"Seriously, Ken. These are delicious. I can see why you and your wife are so successful. Do you cater often?"

"We do some, but the restaurant is the big draw. This is a fun sideline for us. We do it for special people or for those willing to pay a little more for a great spread, but not often."

"I can't decide if I like the chicken and mushroom sticks or the beef better. They're both quite tasty! I can't wait until Wednesday to have more. Thanks again for doing this."

"Anything for my little girl and I wish you good luck. I'd better go help in the kitchen before the boss-woman comes after me."

"He's really quite a good guy, isn't he?"

"Well, he is my dad, but yes, he has a good heart."

"Speaking of dad-types, I don't see Jean-Luc."

"And I haven't heard from him either. He was very tired this afternoon. Maybe I should call him. Oh, there's the

177

doorbell. Let's go see if its him."

"Jean-Luc, I was wondering if you were coming. *Bonsior*, Henri, welcome." Jean-Luc's friend and sometimes chauffeur followed close behind sniffing the air.

"Yes, good evening, Liz. What smells so delightful?" Henri darted his eyes in Jean-Luc's direction and tilted his head as if to call attention to Jean-Luc. "Sorry to be late. Old men such as us, we aren't so fast these days."

"Speak about yourself, Henri." Jean-Luc pointed in Michael's direction. "You haven't met Michael yet."

"*Le plaisir moi le mien.*" Henri extended his hand to be joined by Michael's.

"*Bonsior*, Henri. The pleasure is mine as well. We were just headed over for some more snacks." Michael motioned to the food table. "Please join us."

"I'll get you some wine," Liz offered. "Michael, please find them a seat as well." Relieved that Jean-Luc had arrived, Liz headed to check on Morgan.

"Two Chablis, please, Morgan. And what are you up to?" Liz asked Richard.

"I was just trying to convince Morgan to stop by the store. I have a new shipment of Morganite stones I'd like her to see."

"And I informed him that I don't need another stone." Morgan handed Liz the two glasses of wine.

"Come try the appetizers." Liz bumped Richard's arm with her elbow, and motioned away from Morgan.

"I'll stay right here and enjoy the scenery." Jim saluted Morgan with his drink.

Richard joined Liz with barely a nod to Morgan. "Is she always this stubborn?"

"That ring means a lot to her. She's sensitive about it and would never replace it."

"Women, you are so confusing. I wasn't implying that she should. I simply wondered if she would be interested in more of them."

"Try the Tenderloin Pockets. You'll feel better." Liz patted Richard's back.

With not an ounce of food left over, the evening ended with friends and family well-satiated from not only the food, but from the wine and the company as well. Jim and Richard dragged Will and Michael out the door, extending their appreciation for the event. As Michael looked back, Liz pulled the comb from her hair and shook it out as she closed the door. He wanted to run back to her and comb his fingers through her hair, but forced himself into Richard's Mercedes instead.

"Get a grip, son, she's your employer not your lover. And by the looks of things, that won't be easy," Richard said.

"Yeah, I need to keep a manageable distance and be professional. It won't be easy." Michael shook his head.

Liz and Morgan reclined on the modern low-slung sectional with a glass of wine while Katy told Ken and Nancy all she learned about Will that evening.

"Morgan, what's up with you and Richard? Why does he irritate you so?" Liz asked.

"I have no clue." Morgan raised and lowered her shoulders.

"I do. You like him and you don't want to. You are like little school kids. He pulls your hair and you punch him. Admit it."

Morgan rolled her eyes. "I'll admit no such thing. I'd rather date Jim. Drop this nonsense and let's go clean up."

Morgan walked off and Liz knew she was dead-on with her assessment.

The next morning at his small gallery, Michael selected the paintings he needed and began loading them in his Jeep. As he brought out the last painting, the Jeep seemed to drive off by itself. It took him a split second to realize that someone had just stolen his vehicle.

CHAPTER 18

On Sunday morning, Liz sat in her car in the parking lot behind the gallery and enjoyed the wait for Michael to arrive. They planned to hang Michael's work before the gallery opened. Her thumbs tapped the steering wheel in tune to the sweet songs made by Jean-Luc's birds floating through her partially opened window. Maybe she could actually grow to like them if they quit pooping on her car.

Time passed and Michael had not arrived. Had he changed his mind? Had something happened to him? After 15 minutes, she wondered if she had the time wrong.

Michael pulled in next to her just as her insecurities got the better of her. She left her anxiety in the car when he popped out of his Jeep.

"Liz, I'm so sorry I'm late."

"No worries. Let's go in. I want to show you the spots I've planned for each painting. I brought croissants and we can make coffee inside."

"Shall I unload now?"

"No, I need coffee first. Late clean-up tasks last night. You can pull the Jeep up to the back door and unload later."

Over coffee, Michael explained how he had left his keys next to the paintings when loading them and some kid went joy-riding with his vehicle and all but one of the paintings he intended to bring. He had jumped in his other car, caught up to the kid and forced him over to the curb. The kid took off.

"Are the paintings okay? Did you call the police?"

"Yes and yes. The kid had closed the hatch, maybe to avoid being noticed. Thank goodness for small favors."

"Thank goodness for both our sakes." Liz cheered him with her coffee cup.

With a cup still in hand, Liz led Michael around the front of the gallery. She pointed to the prime spots she had chosen for his work. He admired the way she took charge and the vision she had for what would work best where. Her job truly suited her.

An hour later, most of the art had found a temporary home thanks to Liz. A few pieces would be held as backstock to replace any that sold to avoid possible holes in his presentation.

Liz adjusted the lighting on top of the tallest painting. Suddenly, her Earl-Grey scent slammed into Michael just as hard as she did when she toppled off of the stepladder. He caught her and held her moments longer than he should have. And she let him. He drank in her scent while she regained her footing and righted herself. He'd definitely need to find out who Earl Grey is and thank him.

Liz kissed him. Softly at first, then with more intensity as he responded in kind. Much too soon, she pulled away, although, based on his pending reaction, it was a good thing that she did.

"Thank you, My Earl, for rescuing me once again."

"What did you do, Lady Grey, before I came along to catch you?" He looked in her eyes for some meaning to her actions.

"Well, I didn't have anyone to kiss 'thank you' and as you know, that wasn't my first hospital stay. I've seen several of the urgent care facilities in the area and have quite a supply of ice packs and heat rub at home and at work."

"Will you walk with me outside to get the mail and the paper?" Liz grabbed her keys to the communal mail box cluster and headed out the front door, locking it behind

Michael.

Butterflies ricocheted off the walls of his stomach. Not a masculine picture, but an accurate one. He wondered how Adonia could weave the butterflies into a story that would help transform their destinies. That's a dramatic thought, but Adonia had his head spinning these days.

Liz grinned as she walked beside him as if everything fit in its place in their world. That is until she stepped crooked on one the pavers leading to the mail box and twisted her ankle. Without falling, she did a little one-footed, hop-dance before testing her ankle for damage.

"See, it's nothing." Liz walked in circles.

"How do you get through the day without killing yourself?"

"Some days are easier than others, I will admit." Liz pulled the mail from the box and handed the newspaper to Michael. "Here, carry the paper while I look at the mail."

"I don't think you should walk and look at the mail at the same time." He took the mail from her hand, combined it with the newspaper, and extended the crook of his other arm. "Here, Milady, let's see if we can get you back in one piece."

"A kind gesture once again, Sir Michael." She took his arm and walked back to the gallery under the Chilean Mesquite trees that lined the walkway.

"Sit." Once inside, he placed her behind the antique desk. "Do you have an ice pack in the freezer?"

"Of course."

He returned momentarily with the ice pack, a towel, a folding chair, and a cup of coffee for Liz. After opening the chair in front of her, he laid the ice pack wrapped in the towel on the chair. "Put your ankle here and sit still long enough for me to read the paper without worrying about trying to catch you falling out of the chair."

"A hero with a sense of humor." Liz rolled her eyes at him, but rested her ankle on the compress and picked up her coffee.

"Nice ad. Thanks!"

"Here is the interview for publication on Wednesday." Liz handed Michael a sheet of paper.

He read it and said, "I'm not sure who you wrote about, but he sounds very talented."

"Well, the next few days will identify if that's you or someone that I invented."

"Now who's the funny one. There's Jean-Luc. *Bonjour.*" Michael stood to greet his new friend.

"*Bonjour*, Michael, Liz." He kissed her on the top of her head, looked at her ankle, then her face.

"No comment." Liz waved him off.

He patted Michael's shoulder and headed to the kitchenette. "*Merci*, Michael. I see you have her well in hand."

Michael busted out laughing. "He's used to this scene, I take it."

Liz set her jaw and glared at Michael.

Jean-Luc re-appeared with his own *café*. "Follow me, Michael. Let's see what your painting tells us." Jean-Luc walked a slow circuit from the front door in, following the maze of a path that Liz created with Michael's work. Michael followed in silence.

"Ah, *ma chère*, they do tell a story, just as you said. Michael, what is the story? Not the individual stories, but the whole story."

Michael looked back and forth between the two who both smiled knowing smiles at him. "I know what each one says to me, but I don't get the whole story."

"Go ahead, Jean-Luc." Liz raised and spread her hands as if to display the invisible story.

"The story has two folds, Michael. The first is energy, unlike any other on these walls. To walk this path is to feel energy building inside oneself. The potency to sense what the eyes see. A culmination of the parts into a whole that makes one want to act. To acquire. To own. A feeling beyond the moment." Jean-Luc let that sink in before continuing.

"The second is transcendence. One builds upon another to go beyond the single experience of only one. Again, one builds upon the next to take desire past thinking about one, but about the collection as a whole. A collection is always more valuable and desirable than a single piece of art."

Momentarily mute, Michael's eyes searched the depths of Jean-Luc's eyes, and then the furrows between them wondering what it took to acquire such a skill. "So are you saying, that based on the order, placement, and progression of presentation, you can change the perception of a buyer prompting them to act when they might not ordinarily do so?"

"*Précisément.*" Jean-Luc slapped Michael on his shoulder.

"Do all of you gallery folks know how to do that?" Michael stepped back to look at the other collections further back in the gallery.

"That's the *art* part of a successful gallery, Michael." Liz made 'air quotes' with two fingers on each hand. "Jean-Luc is the very best at vision."

"Ah, *ma chère*, it is a lesson you learned well, obviously." He turned toward Liz, with his hands clasped in front of him, happiness painted on his face. "Michael, she is one in a zillion."

"Yes, she is, and my art is obviously in good hands."

"Okay, enough." Liz stood, collecting her paraphernalia. "I need to go change before we open."

"Handle the paperwork," Jean-Luc commanded, pointing to Liz as she ignored him and walked away. "I have the floor."

"Michael, here is where you should be today. You must listen to what is said. And I'll want to introduce you."

"I'll need to run home and change. I'll return with lunch. What do you want me to wear?"

Jean-Luc motioned at his own attire. "Have you better attire, perhaps a suit?"

Michael bit his tongue. "Not as nice as yours, Jean-Luc,

but yes, I own a suit."

"Then go. I must call someone then open the shop."

Michael returned dressed in a sharp navy suit, cut precisely to fit his frame. A pale yellow tie with multi-blue colored squiggly squares balanced nicely against his pale blue, crisply pressed shirt.

Eyebrows rose high on Jean-Luc's face and his sideways grin spread across his face. "Ah, Michael, store the food and return to meet my friend."

"I'll be right back." Michael's mouth duplicated Jean-Luc's lopsided smile. Did he expect a suit from a discount store?

Passing Liz's office, he stopped in the doorway to say "Hi." Liz's jaw dropped. That was the very reaction he hoped for. "See you later. Jean-Luc needs me."

Liz jumped up from her desk and quickly hobbled to the door to watch Michael walk away. He didn't look back, but wiggled his fingers in the air in goodbye, pleased that she couldn't resist the view. He hoped she liked what she saw.

"Philip Durand, this is Michael Donovan, our recent find."

"Pleased to meet you, Mr. Durand."

"And, I, you," Philip said. "We were just admiring your work. Your triptych provides an awe of grandeur that opens my mind. What was your inspiration for this piece?" They stood in front of his *Color Play*.

In a shaky voice, Michael began, "That one is about thoughts. I like to think that each color is a thought, that is compatible with other thoughts, and that one thought gives meaning to other thoughts. What do you think?"

Philip frowned in concentration. "I think it prepares my mind and mood for the way it plays into this one." He turned to his right to view *Heart Storm* on the adjacent wall. "One could hang them just so to maintain the compelling effect."

Jean-Luc grinned at Michael as if to say, "I told you so."

"The *Heart Storm* beckons me to sense one entity protecting the other entity in *The Guardian*. Those light colors calm me so I can imagine what might be a figure with wings admiring a reclining figure. Much like a musical piece floating me through the notes." Philip moved his hand as if orchestrating a tune. "I want the *Color Play* and *Heart Storm*. They speak to me the most. Jean-Luc, our usual arrangements, if you please."

"Ah, *oui*. I'll see that they are delivered promptly."

"Well done." Philip shook Michael's hand. "I must adjust my current collection to take full advantage of your pieces. You are off to an excellent start. Show me more when you are ready. For now, I have another engagement."

"Michael, will you inform Liz while I escort Philip?" Jean-Luc's eyes sparkled and matched his man-on-the-moon grin.

"Of course. It was a pleasure to meet you, Mr. Durand, and thank you for your commentary. I hope you enjoy the pieces for years to come." Michael practically floated back to Liz's office.

Michael stood in the doorway watching Liz work, barely containing his shock from the unexpected sale. He owed this woman a great deal for this opportunity and didn't know how he could repay her. If he could make more sales to help keep the gallery open, perhaps that would be the thanks she deserves, but he needed to find a way to thank her personally.

Liz looked up from her laptop screen and her smile warmed his heart. Admit it, Dude, you wish she was yours.

What his conscious really wished is for that part of his brain and body to shut up and let him conduct business without the constant interruptions.

"Guess what! Philip Durand just bought *Color Play* and *Heart Storm*."

"Congratulations!" Liz stood up and hurried to Michael as he entered her office. She threw her arms around his neck and planted a big kiss, right on his lips. "Oh, sorry – just between friends. I'm just so excited. I want to hear all about it." Liz walked back to her glass desk red faced, but she no longer limped.

Apparently, the ice worked. Michael had to sit down to hide the part he couldn't ignore. Maybe he needed some ice in his lap.

The art behind her head caught his attention. "That's not the original *Eos* painting, is it? Wings and all? The curtain behind the greyhound is not the right shade of red."

"Good eye. It's a reproduction. We could never afford the original. Now, what about the sale?"

He shared the conversation with Liz, and relayed Jean-Luc's instructions.

Liz explained the usual arrangements to Michael and walked him though the paperwork that needed to be completed and signed.

Jean-Luc received a huge bear-hug from Liz as well when he entered her office. Finally relaxed a bit, Michael stood and shook his hand. "I can't tell you how grateful I am that you called Mr. Durand to see my work. Honestly, I'm shocked that he purchased two of 'em."

"Sit." Jean-Luc took the other guest chair. "I knew he would admire your style. It suits the other work he has in his collection. Thank you for the works to hang. I'll need some replacements. You said you have more. Are they as good?" Jean-Luc raised his eyebrows, waiting for an answer.

"I hope so. We have a couple of extras here, but I can bring more. Do you want them today or when?"

"We are closing soon. Bring two replacements and perhaps some backup is best. Can you come early tomorrow with them?"

"Sure, what time?

"Ten."

"I'll be here."

"I'll come, too." Liz stood up. "I'd like to see what he brings. Or I can meet Michael and help him pick out what to bring."

"No." Jean-Luc waved his hand at Liz. "You rest tomorrow. I insist. Let's see if Michael can assess what we need. I also want to hear his life plans. If this is a hobby or a career. You two go now. Go celebrate. I'll close up."

"I need to finish some paperwork," Liz said.

"And I need to go home and feed the dogs." Michael wanted to celebrate, but he couldn't take Liz out. It would be too much like a date.

"You were going to let me have Duke this weekend. Will you drop him off tonight or should I come get him? I guess I'll be at home tomorrow and would like to get to know him."

"Sure, I'll bring his things and you can meet Pricilla, too. How's 8:00?"

Liz paced her small living room matting down the leaf pattern of her new area rug. She had already pushed back the furniture to make more room for Duke to move around. She even made space next to the couch for his bed. She did the same in her bedroom so that he could be with her at all times. A new water bowl rested in a metal planter to raise it off the kitchen floor, closer to his height. Liz had stopped on her way home to purchase all Duke's favorite foods, according to Michael, and some treats. She couldn't think of anything else to prepare for Duke's arrival.

A short squeal escaped from Liz and she jumped when the doorbell rang. Duke and Priscilla charged in the minute she opened the door. Their leashes dragged beside them. Michael held a large dog bed and wore an amused grin. Duke sidled up and leaned into Liz, his face upturned to gaze at her. Priscilla looked at Liz, then back at Michael, then back at Liz.

"Well hello, pretty boy. And how are you today, Priscilla? Please come in, Michael."

"Thanks, nice place. Where do you want Duke's bed?"

"Over by the couch." Duke wiggled into Liz a little harder when she stopped petting him to point to the bed's spot. She held out her hand to pet Priscilla who didn't seem to mind one bit. "Please sit, can I get you something to drink?"

"Just water, thanks." Michael detached the leashes from both dogs and sat on the cushy sofa. Priscilla took over Duke's bed while Duke followed Liz into the kitchen.

"Make yourself at home. Here's your water dish." Duke took a quick drink while Liz pulled a bottle of water from the refrigerator, then he followed her back into the living room and stood between her and Michael as Liz sat in the leather club chair across from him. Duke whined and looked from one human to the other. "Do you speak dog, Michael?"

"Unfortunately, Adonia is the only one I know that does."

"Well, we'll just have to learn to figure him out. Thank you for bringing him by. Do you think he will be okay here?"

"Probably. Duke, do you want to stay with Liz tonight?" Duke looked at Michael while he was talking. He turned to Liz and then reclined on the rug.

"There's your answer. I don't think it gets any clearer than that."

The two talked non-stop about the dogs and the gallery for the next half-hour with both dogs content to just doze. Michael confirmed what Adonia said about Duke insisting that he wake by six every morning. "He wants his walk right after dinner each night and if I'm home, he wants to eat about five every night. That dog does love his routine. There's a poop bag holder attached to his leash. You'll need that. When you pick a path, he's going to want to go the same way every time."

"Sheesh, does he come with written instructions?"

"It's really not that bad, Liz. At least you know what to expect. If your ankle is okay, let's take a quick walk so you have the feel of him before I leave." Both dogs jumped up and were ready to go the minute Michael picked up the leashes.

"It's fortunate that your condo is on ground level. Most of these guys don't have much experience with stairs. They'd rather jump because their cages were stacked on top of each other at the kennels." They took a left and walked down the street past the ubiquitous desert landscaping. The dogs sniffed mailbox poles, the occasional Mexican Bird of Paradise, and frequent low-growing Lantana plants.

"Oh, don't get me started about their prior living conditions. You should hear Katy ramble on about it. Fortunately many of the racing kennels were good to their animals, but that isn't the case for more than I'd care to know about. Anyway, how often do you walk them?"

"If I'm gone all day, I just take them in the evening. If I'm home, I might take them once during the day just to get us out and about. At least it's not hot yet. One thing that you need to always be aware of is that since they are sight dogs, if they spot a cat, they might take off after them. You'll always need to hold the leash tight so he doesn't pull you down. And never let him off the leash if he's not in an enclosed area because at 40-miles-an-hour, he'll be gone before you know it. I think that's about it."

"Let's cross here and head back. The walk is nice, thanks for suggesting it."

"Yes, it is."

The fact that Michael stared at her with that big grin gave Liz as much pleasure as the feel of the dog in her company. That is, until Pricilla bolted after a tabby, almost pulling Michael off his feet. Liz had seen the cat at about the same time and had tightened her grip, expecting Duke's equal reaction.

"See what I mean." Michael laughed out loud. "Even I get caught unaware at times. You wouldn't think they are that strong, but they are all muscle."

Back at the front door, she thought Michael seemed to hesitate as if to kiss her. "If you need anything, just call. You have my number. I can pick up Duke tomorrow night about eight since you work on Tuesday. I'll bring him back when you have another day off."

"Are you sure it's no trouble?"

"Not at all." Still holding Priscilla, Michael knelt down to talk to Duke. "You stay here tonight, boy. I'll be back tomorrow, okay?"

Duke licked his face, entered the open door, and stood waiting for Liz to follow.

Liz sat on the floor next to Duke's bed and pointed. "Come, Duke." He responded as she'd hoped and reclined on his bed. She petted, scratched, and talked to him until he could hardly keep his eyes open. "Let's watch a movie. I'm too excited to go to bed yet."

She watched Duke sleep which caused her to miss half of the movie, but she didn't care. He was on his back with his feet in the air by the end of the movie.

"Come, Duke. Let's go to bed." He stood up, got his bearings, and looked at Liz for his next instruction. When she reached for the corner of the bed, he stepped off it as if he knew her intentions. He kept pace with her into the bedroom and watched her place his bed next to hers. "Are you tired, boy?"

Duke jumped onto her bed, settled himself at the foot, and looked at her as if to say, 'your turn'.

"You are supposed to sleep in your bed. That's why I moved it in here." Duke dropped his head on her bed and looked up at her with sad eyes. "Okay, you can sleep with me this one time. I'm sure I'm going to regret this, but I don't have the heart to be stern with you on your first night here." Duke remained still and watched her go through her nightly routine. He stayed put as she crawled into bed, ruffled his fur, and turned out the light.

Liz awoke the next morning, amazed that she had another dream-free night. As she reached down to pet Duke, she found herself alone.

CHAPTER 19

Liz checked his bed, she checked the bathroom, and then she ran to the living room. Duke jumped up from the rug that rested by the front door and wagged his tail like a wind-up toy. Liz rubbed him and gave him a huge hug. "You scared me, Duke. I didn't know where you were." He danced on all four feet and touched his nose to the door.

Her heart sank. "Do you want to leave? Don't you like it here?" He didn't move. "Or maybe you have to go outside." He repeated the dance. "I'll be right back." Liz quickly put on some sweats and grabbed his leash.

Duke did his business the moment he got to the right place outside and then pulled Liz back to the front door.

"Whew, that's a relief for both of us, isn't it?" She sat on the floor to talk to him at his level. "Why didn't you wake me up? Or maybe you did and I didn't hear you. What time is it?" The clock in the dining area said five in the morning. "I guess it isn't six yet." She giggled as Duke danced around her, licked her face, and then leaned into her for a hug. "You're one amazing dog, you know that? Let's go get some breakfast."

Liz fixed herself breakfast, but only after she fed Duke. He reclined politely while she had her coffee, bagel, and an orange. "Let me shower and then I'll take you for a long walk." At that, he raised his head and seemed to smile. Liz knew attributing human traits to an animal made no sense, but she didn't care.

Duke rested patiently on his bed in her bedroom during her morning ablutions until she patted her leg and said "Let's go."

The sun had abated the morning chill and it was perfect for a nice long walk. Duke politely nosed other dogs as they passed and behaved like a perfect gentleman *dog*. No cat chasing, no pulling, nothing. He even stopped at cross streets. Two people asked to admire her elegant dog and wanted to know if he raced.

Back at home, Duke rested next to Liz while she called Katy to ask about how to find details about Duke's racing history.

"Do you know his racing name?"

"I think Michael said it was 'No excuses' or something like that."

Katy gave her a couple web sites to search, but needed to get back to her patients. "Let me know if you need more help."

Liz found his stats and wondered why his winning streak ended so abruptly. "Did you break a leg, boy, or did you catch the rabbit?" Of course, Duke didn't answer, but the phone rang.

"Hi, Michael" … "Yes, we had a great night. Hey, does Duke sleep with you?" …

"Because he jumped up on my bed like that was his usual routine." …

"Yeah, I figured I shouldn't have let him, but I wanted him to feel safe."

"Ooof."

"Oh, Duke says *hello*. He is one smart dog." …

"What paintings did you find?" … "Okay, I'll wait to see them tomorrow."…

"Alright. Do you want me to bring Duke to your house

tonight?" …

"Okay, we'll be here waiting. We'll see you about six then. Do you want to eat dinner here?" …

"I know I'm supposed to be resting, but I want to hear about your day. Besides, I have some of my mom's food in the freezer. I'll just add a salad." …

"See you then."

Liz sat wondering which paintings Michael selected for his next installment to the gallery. His other paintings were very good, but not the same caliber or feeling as the ones she had selected the first time.

Duke tipped his head while she puzzled through her thoughts. "What are you looking at, Duke?"

He jumped up, trotted over to her tapestry, and gave a little "Ooof.". Liz joined him to see what caught his attention.

"What is it? There's a black grey just like you. Is he one of your ancestors?"

Duke puffed some air again. "Ooof."

"He's beautiful just like you." Liz stroked his ears. "And look, the rider next to him has brown hair just like Michael."

Duke puffed twice. "Ooof. Ooof."

"Yes, it does look a bit like Michael. Your imagination is as active as mine. Let's get some lunch."

Duke followed her throughout the rest of the day as she went about her business, and he slept when she remained still long enough.

Since Liz had bypassed the remainder of the paintings Michael had hanging in his own gallery, he searched his leaning stack for something to hang. An important task to be sure, Michael needed to put himself in Jean-Luc's head to guess what might be worthy. Not only did he need to think about individual works, but needed to think about what would fit in with his remaining works: the triptych, *The*

Guardian, and *Love and the Maiden, Too*. The right paintings must mesh with the colors and the partnership or multiples themes. Finding what he looked for, he grabbed a couple spares.

♥♥♥

Michael rang the gallery's back-door bell and waited for what seemed like hours before Jean-Luc opened the heavy metal door.

"*Bonjour*, Michael. *Entrez vous*."

"*Bonjour*, Jean-Luc. I've brought the paintings you requested. Should I bring them in now?"

"*Oui*. I'll make you a *café*."

Michael leaned his paintings against some boxes, locked the freight door, and went in search of Jean-Luc and his coffee which were both waiting in the small kitchenette.

"Ah, Michael. Let's retire to my office." Michael shadowed Jean-Luc to the guest side of another Louie XV desk that fit perfectly in the small room. Multiple pedestals held sculptures of all kinds, but no paintings adorned the walls. A scraggly black crow perched on the corner of the desk to his left. Enough spot lights highlighted the sculptures to illuminate the entire office. A small task light shone on paperwork in front of Michael's benefactor.

"How does your day find you, Michael?"

"It is bright and shiny out, and I'm happy that Liz has the day to spend with Duke. How is your day?"

"I am fine for a man so old. Let us continue from our previous conversation. For Liz, what are your intentions?"

"Um, we are business associates and, I hope, friends. Why do you ask?"

"I am blunt. I am not her father, but the same, I don't want her hurt. I need to know that she is in good hands when her father and I are not available. You must forgive my query. I sense you are good, but there is a minor shadow with you and I cannot place it. She is warming to you and you to her, more I think than just friends. Will you hurt her?" Jean-Luc's eyes changed from squinting to raised eyebrows. His hands remained on his coffee cup.

If Michael felt mildly intimidated before, it was nothing compared to his elevated heart rate now. He took a deep breath to hold back defensive thoughts. He needed to select the proper words to express his place in this situation.

"First, let me say that I would never hurt Liz, or you, on purpose. I'm sure you know that, just as I'm sure that everyone, including myself, thinks that Liz is amazing.

"Second, she has a great business head on her shoulders as well as an excellent eye for art. She is a flexibly strong individual, but I know that there is a sensitivity somewhere underneath. Perhaps she's been hurt in some way, other than her clumsiness. I'm aware of that and would not use it against her.

"And last, yes, I want my art career to soar, but not at a cost to anyone other than myself. This has to work for all of us for a lasting solution. Shortcuts don't work for me. Money is not my main focus – it only buys groceries, not happiness." If that answer didn't satisfy Jean-Luc, he didn't know what else to say to prove his point. Michael held his breath and awaited Jean-Luc's response.

"This I believe, but I needed to listen to it. Now let's talk about your work. You have brought more paintings?"

Shit, he couldn't keep up with the old man. "Yes, I have two replacements and a couple of spares."

"I'm going to drink my *café*." Jean-Luc took a sip. "You can take yours. I want you to go place them. Others you can move as necessary. Advise me when you are ready for my viewing. Does this sit well with you?"

Michael stood and picked up his coffee cup. "Tell me, why are there no paintings in here?"

"I have yet to find an adequate replacement." Jean-Luc motioned behind his head with his thumb. Apparently there used to be something hung there, but he didn't elaborate. "Take your time, I have much paperwork."

Having been summarily dismissed, Michael went about his task as directed. He hung *Trident* with its reds representing *will*, greens representing *action*, and blues representing *knowledge*. *Attraction* was next with its amorphous yellow entities moving toward each other through a turquoise background. He rehung *Love and the Maiden, Too* in the next space, followed by *The Guardian*, and then the triptych. He studied the story as he had envisioned it, second guessing himself, and then left them as he hung them in the first place.

CHAPTER 20

Tuesday morning passed slowly as Liz handled the final touches for the auction. Morgan filled in for Liz at lunch so she could run a few errands.

"So glad you returned early," Morgan said to Liz. "I need to prep for a client meeting. By the way, Richard stopped in and purchased a triptych that Michael suggested, named *Heart Storm*. He wanted it for his fireplace and didn't want to risk losing it at the auction."

"Oh, I loved *Heart Storm*." Liz slumped and stuck out her lower lip.

"You didn't inform me you desired it."

"Oh, I did, but couldn't afford it. No worries. Go to work and thanks for popping in to cover for me." Liz hugged Morgan goodbye.

"In the future, elaborate on your cravings." Morgan wiggled her index finger as she stepped out into the sunshine.

After the gallery closed for the day, Liz's volunteers filtered in for final party planning and pizza.

Standing next to the sales desk, Jean-Luc started the meeting. "Liz and I are indebted to you all for this event to be possible. How can I best tell you of my appreciation?"

"There's no need for that, Jean-Luc," Ken shook his head. "We are happy to help and we may get some catering business from it as well or customers to the restaurant."

"Just the same, my heart is full," Jean-Luc touched his chest. "Liz, *s'il vous plaît?*"

"While you are eating, let's go over the plans together. Let me know if you see any holes," Liz continued. "We are going to be closed tomorrow for preparations. If anyone wants to help, and can, we'd love to have you here during the day."

CHAPTER 21

People in black ties and long gowns hurried to prep the last minute event details. The first guests arrived promptly at seven o'clock to find Will taking tickets at the door. He collected the pre-registered printouts and double-checked their names against a numbered list on his clipboard. Katy stood next to Will and handed each guest a copy of their numbered ID as a reminder for the bidding. She also provided a handout containing the names and associated pictures of the paintings for reference. The printer, the restaurant, the artists, and the gallery had all been advertised on the flyers.

Each guest had previously received emails containing thumbnail pictures of the paintings to be auctioned and instructions on how to log their number and bid amount on the bidding list displayed on a small table in front of each painting.

Jean-Luc performed his meet-and-greet not far from the door to welcome the many people he knew and to introduce Michael.

Morgan circulated through the mingling people with a tray to offer sparkling water with fruited ice cubes and wine. She directed patrons to the appetizers and desserts near the few high-top tables where they could pass the time until the auction officially began.

Jim played Bach, some jazz, and some other tunes that Liz didn't recognize, on a baby grand piano in an open area of the gallery. Liz did, however, recognize his talent and hoped it carried the evening on a light note.

After everyone arrived, Will hung the 'Closed for private event' sign on the door sharply at 7:30 PM. Will handed the clipboard to Katy while he remained at the door as a bouncer if need be.

Katy then delivered the clipboard to Liz who needed to log the number for each sale.

Richard began to canvas the room to moderate the proceedings and to help if any questions arose.

During the silent auction, Katy ran between the gallery kitchen, where Liz's mom and dad handled final preparation of the food, and the two food tables to keep them fully stocked.

On his rounds through the gallery, Richard overheard a disconcerting conversation.

"This painter is a hack. His work portents a story that is clearly not present," said a short pudgy man. "I doubt these are worth the canvas he stretched to hold the paint."

"On the contrary," Richard butted into the conversation. "Just this week, I was offered six times what I paid for the tryptic hanging over my fireplace by this artist. I'm planning on purchasing several more pieces as investments and to enjoy as well. So, please don't bid. I would appreciate getting them for a lower price." Richard strolled away smugly, admiring the paintings along his route slowly back to Liz to tell her of the exchange.

"Oh, Richard," Liz covered her mouth with her flyer. "Thank you for backing him up, but please don't tell Michael. I would hate for him to know what was said."

"Ah, but my part is the truth." Richard raised his hands, palms up. "I am planning on making a few purchases for my home as well as for the store. So you see," he dropped his hands to his hips and grinned, "I can continue to stroll about with an honest face."

The wine ran out and people switched to the fruited water, which was good, considering they would be driving home.

At eight-thirty, Jim stopped playing so Liz could make an announcement.

"Attention Ladies and Gentlemen," Liz tested the microphone. "Thank you for attending our gala event this evening. We have many talented artists on display this evening and in attendance, and we'd like to introduce our newest artist, Michael Donovan." She motioned toward Michael and paused momentarily for the brief applause. "We hope you enjoyed meeting him and viewing his work, as well as the fine food from one of the city's best restaurants. As a bonus, the winning bidders will each receive a buy-one, get-one entrée certificate as well as a discount coupon from our printer. Please remember that all proceeds from your evening's purchases will go straight to the charity of your choice, so please be generous.

"Precisely at nine o'clock, all bidding forms will be collected and tallied to determine the winners. Those winners will be announced at nine-thirty.

"Successful bidders will gather at the desk after the auction to pay, log their favorite charity, and collect their paintings or arrange for transport. Jean-Luc and I will take care of all those details. In the meantime, please enjoy yourselves with food and drink and the wonderful sounds from Jim Smith. Thank you."

Jim resumed with a requested jazz number as tips found their way into the vase that Liz had thoughtfully placed on the edge of the baby grand.

Richard overbid on the three pieces he wanted and boosted a couple of others to make his point. It took several rounds to remain on top. He watched and listened for the nay-sayer, but didn't hear any further disparaging remarks. At least nothing that he reported to Liz.

Activity in the bidding war ramped up during the half-hour before Liz called time. "It's now nine o'clock, so make any last bids on your favorite paintings. We will make the announcements very soon. When your number is called, please step up to the antique desk to make your arrangements. And once again, please accept our appreciation for this wonderful cause."

The desserts disappeared quickly while the tally took place.

Light clapping congratulated the winners as they were announced. Many bidders settled for one painting, probably because Michael was so new on the scene.

Richard paid more than expected for one of the paintings, but less on the two others he wanted, so he was happy. He deliberately lost the bids on the other two he padded. He noticed that the nay-sayer got lucky on a painting and he clapped loudly for the man.

Michael shook hands with each attendee as they filed out the door at the end of the evening. A few ladies wanted him to autograph their flyer. One provided him with her phone number on a napkin.

"So, how did we do?" Michael asked Liz as he plopped down in a chair by the desk.

"Everyone gather around," Liz instructed. "I'm happy to announce that we exceeded our anticipated participation by double. We hung 26 paintings, and thought we might sell 6 or 7, based on the economy. We actually sold 15 of yours, along with a couple of others. Congratulations, Michael. You are really out there now. Even though Richard bought 3, that's still 12 of your paintings now in circulation. We had several charity choices against drunk driving, some for our military, and of course, some for pets. YAY!"

"I'm speechless. Truly." Michael rubbed his ear. "How can I begin to thank each of you for your tireless effort? I know, why don't each of you pick a painting from my Glendale gallery with my thanks. I'll bar-b-que for you and you can make your selections. Let's meet Friday night at eight since you close the gallery at seven. If that doesn't work for anyone, let me know and I'll make other arrangements."

After the tear-down and clean up, only Liz and Michael remained. High on success, they opened a bottle of Liz's favorite champagne, which Michael brought, and savored the fizzy bubbles on their tongues. Sitting in her office chairs, Liz kicked off her heels, and as she put her feet up on her desk, her gown slid from her ankles to her knees. Michael's face split into a huge grin. They toasted each others work skills, glass after glass, and started in on personal characteristics. "Here's to the gold sparkle in your hazel eyes when you smile," Michael said.

"Here's to that mysterious glare you give me from your tilted head and that shadow of a beard already starting to grow back." Liz dropped her feet and slid further forward in her seat toward Michael.

"Here's to your pert, soft nose that nuzzled me that time we kissed." He remembered every sensation of having her against his door.

"Here's to your perfectly cut hair that's supposed to look so unkempt. It's long enough to drag my fingers through. May I?"

Michael stood. He wanted her to touch him but panicked as she stood and reached for him, but it was too late. Liz rose to meet him in a tentative kiss. When he couldn't help but respond, she deepened the kiss and pressed herself against him. His libido kicked in full force and she responded to the hardness growing between them. His hands stroked her back and he grinned inwardly when he discovered she wore a thong. He groaned and she opened her mouth to take his tongue, biting and sucking gently. As she came up for air, she closed her eyes and tipped her head back. Michael feathered light kisses down her neck. Liz arched her back in invitation.

He had to stop this before it went too far. Shit, it already had, but he couldn't pull away. He wanted everything she had to give and wanted deseparately to please her until she could take no more. He had to stop. She needed to know.

As Liz ran her hand down the front of his shirt, and then further south, Michael forced himself to break their passion and gently pushed her back a little by her oh-so-soft shoulders. Those naked shoulders that her low-cut green dress didn't cover. Her skin tantalized his hands and invited his mouth.

"Liz…,"

"Yes, Michael?" Her eyes were still half closed and she hadn't pulled her hand away.

"Liz, wait." He backed away from her. "I…"

"It's okay, Michael."

"Please, Liz, stop." His voice rang a little harsher than he intended.

At that, Liz blinked several times and smoothed her dress. "Oh. Um. What is it?"

"Well, I…" Michael turned slightly and rubbed his right ear as he did when he was nervous.

"I'm sorry." Liz stepped away, slipped into her heels, and extracted her gold clutch from her desk drawer. "It's getting late. We should call it an evening." She removed car keys and started out of her office.

"Liz, wait."

"No, Michael." She turned in the doorway and shook her head. "You said we were just friends, associates, and such. I got carried away with the celebration. Don't give it another thought." Liz gave him what he took as a fake smile, turned, and left her office.

Michael followed. He didn't want to leave things this way.

Liz rushed toward the back door.

"I need to tell you something…"

Liz stopped and turned toward Michael who reached for

her arms, but she put both palms up toward Michael and interrupted. "No, you don't. Just leave it. You don't need to say anything. Let's go, I need to lock up."

He let out a long sigh. "Will you just listen to me…"

"Michael, please. Let's just go." She squeaked and held the door open for him to exit.

Her eyes had welled up and he didn't want to make her cry, so he stepped over the threshold without another word.

Liz locked the door behind him, ignored him, and started for her car. She knew she shouldn't drive, but would pull over after he left.

He grabbed her arm to stop her until she looked at him. "I don't want there to be any misunderstandings between us. I want us to have a healthy relationship based on truth."

"Let go, Michael," Liz said through tight lips. "I think we understand each other perfectly." She lightened her tone and flipped out a casual hand. "We are friends who are mutually attracted to each other, but must remain neutral to keep our business relationship healthy. What more is there to say? I'm tired and want to go now. Congratulations. We were a huge success. I'll talk to you tomorrow." She pulled away, hiked her long dress for the walk to her car, and left him standing in the dark.

"Pricilla, Duke, where are you?" Michael looked everywhere. No dogs. No dogs in the house, no doors open, no dogs in the yard. Michael came home to a dark, empty house. Where could they be?

The answering machine blinked. The one he kept for his graphics business. Maybe someone found them. Damn, Bethany's voice. "You weren't home all evening, so I let myself in. It's my turn for Pricilla, and Duke wanted to come as well. He seems to like it here, and I think he falls under our 'dog agreement' so I'll return him with Pricilla Sunday night."

"That bitch!" Michael dialed her number immediately. "I'm coming to pick up Duke right now. I don't care if it's late."

"Well, hello Michael. Good evening to you as well. He's a sweet dog, but not as friendly as Pricilla."

"He's not your dog and does NOT fall under our agreement…"

"Michael dear, sorry to interrupt. That may or may not be the case, but if you want him back, you'll need to agree to give up Pricilla. Since you have a new dog, you don't need her. And she needs me. She's my dog, after all."

"You bitch."

"Now, now, no name calling. So do we have an agreement?"

Michael paused to control his anger. "I'm coming to get him now."

"I thought you'd see it my way."

CHAPTER 22

On Thursday morning, Michael called the locksmith. "Can you come now? I need all new locks and deadbolts in both locations." Michael listened to the locksmith's response.

"Bring whatever you have or can get. I don't care how many different keys I have to use. Do you have enough?"...

"Good I'll meet you at the home location first at 11:00 and then we can drive over to the second location. Thanks for the rush job. See you soon."

Michael answered the door. "Want a beer?"

"No thanks," Richard said. "It's a little early and I still need to go to work. Aren't you working today?"

"Hardly. Come in. I've got your locksmith coming soon." Michael stomped into his modern living room, stepping around the construction materials.

"You haven't done that yet?" Richard asked Michael's retreating form.

"I've been a little busy. Sit. The bitch is back." Michael sat on a stack of wood flooring, giving the only chair to Richard. He then told Richard about Bethany's latest trick. "I'm done with women. I've called my attorney. He assures me Duke is not part of the deal."

"That's a relief. You can't swear off all women."

"Like you have anything to say on the matter." Michael threw up his hands. "Where's your woman? What happened to 'women are gold-diggers' and all that rot?"

"I haven't found the right one, but she's probably out there."

"Don't find one named Bethany! Look, sorry, man. Did you need something?"

"I was going to ask you about Morgan, but it can wait. I've got to get to the store. You okay if I leave you?"

"Yeah, catch you later. Stop by for a beer tonight if you want."

♥♥♥

Thursday rolled on, business as usual. Then Liz made another sale and had a call to hold another piece using the customer's credit card. Michael's art was actually selling. He might just help the gallery make a profit this month.

Liz's elation over the two sales was short lived. In her office a little bit later, she sat with her head in her hands. She had made such a fool of herself the previous evening and had stewed about it on and off all day. Michael had reacted exactly the way she wanted him to until…until he didn't. Most guys would jump at the chance to get what they wanted, but Michael didn't want her. Not in that way. She thought he did, but it was business—all business. At least he behaved like a gentleman. Too bad she hadn't behaved like a lady.

Oh, well, after a little embarrassment, they'd continue normal business. Somehow.

It mortified Liz to think about going to the bar-b-que. She had to go and figure out a way to face Michael. Everyone would expect her and worry if she didn't attend. She couldn't think of a valid excuse. Plenty of lame ones came to mind, but someone would catch her in a lie. She'd just have to pretend that nothing had happened. Nothing had happened, so it should be easy. Yeah, right.

"I never thought I'd say this," she said to herself, "but I need a drink."

Liz finished the paperwork to transport the auction

paintings to their owners. She emailed coupons to each of the winners and finished up some remaining gallery paperwork.

"Jean-Luc, I need to speak with you." Liz said after checking to see there were no customers. "Two of our artists called to complain that I removed their work from the display window before their contracted display dates. I had removed them to make more room for the people who watch Michael paint."

"Such a *faux pas*, Liz. I'm surprised."

"I apologized and agreed to move their work back and give them a couple of extra days display." She told Jean-Luc that she needed a nap when he asked about her mistake and her mood.

"You must go home and rest, but after you replace the paintings." Jean-Luc shushed her away with his hand.

CHAPTER 23

The little back yard behind Michael's gallery held everyone with room to spare. Some stood, others sat in the teak lounge chairs, and some watched Michael grill. Beer, wine, and sodas chilled in a cooler on the patio. Michael made the classic potato salad, pork n'beans, chips and dip, and a few other items, along with green chile to add to the burgers for those who wanted a more Southwestern flavor.

"This is no gourmet feast," he told Ken and Nancy as Morgan and Katy brought out the cold foods, "but I do know how to grill meat well."

"It looks lovely," Nancy handed more raw burgers to Michael. "The classics are always a nice change for us. We don't find time to grille often enough."

Will and Richard were tossing horseshoes in the side yard. Liz and Jean-Luc walked around Michael's gallery viewing his latest hangings.

"Michael," Jim asked, "did you tell your brother your good news?"

"Not yet."

"So you aren't an only child?" Nancy asked.

"No, my brother works in Boston as an engineer, and my parents live in Spain now. Dad is an English professor and wanted to spend the second half of his life traveling, so he teaches here and there in Europe."

"Then I can see why you are so close to the guys here. They are your extended family."

"Yep. Burgers and dogs are ready. Nancy, will you mind rounding everyone up to eat?"

After eating, Michael followed Liz back into the gallery when she asked to see more of his work. "Liz, about the other night…"

"Stop, Michael. It's fine. We were both a little loaded. Please, just forget it. I'd like to see some of your older works. Where are they?"

"Okay, for now." He gave her a sideways glance, but let it go. "Come into the back room." Moving from the end of his hangings, Michael motioned to some paintings leaning sideways against the back wall. As she flipped through the heavy framed paintings, studying each one, Liz noted a different complexity of skill and subjects. "How old is this grouping?" She asked as she began eyeing the paintings.

"Probably 3-4 years." He rocked his hand in a so-so motion. "Anything older is in storage or hanging somewhere."

Dog subjects moved on to stills, that flowed to various landscapes, that transitioned to nudes…he wasn't kidding. "So, who is the blonde nude?"

"My wife." Michael answered and then suddenly looked up at Liz with wide eyes.

"Your WIFE!"

Colors flared around Liz, each one turned to red, blood red. Heat built in her face and flowed down her body, a volcano ready to explode. It took all her energy to remain standing, facing the man she had dared to hope might become something in her life.

"No, no, no! I mean my soon-to-be ex-wife. I've been trying to tell you, but you never let me finish." Michael shook his head and put his hands in his front pockets.

Liz let the paintings go, not caring if one banged into

another as they fell back to their original leaning position. She crossed her arms as Michael crossed over to her. "I think you'd better tell me now! Don't you think that's a small detail I'd have been interested in knowing before one of our kisses!" She glared at Michael through scrunched eyes. "Well, no matter," Liz raised her shields once again and threw her hands in the air. "It shouldn't affect our business relationship, right?"

"Our divorce should be final this week or next week." Michael said in a volume that matched hers. He reached for her arm and his tone softened. "That's what I've been trying to tell you, and why I wouldn't do more than kiss you. I couldn't start anything under these circumstances."

Liz pulled back. "What else are you hiding?"

"I didn't hide it, damn it." Michael rubbed his ear, again.

"Same difference!" Liz snapped.

"Originally, I was waiting for the right time. We had just met, and then you were hurt, then everything else." Michael leaned against a short wall, nearly knocking down a painting. "I didn't know if it would matter anyway. We were just supposed to be business partners, then just friends."

"Well, it's of no consequence to our professional relationship to be sure." Liz started walking toward the front door. "And since our personal relationship appears to be set around sharing a dog that you stole from me, that shouldn't matter either." Liz turned slightly and flipped her hand at the stack. "Just get some pieces to the gallery tomorrow, not your naked wife, and everything will be just peachy."

"Liz," Michael followed her into the front yard and said in a soft tone, "We were married only two years when she left me for her boss. It's not pretty, and not something easy to share." Michael stuffed his hands in the pockets of his jeans again.

She looked into those *café au lait* eyes of his, and melted in turn. Her face softened. "I didn't realize." She wanted to drop her shields and run to him, but stopped herself. He still kept it a secret while flirting with and kissing her. This must remain business. It MUST, her head kept reminding her heart.

"I would have preferred to tell you, rather than you find out this way." Michael looked down at his shoes.

"That must have been a terrible experience. I'm sorry for your pain." Liz closed her eyes and took a deep breath. "Let's just put it all behind us, and move forward. Come on." She moved back into the gallery unsure how to proceed, unsure how to feel. She went to a different stack next to the nudes. "I think these will bring a good price, especially this triptych," she said motioning to a typical fireplace favorite.

"That one's call *Hearts Afire*."

"Yes, that's appropriate," that's how she felt, or at least had wanted to feel. "I'll work out the sales price and see if you agree. We need to get those hanging by tomorrow if possible. Does that work for you?"

Michael moved closer. "Of course. Thanks for understanding."

Speechless, yet still drawn to him, she held back. He reached for her hand to shake it in an official fashion. Part of her still wanted that hand touching her body elsewhere; another part of her wanted to break it. She forced herself to shake his hand and then headed toward the back door to the crowd waiting there. She couldn't leave now. "Time to get back to the crowd," she reached for the door knob.

"Liz,…

"Michael," she interrupted with her hand on the knob, "I'm sorry for your troubles. We'll keep our business relationship totally professional to avoid any complications."

"You don't really want that, do you? What about being friends?"

"Yes, I do. Just business."

"Then how will you get to see our dog?"

"Oh, that's low. Tell my parents I had to go. My stomach is upset. I'll talk to them later." She turned, ran out the front door, and left Michael to face the group alone.

"Ah, shit. Why the hell is this so difficult?"

The party continued for another half-hour and only Richard remained to help clean up. "What's eating you, Michael? Why did Liz really leave so abruptly?"

Michael placed the condiments in the refrigerator. "Can't get anything past you, can I? She saw Bethany's nude and I told her everything."

"I take it that didn't go over well. Why did you wait so long?"

Michael washed and dried his hands, and then sat in one of the kitchen chairs with Richard doing the same. "I wanted to find the right time and when I tried, she kept stopping the conversation. I made sure she knew we were only friends and business partners. I tried not to kiss her, but we are so damn connected. I can't seem to stay away from her, as hard as I try. I even dream about her, but I don't want to get involved."

"Out of the frying pan and into the fire, as they say. Look Michael, you need to figure out what you do want. Where does she stand?"

"I think she's confused, angry, and feels rejected. It's all my doing. I didn't handle things well. Everything is still so raw."

"So what are you going to do now?"

"I'll think of something." Michael blew out a sigh. "Come on, let's get this mess finished."

CHAPTER 24

"It's about time, Michelangelo." Adonia invited Michael into her home.

Michael and Duke greeted Adonia's grey-pack that danced around them in her elegant foyer. "I know it's been a while. Duke wanted to see you."

"I know. He has a lot to tell me about what's been happening." Adonia pinched Michael's right ear when she hugged him hello. "Sit while I love on Duke for a bit." Duke telepathically told her his version of the latest activities.

"So, what's up, Michael?"

"I finished the updates to the website and I wanted to share them with you."

"Wonderful. Plug your computer in by my desk. Then you can tell me why you two are jeopardizing your relationship." Adonia raised her eyebrows at Michael.

The unexpected doorbell caused Liz to spill the wine she had started to pour. She sat the bottle down next to her near empty glass. A fitting end to a crappy, slow day. She ignored the bell, wiped up her mess, and poured herself a full glass.

She pressed on her eyes as the bell pealed twice more. "It's 8:00 at night. Who could that be?" she asked herself.

Curiosity overrode frustration. Michael stood on the other side of the peephole. He called out her name as she debated opening the door. "Michael. HI DUKE!" She smiled and squealed the dog's name as she opened the door.

"Can we come in?" Michael asked as Duke ran into Liz's dog-rubbing hands.

"What a good boy. I've missed you so much."

Duke whined softly in response and rubbed his face on her leg, so she bent further to hug him and talk doggie talk.

"Lucky dog. Can I come in, too?"

"Sure." She stepped further back into her apartment with Duke glued to her. "Looks like he missed me."

"Of course he did." Michael closed the door behind him. "I knew you'd miss him, too, so here we are."

Liz looked up at Michael through misty eyes. "Thanks."

"Would you like me to leave him for a few days?" Michael asked as he rubbed his ear.

"Yes, please."

"Look, can we talk? I don't like how we left things."

Liz tried to read Michael's face and sensed sincerity. "If you'd like a glass of wine, have a seat." She headed back into the kitchen to retrieve hers. She took a deep breath and returned with two glasses. "What's on your mind?"

Duke settled next to Liz as Michael stood and paced in the small living room. "I've been hurt, I have trust issues, and we aren't communicating as well as we should be. I think we are both attracted to each other and maybe afraid of it. Being in business together complicates things and so does Duke. There's enough stress there, on top of the gallery, to explain why we are having difficulties. I'd really like to work through this and come up with some sort of comfortable relationship. Is that possible?"

"Wow." Liz blinked. "That sounds well thought out for a guy."

"Yeah, funny girl." He sat on the edge of a chair. "Actually, I had a meeting with Adonia tonight and she helped me talk it through. Get in touch with my feminine side as she said." He rubbed his ear, like he was prone to do. "Have you had a chance to think about things?"

"Today dragged so much that I couldn't help but rehash

all of it. I'm exhausted."

"Look, we need each other at the gallery and Duke needs us both, so there's no reason we can't work out that much right now. We haven't screwed it up that badly. Do you agree?"

Liz took a sip before answering. Duke rubbed her arm as if to spur her on. She draped her arm over him in acknowledgment. "Okay, yes, on that much I agree."

"Good." Michael placed his glass on the end table. "I'd like to apologize again for not finding a way to tell you about Bethany sooner. I tried, but not hard enough."

Liz pursed her lips. "That's true, and perhaps I should have told you about my x-fiancé who cleaned out our joint bank account, mostly my money, while I was out shopping for my wedding dress, and then he skipped town. I was so naïve."

Michael rubbed his ear. "Man, that's the lowest." He finally sat back in his chair. "I can't imagine how you dealt with that."

"It was a year ago. I've fixed my financial mess, but am still fixing me. Maybe that will explain why I can be so sensitive."

"Since we are getting things out in the open, I also need to tell you about Adonia. I have her permission, but first you need to promise to keep her secret."

"What about her?" Liz tipped her head. "More secrets?"

"Yes. Promise first, even from Katy and Morgan, at least for now."

"It looks like we have another trust opportunity." Liz searched Michael's eyes before she agreed.

"Please keep an open mind. She has this theory that we have belonged together for eternity, in past lives and now, and that Duke is a gifted dog that will bring us together. That's her story and she'll probably tell you her thoughts if you want to talk to her. Whether we get together as a couple eventually or not is up to us, as far as I'm concerned."

"Seriously? I guess in a round-about way, he has brought us together, but past lives, gifted dog? I need more details."

"This will sound even crazier," Michael said. "Adonia is from a long line of descendants of Cupid, the god, and Psyche, his mortal wife. That makes her a demigoddess; half human, half goddess. She has the ability to telepathically communicate with certain Greyhounds that are descendants of two greys that the goddess, Diana, gave to Psyche. These greys can awaken lovers by kissing them at the right moment in time. This special kiss causes the lovers to have memories of being with the other person in past lives. The couple may think they are dreaming, but they are really memories. Duke has kissed me, it tingled, and I do dream of you often, which could just be a coincidence since we work together." Michael paused and waited for Liz to say something. She just stared at him for a bit with her mouth open. "She says she'd like to talk to you and answer any questions you may have."

"I see. Do you believe her?"

Michael shrugged his shoulders. "Honestly, I think I do. I've known her for a long time. I've seen many other couples come together after adopting a grey. You are looking at me funny. Do you think I'm nuts or that Adonia is nuts?"

"Neither. I've been kissed by Duke, and another greyhound many years ago, I tingled both times, and I do dream of you often. I was sure I remembered you the first time we met. I bet you thought I was nuts back then."

"I wondered what was going on with you, but I also wondered why you also seemed so familiar. Since then, Liz, when I touch you, I remember the feel of you."

"And I, you, but I need time to think this through and I may want to speak with her. It's been such a crazy time and I'm a little fried."

"Okay. I should probably go and let you have time with Duke. Please remember to keep her secret. I'll see you at the gallery tomorrow, okay?"

"Sure. Can you come mid-afternoon sometime?"

"I'll be there. Bye Duke, sleep well." He hugged Duke and made for the door. "Lock this after me, please."

"Hi, Liz." Katy returned Liz's call at 9:00 PM "Are you doing okay?"

"Hey, Katy. I'm fine. Michael just dropped off Duke and we covered some trust issues." Duke perked up at his name so Liz rubbed his ears.

"I'm at a bar with Will at the moment. He agreed to stop by and talk to you if you like. He confirmed everything Michael told you about Bethany. It's had Michael messed up for quite a while. I thought you should know."

"Thanks for the confirmation. I'll let you get back to Will and we can talk later. I'm so tired I'm going to crash now— that is, if I can sleep."

CHAPTER 25

Early Sunday afternoon while wrapping up a small sale to a customer, Liz noticed a well-groomed man who strolled into the gallery in what had to be a high-end designer suit, or at least a marvelous knock-off. As he turned, she recognized him as Jean-Luc's attorney. She returned his wave, but noticed he didn't return her smile as he usually did.

Matthieu Mausset perused the artwork while waiting. "Hello, Liz." He approached her after she finished speaking with her customer.

"*Bonjour, Monsieur Mousset.* You are dressed up for a Sunday. It's a pleasure to see you again." Liz extended her hand to shake his. "Jean-Luc is not in yet today. Is there anything I can do for you?" She didn't like the frown between his eyes and her stomach turned a little flip.

"Call me Matthieu, remember. I was hoping that you could take a break. Is it possible to close the store for an hour?"

A sharp pain stabbed Liz in the pit of her stomach. She hoped his visit meant nothing, but her gut told her otherwise. "Um sure, if it's important. What did you have in mind?"

"It will keep until after you have locked the door."

"Okay, I'll be right back" Liz's step faltered here and there as she headed across the hardwood floor. She flipped the sign over to CLOSED. Jean-Luc loved the old hanging sign. He said it reminded him of simpler days.

Matthieu had wandered over to the antique sales desk by the time Liz returned to him. "Can we sit for a moment?" He motioned to her chair and he moved to the guest chair while he waited for her to sit first.

Liz nodded and waited for him to continue with this mystery visit. Sadness emanated from his pale gray eyes. Her gut tightened another notch.

"I'm afraid I have some bad news. Jean-Luc's maid found him still asleep when she arrived this morning, or so she thought. Sadly, he passed in his sleep. She called me right after she dialed 911. My business card was in his wallet and she knows who I am. I wanted to come tell you in person as soon as I could."

"Noooo, that can't be." Silent tears instantly chased one another down Liz's face while he continued.

"I know how close you two were so this must be quite painful. I'm so sorry for your loss."

"What happened?" Liz sniffled.

"It might be a heart attack, but we don't know for sure. An autopsy might be conducted and could be scheduled this coming week if need be. I'll provide you with details upon receiving them." Instead of a handkerchief, Matthieu handed her his plaid pocket square.

"Thank you."

Liz wiped her tears away with the silky fabric and inhaled some much-needed air. "What do I do without him? Do I keep the gallery open? Can I close for the afternoon? What will happen in the long run?" Her stomach cramped even more and her mind went in several directions at one time. Her eyes darted with her thoughts. "He can't be gone. I need him."

"Liz, as the manager, you have every right to open and close as you see fit. I'm Jean-Luc's executor, his personal representative. I will handle all the legal matters. You'll need to work with me in that regard."

"Yes, of course. What happens next?"

"As you know, he has no remaining family. There is a will and we'll need to discuss it in regard to the gallery. In the meantime, one of his wishes was for you to keep the gallery running, provided you are willing. Are you willing and able?"

"I'm willing, yes. I'm not sure about able." Liz pressed her fingertips to her eyes and exhaled. "Yes, I can run it, but what about money to pay the bills?" The responsibility pushed aside the shock. Momentarily, anyway.

"You're a signer on his accounts so banking is no issue. The money won't be frozen, but every penny must be audited going forward. Your authority to conduct business with the CPA remains as do your agreements with other vendors. You can continue to make sales, as always. If you run short of funds, advise me before you run out. Contact me for any reason, especially for questions or problems. That's my job."

Liz remained speechless. She tried to absorb the volume of information and manage her heartache at the same time. She grabbed her stomach and leaned back against the soft tapestry of her chair. A deep breath held back her tears for the moment.

"Is there someone you'd like me to contact?" Matthieu's sharp business eyes turned a softer shade of gray. "I can remain another hour, and then I'll need to return to the office. I'm sure you must be in shock and I don't want to leave you alone."

"That's very kind. I'll be okay. I can call…"

A sharp knock against the front windows interrupted Liz. She had forgotten her appointment with Michael.

Liz held on to the edge of the old desk and stood up, but then stopped. "This is an artist friend of mine, Michael Donovan. We have an appointment and I need to let him in. Is this public knowledge?"

"You may tell him, and your family. It will make the local news soon enough. Before you let him in, there's one more thing. The police may want to question you."

"ME?" Wide-eyed, Liz fell back into her chair. "Why me?"

"Because you worked for him and your name is in the will. It's standard procedure. Depending on what they find if

225

they do an autopsy, they may want to talk to you further. The police may want to interview you anyway. I just wanted you to be prepared in case."

"How can you prepare for something like that?" Her voice broke along with her composure. Michael banged harder on the glass. She could see the bug-eyed expression on his face. She held up one finger hoping he would wait a minute. "Why would they think I had any information?" Liz stood and paced the floor now.

"That's all I can say at this point. You may be a suspect if they find foul play. If not, then there's nothing to worry about. If you need an attorney, I can recommend someone."

"What? I don't need an attorney. I didn't do anything." Michael must have seen her distress, because he rattled the door handle and yelled her name.

"I'm sorry if I scared you." He stood with his hands splayed out. "It's my responsibility…"

"I'm going to get the door," Liz interrupted as she walked away, not listening to Matthieu any longer. "Just wait a minute."

Michael pulled the door open as fast as Liz could unlock it. She stumbled back, but remained on her feet. "What's going on? Why are you crying? Did he hurt you?" Michael stood rigid with his fists tightened by his sides and wondered what to do.

Liz wiped her face. "That's Jean-Luc's attorney. He…he died last night in his sleep." She started to wobble.

Michael pulled her close while she shed a multitude of tears. He stroked her hair while the sobs kept coming. "I am so sorry, Liz. What can I do?"

Liz hiccupped. "I…don't…know." She wrinkled her brows. "You can join us." He followed her and shook the attorney's hand as she made halted introductions.

"We were just about finished," Matthieu said.

"Let me get you some water." Liz nodded and Michael went to the kitchen to give them some privacy.

Michael didn't know how she would handle this. This man was more than a second father figure. He was mentor, employer, and friend. Regardless of what this meant to Michael's career, he didn't care, but he would be there for her no matter what she needed. His other work was flexible enough to juggle. He didn't need to paint for a while either. He could, and would, make the time for her. He took a deep breath.

Jean-Luc had touched Michael's life as well, both in college and most recently. His firm kindness made Michael think more about what his paintings meant, both to himself and how they affected others. And, of course, how he felt about Liz. As much as he tried to keep his distance, to keep things just business, he had to admit that she touched his heart in a way that no one else had ever done. As his heart clenched, he dropped the bottle of water he had pulled from the refrigerator.

Matthieu held Liz in a tight embrace as Michael walked out to the front. The plastic water bottle made a crunching noise as Michael squeezed it a little too tight.

"Call me if you need anything, Liz," Matthieu said as he stepped back. "I'll be in touch. Hope to see you again, Michael, under better circumstances." He handed Michael his card.

Liz took the water from Michael after she let Matthieu out. "Thanks. I'm glad you are here. What do we do now?"

He liked the sound of that, the WE part. He handed her his plain white handkerchief and dropped the soggy silk one in the waste paper basket.

"Hey, that's silk. I should probably have it cleaned and returned to him."

It was like her to be so concerned of others, even now. "I doubt he'll want it. He probably has many more. Are you okay?"

"I can't think straight at the moment." Liz rubbed the side of her head.

"Are you expecting any clients?"

"No."

"Then can you close for the afternoon?"

"I don't know. I suppose so. It's been a slow day so far."

Michael disappeared into the back room and came back with a piece of white mat board and a marker. He wrote:

Closed Tuesday afternoon.
Please excuse any inconvenience.
Unexpected emergency.

"Is this okay?" When she nodded at the text, he placed it in the window near the normal closed sign. "Shall I take you home or somewhere else?"

"I want to see Duke."

"He's at my house. Do you want to go there?"

"Do you mind? I can't go home right now and I can't stay here. I need to be somewhere else." She looked at him with watery puppy-dog eyes.

"It's okay." How could it not be okay? She's never been there. What would she think? Is it a mess? Oh well.

CHAPTER 26

Within a half-hour they arrived at Michael's house in North Arrowhead Ranch. "You live on the lake?" Liz looked at the large house on the gently sloping hill.

"It's my uncle's house actually. We're remodeling it for sale so please ignore the mess. I'm between houses at the moment."

They shared a look between them. Liz wanted to ask if the divorce caused that situation, if his wife was in their house or what, but on second thought she didn't really care at the moment.

"Come on in."

An ecstatic Duke waited to greet her on the other side of a child's gate intended to keep him out of the construction areas. He placed his head on top of the gate while he waited. He could have easily jumped over it had he not been such a polite dog.

Michael opened the gate to let Liz into the family room to see Duke. "Make yourself at home and I'll get some wine. Sorry, but as you saw, the formal living room is full of wood flooring waiting to be installed."

Liz sat cross-legged on the gray carpet and nuzzled Duke at his level. He repeatedly licked her face to wash away the tears. "You are exactly what I needed at the moment boy. How could anyone not love you to pieces?" Duke knelt in a play bow stance then ran circles around Liz. Next, he jumped on the leather couch and ran from side to side, stopping in the middle, panting hard. Liz laughed so hard she cried, again.

"That's quite a feat for such a large dog, isn't it?"

Michael stood in the opening between the shiny kitchen and the family room watching Duke's antics. "He's a blast, isn't he?"

Liz went to sit by Duke on the black leather couch and ruffled his ears. He settled in next to her. "Does he do that often?"

"Only when he wants my attention." Michael held up a bottle. "Is Sauvignon Blanc okay? I'm running low on wine."

"Sure, the grapefruit notes are nice." Silent tears ran down her face again.

Michael fetched a box of tissues before pouring the wine. "What else can I get you?"

"Nothing, just sit, please." Liz wiped her tears and sipped her wine. "Thanks for bringing me here. Matthieu said he'd notify Henri, Jean-Luc's friend. I don't know who else needs to know right away. My parents. Morgan. Katy. I need to call them."

"Of course. I can take you to your parents or home whenever you like."

"Soon. I can't believe he's gone." She sniffled.

"How long have you known Jean-Luc?"

"Over five years. I first worked for him part-time during my senior year and then he hired me right out of college. I had hoped for a position at the Phoenix Art Museum, but his offer felt right. More like home."

Duke put his head in her lap and looked up at her.

Liz wiped at the tears that wouldn't stop. "He trained me, but always treated me like an equal, not an underling. I knew art, but I didn't know business. Not really. He taught me that and more. He taught me vision. You know that. Oh, God, how can he be gone?" Liz put her face in her hands and bawled. Duke stuck his nose under her hands and pushed. She hugged him and cried against his fur.

All Michael could do is sit there while she cried it out. She needed Duke more than she needed him at the moment. A dog was safer than a man, more honest, less intrusive, pure comfort.

Liz gained composure after a time and several tissues. "I'm sorry, Michael, I…" Liz looked around with a pile of tissues in her hand.

Michael jumped up and brought over a wastebasket for her tissues. "Don't be. This is one of the hardest things to ever deal with. I'm here for you. I can drive you around. I can cover the gallery. Whatever you need."

"Thanks for being so kind. I need to think about the gallery, but not right now. It can wait. We're closed on Mondays so tomorrow won't be a problem. Can Duke come home with me today?" She hugged the special dog.

"Of course, whenever you are ready. Just let me know."

"Do you mind if I call everyone from here?"

Michael picked up her purse from the floor by the kitchen doorway and brought it to her. "I assume your phone is in here. Do you want me to give you some privacy?"

"No, stay please. I don't want to be alone."

CHAPTER 27

While Liz made her calls, Michael called Adonia.

"Hello, Michael. How is Duke doing?"

"He's enjoying being able to spend time with both Liz and me. We switch off every few days." Michael leaned back in his desk chair in his gallery office. "She has him now. Duke is providing great comfort to her. I don't think I've told you that her boss died on Saturday night and she found out Sunday. She's having a rough time of it.

"Maybe I should visit to see if Duke has anything to say to her."

"She might like that and she may want to talk to you otherwise, eventually anyway. We are heading over to her parent's house soon, so I'll ask her to schedule a visit if she's up for it."

"Now what about you? Give me all the details."

Michael sat forward and started to doodle. He filled her in on the status with Bethany and the divorce, his workload, and his relationship with Liz. "I'll have to admit, things are crazy at this point. What about you?"

Adonia cleared her throat. "Well, another race track closed leaving me with five new greyhounds to foster. I need to get their pictures and details up on the website soon and there's one to be taken down. It sounds like you'll be too busy to do that right now, so it can wait. Someone else can foster a couple of them and I had adopted out the last one so the timing is fine. Otherwise, all is well."

"Maybe Katy could help with the dogs if you get in a pinch. I could probably get the web work done on Wednesday if you have all the pictures and copy written. It won't take long. Email me what you have."

"I have everything, but there is one picture I don't like. I'll see if Richard can come take another one. If not, it will do for now."

"Sounds good. Hey, I wanted to ask you about Love at First Sight. Does that have anything to do with your abilities?" Michael rubbed his ear.

"Well, there's Lust at First Sight, but that skill belongs to a different demigod, not me. Love at First Sight is really just a memory of a feeling from a past-life love. The sense is there without the conscious memory that goes with it. Some couples never fully remember a past love, but still live a long happy life with their partner."

"Then why is it important for you to have us remember?"

"It comes down to free will, which we all have. Some people ignore the chance to connect with their true soul mate if they don't really believe in Love at First Sight. If you are aware of all the facts, then you can make an informed decision."

"That sounds quite logical for a demigoddess."

"I'm not all wands and fairy dust, my boy. I'll send the email and you can get to work whenever you finish pondering your life." Adonia chuckled. "Talk to you soon."

"I just don't understand how he could be gone." Liz sipped from the glass of water her mom had handed to her after she and Michael arrived at her parent's home. She turned the glass in circles before taking another sip.

Ken squeezed her hand lightly. "He was getting on in years, Liz. It happens to us all."

233

"Don't even say that." Liz squeezed his hand back. "I knew he was extra tired lately. I should have insisted he go to the doctor. Why didn't I see how bad he was? Maybe I could have saved him instead of trying to save the gallery." Liz searched her Dad's eyes hoping for an answer.

Ken pulled her close while her tears flowed freely. "You were doing exactly what he asked you to do. We are each responsible for our own health. Jean-Luc wouldn't have wanted you to mother or baby him."

While Nancy and Ken flanked Liz on the leather sofa, Michael, Morgan, and Katy sat subdued in club chairs nearby, each grieving in their own way. "We all noticed his exhaustion," Morgan said. "Any one of us could have interfered, but he was a private man. Besides, he would have dismissed any of our assistance as unnecessary."

"That's true." Katy pointed to Morgan. "He would have blown it off as nothing."

Duke sat next to Michael and whined in agreement. Everyone else sat in silence for a bit letting Liz have a moment.

"What happens next?" Nancy asked. "The gallery is closed tomorrow, but what about Tuesday? Are you going to keep it closed for a while?"

"I don't know what to do."

"I suggest you keep it closed for a couple of days," Morgan said. "I can go in tomorrow and change the phone message and add a sign to the door."

Liz sniffled. "Maybe Tuesday. I don't want the customers to think I'm shutting down the gallery."

"I can probably make myself available for Wednesday and Thursday." Morgan checked the calendar on her phone." I need to adjust one appointment or leave you alone for an hour."

"That would help me catch up on my workload," Michael said. "Friday may or may not work. I'll have to let you know later."

"Sorry I can't help," Katy said shaking her head. "The other vet tech is on vacation. I'm scheduled. I can stay with you overnight though for as long as you need me."

Liz sat up straight, blew her nose, and said, "Okay."

"Okay to what?" Nancy rubbed Liz's back.

"All of it." Liz waved her hand in a circle. "Thanks for your usual support. It means the world to me. I'm honestly scared about the autopsy. What if they find something wrong with Jean-Luc? Matthieu, his attorney, said they may have to question me. What if he was poisoned or something? I don't have an alibi; I was home alone last night, except for Duke." Liz reached out her hand to him and he immediately came to sit at her feet.

"It's easy to think the worst, Liz, but I'm sure he didn't have an enemy in the world." Nancy put her arm around Liz again. "Matthieu was just covering all possible scenarios as attorneys are prone to do. He had your best interests at heart as well. If anything untoward did happen, we are all here for you and I'm sure it would be cleared up in no time."

Liz laid her head on Nancy's shoulder and the group sat in silence for a while.

"Hey Liz, do you remember the career fair? When you first met Jean-Luc." Katy moved to the edge of her seat. "Morgan in her suit and me in my scrubs, we pretended we weren't with you. Jean-Luc saw right through that and waved hello to us." Katy waved high in the air. "He was always so perceptive."

"And when he interviewed me after his accountant quit," Morgan snickered, "he asked me what one-plus-one equaled. I answered 'Two, unless the ones were deductible, then the answer was three, because it was like acquiring an extra one tax-free.' He laughed so hard I thought he was going to pee himself."

"The first time I made Macarons for him," Nancy sighed, "they came out flat. He ate them anyway and said he loved the strawberry cream filling. Then he offered to show me how his wife made them. That was the first time he had ever mentioned her to me." A tear ran down Nancy's face.

"He once thanked me for instilling in Liz a sense of wonder for art." Ken pursed his lips and nodded his head. "He said you told him about your first paint kit, the Louvre, and other things we did to help you in the beginnings of your career." Ken hugged Liz.

Hours went by while they talked, laughed, cried, reminisced, and paid homage to Jean-Luc's memory. Nancy warmed up some leftovers with Katy's help. They ate in silence before they parted for the night.

"I'll take Liz home." Katy pointed her thumb at Liz who stood behind her. "I need to pick up a few things first."

"Do you want Duke for the night?" Michael picked up his leash and Duke came running to be attached.

"I guess I do. Apparently, he wants to come with me."

Back in the kitchen, Nancy and Morgan washed dishes. "You are quiet tonight, Morgan. Are you okay?"

"Another person I loved died. You guys aren't safe around me." Morgan's tears flooded out.

Nancy grabbed Morgan's shoulders with soapy hands and turned her so she could look in her eyes. "Morgan, we've talked about this before. This idea you have about being responsible for your loved ones' dying is not healthy and it's not true. Death just happens. We each have our time. It was Jean-Luc's time. I know you feel responsible for your little sister's death, then your parents' death, and who knows how many others. You simply cannot blame yourself. You are no more responsible for them than Liz is for Jean-Luc's death. It was his time as well as their time. People can't live forever."

Morgan just shook her head as the silent tears fell. There was nothing more Nancy could say on the matter that would change the way she blamed herself. They'd been through that

before. Nancy hugged her to provide all the comfort she
could hope for at the moment.

CHAPTER 28

Liz checked the peephole and answered the door in her pajamas. "Hi, Mom. Come in."

Nancy rubbed Duke's ears. "Did I wake you?" She followed Liz and Duke to the cushy couch where Liz plopped down and Duke jumped up beside her.

"No. I can't sleep. I was awake all night. I keep rehashing everything in my mind." Liz closed her eyes and tipped her head back on the sofa. "If Jean-Luc did die of a heart attack as his attorney suggested, couldn't it have been prevented? There are pills, surgery, pacemakers, and all kinds of things that can help. I never saw him take one pill, not even an aspirin or a vitamin as I suggested. Was he even under a doctor's care? I had asked that he go see someone one day when he looked so tired. Did he go? And how could I not know?" Liz lifted her head to look at Nancy.

"We probably won't ever have answers to those questions unless Matthieu knows and will tell you. When do you hope to hear anything further?"

"I don't know. Matthieu said he'd call as soon as he knew anything, but didn't give me any timeframe."

"I can stay as long as you need me, or want me to stay. Have you eaten anything yet today?"

"No, and I don't want anything right now. I'm not hungry. Help yourself." Liz tipped her head back again and stared at the ceiling.

Duke whined and licked his lips.

Nancy went to the kitchen and brought back two glasses of orange juice, a sandwich, and a dog biscuit. Liz was still staring into space.

Duke rubbed his face on Nancy's leg as if to say thanks for the treat.

"Why don't we watch a movie?" Nancy picked up the remote.

Liz didn't move an inch. "Sure, find whatever you want."

Nancy found an upbeat romantic comedy, but Liz paid no attention. After about a half-hour, she finally dozed off.

Michael arrived at Richard's jewelry store at lunchtime. "Can you take a break? I need to vent. I brought burgers." He raised the bag and then set it down on Richard's desk.

"Sure, I have enough people on the floor and this paperwork can wait." He lifted the bag and wiped the grease spot with a napkin. "Let's go to the breakroom. I can close the door and we won't be bothered."

Richard grabbed more napkins from the fully stocked counter and they sat at the small, contemporary-style break table.

Michael ignored the food. "So, we had our last settlement meeting this morning before the divorce is final. It's been pushed out again. The damn gold-digger now wants half of all proceeds from the sale of my paintings. She claims that she supported me while I was painting and, therefore, is entitled to a share of the proceeds. If I don't cooperate, she won't settle and we have to go to court. And you know that will cost an arm and a leg."

"So what are you going to do?" Richard shifted in his chair and took a sip of his soda from the burger joint.

"What choice do I have?" Michael stood and paced in the small room. "She saw the auction in the newspaper and jumped all over the fact that my paintings are out there now.

I have to inventory every painting I sold between the time she left and now, and provide that to her attorney by tomorrow. I agreed to do that, but I forced her hand to one-quarter of the amount, thanks to my attorney. She didn't do any of the work and I'm not giving her half of my profits. I have two days to come up with the money, which I have, so that's not a problem. I also insisted that the divorce is final no later than Friday. If she pushes it out again, she's doesn't get that money, and she can't claim any further money from my work or for any other reason. Maybe that will make her stop the insanity." He finally sat down.

"Sounds like her. What can I do to help?"

"I don't know. Maybe come keep me company tonight. I have a list from my few gallery sales so that will make it easy. I'll get that list and a check to my attorney today to get this going. He doesn't think it will delay the court's processing time by more than a day, so we should be on track for Friday. Keep your fingers crossed."

"What can I say? That's a rough blow right now, especially with everything else going on."

"Yeah, I haven't called Liz yet today. I want to be more supportive, but Bethany's got me so pissed off that I'm likely to say the wrong thing to Liz."

"Maybe you should give yourself a couple of hours and then call her and explain what's happening. It might help for you both to be more open with each other going forward."

"You're probably right. Thanks. I should let you get back to work." Michael rose to leave.

"Don't forget your burger." Richard handed the bag to Michael.

"Thanks. Later." Michael waved as he turned to go.

The ringing phone jarred Liz, Duke, and her mom awake to find the movie had ended. Liz found her phone under her stomach where it slid after she tipped over in her sleep. "Hello." Liz covered the microphone and whispered to her mom that it was Matthieu.

"Yes, you can come by, or save yourself a trip and just tell me over the phone?"... Liz placed her hand on her stomach and held her breath.

"I'm not alone. My mom is here."...

After a few moments, Liz replied. "Oh, that is such a relief." Duke laid his head in her lap as Liz let out a deep sigh. "What do we do next?"...

Liz glanced at her mom.

"Oh, that soon. Do we need to be there?"...

"I'd like to make arrangements for a memorial service. Can I do that anytime?"...

"Unless you want to do it, I'd like to spread his ashes. Or we could do it together."...

"Ok, let's talk tomorrow." Liz ended the call, took a deep cleansing breath, and turned to Nancy.

"It looks like I'm out of the woods, as they say." Fresh tears quietly rained down her face as she petted Duke's face. "The pathologist spoke to Jean-Luc's physician. Apparently, he's been having heart issues for a while, but refused surgery or any other treatment. So a major heart attack is the assigned cause of death. They don't need an autopsy; the Coroner's not concerned about foul play." Liz reached for a tissue. "There's no one else to contest the autopsy decision."

Nancy moved to sit by Liz on the couch and took her hand. "That's good news, in a way. I'm sure that's a relief to you, even though I didn't think you needed to worry about it. What's the next step?"

Liz wadded her tissue and threw it in the wastebasket by the couch. "Jean-Luc's will calls for cremation and it's already paid for and arranged. Matthieu said it's scheduled for tomorrow morning. We don't need to be there because there's nothing we can do." Liz tipped her head back and took another deep breath. "He will let me know when the ashes are available and we can spread them, although it might take up to a week to get them. Jean-Luc wanted them airborne so they can float on the wind back to France. Matthieu needs to be there to ensure his wishes are carried out, but he said I can actually do it if I want." Fresh tears started anew.

Duke whined and snuggled closer to Liz.

"We can be there if you want us, and I'm sure others may want to attend as well," Nancy said, "unless you'd prefer to do it by yourself."

"I'll think about it. I should probably plan a memorial service for some of his friends and maybe special customers." Liz rubbed Duke's ears. "Will you turn on another movie, please? I need to veg."

"Of course. Do you mind if I call your father and fill him in? I can go in the other room."

"Thanks for doing that. I'll call the girls and Michael later." Just then the phone rang, so Nancy paused the movie she had just started.

"Hi, Michael"... Duke raised his head and looked at Liz.

"I'm okay. Just vegging."...

"Sure, come on over. Bye."

"Looks like I should change out of my pajamas." Liz threw off her lap blanket and headed to her room, Duke right behind her.

"Really? That's what you are going to wear?" Nancy pointed to the sweats Liz wore when she returned.

Liz turned on her heel without a word and then came back in yoga pants, a t-shirt and flip flops.

"At least you brushed your hair this time. I've yet to adapt the super-casual style of your generation." Nancy laughed and shook her head. "I'll go see if there's anything to serve him." Nancy picked up the stale sandwich that Liz had not touched and her partial glass of orange juice.

The doorbell rang as Nancy returned with chips and dip. "I'll get that." Duke beat Nancy to the door and 'Ooofed'.

"Come on in, Michael."

"Hi, Nancy. Hey, Duke ol' boy." Michael gave his dog the desired attention before turning back to Nancy. "I came by to check on Liz and Duke."

"I've been here all morning; however, I do need to run some errands. Do you plan to stay for a while?

"Sure, if that's okay with Liz."

Liz approached then. "I'd like to spend some time with you. Can we walk Duke? He hasn't been out much today."

Duke turned circles at the word 'walk' and did his 'jabber-jaw' thing.

"I guess that's your answer. He does that soft teeth-clicking thing when he really, really wants something." Michael reached for the leash hanging by the front door. "I can stay until Katy comes home or whenever."

Nancy looked to Liz for approval; Liz nodded slightly, completing the silent mother-daughter communication. "Then, I'll leave you two, sorry, three to your walk. I made a grocery list for you, Liz. I'll pick up a few things and be back in the morning. Call if plans change or you need anything." Nancy went to the kitchen for her list and purse.

Liz smiled at Michael and grabbed her house keys and poopy bags from the antique table near the door.

Michael returned her smile, stepped outside, and held the door for Nancy.

CHAPTER 29

The sun had begun its slow descent, painting the western sky with its usual fuchsia and citrus tones. Liz, Michael, and Duke walked toward the green area of her apartment complex.

"Thanks for stopping by." Liz looked at Michael as they walked along. "It's been quite the day. The good news, if you can call it that, is that Jean-Luc died of natural causes. He had a massive heart attack. His doctor confirmed it, so there's no cause for an autopsy."

Michael took hold of Liz's hand, the one that wasn't holding Duke's leash. "I didn't think you had to worry, but I'm glad the news came so quickly. You can relax now, right?"

"Yes. I didn't do anything to him, but I didn't want to try to prove it if it came down to that. His cremation is scheduled for tomorrow morning. We might not get his ashes for about a week and he wanted them spread on the wind from Piestewa Peak. Luckily, it's an easier hike than Camelback Mountain."

"Do you want me to come with you?"

"Matthieu will be there, but it would be nice to have you there as well. Also, I want to plan a memorial for Saturday morning for whoever wants to come: family, friends, and some customers like Philip Durand. There's a park near the office. I can reserve the ramada there from the City of Scottsdale and provide light snacks and drinks, but no alcohol. What do you think?"

"It's a great idea. I know where you can get lots of help."

Michael grinned and put his arm around Liz.

She smiled up at him, so grateful for his support.

As they walked on, Duke did his business on the grass, and Michael took care of the results and told Duke he did well. A nearby trash can came in handy.

Liz asked Michael. "What's new with you?"

"I had quite a day as well." Michael sat on a nearby bench and Liz followed. Duke plopped down in the grass and panted. Michael then filled her in on Bethany's latest antics. "I had naïvely thought this would be all behind me by now. Cross your fingers for a good day on Friday."

Liz lovingly touched Michael's face. "I guess we are both naïve. Better that than suspicious all the time, I suppose."

Michael leaned in to kiss her, just a quick one. "Thanks for listening. I'm glad we are improving our communication skills." He put his arm back around Liz and they watched the sunset for a bit. "I know that we, or mostly me, kept talking about keeping our relationship *just business* and *just friends*, but I have to admit I have stronger feelings for you than that. And they aren't based on Adonia's powers as a demigoddess or Duke's gifts to awaken my dreams and memories of you."

Liz blinked back emerging tears. "That means a lot considering what you went through today and recently. I'm happy that you hung in there after all my moodiness. I care for you more every day and I'm working through my trust issues. Apparently, you are as well."

"Does that mean we can move forward with a romantic relationship?"

"There you go again getting in touch with your feminine side. Yes, I think we should try a little romance." Liz reached up and pulled Michael in for a soft kiss that deepened like the colors in the sky.

CHAPTER 30

"I bring the gift of Greek salads." Morgan entered Liz's apartment Tuesday at lunch and glanced around.

"If you are looking for Duke, my mom took him out for a walk." Liz wandered to the dining table and sat down. "Thanks for lunch."

"I failed to bring the right quantity, not remembering your mom was here. She can have mine and I'll pick up something on the way back to the office." Morgan pulled the food from the bag.

"She can have mine or I'll split mine with her. I'm not really very hungry." Liz rose to go get bowls from the kitchen.

"Why aren't you hungry?" Morgan divided the two salads into three equal portions.

"Yesterday I was sad. Today I'm mad. If Jean-Luc knew he was having such serious problems, it wasn't fair not to tell me. He had plenty of opportunity. We could have bought him some more time. He had me become a signer on everything under the false pretense of him wanting to go to France. At least I'm assuming he lied. Plus, he asked me if he had taught me enough about the gallery. I should have seen this coming, but how is that even possible?" Liz pushed the tomatoes around in her bowl.

"It's understandable that you feel abandoned. But how can you resent the man for making your life easier? That's unfair to him, Liz. Perhaps he misjudged the amount of time he had left. Going home has been his desire for some time now." Morgan crunched on a bite of salad and stared at Liz.

Liz dropped her fork in her bowl with a clank. "I can't help but be angry. I thought we had more honesty in our relationship."

"He desired to protect you in every possible way. Can't you comprehend that concept?"

Liz speared a tomato and turned her fork over and over so the tomato turned in circles.

"Are you listening to me? Will you please eat that tomato; it's driving me insane watching you play with your food."

"Ugh, you sound like my mother." Liz popped the tomato into her mouth.

"Besides, men avoid appearing weak above all things. He wanted you to concentrate on saving the gallery, not fret about him."

"In my mind, I know you are right. In my heart, I hurt and can't make sense of it all. I suppose I shouldn't be angry. He didn't die on purpose. Okay, let's change the subject and eat these salads. The tangy dressing makes my mouth water."

Nancy returned, greeted Morgan, and told Duke not to drool on Morgan's pretty pink suit. She grabbed a dog biscuit for Duke and sat down to eat. "Did you tell Morgan about the Memorial?"

"I was getting to it," Liz said. "I want to hold a memorial in the park near the gallery on Saturday morning. Mom has agreed to provide some finger foods, coffee, and such that we can offer after the ceremony. I can send an email to everyone with the details. We can order a couple of flower sprays and have the printer provide a large poster of Jean-Luc, and some handouts. I can start off and then anyone who wants to speak about him can. Am I missing anything?"

Nancy had started eating her salad and paused. "I also offered our tables, chairs, and all the usual. There are some shade trees, but I know where we can rent a tent as well. I'll need to know how many you think will attend."

"I'll order the flowers and coordinate with the printer if that's okay," Morgan said. "I'll require your thoughts on the contents of the handouts. Perhaps the guys can usher people in and keep kids out of the area. Katy could purchase ribbon for marking boundaries; I'll ask her. That should be sufficient. I need to return to work."

"Sounds like a plan." Nancy offered her thanks for the food and started cleaning up.

Katy plopped down on Liz's couch after work. Duke sniffed her up and down. "He must wonder about all the pets he smells." Katy snickered, pointed to her scrubs, and gave Duke a good ear rub. "Is Nancy still here? Something smells good."

Liz sat at the table working on the email list. "Good nose. We're having pasta and then she's leaving to spend some time at the restaurant. Michael is coming over later to pick up Duke since I'm going into the gallery tomorrow."

"Will she mind if I skip dinner? Will asked me to go out tonight. We've been getting to know each other slowly. I don't plan to get too serious." Katy shrugged her shoulders. "But I'm anxious to have a little fun."

"You should go. Mom won't mind a bit. Maybe Michael could come eat instead. There's something you should know, Miss Matchmaker. Michael and I are getting closer, albeit slowly as well. We've changed our minds about remaining friends only."

"Ooooh, congrats. That's wonderful. Since you'll be alone tonight, maybe you can get even closer."

"Alright. Enough of that! Go say hi to Mom and then shower so you aren't late."

"Is there anything you don't cook well?" Michael rubbed his stomach as he licked his lips.

"I find Chinese food to be a bit challenging." Nancy smiled as she got up to remove the dirty dishes from the table. "I can't quite get the sauces right. I gave up trying, so we go to a local place not far from ours. We really like the owners. Speaking of food, I better get to the restaurant soon."

"Leave the dishes." Michael stood and took the dishes from Nancy's hands. "I grew up with dish duty. I can make quick work of this task so you can leave now." He kissed her cheek. "Thanks for another tasty meal."

Michael washed and Liz rinsed. "I have to catch up on some graphic deadlines tomorrow and Thursday. I'll keep Duke both days. Morgan will be at the gallery with you, right?"

"Yes, she insisted on taking two days of vacation to help. It's nice to have my friends and family around right now, but I won't fall apart if I'm alone."

Michael put his soapy hands on both sides of her face and kissed her thoroughly. "Enjoy the company. We are here for you whether you need us or not."

"Oh, I'm enjoying the company all right. I hope you aren't leaving soon. I'd like to enjoy it a little more." Liz reached her arms around his neck and went back for a second helping of enjoyment.

CHAPTER 31

Morgan helped reopen the gallery. She dusted, gathered the mail, and conducted other routine duties for Liz.

The first two hours were quiet, which gave Liz time to adjust being there without Jean-Luc. She had sent the invitations for the memorial service on Saturday and had asked for RSVPs. She needed to provide a head count to her parents for the snacks. Liz didn't need to address any other emails immediately, except the one from Emilio which included their baby announcement. Their little girl was born on Monday. When Liz looked at her name, her eyes watered. A few happy tears escaped.

"Hey, Morgan." Liz waved her over to the desk. "Look. Emilio named his baby girl, Jeanne Lucinda."

Morgan pulled a guest chair over next to Liz to read the email. "Jeanne is the female equivalent of Jean in French, but I've never heard of a female version of Luc."

"Lucinda is his mother-in-law's name." Liz wrinkled her nose. "He doesn't care for her and probably only agreed to it because the name is so close to Jean-Luc."

"Perhaps she is a reincarnation of him. If so, that was fast."

Liz smiled at the thought. "Who knows, but it's something to think about." A customer walked in, so Liz closed the email and went to greet the woman.

"I'm not an art connoisseur, but I'd like to find

something that might appreciate in value rather than throwing my money away on junk. Can you recommend something?" The woman motioned at the paintings around her.

"I'm sure we can find you something of value. Did you have anything in mind? Size? Color? Subject?"

"A good size would be forty inches wide by thirty inches tall, or something near that size." She used her arms to diagram the dimensions. "It's to go over my aqua suede couch, so I guess color is important. Maybe something with a sky or water scene. I'm not really into modern art, although it would match."

"Follow me. I have two excellent artists who paint landscapes." Liz took her past the Native American art and past Michael's art. The woman stopped in front of one of Michael's paintings. "This is amazing. Too bad it doesn't meet my parameters. Maybe it would go in my bedroom, but I'll need to think about it. Lead on."

As they perused and discussed each aqua one, the woman stopped before a lake with a red boat just off center. A man and a child sat there fishing. The woman began to cry.

"Are you okay?" Liz produced a small packet of tissues out of her jacket pocket.

"This is my grandfather and me. Or it could be. He died the day after we caught lots of fish in a boat very similar to this one. I was ten years old. I loved everything about that man."

Tears ran down Liz's face too, thinking about Jean-Luc. She, too, loved everything about *that* man. "Some paintings are felt, rather than seen. They can produce happy tears or sad tears, depending on the perspective of the viewer."

"Oh, these are happy tears from a happy memory. I have to have this one, regardless of value. Plus the water and the sky behind all the trees match my couch. The size is about right, too."

"Then it's all yours. We can have it delivered or you can take it with you today. Right this way." Liz directed her to the desk where the sale could be concluded. "Let me tell you about the artist. Although he isn't our top artist, his work appreciates more than the best landscape artist, by 20% per year for the last three years. So this piece meets all your criteria."

"I'm so happy I came in today. Thank you for helping me find this special painting. I'd like to take it with me."

"I'm very happy you came in as well. If you have a minute, I can box it up for you so it travels safely in your car."

Matthieu stopped by after lunch. "Hello, how are you two beautiful ladies today?"

Liz and Morgan both said "Fine" at the same time.

"Excellent. Liz, can we talk about Jean-Luc's condo?"

Morgan pointed with her thumb over her shoulder. "I'll go watch the floor." And she turned to leave them alone.

"Let's go to my office." Liz passed Jean-Luc's office on the way to hers. She couldn't look inside.

"We haven't discussed Jean-Luc's will yet, but I do need to discuss one point with you now. His maid is wondering about her job and will need to fill his slot if she is out of a job. She came once a week on Mondays, all day, and cooked his dinner. This concerns you because Jean-Luc left the condo to you."

Liz raised her eyebrows and couldn't speak.

"I'm sure this is a shock, based on your expression, but it's a good deal. It's fully paid for, so there are only the annual property taxes and insurance to be addressed. We can discuss that more at our next meeting. What I need today, is a decision about the maid. She is quite reasonable as domestic help goes. Perhaps she could help you with boxing up any of Jean-Luc's things that you might not want."

"Um, can you give her a paid week off, and tell her I will

keep her on for now. I'll come meet her the following week."
Liz slumped back in her chair. "I don't know about Jean-
Luc's things yet."

"I'll handle the arrangements. I know this is a lot to take
in right now, but as food for thought—I would imagine that
the taxes, insurance, and maid are less than the rent of your
apartment. Plus, it's closer to the gallery. Forgive me, but he
shared those details with me. Anyway, think about it. I need
to get to my next appointment. And thanks for the invitation
for Saturday. I'll be there."

He reached to shake her hand, but she hugged him, and
then walked him out.

"You appear as white as a ghost. What happened?"
Morgan walked Liz to the desk to sit her down.

As Liz explained the reason for Matthieu's visit, Morgan
smiled. "That's excellent news. That condo will only
appreciate in value. Plus, it's full of special memories.
Retaining it or selling it is a win-win either way."

They chatted through the remainder of another quiet
afternoon, and then closed up shop.

CHAPTER 32

On Thursday, Michael went to the court proceedings with his attorney—whose extra cost gave Michael reassurance that Bethany couldn't pull something at the last minute. He rubbed his ear frequently while he waited for her to show up for their turn with the judge. He turned in his seat and watched the heavy wooden doors.

"I doubt she'll show." His attorney shuffled papers. "She knows she's bled you dry and more attorney fees aren't going to produce further results. And she does know we are scheduled a day earlier because of your quick payment and a quiet day on the docket."

"I hope you are right."

Michael's turn came and went quickly with no one there to contest any part of their agreement. He let out a heavy sigh and shook his attorney's hand. "Thanks for all you've done."

"As soon as the paperwork is recorded, my office will send your copies to you."

Michael drove to a bar close to his home. Not a big drinker, he ordered a beer. "No, make that something stronger. I just came from court."

The bartender nodded. "Do you like Scotch or Whisky?"

Michael looked at the rows of bottles behind the bar. "What can you make with Vodka?"

"I assume no girly drinks so what about an Old Fashion, a Martini, or a Moscow Mule?"

Michael's eyebrows drew together. "What's in a Moscow Mule?"

The bartender counted off the ingredients on his fingers. "Vodka, lime juice, and ginger beer over ice."

"Let's try that."

While the bartender made his drink, Michael texted Richard and Will. He relayed that the divorce was final and where he had stopped to blow off some stress and celebrate. Of course, he invited them to join him when they finished working.

"Here you go. Let me know what you think."

"That's a fancy cup." Michael picked up the copper mug and checked it out.

"It's the traditional way to serve it. People steal the mugs so I don't often use them. You looked like you needed a pick-me-up today. You okay?"

"Yeah. My divorce was final today."

"Your choice or hers?"

"Hers, but I'm glad it's over. She did everything she could to clean me out."

"Then your first drink is on me. Did she leave you enough to start a tab?"

Michael laughed out loud. "Yep, I stopped her just in time."

"Let me know if you want to talk." The bartender walked away to server other customers.

Michael sipped his drink to savor the flavors. He eventually chugged it and asked for another.

Will arrived first. "What on earth are you drinking? Where's your beer?"

"There's ginger beer in here, so it counts. Here, try it."

Will took a sip and made a face. "That's a little strong, buddy. How many have you had?"

"This is my second. I nursed it hoping one of you would show."

Will ordered a beer just as Richard arrived.

"Michael, did you get *class* in the divorce decree? Quite the drink. I'll have what he's having." Richard pointed to the copper mug and sat on the other side of Will.

"You got here fast. You must have left the store early. Here's to the three single Musketeers." Michael raised his mug when the other two received their drinks.

"*Congratulazioni*—which is Italian for congratulations. That should be obvious, or *Felicitări* in Romanian which is not so obvious." Richard touched his mug to Michael's.

"*Lloniannau*—which is cheers in Welsh. To it being *done and dusted* as they say in the UK." Will tapped his mug to Michael's next.

"Thanks, guys. I can't believe it's finally over. Good riddance. Enough with women." Michael chugged the rest of his drink.

"Speaking of women, did you contact Liz?" Richard gave Michael the evil eye when Michael shook his head.

"I'm done with women today!" Michael ordered another drink while the other two sipped theirs.

Will pushed his empty bottle back on the bar top. "Seriously, man. At least text her."

"Yeah, I should." Michael pulled out his phone, sent a short text, and then chugged half his drink. "Happy now? Thanks for the reminder, I guess."

Richard had barely touched his drink. "Let's get you home and we can celebrate more there." He put his hand out for Michael's keys. "Will and I can come back for your car later."

"Thanks, I need to feed Duke anyway."

Liz showed Morgan the text from Michael. "He must be relieved, but I wish he would have called me. I guess I can understand why he wants Duke back for a few days."

"He undoubtedly requires a day sans women. He'll arrive

tomorrow and provide the details soon enough. You should exercise patience until then and with him tomorrow as well."

Liz shook her fists. "I've been patient all day for his contact and for someone to walk through the front door. One measly sale yesterday is not going to keep the doors open."

"What about arranging a sale on sculptures after Saturday? We can advertise using your usual methods. You haven't sold any of those in an eon."

"Okay, that might be a good idea. I'll go prep it now. I should keep the stupid black crow. Jean-Luc loved it so."

CHAPTER 33

Michael arrived at the gallery on Friday wearing sunglasses.

"Glad you got here safely." Liz pulled off his shades and grinned at him. She closed the heavy back door behind him.

"Yah, well, I won't be painting by the window today, I can tell you that. Look, I'm sorry I didn't call or come by yesterday. I needed some space and time to wallow in the finality of it all. Maybe we can talk at lunch. I need quiet for a bit."

"No worries, I can move you to the landscape area. I made one small sale there and can adjust the wall."

Liz paced the remainder of the morning on the other side of the gallery to think about sales and to give Michael his space. She spoke to herself in a whisper. "Maybe no one is coming because Jean-Luc is gone. I need them to see that I can provide what they need and want. Maybe I need to hold some kind of promotional event. It's too early for another charity auction, but what? Something that keeps the upscale vibe—not a cheap sale. My apartment lease is up next month and Jean-Luc's condo would be less expense than my apartment. I could use the extra savings to stay open. My money is minimal and Jean-Luc's money will probably only go so far. I guess I just made that decision—I'm moving to his condo. Whew!"

♥♥♥

Liz closed the gallery for lunch and went to peek at Michael's progress. "You never cease to amaze me with your work. This one feels cheerful and comforting at the same time."

"What do you see?"

"It's almost as if something is rising up through the light in the middle of the painting."

"I call it Ascension. I hope it honors Jean-Luc's latest journey. It won't be dry enough, but if we took it to the service tomorrow anyway, do you think the other artists would get mad?" Liz had tears trailing down her cheeks when he turned to look at her. "I'm sorry if I upset you." He pulled her close to him and held her until she stepped away.

"Jean-Luc would be honored and I love it. I know just where we could hang it in his condo."

Michael raised his eyebrows at her sudden show of strength. "So you are not selling?"

"No, I'm moving—and I'm happy about it. It's paid for and the money I save every month could go into keeping the gallery open and into buying this masterpiece."

A sudden surge of warmth infused Michael. He smiled and tucked a stray lock of hair behind Liz's ear. "This is already yours." When her eyes flew wide he said, "Free of charge. I painted it for you from the beginning. I was never going to let you sell it. At least I hoped you wouldn't want to do so. I'm pleased that you like it."

"Like it—I love it." She hugged Michael and reached up for a kiss.

"I added the finishing touches today and it needs to dry now until tomorrow."

"We can put it closer to the window but out of direct sunlight. It's warmer there. Let's go eat. I'm finally hungry."

"P.F. Changs? My treat." He put his sunglasses back on. "Do you mind driving?"

♥♥♥

"Did yesterday go well? You wanted to talk about it, right?" Liz picked up a forkful of Kung Pao.

Michael shared the court details with her and expressed his feeling on the matter. "I'm afraid I might be weird for a few days."

"Weirder than usual?" Liz lifted her shoulders. "Sorry, trying to make you feel better. It's one of the big adjustments in life. You've put up with me during my Jean-Luc ordeal. I'm here for you as well."

"Thanks. Let me know if my attitude gets out of control. To purposefully change the subject, I have a gallery question. Do any of your customers bring their paintings in to sell on consignment? I know I wouldn't like it if one of my paintings came back, but better that than to be sold for pennies on the dollar at a yard sale or online. Again, it would get more eyes on my work and sell higher and if you took a small commission, it would be a win-win-win for all concerned." Michael pushed his food around on his plate.

"I don't know if Jean-Luc ever thought of that, but he never mentioned it to me. I could ask the other artists what they think of the idea. The buyers would never know it was a resale unless they knew who owned it prior or had seen it in the gallery before. Thanks for the idea. I'll run it by Morgan, too, to see if there are any accounting implications. Let's get back and I'll call her."

Back at the gallery, Michael moved his new painting close to the front window. Fading wouldn't be a problem because of the special coating Jean-Luc had added to the glass.

Liz told Michael that she and Morgan had worked out all possible details via email, including a consignment agreement to run by Matthieu.

With no customers and nothing to do, Michael paced

looking for any possible changes that might help matters. "Hey, Liz. What would it cost to replace the signage outside—on the street and on the front of the building? Can you go any bigger at the street? And maybe change the font. Your branding with French Blue is nice, but the script is hard to read. People might notice it sooner with a simpler, larger font." Michael rubbed his ear. She might not like him offering suggestions, but he had to try to help.

"I guess that's my next call since there's no one walking through the doors. Do I owe you a consulting fee for all these ideas? So far, they are possibilities, but I don't want to make any final decisions until after tomorrow."

Michael released a breath he didn't realize he had been holding. He paced more while Liz took to the phones.

"The city says the sign can only be two feet higher and one square foot larger. Changing the font is not a problem and adding a phone number is okay."

"That's a good idea. What about cost?" He stood in front of her sales desk.

"There's an inspection fee and I'll need to see if I can find who we used before or get some quotes. But right now, I'll need to confirm all the plans for tomorrow before we leave. If you come up with any more ideas, we can discuss them later."

CHAPTER 34

Saturday dawned bright and sunny with just a few clouds dotting the sky. The temperature had warmed nicely for Jean-Luc's service. Cool enough to be comfortable in dress clothes, but warm enough to go without much outerwear. His many friends and customers filled the chairs and a few stood at the back of the tent that Liz had ordered for the event.

Liz began the service thanking everyone for coming. "Jean-Luc would be deeply touched to see so many familiar faces. His bird friends have also gathered by the hundreds to honor him with song, so we have eliminated the music portion of this service. I'm sure they will hold off pooping on us or our cars, which would honor me, since it's usually my car that they grace with their presence." The crowd chuckled with Liz. She proceeded to talk about her mentor and friend for the next ten minutes. "Not to commercialize this event, but I have been asked if the gallery will remain open. If you were wondering, Jean-Luc left it to me in his will and I'm sure he will be watching over me daily. Philip Durand mentioned that he would like to say a few words. If anyone else does, please form a line next to the chairs on my left." Liz pointed in that direction.

Philip spoke about his long-term friendship with Jean-Luc and Jean-Luc's skills as an acquisition expert. "As an aside, Jean-Luc would want all of us to continue to support Liz and the gallery. She knows art and knows the business—he taught her well. Liz, I for one, will be by to visit soon to add to my collection. Thank you for keeping his dream alive." He bowed in her direction.

Liz returned his bow and sat down hard on a nearby chair. Her heart raced as nearly a third of the quests lined up to speak.

Michael spoke last. "To honor Jean-Luc, this painting goes to Liz for her personal collection." He motioned to the painting he had set up next to the picture of Jean-Luc. "I call it *Ascension*. Although I didn't know Jean-Luc long, I do know that he was one of the finest men I've ever met, so I know he ascended to a happy place, maybe back to his native France." He started to step away, and then asked the crowd to please avoid touching the painting because it was still somewhat wet.

Liz concluded by handing out small cups of bird seed. "If you would like to honor Jean-Luc by feeding his many bird friends, please walk in the opposite direction of the food and cars, and then join us for a snack." Liz led the way to the birds. "Jean-Luc is going to miss you birds. Thank you for bringing him joy." She threw the seeds in the air, watched the hungry birds descend, and then she walked to the food ramada to help serve drinks.

"So many people loved Jean-Luc and I love each of you." Liz hugged her mom first, her dad second, and then each of her friends in turn. "Thanks for your hard work to make this remembrance so successful."

Philip approached Liz and thanked her for such a memorable service. She hugged him and thanked him for his comments about her and the gallery. "You can't know what it means to me that you asked for support from everyone."

"I meant every word I said. I'll be in to see you next week. Michael, I expect to see something new from you then." Philip shook hands with Michael and then her family and friends. He smiled at the memorial wrapper that Michael had created for the bottled water. "Thanks for the drink."

Back at Liz's apartment, her family and friends relaxed

after unloading. Liz opened the many sympathy cards the attendees had left, and read each one out loud. She used several tissues in the process.

After a while Liz grew quiet. "I'm kind of tired. Would anyone mind if we called it an evening?"

"Of course not. I'll leave Duke with you tonight if you like." Michael rubbed Duke's head when he jumped up and looked at him. "That's okay, right boy?"

Duke walked over to Liz, looked at her, and then sat beside her.

"I guess he's okay with it." Michael gave Liz a bird peck and led the crew out the door.

Liz curled up on the sofa with a blanket and went right to sleep with her dog curled up beside her.

CHAPTER 35

Michael arrived on Sunday with breakfast in hand.

Duke got a whiff of the large food bags, but stood patiently while his humans hugged and kissed. Finally, Liz took the food bags and Michael turned his affection to Duke. He knelt down and hugged Duke and then rubbed his ears. "Would you like to go to the park after we all eat?"

Duke wagged his tail and whined "Yes."

"There's your answer." Liz laughed over her shoulder as she walked toward the dining table.

On the way to the park, Liz asked, "Do you think it's too late to ask everyone to dinner tonight? I rested well and would like to cook this time. I've picked up a few skills from my parents over the years and I make a yummy spaghetti."

Duke's ears perked up at the word 'spaghetti', but his humans ignored him.

"Will is working tonight, but Richard might be able to make it. I'm sure everyone else will come if they can."

"Great. Do you want to go grocery shopping with me?"

"That sounds a little domestic."

Liz poked him in the ribs when he burst out laughing.

"Sure, I'd love to go. I have all day free."

Duke followed his usual walking routine at the park while his humans walked hand-in-hand. Eventually, they took him home.

♥♥♥

Back at her apartment, Liz looked in the refrigerator as she put some of groceries away. "It's noon, are you hungry?"

"Not after that huge breakfast. You?"

"Not yet, but I'll set out some crackers and cheese. We can nibble while we cook."

"Come here, I'd like to nibble right now." He pulled Liz to him and bit her neck gently. "Your neck is amazingly soft." He ran his tongue up from shoulder to ear. "I could nibble all night long."

Liz giggled and pulled away. "Oh, that's cheesy. Back to work, Mister."

"I can make the salad. I have skills, too, you know." Michael picked up the lettuce and went to work. He whistled a light tune and thought maybe he could get used to being domestic with Liz.

"Thanks. I make my sauce and meatballs from scratch so it takes time to prepare."

"When do you plan on moving to the condo? I can help with packing and moving if you like." Michael continued to chop vegetables.

"I need to donate Jean-Luc's suits and a few other items, and then clean. His maid will help me with that. Not sure how long that will take."

"Maid? Cool. I could still help with the heavy lifting, furniture moving, and whatever else you might need."

"Are you always this nice?" Liz tilted her head. "It's a serious question."

"I try to be, to the point that some people take advantage of me." When Liz frowned he added, "Not you, of course. Or Adonia, either. Sorry, I'm still a bit raw. I hope that didn't sound the way it sounded to me."

Liz stopped stirring her sauce. "It's okay. I know to

whom you were referring. I imagine that both Bethany and Jack will enter into our conversations from time to time. Let's just hope it's not too often. I've had a year to deal with my issues and I still have a bad day once in a while, as you well know. I'll try to be as patient and supportive while you deal with yours." She walked over and hugged Michael.

"I can't tell you how much that means to me. Liz, I'm pretty sure I love you."

"Pretty sure?"

"Pretty darn sure. It's just this thing with Adonia makes me nuts. I need to be sure it's us, not just some magic spell or something."

Liz laughed and gave Michael a quick kiss. "I'm pretty sure I love you, too. I guess time will tell."

A continual plopping noise brought Liz back to the stove. "The sauce is ready for the meat balls that I should have made already. All this hugging and nibbling has thrown me off my game. I need to make them now."

"Go ahead, I'll watch and learn."

Ken and Nancy arrived first to dinner, with a New York-style cheesecake in hand. Michael took it from Nancy. "Yum, I'll pay you to teach me how to make one of these."

Nancy laughed. "I'll trade you a cooking lesson for a painting lesson one day soon. I'm looking for a new hobby."

"Anytime," Michael said and then took the dessert into the kitchen.

Kathy arrived next and grabbed a glass of white wine. "When is Will coming?" Katy pointed at the wooden clock hanging in the living room and then sipped her wine.

Michael shrugged his shoulders. "He's on an extended shift tonight so he won't be coming. It's busy and they are short-handed right now."

"Okay. Duke can be my dinner date." She walked away

to find him.

Morgan and Jim arrived together. "Hey you two!" Liz said by way of greeting. Everyone turned, surprised to see them.

"Yes, yes." Morgan answered, to all the curious faces. "We are going out for drinks afterward and this is our first official date. Any other questions?"

"That's great. Come in and get a drink." Liz pointed to the make-shift bar she had set up on the coffee table.

"Thank you for coming," Liz hugged Adonia when she arrived. "You'll find Michael talking to Morgan and Jim on the couch. Also, do you have time to go to lunch tomorrow? I'd like to talk to you about the greys and other things."

Adonia took Liz's hand and held it. "I wondered how long you'd hold out with your curiosity. Come to my house tomorrow at noon and you can meet some of my other grey family."

"Thanks, I'll be there."

Richard arrived last and headed straight for Morgan. "Hello, everyone. Hey, Jim. Good to see you." They clasped hands. "You look lovely tonight, Morgan."

She simply smiled and dipped her head in thanks.

Liz served dinner on folding tables in addition to her small dining table. "Jean-Luc's dining room is bigger, so we won't be so cramped after I move."

"I'm still in shock that he left his condo to you. I guess I shouldn't be." Nancy pointed to her plate. "You sure did a great job on this spaghetti and salad."

"I second that." Richard raised his hand. "I have a thought about the gallery if you are interested."

"Shoot. I'm always open to new ideas, right, Michael?" She laughed when he blushed ever so slightly.

"I have a nice jewelry case in storage that is in my way. I would love to loan it to you or give it to you, for that matter. I also have a collection of high-end silver jewelry I make in my spare time. I use high-quality gems and stones, such as

Herkimer diamonds and amethysts, but the unique styles don't work for my jewelry store. My custom pieces might just sell to an art crowd. I know some other silver smiths who might be interested in supplying items for sale. I wouldn't expect you to say yay or nay today, maybe just think about it."

"Richard. How perfect—a wonderful suggestion." Morgan gave him what may have been her first heart-felt compliment ever.

He simply raised his glass in appreciation and ate his last bite of spaghetti.

"I appreciate the suggestion. I'd like to see some pieces before I make a decision. Is that okay? Could we schedule a time?"

"Sure, just let me know when. Take your time thinking about it. I know it's a different direction perhaps than a typical art gallery, but it could draw a crowd if done right."

"I wanted to feed you all tonight to thank you for your continued support. I know it's not much, but I'll always be there for each of you whenever you need me. Don't forget that. Please relax the remainder of the evening. Mom…Michael and I will do the dishes."

Duke yawned. Katy pointed to him and said, "My date is tired. That's my cue to leave. Bye, my love." She kissed Duke on the nose.

Everyone but Michael filed out the front door laughing, saying they had full bellies.

"I need to sit down." Liz plopped down on the sofa. Michael sat next to her while Duke had already fallen asleep on his bed. Michael slid his arm around her shoulders so Liz reached up to kiss Michael. She deepened the kiss and pulled him toward her, ready for more.

Michael pulled away. "I'm sorry. I can't yet. Can I take a rain check?" Michael rubbed his ear.

Liz had recognized that motion by now. "Rejection is never fun. You can go, I'll do the dishes." She stood and adjusted her blouse.

"Are you sure? I don't want to hurt your feelings." He stood and looked into her eyes.

"Come on." She reached for his hand and walked him to the door. "We'll pretend this never happened and when we are both ready, it will. Good night." Liz closed the door, leaned against it, and closed her eyes. That's twice. He's going to have to make the next move.

CHAPTER 36

"Thanks for coming with me, Dad." Liz closed the car door. They had parked in front of the lawyer's office on Monday morning.

"I'm glad to be here with you. Why are you shaking? You already know Jean-Luc left you the condo, so it's just the formalities, right?"

"I need to sign a bunch of papers. I don't know what to expect. Matthieu didn't say much else. There's no official 'Reading of the Will'," Liz made air quotes with her fingers, "like they do on TV. There's no one to contest the document, so it should be straightforward."

"See, nothing to worry about. Now, let's go in and say hello to Matthieu."

"Thanks for taking care of all this, Matthieu."

"It's my pleasure. This is both an informal and a formal meeting, but don't worry about it. First, I need to officially ask you, Liz, if it's your desire to have your father present at these proceedings. A yes or no is sufficient."

"Yes."

"Good. Jean-Luc left a small note that he'd like for you to read before we continue."

Liz took the note and began reading:

Liz, the joy you have brought to this old man is beyond measure.

You are the daughter that my wife and I could never have. Thank you for sharing your many years with me.

Please mourn for me very little as my life has been filled with love, friends, good work, and much luck. You must remember that work is not everything. When you find someone special, hold on to him with all the love in your heart, through happy and not so happy times. Make most of them happy. I didn't make it back to France, but I had France in my heart. You should go one day and visit my home town. Matthieu has the details.

It brings me great joy to give all that I own to you, my special one. Please pick out something to give to Morgan and Katy if there is anything in my possessions that would bring them joy. Please keep my maid if she meets your requirements, as she is a gem.

I will smile at you all the way from France if my soul gets to go there. You should find an art student to replace yourself at the gallery, it would be good. I have always been extremely proud of you and you would be a good teacher.

Remember me fondly,

Jean-Luc

Tears flowed freely down her face and onto the note. She handed it to her dad.

Matthieu passed her a box of tissues and waited patiently for her to compose herself.

"What did he mean when he said, all that he owns?" Liz wadded her collection of tissues.

"He literally left you everything he owns. We've already discussed the condo, which also includes all the contents, including his art. The gallery is yours—everything he owns in it, along with the money in the business accounts to run it. There is money in a personal savings account and checking account. His little foreign car is yours. And there is a life insurance policy he took out two years ago in the amount of $200,000.00. That usually takes weeks to clear, however. My costs for administering his estate and transferring all paperwork are also included."

Liz dropped her head between her knees and took

several deep breaths.

"Are you okay?" Ken placed a hand on her back and one on her arm to steady her.

"She probably needs a minute to absorb it all." Matthieu's assistant, Jeni, poured Liz a glass of water from the pitcher on his credenza.

"There's still the deed and other paperwork to sign. If you feel up to it, Liz, we should take care of that today so we can switch the insurance policies over. You don't want to be without coverage."

"Okay." Liz sat up and took a sip of water. "Thanks." She nodded to Jeni. "Can my dad help me read them so I know what I'm signing?"

"Of course. I'd also suggest that you send an email to your client base advising them of the change in ownership. The people at the service know you are keeping it open, but I assume there are others who don't know that you now own it. Are you up for signing?"

It took almost an hour to work through all the details.

"Are you sure there isn't anything else to sign?" Liz laughed uncontrollably until she had hiccups.

"Not today, anyway." Matthieu laughed with her, so Ken joined in. "Do you plan to keep Morgan on as your accountant?"

"Um, probably. I'll have to ask her."

"I'll make sure you have copies of everything by tomorrow. I'll need to record some of the documents and get back to you."

"Thanks, Matthieu, for everything. Would you be interested in being my attorney? I'm not sure what all I'll need, but if Jean-Luc needed you, I probably will, too."

"Of course. We can set up a meeting to discuss it later when you have less to think about."

Liz and Ken shook Matthieu's hand and left.

♥♥♥

Ken opened the car door for Liz. "Dad, will you take me home and have a glass of wine with me?"

"Yep, let's go. You can afford an expensive bottle now, but let's stick with water since you are driving shortly." He chuckled and closed her door.

On the way, Liz asked Ken, "I don't need Jean-Luc's little car—do you want it?"

"It would be fun to have a car to tinker with, if you are sure?"

"I think you'd need to buy it from me to transfer the title, but I'll sell it to you for a dollar to avoid sales tax." Liz poked her dad in the arm. "And you can take me for a drive now and then."

"You are in better spirits."

"Oh man, I'm so glad you were there. I don't think I could have gotten through all that by myself."

"You sell yourself short. You are an intelligent, level-headed woman. You would have done just fine. I'm glad you asked me along though. Your mother is in for a surprise."

"Yes, she is. Can she tear herself away from the restaurant for dinner? Or better yet, let's go surprise her. It will be easier for her to take a half-hour off."

"Can you believe that old guy? You were lucky to know him."

"It's not the stuff that made me lucky. It was the knowing him."

♥♥♥

Liz arrived at Adonia's house promptly at noon. Her house stood with Doric columns in the front. Not wood painted white, but made of stone like on the Parthenon. Fit for a demigoddess.

The door opened before Liz had a chance to knock. There stood Adonia with four greyhounds lined up behind her. "Welcome, Liz. I'm glad you decided to talk to me.

Please come in and greet my babies." The greys wagged and wiggled waiting for their turn to be petted. "The red fawn and light brindle are mine. The white and black, and the black and white are both foster dogs."

"They are beautiful and so well behaved. What's the difference between the white and black and the black and white?" Liz pointed at the two dogs.

"Please, come and sit down." Adonia led Liz to her living room and sat in one of the two wing-back chairs facing the wall of windows. Her dogs sat, one of each side of her. The rescue dogs sat nearby. "To answer your question, the dominate color is always listed first. You may already know that there are 18 official colors and the gray color is the rarest. It is really called a blue dog. There are no gray greyhounds. Listen to me, I sound like Wikipedia. Let's get to the point and then perhaps we can relax and have lunch. Ask me anything."

Liz took a deep breath. "Thanks, Adonia. I know you know that Michael told me that you are a demigoddess and your two greys are gifted. My life is weird enough to believe all that is true, no offence intended." Liz raised her palms and held her breath for a moment.

"None taken. I'm used to that." Adonia shushed the thought away with a wave of her hand.

"The part I want to discuss is free will versus destiny or fate. I've dreamed of Michael, or who I now know is Michael, for most of my life. Suddenly, here he is. Is that fate? Do I just accept that he is my soulmate, in past lives and in this one? Are we forced to be together? How can I trust what I'm feeling versus what I'm supposed to feel? It's all so confusing. I trusted an ex-boyfriend and that got me nowhere. I'm having trouble blindly trusting all this." Liz covered her face with her hand momentarily before dropping it to her lap. "I'm sorry, I'm rambling." Her heart thundered in her chest, but she had to ask these questions.

"Don't be sorry. I deal with uncertainty all the time. Liz,

we are all given free will from the moment we are born. We choose to exercise it in everything we do. This is no different. Yes, destiny or fate put Michael in your path, but as with other things, we freely choose what to believe and what to do. You can believe or not. You can trust or not. These are your choices. Just because you and Michael were together in past lives, doesn't mean you have to be together in this one. I will tell you that I know your lives will be happier together, but you both have to voluntarily make that choice." Adonia relaxed and put one hand on each of her dogs while she let Liz think.

Liz tilted her head. "So you and Duke can talk to each other. Do you talk to all the greys?" Liz glanced at the two sitting by themselves, and then turned back to Adonia.

"The simple answer is, no. Most greyhounds are just dogs. Most adoption agencies deal with normal dogs. Just as there are few demigods and demigoddesses, there are few gifted greyhounds. They find their way to us."

"Wait, there are more of you?"

"The simple answer to that one is, yes. Again, we are few and far between."

Liz squinted. "So," she thought for another moment, "you have a birthmark and you asked Katy about hers. Katy said her aunt had one."

"You want to ask me if Katy and her Aunt are demigoddesses."

"Yes." Liz shrugged her shoulders. "Is that why Michael swore me to secrecy?"

"What I can tell you at this point is that Katy has free will as we all do. What happens with her is yet to be seen. But if she is given preconceived notions, who can tell what might happen."

A strange vibration buzzed through Liz when Adonia looked directly into her eyes. It didn't scare her, but it did make her think she should keep her mouth shut around Katy. "Okay, well, you've given me a lot to think about. Thanks for being open with me. Would you mind if we take a raincheck on lunch? I don't think I could eat right now." She put her hand on her stomach.

Adonia stood and her dogs went to Liz and rubbed their faces on her jeans.

It scared Liz at first, but then she felt a wave of calmness.

Adonia held out her hand to Liz. "Of course, I understand perfectly. Let's plan to get together soon." Adonia put her arm around Liz when she stood and walked her to the door. "My home is always open to you and yours. Come by anytime. But, maybe call first to make sure I'm not busy with someone else." Adonia chuckled.

Her smile put Liz at ease. "Thanks, again. I hope to see you soon."

CHAPTER 37

Liz knew every inch of the gallery, but it looked and felt different. It belonged to her now. She strolled through every part and touched everything. Tuesday mornings rarely saw much foot traffic, so she took her time. She finally had her own gallery. It felt wonderful, on one hand. On the other? She'd rather have Jean-Luc here and wait a few more years for her dream to come true. A couple of bittersweet tears escaped. She wiped them away, took a deep breath, and decided she'd have to put on her *big-girl panties*, as the saying went. He wouldn't want her to wallow in grief and let the business fail.

She had a short reprieve with the inheritance money, but she still needed more of a plan. She'd check again on the cost of ads in the hottest Phoenix and Scottsdale magazines. Jean-Luc had balked at the expense, but she needed fresh eyes in the place. Existing customers will only buy so much and competition is fierce in the art world.

The airport has a section for brochures at the information desk. Maybe Michael could help design a new one, with her name as proprietor. The gallery's name would always stay *Notre Maison* (Our House)—quite fitting—hers and Jean-Luc's. A warmth filled her chest and she smiled.

He had wanted her to find an art student. Maybe she could rotate one each semester from after school until closing. She needed to 'pay it forward'.

She could ask Jim to play the piano one night a week. People seemed to like his music at the silent auction. Or maybe she should audition some music students.

Liz walked to the sales desk and sat down. She needed to make a list and prioritize all of the ideas, and then come up with a plan. Their website needed updating as well as their mailing list.

Not *theirs*.

Only *hers* now.

Another set of tears flowed unbidden.

Liz stood and stomped her foot. "Shit, where is everyone? Do I have to go out to the sidewalk and hold a spinning sign to get people in the door?"

Liz arrived promptly for her lunch-time appointment at Morgan's office, which was painted light pink with feminine accents, Morgan's typical style. Liz had her to-do list completed now, and asking Morgan to be her accountant occupied the number one spot.

"Of course I'll continue as your CPA." Morgan tilted her head. "I do find it interesting that you requested a meeting here though. Wouldn't you assume I'd be agreeable?"

Liz shrugged. "I wanted it to be official. Do we need to do any paperwork to make the change?"

Morgan smiled. "I don't require a contract or a retainer. If you'll provide me with an email from the gallery, or a letter on your letterhead, stating your requirements, that's all I'll need. Has everything been transferred per your attorney?"

"It's all done or in the works."

"It's early in the year, so I don't expect any complications. Now, what are your plans this evening?"

"Michael is taking me over to Richard's to look at his art jewelry. You should come along. I could use your keen eye and good taste. Maybe Katy would like to come as well."

Morgan sat back in her office chair and briefly placed one hand over her eyes. "Alright. I suppose I'm curious to view the jewelry, so if it will help you, I'll come."

Liz giggled. "And maybe you're slightly curious to see how Richard lives?"

"Not particularly. Will Jim be there?"

"I don't know. Shall we pick you up, say, 7:30 or 7:45?"

"Welcome, come on in." Richard hugged Liz and stepped back to allow her entry past the arched double doors. He greeted Michael, Katy, and Morgan in turn. To Morgan, he said, "Ah, I finally have you on my turf. Welcome."

"Funny guy," she replied and walked on in. "You have a lovely home. I wouldn't have expected you to live in Fountain Hills."

"Funny girl," he smirked. "Liz, everyone, I'd like you to meet my fellow jewelry artists—Adrian and Roberto."

After greetings all around, Katy asked, "What's that wonderful smell?"

"We had Greek food while we were waiting. Please sit. Michael, please fix everyone a drink and I'll grab some appetizers. Morgan, would you please lend me a hand?"

Morgan rolled her eyes at Liz and went quietly as requested.

Richard had returned to the living room in record time with plates, utensils, and napkins, followed by Morgan, carrying a tray of snacks. "Here we go. Let's talk here before we adjourn to the game room to view our work."

Two modern sectionals faced each other in the large living room with a stunning glass coffee table in between, which now held a tray of olives, humus, pita bread, cucumbers, lemon slices, cheeses, and dried fruits. The group snacked and drank while getting to know each other. They discussed their histories, their customer following, jewelry trends, and, of course, food.

"Liz, would you care to look at some of our pieces now?" Richard stood when she simply nodded. "Please follow me." He led them down a set of curved metal stairs to a second level of the home which obviously sat on a hill. This room had one wall of glass leading onto a well-lit patio with a negative-edge pool beyond that. From the indentions in the carpet, the gaming table had been moved aside. "We have set up three folding tables—one for each of us—showcasing some of our available work. Please take your time browsing and we can discuss any interesting pieces."

Michael stood off to the side out of the way. Morgan and Katy quietly followed Liz while she browsed. The room was well-lit and the jewelry artfully displayed.

As she stood in front of Roberto's table, Liz thought about the jewelry she remembered her customers wearing, trying to determine which pieces, if any, would sell in her gallery. "Please feel free to pick up anything you'd like to see in more detail. This is my latest thumb ring." He handed it to Liz.

Obviously sized for a man, the domed ring had a rectangular surface. "It's chunky, yet elegant in its simplicity."

"Thank you."

Next, she picked up a sugar skull necklace—its face completely studded with small pearls. "This must have taken some time to complete. Again, you kept it elegant by avoiding a riot of colored stones. Quite nice."

"I see you've captured my style. I make substantial pieces that say 'I'm here' but don't overwhelm the owner at the same time."

"Exactly." Liz picked up a few other pieces she liked.

She then moved on to Adrian's table. "Your work is substantial, but lighter. For example, this necklace has size, but not weight. The silver looks like torn strips of paper overlapped and adhered together at odd angles. It's certainly a statement piece that could be worn by even a smaller woman. Morgan, put this on, please." Liz helped her hook the chain around her neck. "It contrasts very nicely against your black sweater." Morgan nodded her approval and removed it as Liz moved to examine a few more pieces, including a pair of earrings that looked like pop tops from a soda can. "Your work has an Avant-garde flare not found just anywhere. One-of-a-kind pieces sell well to the right buyer."

Adrian nodded once. "Thanks, Liz. I've had good luck so far."

"Ok, Richard. What do you have to show me?"

"As you can see, my work involves stones along with the silver."

"How did you make these earrings?"

"I first carved the lapis into a single link of a chain, then made a silver knot to interlink with it, and then attached that to a stud earring base."

"Richard, you own a jewelry store. Where do you find time to make jewelry, let alone carve stones?"

He shrugged. "It's a hobby."

"Okay, gentlemen, I like your work very much. I'm interested. I've brought along my standard agreement which includes the percentage I'll take as part of the sale. If you are interested, please read them and then we can talk about sales prices. I'd like to display some of your work for a trial period of three months. If you sell well, we can discuss more at a later date. If you don't sell, frankly, I'll need the floor space for something else. Does that make sense?"

Each man nodded and smiled at Liz. She dug the agreements out of her tote bag and passed them around. "Richard, you mentioned that you had a display case. May I see that?"

"Sure, it's in the garage. Follow me."

"Morgan, will you please pick out a few more items from each table for the store. Katy, if you see something you like, add that, too. I'll be back in a minute and then we can go."

CHAPTER 38

Early Wednesday morning, Matthieu met Liz and Michael in the parking lot of Piestewa Peak.

After the usual greetings, Liz said, "Thank you, Matthieu, for bringing Jean-Luc's ashes." She pointed to his clothes. "You aren't dressed for the climb. Not going?"

"What climb? I don't know what you are talking about."

Michael laughed. "So, I take it that this is not especially legal?"

"I'm just here to work in my car while I watch the beautiful sunrise. This location is close to my office, and I don't have this view from there."

"I've made this climb before and it usually takes me about 35 minutes or so for the ascent and less to come back down," Michael said. "Do you have enough work for an hour or so?"

"I do. I need to make some calls as well. It's a beautiful morning, isn't it? I'm sure Jean-Luc would have been pleased that you are both here to receive his ashes." He produced a document out of his brief case. "Liz, please sign the receipt here."

"Shall we get started?" Liz took the urn from Matthieu, placed it into her backpack, and started toward the trail head. Michael followed close behind. The first half was easy going for her, but the second half was more challenging.

"Do you want me to carry your pack?" Michael asked when they stopped for a breather.

"Thanks, but this is something I have to do. Just catch me if I slip." Liz chuckled. "I'm in shape, but it's surprising how much difference a little extra weight makes. I'm not sure if the pack or the urn is heavier." Liz stubbed her toe, but kept upright. "I'm glad that they installed the hand rails in a couple of these tricky spots."

When they reached the top, a couple greeted them and turned to go back down. Liz and Michael were alone then. The sunrise had changed from its multi-hued glory to a brilliant gold and the view of the valley shown magnificently, as always. "We are here, Jean-Luc. Are you ready to travel on the wind back to your native France? There's a nice little breeze to aid your travels." Liz turned to Michael. "I think I've said all I need to say up to this point. Do you have anything to say?"

"No. I'm here to support you. There're more people coming up, so if we are going to do this, we should get going before they see us. Turn around and I'll get the urn."

Liz turned to the back side of the mountain, opened the lid, and spilled the ashes on the wind. "*Adieu mon autre père. Vive la France.*" The breeze took the ashes on a little spin and then disbursed them on their way down. Liz waved, capped the urn, and Michael put it into her backpack before the next group of people arrived at the top.

Liz took one last deep breath before they started their descent.

♥♥♥

Michael kissed Liz goodbye before she exited his Jeep. "Are you sure you'll be okay if I just drop you off? I could go get my computer and do my graphic work at the gallery instead."

"No, really, I'm fine. It was a very special morning." Liz stepped out. "I'll just talk to Jean-Luc's spirit while I'm opening for the day and then I'll be busy. I'm glad you came with me. See you later."

He watched Liz open the ugly back door and step inside.

He didn't have a good feeling about the day. He'd check on her later. Being protective brought him comfort.

♥♥♥

At 10:30, a long-time artist stopped by to talk to Liz. Since there were no customers, they spoke freely.

"I've come in to remove my paintings as per our agreement." The artist told her. "Nothing has sold for over six months and I think I need to do something different."

Liz bit her lip and raised her eyebrows. She thought for a moment. "Before you do, I'd like you to consider something. I've been thinking about having a monthly open house with one featured artist each month. The artist would need to be present to talk about his or her work. All your work could be moved to the front for that evening and that month. After that, I'd move things around for the next artist. I'd advertise the event and you could do the same in your social media. You could be first and I can do a random drawing for the remaining months for other artists. What do you think? Maybe sometime in the next two weeks?"

"I suppose. I haven't made any other arrangements, so it wouldn't hurt to try it. Would a Wednesday evening work?"

"Sure. Thanks for being willing to try. Let's go look at your work and discuss it more."

Liz sat with her chin in her hands after he left. If that didn't work, it wouldn't be any more of a loss other than a few advertising dollars. His work didn't sell well anyway. Maybe this will help move it along.

A little later, another artist phoned and wanted Liz to email him a copy of their agreement. When she asked him why, he told her that he couldn't find his copy and he was concerned because his work wasn't selling. She sat back in her chair and took a deep breath. Liz made him the same offer and he accepted.

At lunch, she decided to get an email out to the other

artists with the open house offer before someone else got the idea to pull their work. If they all left, she'd have nothing to sell. She shook her head. Where would she be then?

With that task complete, she looked at the books. Michael's work had definitely saved the gallery this past month. Maybe it would continue to do so, but right now it was entirely too quiet. Perhaps some of her other ideas would reap some benefits soon. Something had to work, and soon.

Not hungry for lunch, Liz decided to nap at the desk in her office. She definitely needed a little shuteye.

When she reopened for the afternoon, Liz yelled to the empty store, "Hello, customers. Where are you?"

There were too many events happening in the valley every March that kept people busy. Maybe that's where they were.

Liz repositioned a couple of walls to make room for the display case that Richard planned to drop off that evening. She normally didn't do that type of thing during open hours, but there were no customers there to wait on.

Richard and Adrian arrived at five o'clock to unload. They positioned the case next to the sales desk, dusted it, and set up their displays. Richard completed the work for Roberto, who couldn't make it. The glass and wood cabinet was longer than she remembered, but that offered room for some displays on top. She stepped outside and looked at it through the main window. The location offered a pleasing addition from the outside.

"Does this look okay?" Richard asked. "We selected some pieces to display, but you can change the arrangement any way you like."

Liz lightly patted his arm. "It's perfect just like it is. Thank you both for setting it up. The jewelry looks amazing. Do you have the signed agreements?"

"They're over here." Richard moved over to the two remaining boxes, opened one, withdrew the documents, and handed them to Liz.

She looked them over, signed them, and said, "I'll go make copies for you."

Back from her office, she handed them back to Richard. He handed one to Adrian who thanked Liz and shook her hand.

"I'll make sure Roberto gets his. Where do you want this back stock?"

"Bring them to the storage room. I can unload them into the safe. There's plenty of room." When she completed that task, she asked Richard, "What do you think of this sandwich board? I'd like to get a poster printed showing some of the pieces. I'll put it on the sidewalk for passersby to see."

"That's a good idea," Richard said. "I take pictures of all my pieces…"

Adrian interrupted, "So do I."

"Great, will you both send them to me tonight, please, and I'll get right on it. This is coming together quite nicely." Liz offered her biggest smile.

"What is?" Michael asked. He had arrived through the front door.

"Hey, Sneaky." Liz waved him over. "Come see the display cabinet."

"It looks great." Michael gave Liz a quick hug and then greeted Richard and Adrian with handshakes.

Michael bent to see the items on the shelves. "I recognize a couple of these pieces, Richard."

"Yeah, I'm glad to have a place to sell them. I need to hit the road. Thanks again, Liz." Richard hugged Liz and she shook hands with Adrian.

"I'll talk to you both soon." Liz locked the door behind them.

Liz returned to find Michael sitting in a guest chair with his hands steepled in front of his mouth.

He lowered his hands. "You know, I could give you a loan to tide you over."

She sat in the desk chair. "That's sweet, but I don't know

287

if I could pay you back."

Michael nodded. "If you'd rather, it could be an investment. We could be partners."

Liz stood, pursed her lips and crossed her arms. "No. I'll never co-mingle funds with a man ever again. Let's go." She grabbed her purse, headed for the back door, and unlocked it.

He followed. "Don't you trust me?"

"Yes and no. It's a matter of principle." She lifted her chin and pursed her lips.

"Fine. I'm outta here." He got in his car and drove away.

CHAPTER 39

That evening, Liz entered her front door, slammed it shut, threw her keys and purse on the table, and flopped down on the couch.

"Why is everything so dammed hard?" she yelled at the walls. She took several deep breaths and went into the kitchen to pour herself a glass of wine.

Back on the couch, Liz rehashed her roller-coaster of a day. It started out wonderfully, albeit emotional. Spreading Jean-Luc's ashes with Michael seemed like exactly the right thing to do. She imagined that Jean-Luc's ashes had waived at her before they dissipated. At least that's what she wanted to believe.

Then, the day took a nosedive when two more artists wanted to pull their work. Why does it take so much work to try to earn a little money? Art just didn't sell itself anymore.

Next, the jewelry from the guys looked amazing. Each piece shone with elegance. If she could get someone in to see them, they would sell, she just knew it.

Lastly, the tiff with Michael upset her. She knew she was harsh. She really did trust him. It's just that her hurt wouldn't let her accept his offer. Did that mean she really didn't trust him completely yet? How did that saying go? Shame on him once and shame on me twice? Something like that.

Liz kicked her shoes off and covered herself with a throw while she finished her wine, which helped take the edge off her mood. Maybe she could think straight now that she calmed down. At least she would try. No matter what, she wouldn't put herself in a difficult financial position again if she could help it. Michael would just have to understand that. And if he didn't, where would they be then? She trusted him with her life, but not her finances. How could she help him understand that concept?

He didn't, or couldn't, commit himself to her yet, even sexually. Most guys would jump at the chance, but that made her respect him more than she already did. Maybe that's how to explain it to him. If he wasn't ready sexually, why should she be ready financially? That's something a guy should understand.

She retrieved her phone from her purse and called Michael. No response. She hung up. Truly not something she wanted to leave in a message. She tried the call again later with still no response.

Liz missed Duke. She wanted to snuggle and pet him. She expected a long sleepless night ahead of her.

Michael called Richard the minute he got home. Well, after he fed Duke and gave him some love.

"I'm done!"

"With what?" Richard asked.

"With women. They are entirely too much trouble." Michael shared the loan discussion with Richard.

"You don't mean that, again. Didn't you tell me that her ex-fiancé stole all the money from their joint checking? Don't you think that would make her wary of anyone financially? And why would you want to do that anyway when you just untangled your finances with Bethany? Surely, you better than anyone, should understand that. Do you love her?"

"I do. I guess I have to admit that my pride was hurt. I was only trying to help her."

"What if she wanted to buy a house with you now? Would you do it?"

"Probably not." Michael went silent for a moment. "I

guess I get it."

"Have you talked to Will?"

"No. I usually call you first. You're more logical. Plus, he's getting close to Katy and I don't need my thoughts getting back to Liz before I can share them with her."

"Why don't you sleep on it and talk to her tomorrow."

"Yeah, I guess I will."

CHAPTER 40

Michael answered the ringing doorbell on Thursday morning, only to be crowded out by Duke trying to investigate who had arrived.

"Hey, Duke. How are you, buddy?" Liz scratched his ears until he started rubbing his face on her jeans. "Hi, Michael. Can we talk?"

Michael hesitated slightly, before opening the house door wider. "Come on in before Duke gets out."

They stood quietly in his entryway until Liz spoke. "I wanted to apologize for being so harsh with my response to your kind offer last night."

"Maybe you were a little defensive, but you were right. Let's go sit down and talk." Michael led her back to the family room and offered her some cranberry juice.

Duke parked next to Liz's feet and looked up at her wanting attention. She complied and then took a sip of her drink. "Thanks for the juice. What do you mean, I was right?"

"It's probably is too early in our relationship to co-mingle funds, no matter the reason." Michael shrugged his shoulders. "As I mentioned before, I'm still sensitive, and I took your rejection personally. Now that I've had time to think about it, I understand your reasoning."

"I appreciate that and I'm truly grateful for your thoughtful offer."

"So we're good?" Michael tipped his head.

Liz chuckled. "Yes, we're good."

Michael rose and approached Liz. She stood, put her arms around his neck, and planted a sweet kiss on his lips before stepping away.

"I need to go get ready for work. Can we have a late dinner tonight?"

"Sure, why don't you come here?" Michael raised a thumb over his shoulder. "The construction in the kitchen is done and I can cook for you. It might be simple, but it will be easier that way."

Liz peeked around Michael at the shiny stainless appliances, the black granite countertops, and the new grey paint. "It looks amazing. Are you sure you want to get it dirty?"

"Silly girl. Call me when you leave and I'll have something ready. Come on. I'll walk you to the door."

Duke wedged himself between the two at the door which knocked Liz sideways. She lost her balance and fell over a stack of wood flooring beside her. She hit her head on the wall near the same spot where she landed at the Renaissance Festival.

Michael rushed to her side, ignoring the fact that he stepped on Duke's foot in the process. Duke literally "yipped."

Liz seemed disoriented as he picked her up and took her to the couch in the living room. He didn't care if she bled on the carpet or the furniture.

He examined her head. "I don't see any blood. Does it hurt?"

"I'm fine," Liz said.

Duke danced around wanting in on the attention.

Michael angled himself to check out her eyes. He couldn't remember, but he thought they shouldn't be dilated.

"I'm fine." She said again.

"I'm calling 911." Michael pulled his phone out of his back pocket.

Liz put her hand over the key pad. "No, you're not. I said I'm fine." She glared at him and then reached to pet Duke. "It's okay, boy."

"Then I'm taking you to urgent care. You need to be seen, just to be sure. I'll get the car out of the garage. Stay here and then I'll come get you. Don't argue."

"Fine! My parents would insist anyway," Liz yelled to Michael's back as he went outside.

"Fine," He said over his shoulder.

On the way, Michael suggested that Liz call her parents. "Can Morgan watch the store for you today or at least go put up a sign?"

"Let's see what happens first before we get everyone all excited." Liz rolled her eyes. "I'm sure it's nothing to worry about."

The staff at the urgent care took Liz back right away and set her up for an x-ray, thanks to Michael's big mouth about her last head bump.

Liz glared at Michael and shook her head. "This really wasn't necessary you know."

"How do you know? They might find something. I'm not going to take the chance with you. After they read the x-ray, then you can scold me, okay?" Michael paced in the exam room while she sat on the exam table watching him.

While they waited for results, they chatted about Michael's recent graphics work and the possibility of profits from the sale of the jewelry.

The doctor knocked and entered the exam room. "Everything looks good, Liz. The radiologist on staff doesn't see anything that might suggest a problem. You should probably stay home and rest today. Watch for any signs of a problem such as dizziness, and so on, and follow up with your regular doctor as soon as you can."

As they left, Michael took her hand to walk to the checkout station. "You really need to quit falling. I'm beginning to think you like the attention."

Liz socked him in the arm lightly. "You're a funny guy. It wasn't my fault—either time—it was the boy and then it was Duke."

"That's true. But seriously, I worry. I still want you to call your parents and take the day off. You can stay with me or your parents, but I don't want you to be alone."

"Are you bossing me?" Liz raised her eyebrows. She didn't want that precedent to get started.

"No. Absolutely not." Michael raised his free hand, palm out. "I'm just telling you what I would like to have happen. You'll do whatever you want. I know that."

"Thank you. For everything. I know you need to work today. I'll see if one of my parents can stay home. Just as a precaution." She pointed at him. It would be fun to have a day off with one of them. "And I'll call Morgan."

Ken couldn't believe she fell, again. "Liz, I swear, sometimes I think you must be a Slinky toy, ready to plunge down a steep set of stairs, unable to stop."

"That's not funny. But it is a fairly accurate description, Dad." Liz snickered. "Thanks for today, even though I'm sure it's not necessary." She walked to the couch, pulling Michael by the hand.

"Thank you, Michael, for bringing Liz to our house. I needed a day off anyway." Ken sat in his recliner.

"I'm glad you are available. I offered, but she wanted to come here since I have to work."

"You should stay over, Liz, and I'll take you home early in the morning. Let's go play cards." Ken stood and so did they. "We'll see if your brain still works and it will keep you awake and alert." Ken put his hand on top of Liz's head. They loved to play Canasta and did so every chance they got. "Do you want to join us, Michael?"

"I'll take a rain check and leave you both in each other's

good hands." Michael hugged Liz, shook Ken's hand, and made for the front door.

Ken walked him to the door while Liz went to find the cards. "I'm glad she has you looking out for her, Michael. You make a good addition to our group of crazies."

"Thanks, Ken. I'll take that as a compliment."

"Take that as my blessing if you like. You are welcome here anytime."

They talked quietly for a few minutes before Liz returned with the playing cards and then Michael left.

CHAPTER 41

Michael managed to get his work done on Friday morning, even though he thought about Liz the whole time. Maybe thinking of her enhanced his creativity. He couldn't imagine his life without her in it. Maybe he should think about that thought a little more.

After emailing his graphic work to his customer, he didn't know what to do with himself. Since he'd been working at his office space in his gallery, he stood up and paced around studying the paintings he still had hanging.

Michael stepped in front of the painting he had done of Liz and Duke. "All that's needed is my signature and then it's done," he said to himself out loud. "I should try to get another painting done this afternoon for Liz's gallery."

Liz unlocked the back door of the gallery just before ten and went through her opening routine. A customer waited outside the front door as Liz unlocked it.

"Hello and welcome. Have you been waiting long?" Liz held the door for the lady to enter.

"No, my husband is at the car show, so I'm shopping. I've never been in here before."

The woman looked around with a smile, which gave Liz butterflies in her stomach. Finally, a customer. "You can take your time and look around or I'd be happy to help you find something."

"I'll just look…oh, you have jewelry?" The lady headed straight for the display case.

"Yes, I have wonderful pieces from three of the top silversmiths in the area." Liz walked to the back of the case and unlocked it. "Let me know what I can show you." She pulled out two necklace displays and positioned them at opposite ends on top of the case and waited while the lady browsed. Liz had to stop herself from fidgeting.

The woman asked to see seven pieces and decided on four of them without even asking about their prices.

"These are originals, right?" The woman asked. "I only wear custom pieces."

"Yes, of course, they are one of a kind. The artists create them right here in Scottsdale." Liz wrapped the jewelry while the lady walked through the remainder of the gallery. Liz laughed to herself. At least they are cheaper than the cars her husband is shopping for at the auction in town.

The lady's friend then entered from the store next door and bought several pieces as well. They left laughing, and left Liz smiling. She couldn't wait to call Richard and Michael.

Michael called Adonia, picked up deli sandwiches, then stopped by her house at lunchtime. "Duke wanted to some see you." Michael said. He held the food up and away from Adonia's greyhound pack.

Duke sent to Adonia, "I do, but Michael is really struggling with some thoughts about Liz."

Adonia suppressed a giggle. "And I'm happy to see you too, Duke. She rubbed his ears. "Let's go in the dining room and eat while the food is warm. The dogs can play and I'll give them a treat when we are finished. How are things with you, my boy?"

"Work is busy. Duke is happy. Liz is still alive, in spite of her clumsiness."

"What happened now?" Adonia unwrapped the sandwiches and provided drinks while Michael told her of the latest urgent care visit.

"It's a good thing she has you around to pick her up. What are your plans regarding that lovely girl?" Adonia pointed her sandwich toward Michael then took a bite.

"That's what I'm trying to figure out." He took a sip of water.

"And you came to me to listen or to provide answers?"

"Yes."

Adonia broke into a full belly-laugh.

Morgan showed up at lunch and Liz told her the good news. "She didn't buy the necklace with the Herkimer diamond, did she?" Morgan asked and headed to the case.

"She looked at it, but didn't buy it." Liz unlocked the case again and handed the necklace to Morgan.

"This is mine, but don't tell Richard I purchased it."

"Why not?" Liz frowned. "I bet he'd give you a discount."

"His comments set me on edge. I'll need to be careful when and where I wear this beauty." Morgan angled the necklace in the light to enhance its sparkle.

"Well, I'll give you a discount anyway." Liz walked to the sales desk to enter the sale.

"No you certainly will not. I can afford it and I don't want him to see a discount on the invoice."

"You are so silly, Morgan. Then I'll buy you a nice lunch somewhere."

"Are you available now? I'll show this off at the restaurant and maybe generate more sales. I'll be your model and you can dispense business cards to the adoring public." Morgan laughed and Liz joined in her silliness.

"Katy. Hi, it's Michael." He had called her cell mid-afternoon on Friday to catch her before the end of her workday.

"Hey, Michael. Is everything okay?"

He briefly told her what had happened. "Can I take you out to dinner? Morgan, too. I want to discuss something with you both."

"Um, sure. I'm off at 5:30 today. I can meet you somewhere. You sound nervous or something. Are you sure Liz is okay?"

"Yes, this is about something else." Michael hung up after making their arrangements for dinner. He then called Morgan and did the same.

Liz stopped by her parent's house on her way home from work.

Ken placed his crossword paper on the end table, stood from his recliner and greeted Liz as she walked in the door. "Hi, Sweetie. Where's Michael?"

Liz kissed Ken on the cheek when he hugged her. "He worked at his gallery today and said he had something to do tonight, so here I am."

"Did you see him today?" Ken put his hands in his pockets.

"No, Dad. I just talked to him on the phone. What's up?"

"Oh, nothing." Ken waved one hand in the air. "Just curious that's all. Can I get you something?" Ken motioned toward the kitchen.

"Not right now. Where's Mom?" Liz sat on the couch and placed her purse on the coffee table.

Ken sat back in his chair. "She's still at the restaurant. I expect her soon. She's bringing home dinner. Are you staying? She can bring home an extra one."

"If she doesn't mind. I'll call her."

"Ok." Ken got up and went in the kitchen.

♥♥♥

"Did you ask her yet?" Ken whispered into his cell phone with Michael on the other end.

"She is here now." …

"I can try." Ken said. "I'll let you know." …

Liz walked into the kitchen.

"I'll talk to you later." Ken hung up and stuffed his phone in his pocket. "Want some wine?"

"Sure. Who was that?"

Ken stuck his head in the refrigerator stalling for time. He finally pulled out a white for Liz. "Oh, um, just a working man. I, uh, have a waiter at work that makes mesquite benches. Do you think one or two would look nice in your gallery? Either to sell or just for people to sit on?"

"I don't know. Are they rustic or polished?" Liz took the glass Ken handed to her.

"Um, I don't know. I'll have to ask him. I overheard part of a conversation at work before I came home." Ken picked up his glass and headed back into the living room.

"Are you okay, Dad? You are acting a little weird."

"Yeah, I'm a little tired, is all. I came home from work early and tried to take a nap." He waved his hand to dismiss her concern. He turned on the news. "Let's see what's happening in the world."

♥♥♥

Liz helped her mom with the food bags when she came in the door a few minutes later, bringing with her the scent of tomatoes and garlic.

During dinner, Nancy refilled Liz's wine glass.

"Thanks, Mom. Do you know anything about the mesquite benches your waiter makes?" Liz sipped her wine.

"No, which waiter?" Nancy looked at Ken.

"Not to worry about it," Ken said, "I'll look into it tomorrow. So, how was work today, Liz?"

"I sold some jewelry. Some lady, whose husband was at the car show, bought some. So did her friend and Morgan bought a piece—but that's a secret. For some reason, she doesn't want Richard to know."

"Congratulations." Ken added more wine to Liz's glass. "Let's make a toast to your success. Cheers."

"Is Richard happy?" Nancy asked.

"He's thrilled and so is Roberto. One of the pieces was his. I called them both right away." Liz drank more wine. "I hadn't even put the new sidewalk sign out yet. The shoppers were a lucky fluke."

"Here's to lucky shoppers." Ken raised his glass.

"Dad, you're going to make me drunk."

"Why can't we celebrate with our girl?" Ken said and poured the remainder of the bottle in Liz's glass. "You can stay here tonight. You shouldn't drive after most of a bottle."

"Your dad is right, Liz. Stay here and relax. It's nice to have you visit now and then."

Liz's phone rang. "It's Morgan."

"Go ahead. Your dad can help me clean up." Nancy said and Ken nodded.

♥♥♥

Liz answered her phone. "Hey, Morgan. What's up?" ...

"Early breakfast? Sure. I'm at my folks so I can meet you somewhere." ...

"Okay, that's near here." ...

"Sure, you can pick me up here and drop me off later so I can get my car before work." ...

"See you then."

Liz hung up and went into the kitchen where she found her parents whispering and smiling. "Okay, what's up in here?"

"I'm whispering sweet nothings to your mom." Ken wiggled his eyebrows.

"Yes, I was saying the right love can last a lifetime."

"I'm so happy for your two." Liz hugged her parents. "When you are finished, come out and watch a movie with me." Liz left them in the kitchen and smiled all the way to the living room.

CHAPTER 42

Michael woke up early on Saturday morning to meet Morgan and Katy at Liz's apartment before they went to work. "I'm so glad you have a key, Katy, thanks," Michael said.

"Are you kidding? Liz is going to be so surprised. The balloons are a nice touch." Katy pointed to them. "Let's get this done."

"Morgan, are you sure it's okay if Duke and I wait here while you go get Liz?" Michael squinted and rubbed his ear.

"Yes, I phoned her last night and I offered breakfast at one of her favorite spots. After I pick her up, I'll ask her to run in and change first. That way, she'll come in solo and I'll depart for work."

"That sounds perfect."

Liz stumbled as she walked into her apartment, not expecting Duke to greet her in a rush. "Hi, Boy. Michael? What are you doing here?"

"I came to deliver this painting." He pointed to the wall near the door where he had hung a painting.

"When did you paint this? It's Duke, and me, in a castle!" Liz reached out and pointed at the oil-painted dog. "My hand sits where I always rest it on his shoulder." She took in the braided hair and the green medieval gown. Her hazel eyes turned in Michael's direction. "I once had a green gown in one of my dreams."

"I've been painting your portrait for some time. I had that same dream, or memory. At least I remembered that dress."

Her lips parted and she said, "But this is not your signature. Who painted this?"

"Read the signature out loud."

Liz rubbed the moisture from her eyes for a second look. "It looks like, *Willieu Meramee.*" She turned to Michael as he got down on one knee.

"Duke and I have something for you. It's on his collar."

Liz retrieved the engagement ring tied to Duke's collar with green ribbon and simply stood there staring at it.

"The ring is temporary. I thought you might want to pick out your own ring since you have such good taste." Michael stood and retrieved a parchment scroll that was tied to the 'I love you' balloons. They floated to the ceiling without the weight attached. "Please read this before you answer."

Liz slowly unrolled the document. "A blank prenup?"

"I got it from Matthieu yesterday. We can fill it in later. Liz, I don't need or want your money, your gallery, or anything except you. We could, and should, always keep separate bank accounts. I don't want you to worry about my intentions. I suggest we take some time. Get to know each other better in this life and learn to trust again. We both have baggage and issues, but I think our dreams, and Adonia and Duke, tell us that we belong together. What do you say?" Michael reached his hand out for Liz and she let him put the ring on her finger. Duke whined and licked her hand.

"Do you want us all to be together in a Forever Home, Duke?"

He barked once, quite loudly.

"How can I argue with fate and a dog who knows us better than we know ourselves. Yes, I'll marry you—maybe after we've had time to deal with our issues. I'd like more than a month to get to know you again." Liz rubbed Duke's shoulder, pressed herself against Michael, and sealed the moment with a kiss.

"I asked your dad for your hand last night. I'm sorry your mom wasn't there as well."

Liz leaned back and raised her eyebrows. "What did he say?"

"He kind of gave me his blessing to come around anytime, so I thought it was a good time to ask. He said, yes, of course."

"Ah! He never gave it away." Tears flooded her eyes.

"When did you have time to do all this?" Liz pointed to the painting and the balloons. "And when did you decide you wanted to get married?"

"I signed it yesterday, and I also picked up your ring from Richard's store. And I told you about the prenup. I decided that I don't want to live without you in my life. I want to be so much more than an artist in your gallery. I want to be the artist of our future. I love you, Liz."

Duke whined and rubbed his face on her leg as he loved to do.

"Sold! I love you, too. Both of you." She kissed Duke's nose and hugged Michael again. "You are my artist, my friend, and the love of my life, or our many lives. Let's paint our future together."

Liz reached for another kiss, but stopped midway. "Oh, no." Liz stepped away from Michael suddenly, turned, and reached for the door knob. "Morgan is still waiting for me."

Michael grabbed her hand. "No. She isn't. She drove away the moment you closed the front door. She and Katy let me in this morning to arrange all this. We planned it last night." Michael grinned.

Liz put her hands on her hips. "So, am I the last to know?"

"Pretty much. It's good that you said yes. Otherwise, I'd have some explaining to do. Shall we have everyone, including Adonia, over for dinner tonight to celebrate?"

"Yes. Let's take Duke for a walk to celebrate now. We can plan dinner on the way." Liz reached for his leash and Duke let out a full volume bark.

CHAPTER 43

Duke jumped and danced around when Adonia arrived at Liz's apartment. "We did it!" He sent to her telepathically.

"Duke, my Boy. How are you?" Adonia asked Duke out loud and rubbed his face. Then she telepathically sent, "Yes, we did. Good job with the dream kisses. Liz and Michael will be as happy together in this life, as they were in their past lives."

Duke said "Ooof."

"Liz, Michael, congratulations." Adonia hugged them both. "I was so pleased to receive your call. I want to hear all about it. And I want to see the lovely engagement painting."

"Thank you," Liz said. "Come see, it's on the wall to the right. I think you know everyone here. Help yourself to a drink over on the table." Liz pointed in the direction of the dining table.

Matthieu stood inside the doorway, right behind Adonia, awaiting his greeting as Adonia stepped away. "Congratulations, you two." Liz hugged him as Michael closed the door and then shook his hand.

"Thank you, and come in. You know Michael and my dad. We'll introduce you to everyone else right after our speech. Everyone has been impatient to hear our story. Please, grab a glass of champagne."

"Now that you are all here," Liz began, "Michael can tell you all about his romantic proposal."

And so he did... "And I'm happy to announce that she said yes—maybe." Those that were sitting down, stood up, and everyone clapped.

"Just to clarify," Liz added with a hand in the air and a smile, "We agreed to a long engagement, with no date set. It's been crazy lately and we both need some time to handle things before making a life-long commitment."

"Or a present-life commitment," Duke sent to Adonia who smiled at him.

"A toast," Michael added, "to our friends and family who have been patient with us and who have offered us unconditional support. Cheers." Michael reached an arm around Liz and planted a big kiss on her lips.

"And now," Adonia sent to Duke, "My next task is Katy."

Duke simply sent, "Ooof."

ABOUT THE AUTHOR

Hope was a Technical Writer before starting a career as a Fiction Writer. This book started when she documented a recurring dream that wouldn't leave her alone. As the dream became a story, the story became a book: *Greyhound Dreams*.

Hope and her husband have two loving greyhounds. So, how could her first books not include such a wonderful breed!

She is a member of the Romance Writers of America, along with two chapters, the Land of Enchantment Romance Authors and the Valley of the Sun Romance Writers.

Stay tuned for the next two books in the *Greyhounds Thru Time* series.

Find Hope at *https://hopechase.com* and connect with her through her email newsletter for book news, free stuff, and interesting tidbits.

You can also find Hope on Pinterest at *Hope Chase Author*.

Before you finish, please consider leaving a review on Amazon which is helpful to Hope, of course, but also to other readers deciding on which books to read next. Thank you.

Made in the USA
Monee, IL
13 August 2020